THE CONVOCATION

THE SUNDERING SERIES

BOOK 4

D RAE PRICE

DRaePriceBooks

Book Cover Design &
Illustration © Tom Edwards
TomEdwardsDesign.com

Library of Congress Control Number: 2023911402
979-8-9852043-9-1 (Paperback)
979-8-9884371-0-9 (e-book)

First Edition August 2023
Published by: DRaePriceBooks, Concord CA, USA
Contact: DRaePriceBooks@gmail.com

 Formatted with Vellum

For my Family

CONTENTS

LAGRANGE POINTS

Not to scale

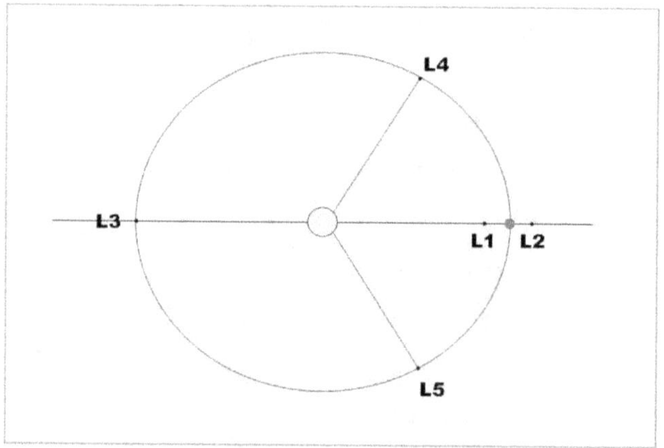

In space, for a planet orbiting its central star, there will be five places, called Lagrange Points, where gravity balances. A small object, such as a space station or asteroid, could be placed in those spots and stay there. This also works for some planet and moon systems. These points were discovered in the late 1700s by the mathematician Joseph-Louis Lagrange.

Three of these points, L1, L2, and L3, are "metastable." It's similar to a ball balancing on top of a hill. A small push will send it down the hill.

However, the L4 and L5 points are stable, as if the ball were inside a bowl. A little push will make the ball roll around in the bowl, but it won't get out. In fact, there are asteroids that ended up in the L4 and L5 points of many planetary orbits, especially the bigger planets like Jupiter. These asteroids are called Trojans.

To see maps and diagrams, go to: https://www.draepricebooks.com/maps-diagrams

The Bahá'í Faith

The Bahá'í Faith is a real religion, founded by Bahá'u'lláh in the mid-1800s. The quotes used are real quotes from the Bahá'í Faith. For more information: https://www.bahai.us/.

The Badí' Calendar

The Badí' calendar, used by members of the Bahá'í Faith, is also a real calendar. New Year's Day is set on the spring equinox on Earth. It has 19 months of 19 days and 4-5 intercalary days, known as Ayyám-i-Há, so the calendar will match the solar year. The day begins and ends at sunset.

Names of the Months

(On Earth, dates vary slightly with the equinox, but these "set" dates are used in the sectors.)

Splendor: Mar 21 - Apr 8

Glory: Apr 9 - Apr 27

Beauty: Apr 28 - May 16

Grandeur: May 17 - June 4

Light: June 5 - June 23

Mercy: June 24 - July 12

Words: July 13 - July 31

Perfection: Aug 1 - Aug 19

Names: Aug 20 - Sept 7

Might: Sept 8 - Sept 26

Will: Sept 27 - Oct 15

Knowledge: Oct 16 - Nov 3

Power: Nov 4 - Nov 22

Speech: Nov 23 - Dec 11

Questions: Dec 12 - Dec 30

Honor: Dec 31 - Jan 18

Sovereignty: Jan 19 - Feb 6

Dominion: Feb 7 - Feb 25

Ayyám-i-Há: Feb 26 - Mar 1

Loftiness: Mar 2 - Mar 20

Ships

    Drumheller—abandoned at the rogue planet

    Cheetah—destroyed and abandoned outside of Friendship

    81-Petals—Incoming to Harbor Station

    Watcher—In Chike space

    Sandstorm—searching for Harbingers

    Wheel of Fire—Tiati and crew were last known to be jumping to Firelight

    Kingfisher—unrepairable, docked at Tektite

    Enkindler shuttle—damaged, aboard the *Watcher*

On the *81-Petals*, at Harbor

    Beezan—former captain of the *Drumheller*, pilot

    Jarvie—Beezan's son, pilot in training

    Iricana—deputy of Oatah, captain of the *81-Petals*

    Katie—doctor

    Thunder—mechanic, husband of Iricana

    Kelson—professor of botany, counselor, founder of the One Tree movement

Sequoia—long jump pilot, Kelson's daughter
Terina—journalist and historian, Sequoia's daughter
Taj—former Tundra acting commander
Ra'Tama—captain of the *Kingfisher*, pilot
Vante Kay—Ra'Tama's crew, spouse of Kay Ling
Kay Ling—Ra'Tama's crew, spouse of Vante Kay
Falcon—former Tundra monitor
Teeve—former chief mech at Tektite, spouse of Maura
Maura—former acting commander of Tektite station, mech crew, spouse of Teeve
Mika—former Tektite mech crew, spouse of Cooper
Cooper—former Tektite mech crew, spouse of Mika
Danny—former Tektite mech crew, spouse of Sunny
Sunny—former Tektite mech crew, spouse of Danny
Chip—former Tektite mech crew, little sib of Sunny
Kente—former Tektite mech crew, little sib of Danny
Sky—Beezan's black podpup, sister of Star
Star—Jarvie's white podpup, brother of Sky
Rocket—Terina's coffee and cream podpup
Cookie—Ra'Tama's gray podpup

On the *Watcher*, taking the Exempt home
Lanezi—long jump pilot, shuttle *Enkindler* commander
Euro—*Enkindler* crew, brother of Io
Io—*Enkindler* crew, brother of Euro
Raykatoo—the Chike Exempt
Neah—Ramian ambassador to humanity
Sontula—Neah's tan
Getti Drann—captain of the *Watcher*
Shiwelna—chief pilot
Widinmay—pilot
Tuladar—pilot

Gosikeen—pilot
Kells—pilot
Whisper—Lanezi's silver mist podpup
Summer—Io and Euro's pastel yellow Ramian podpup
Dusty—Io and Euro's pastel pink Ramian podpup
Blueberry—Io and Euro's pastel blue Ramian podpup
Purple Friend—Sontula's podpup

On the *Sandstorm*
Pascal—the Chike Exempt
Quay—the Ramian Harbinger
Zahar—former captain of the *Cheetah*
Caspia—doctor, spouse of Evan, former *Cheetah* crew
Evan—pilot, spouse of Caspia, former *Cheetah* crew

Colony Planet, Paradise Valley Human colony
Nkiroo—engineering crew in Nile, former *Cheetah* crew
Grace—council member
Jagger—cart driver

Colony Planet, Ramian colony
Danumae—Quay's father
Zhenulell—Quay's mother
Danulell—Quay's brother
Zhenumae—Quay's sister
Kavilor—Zhenumae's spouse
Zhenulor—Zhenumae and Kavilor's baby

Dragon's Den on the colony planet
AnnaLee—Dragon's Den leader
Thayne—former captain of the *Cheetah*

On the colony planet, walking to the western coast

Melawn—Grace's assistant

Tenshi—doctor

Ellant—AnnaLee's right hand

DeeZann—Thayne's student

Others

Oatah—the Human Harbinger, captured by the Chike

Veez—returned to his planet in GenThree space

Kiwi—Zahar's pastel green Ramian podpup, relocated by the Chike

Note about pronouns

The Humans of the outer sectors use gender inclusive pronouns if they don't know the person's gender, if the person does not have a binary gender, or by request.

Ze/He/She

Ziz/His/Hers

Zir/Him/Her

Zirself/Himself/Herself

Sector Map

Sector 1
San
Sector 2
Indigo
Sector 3
Malachite
Sector 4
Tropica
Azure
Athabasca
Sector 5
Cove
5, 15
Jump Days
Firelight
Luminesse
1, 11
4, 14
Coralia
Friendship/
Destroyer
Sector 6
Canyon
3
8, 18
2, 12
Petrichor
Atikameq
9
Harbor
Sector 7
(abandoned)
7D
Windswept
6
1, 11
Mirage
Redrock
7, 17
Sandune
4,14
Terrace
Tektite
2, 12
4, 14
Tanuki
3, 13
Tundra
5, 15
6, 16
Tetra
5, 15
Hamada
8, 18
Tyee
Radium
Junction
7, 17
Sector 8
(abandoned)

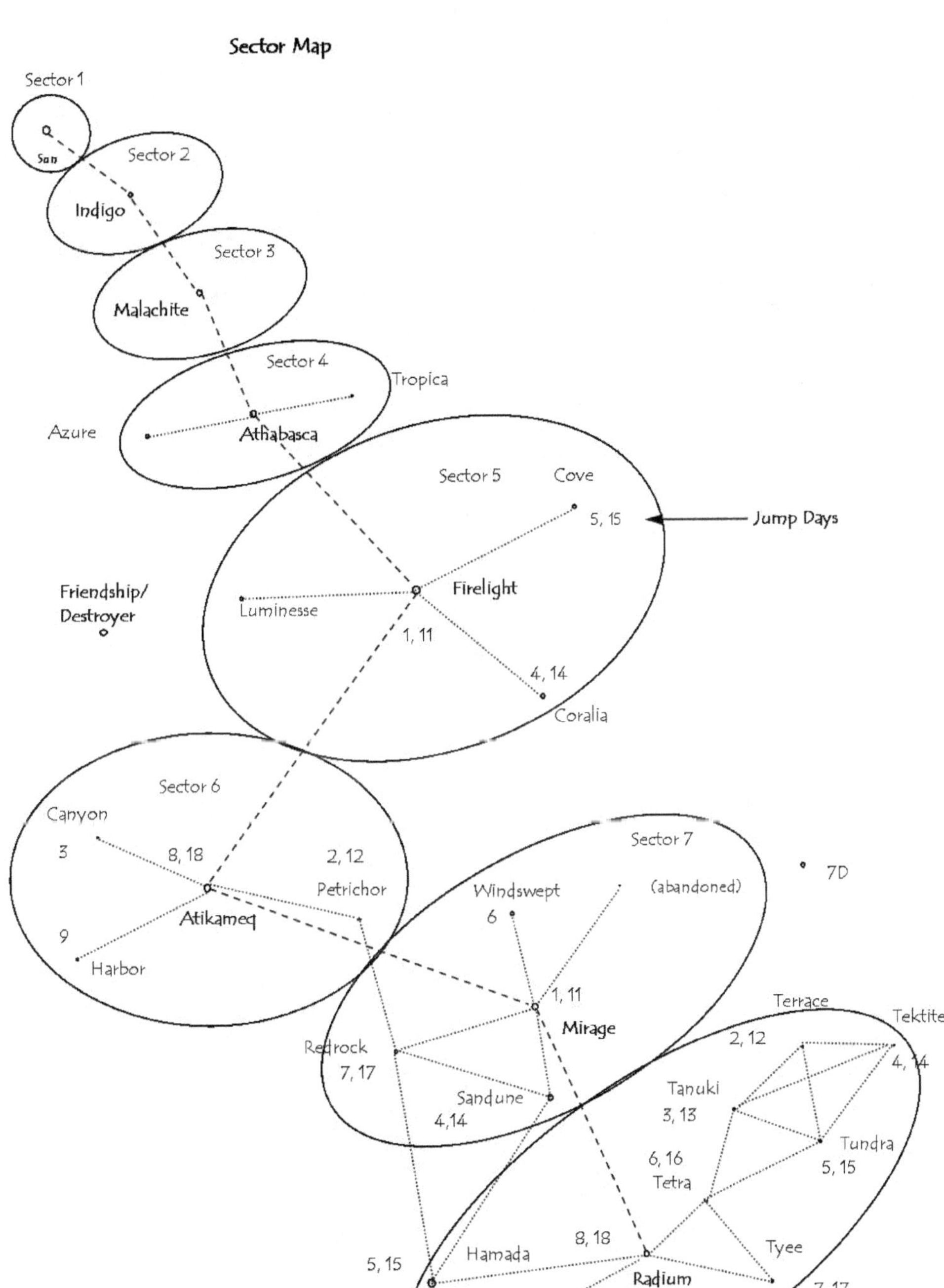

Date: 12-Honor-1084

81-Petals, incoming to Harbor System

Jarvie's eyes flew open when they dropped into normal space. He knew they were at Harbor, but he'd forgotten he was in the scanning tube, and it was only lit by his s'link. Immediate claustrophobic panic set in. He pulled his hands from the restraints and pounded on the tube with his forearms. "Let me out! *81!* Let me out!"

"Remain calm."

"Terina!"

"Jarvie, are you okay?" she answered over his p'link.

"I'm trapped in here!"

"Stay put! We're burn—"

Falcon's voice cut in. "All crew! Remain secure. We are burning for OSRI—the Outer Sector Research Institute, orbiting the fourth planet."

He wasn't in as much pain as he expected. Jarvie realized he must have received some pain meds during the jump. He pressed his hands against the dim curved walls to stay calm. *Breathe. Listen.*

Katie: "Captain, 47 yellow lights. No red lights."

Kelson: "Praise the Lord."

Iricana: "Beezan?"

Katie: "Yellow. Also no light for Jarvie."

Terina: "I've got Jarvie on comm. He's conscious."

Falcon: "Captain, I have Harbor Inbound Authority for you."

Iricana: "H.I.A., *Drumheller*. We are incoming from Redrock. Urgent! Do you have Chike in system?"

H.I.A.: "Not unless you brought them with you."

Iricana: "They may be right behind us. I need an emergency secure link with the council and OSRI command."

H.I.A.: "Stand by."

H.I.A.: "*Drumheller*, please provide your departure clearance."

Iricana: "We're not aware of the requirement for any clearance."

H.I.A.: "You should have been provided a code when you entered the a-rings."

Iricana: "H.I.A., we made an emergency jump. We don't have a code."

H.I.A.: "Very well. Send your departure log."

Falcon: "Stand by."

Falcon: "Captain, there's a giant yellow spider on the departure log!"

Thunder: "And being declared rogue."

Iricana: "There's no hiding it. Send it. Tell them it might take some explaining."

Iricana: "Sequoia, run the spin-up."

There was a clamoring of voices, and of the sucking sound of helmets being pulled off. "What was that yellow gravity ball thing?" "What will happen to Redrock?" "How close behind us?" "How much time?" "Twenty hours to OSRI." "We won't make it if the Chike are after us."

81: **"Burns complete. Stand down from blue zones."**

Iricana: "Please. Thunder, can you get Beezan to the Med Bay?"

Thunder: "Yes, Captain."

Iricana: "We'll reconvene in Consultation Hall in an hour."

As soon as the spin-up was complete, Terina crawled out of her cocoon. Ducking down, she released Star and Rocket. "Come on!" The three of them took off down the rimway, Terina racing to help Jarvie, and the pups in excited chase. She almost slipped past the Med Bay stairway in her socks, but she grabbed the holdbar and reeled up. She beat Katie and the other med personnel; the only person there was Ulf, still strapped in his exam bed.

Facing the wall where Jarvie's scanner was hidden, Terina said, "Medbot, move." A light blinked on. "Medbot, stand over there." She pointed. It didn't budge.

"It's not going to obey you," Ulf grumbled.

"Why? I tell it what to do all the time."

Ulf sighed. "The doctor gave it a priority order. It requires authorization from the same person, unless you have an override code."

"*81*, please tell the medbot to obey me," Terina requested.

"Stand by."

"*81*?" Ulf asked, confused. "As in *81-Petals*? I thought we were on the *Drumheller*? Am I hallucinating?"

"No. Look around!" Terina was getting frustrated. But she remembered that Ulf hadn't been in his right mind all this time and tried to be more compassionate. "Sorry. This is the *81-Petals*. The *Drumheller* is just a cover name for the Ship Tracker."

Ulf unbuckled and sat up, looking around in awe. "*81-Petals*? The most advanced AI in—"

"Make way!" Katie, Thunder, and a med crew came charging up the stairs with two stretchers. Terina rushed to the exam beds and pulled two more down. "Hang on Jarvie. You'll be out of there soon!"

Terina helped get Beezan settled and stood next to him as Roza, the Tundra medtech, did an initial exam. While Katie tended to the other patient, Thunder headed back to the Command Bay. "He's probably just wandering," Katie called over.

"Pulse is way up though," Roza said.

"Terina, please get Sky out of the podpup scanner," Katie said.

Terina unburied the podpup scanner and peered in. Sky's readings were good, except her pulse was also up. Carefully, Terina opened it and scooped her out. She tiptoed back to Beezan and nestled her in his arm. Beezan's pulse immediately started to go down. Roza smiled and said, "Podpup cure." And then they were bombarded by Star and Rocket wanting to jump up onto the bed. "And the podpup curse!"

"I'll take them out. Doctor?" Terina called over her shoulder to ask Katie to move the medbot, but it was already moved, and Ulf was helping Jarvie out.

"Thank you!" Jarvie said, actually hugging Ulf, to his surprise.

"Sorry Jarvie! I was getting there! I'll take care of these two and see you at the meeting."

"Meeting. Right," Jarvie staggered behind her.

After unloading the unruly pups, Terina got her uniform on and went back to the Med Bay to help before the meeting. While she waited for instructions from Katie, Ulf whispered to her, "Where are we?"

"Harbor." Terina edged closer to Ulf while keeping an eye on Honor Beezan and Sky.

"How did we get here?"

"Jumped from Redrock."

"Redrock? I don't remember."

"You've been . . . confused. Adisa and Sho have been here every day, working with you."

He frowned and blinked, as if to clear his mind. "Harbor, Redrock . . ."

"Hamada, RJ, Tyee, Tetra, Tanuki, Tundra." He flinched when she said Tundra. *So he does remember his attachment to the Tundra AI.*

"Seven jumps. So many. So you're using the *Drumheller* call sign to be incognito. But what if the *Drumheller* shows up?"

Beezan started to toss and turn, "*Drumheller?*" he mumbled.

"It won't," she said sadly and lowered her voice, glancing at Honor Beezan. "We had to leave it behind when we found the *81.* Way out there."

"Oh, I see," Ulf said, looking at Beezan with real compassion. "I understand." He nodded.

Beezan seemed calm for the moment, so Terina hung around while Katie scanned Sky. "There's nothing," the doctor reported. "No alien tech, no microbots, nothing." Holding her hand on Sky's side and peering at her scanner, she added, "But her pulse is up. She's agitated or in pain, even though she's asleep."

"No. No. *Drumheller*," Beezan mumbled. "Sky."

"He seems agitated too," Terina said.

"Put Sky back with him," Katie whispered. "Then you can get to the meeting. Thanks for helping."

"Yes, doctor."

"Falcon to Med Bay."

"Katie here," she said quietly.

"Doctor, we're going to do another burn in about five hours. No chairs, but everyone will need to be secure. Just giving you a heads up so Med Bays won't be blasted with multiple announcements."

"Thank you." Katie glanced at her sleeping patients as Terina lingered by the stairs. "Why?"

"Because of the nanos," Falcon answered. "Harbor Inbound Authority declared a clean zone. We can't dock. We'll have to go into a wide orbit."

Katie frowned. "Understood. Thank you."

Terina came back over. "Does that mean we can't dock *anywhere?*"

"I—well, there must be a way to sort it out."

"There was a movie once," Terina told her. "About a ship infected with bad nanos. Did you see it?"

"No," Katie said. "What happened?"

"I don't know. Mom wouldn't let me watch."

"Nanexile," Maura was saying, looking at her p'link, just as Terina got to the meeting.

That's it! she thought. *The name of the movie.*

"Should we remove it from the catalog?" Iricana asked the assembled command crew.

"Way too late," Maura answered. "It's already hit the junk news."

"Can someone give me a summary?" Iricana asked.

"I've seen it," Jarvie answered, and Iricana nodded at him to go on. "Well, it's science fiction. They had these really powerful nanos that could do anything. Some of the nanos went rogue and took over a big ship. So the ship got exiled. They couldn't dock anywhere. So they jumped—using freejumping, even though no one could freejump then. They went from system to system, looking for a new home. It became a generation ship and all this strange cultural stuff happened. But they never found a good, uninhabited, planet to settle on.

"So the ship starts to break down, because it's several thousand years old. The secret group of people, the only ones who know the truth about the ship, decide to program it to fly into a star.

"But some people find out and they rebel and steal a shuttle and land on this ocean planet that can't sustain human life. But the nanos rebuild the whole planet for humans, destroying the original marine civilization."

"And?" Kelson asked.

"That's the end."

"Genocide is the end?" Iricana asked.

"I think it was meant to be a cautionary tale," Jarvie shrugged. "But it's just a story. We don't have nanos like that."

Thunder spoke up in a grave voice, "We do now."

The next day, the command crew, minus Sequoia and Katie, met with the two AI experts to see if they had any insights into getting robot #9 under control.

"Thank you, Sho and Adisa, for coming," Iricana said.

Beezan, after a night of wandering sleep and a good breakfast, felt relatively normal, except for his concern about the unhappy Sky, who could not articulate what was bothering her. He didn't even try to drop her off at the podpup nursery or the kitchen for fear of more whining. He was thankful she now slept quietly in his lap.

After a prayer, Iricana asked, "Would you mind explaining your areas of expertise?"

Sho, the young man, deferred to Adisa, who was about 50. "Greetings, friends," she said formally. "I am Adisa, senior AI counselor, most recently working at Tundra. My area of expertise is human attachment to individual AIs." Beezan suddenly felt self-conscious. Could she see attachment just by looking at people? He slowly leaned back to try to appear casual.

"Is that a psychological condition?" Kelson asked.

"It can be. Some attachment is normal. Even strong attachment can be healthy. Extreme cases, which are medically confidential, only come to us when Human judgment is hampered, programming is compromised, or there's a safety issue."

They all nodded.

"I'm Sho, last stationed at Tundra. My area of expertise is Exemplar Processing." He hesitated. "I am, well, was, Ulf's assistant." Beezan nodded sympathetically.

"So you work on the AI side and Adisa works on the human side?" Teeve asked.

"Correct." He nodded once.

"Do either of you know much about the AI's management of micro and nano bots?" Iricana asked.

"Yes," Sho answered. "That's part of what Ulf and I do. Unfortunately, he isn't cleared for work."

"But he was discharged from Med Bay this morning," Terina added. All heads turned to her. "He has to check in every day, but he's been assigned to a cabin in Arc 1."

Sho and Adisa looked at each other and gave the barest frowns. "We'll speak to the doctor," Adisa said. "I doubt he is objective enough to assist us."

"With the help of *81*, we should be able to get the microbots under control," Sho said.

"It may not be that simple," Thunder said. "The microbot configuration on the hull, called #9, was from the *Drumheller*. Those microbots seem to be influenced by the programming of older microbots."

"How much older?" Sho asked.

"Five hundred years," Thunder said.

"Five hundred!" they both exclaimed.

"And the old bots were programmed by a young man trying to evade a Chike search aboard his ship. He gave them a strong protect order. We'll show you the record of what happened at Redrock."

The screen went on and replayed the morphing of the Chike shuttle and gravity ball. "We've reviewed the feeds from Redrock," Iricana began. "It seems that the Chike shuttle was converted into a human-like shuttle, and then a rocket, which carried the bots to the ship's little gravity ball, and transformed that into a spiderlike thing. The feed ends before there's any other interaction."

"According to reports," Falcon added, "Redrock still has their gravity ball at the a-rings, and it is still possible to jump."

"So what happened out there?" Iricana asked Adisa and Sho.

The two counselors sat dumbstruck. They watched it four

times. They asked for a transcript of the argument between #9 and the *81* crew. They asked *81* for a summary of procedures it used to attempt to control the bots and puzzled over those. "I don't understand," Sho admitted. "How can the greatest off-world AI succumb to 500-year-old microbots?"

"There may be contributing factors," Thunder said. "*81* is a relatively young ship. It spent 15 years abandoned by Humans. And it was under the influence of an alien for those 15 years."

"Alien," they both repeated, eyes wide.

"So you're saying," Sho said, shaking his head in astonishment, "that old microbots took over the programming of new microbots, and together, they hijacked the Chike nanos and used the Chike's own engineering knowledge against them—all under the direction of the *Drumheller* robot config that you call #9."

"Yes," Iricana confirmed.

"What does *81* think?" Sho asked.

"We want to know what you think," Iricana answered.

Adisa and Sho reviewed a lot of data while the others took a break. They consulted with a couple engineers. After two hours Sho shyly shared their recommendation.

"Maybe you all know that 500-year-old bots didn't have the same basic programming that bots do now." They shook their heads no. "Current replicating robots have an AI template built in, certain patterns and restrictions. When necessary for bigger jobs, they build an AI based on that template."

Remembering what had happened in the *Drumheller* rimway, Beezan feared he knew what Sho would say. "The old bots had goal-oriented programming, but very few restrictions. All manner of AIs arose from this. Some were not what we would consider benevolent."

"What sort of termination programming did they have?" Iricana asked.

"As soon as the goal was completed, the AI would report and dismantle."

"Did they always dismantle?" Kelson asked.

"The key," Sho answered, "was in defining the goal or setting a dismantle option if the goal was calculated to be unattainable."

"So whoever programmed these 'protect' orders didn't define an end program properly," Iricana said.

Sho shook his head sadly. "I would say this Azann had no idea what he was doing. As you say, he set the bots to 'protect' his cabin log in a very broad manner. Something like protect from the Chike, without specifics."

"But how is it possible," Thunder asked, "that Human bots could overcome Chike bots?"

Sho became excited now. "I think what's happened is that there were remnants of old Chike nano builders on your ship, which had a battle with your bots in the rimway and ended up on the hull. Most of them were destroyed. But a small number of Chike bots must have survived, intact with their knowledge of Chike engineering. With the help of a real AI in your robot #9, our bots were able to take them over and bring them to the *81-Petals.*"

"So as we suspected, our bots hijacked theirs and re-engineered their gravity ball," Iricana summarized.

"Yes. And they're still out there, with no precise end program in mind," Sho said.

"Will the Redrock people be able to deal with it?" Kelson asked.

"And will we?" Iricana added.

"We have a jump on them," Sho said. "We know about

Azann and what got this going." He gulped and looked around. "We think we need to take over the command chain at robot #9. And that would require the *Drumheller* AI." Beezan sat up. Could they go back for the *Drumheller* somehow?

"However, since that's impossible," Sho said, and Beezan closed his eyes, angry with himself for even getting his hopes up, "the next best thing would be for the *Drumheller* exemplars, if they are alive and can be found, to go face to face with #9."

"They are alive and in this room," Iricana said, indicating Beezan and Thunder. "But what do you mean by face-to-face, with a robot config?"

"They have to go on the hub," Sho said gravely.

81-Petals, incoming to OSRI

"*Drumheller*, lights." Nothing happened. Beezan pushed his blankets down and gently moved Sky away from his neck. "*Drumheller?*"

"How may I assist, honor?" Beezan jerked at the voice of *81*, waking up Sky, who immediately started whining, filling his veins with fire.

"No, no." He buried his head under the blankets. *No Drumheller. Sky sick. Crew of thousands. Rogue nanos. I'm supposed to be at a meeting. No.* "Sky, please," he begged. And the burning faded to a dull ache.

He couldn't face the meeting with a command crew bigger than any full crew he'd ever had. And he didn't want to go to the tram-sized prayer room. So he took Sky to the One Tree garden where they'd first met Veez.

The artificial "sun" was low in the "sky." Beezan sat on a bench with his back to it. His long shadow stretched out before him, mingling with the shadows of the bare tree branches. An unnerving, chilly breeze made him hug Sky close. But, to his great relief, she sighed and breathed more evenly.

Is the tree even alive? Beezan wondered. He got off the bench and sat down on the clear plates that held the dirt in, settling Sky beside him. He leaned forward so he could put his hand on the tree.

His absence from the meeting nagged at him; they would worry. But soon enough, there were graceful footsteps on the stairs and a gentle hand squeezed his shoulder. Ra'Tama sat down next to him, snuggling Cookie beside Sky.

"I'm sorry," Beezan said. "I know you lost your ship too."

"A loss, true, but *Kingfisher* was not my home," Ra'Tama said. More resounding footsteps came up the stairs and Jarvie plopped down on Beezan's left, folding his long legs crosswise. And then Sequoia came, practically tip-toeing. They all reached out to the tree, pressing their palms against the trunk. Ra'Tama chanted a prayer that sounded like Earth, like wind and waves and trees with branches reaching to heaven.

"So far, no sign of the Chike," Falcon reported from the Command Bay.

In the Consultation Hall, Iricana breathed a sigh of relief, but Terina's grandpa shook his head and cautioned Iricana to "Put the pedal to the metal." She must have known what that meant as she nodded.

Terina tried to write her newsfeed while they waited for the pilots. "Next destination: Firelight" was as far as she got. She wasn't allowed to say that they didn't have enough ships to evacuate Harbor, or that Jamez was looking over Veez's specs for the shimmer shield.

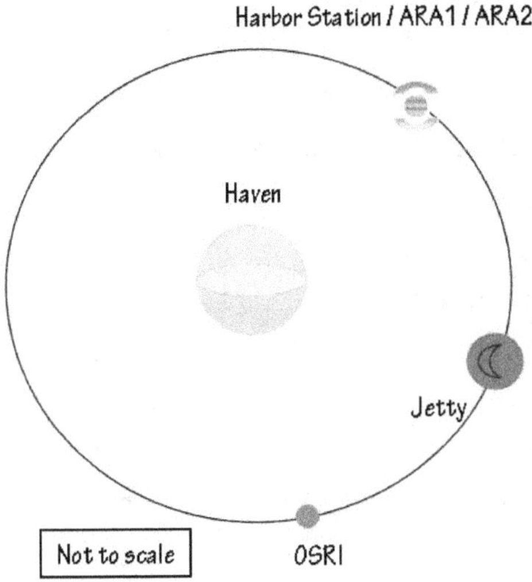

When the pilots arrived, along with two pups, Falcon put Jamez through.

"God is Most Glorious, Captain." Jamez sat facing them through the screen.

"God is Most Glorious," Iricana said and introduced the command crew.

"Greetings everyone. I'm sorry," Jamez said, "I know what you want. It's the staple of science fiction: a mysterious coating that makes a ship invisible. And that's what this is. It's instructions for using nanos to assemble a flexible, detached shield made from this magic material. But we don't have any such material that absorbs all signals and returns nothing, or scatters signals in all ways but the incoming direction."

"Kind of like a gravity ball," Jarvie said.

Everyone turned to look at him, stunned.

"Well, yes. That's as close to invisible as you're going to get," Jamez said. "But that still wouldn't work. You can't take a gravity ball with you."

"We have," Iricana said. The *81* people were thinking and looking at each other. "And you have a spare gravity ball," Iricana pointed out.

James sighed. "We have several. But we have no idea how to manipulate that material."

"We do," Iricana said. "Kind of. We have Chike nanobuilders."

"Yes," Kelson agreed. "If we could get control of Azann's bots, who control the nanos, we could most likely build whatever we want."

"Are you serious?" Jamez objected. "Let rogue nanos take a gravity ball apart? Make a shield that folds up? Stick it in your cargo hold and jump? Deploy it the second you drop into normal space? Hope they don't feel the resonance anyway? That's not engineering! That's dreaming!"

Terina agreed with Jamez. It was crazy, Ramian-like thinking. But then she saw Beezan looking towards the top of the ship.

"That's the angle I need," Beezan said quietly. And everyone turned to him. "The protect order that will bring #9 to our side and finish the command." He looked at Iricana. "I'm going up there."

She put her hand on his arm. "Tomorrow."

The next day, Beezan took a work tower lift to the transfer ring and pulled the rest of the way to the hub top hatch, Thunder and Teeve close behind him. They crosschecked their suits and he and Thunder went out, leaving Teeve behind. Focusing only on tethering and checking the safe zones, it was a moment before Beezan could take in the full view of the *81-Petals*.

Bigger on the outside. The *Drumheller* had a big cargo hold, much bigger, but the torus of *81* rivaled the smaller space stations. He was glad he didn't see it before going through the a-rings.

It's so new! All the panels were the same color, with paintings of flowers. With the golden light of Harbor glinting off the hull, it was beautiful. *In its own way*, he thought guiltily.

Knowing he was being monitored, he tried not to gaze about too long. Walking carefully along the gripstrip, he came to the last known location of #9. It was awkward to turn around and look for Thunder, who was reporting to Adisa, Sho, and the Captain, but he had a sense that Thunder was right behind him.

Beezan took a few deep breaths and set plans A-E in mind. "Robot #9? It's Beezan. Do you know me? Do you know the *Drumheller*?"

Beezan suddenly felt disoriented, as if he were falling, or the surface was sliding out from under him. Thunder grabbed his arm and whispered, "The bots. The bots are assembling."

They were moving, sliding across the hull, and building themselves into a human shape, but sleek, not the clunky type that had saved them from the alien fever. A facsimile of the human suit control appeared on its chest and frequencies were matched. "I am Drumheller."

You are not! Was Beezan's gut reaction. *Maybe some wayward strand of the real Drumheller. Focus. Plan A.* "#9, acknowledge that we are on the *81-Petals*."

"Acknowledged. *Drumheller* beacon was transferred to *81-Petals*."

"Therefore, programming is now supervised by the *81-Petals*."

"Negative."

Well, it couldn't have been that easy. "Explain logic."

"Program incomplete. Program goal transferred from *Drumheller*. Program goal transferred from *Ultrasoar*."

There were more gasps over the s'link. *Plan B.* "Acknowledge original programmer Azann."

"Acknowledged."

"Estimate current status of Azann."

"Deceased."

"Acknowledge that I am the next living human in his command chain."

"Databases are insufficient."

"Acknowledge that I am a *Drumheller* exemplar."

"Acknowledged."

Beezan switched channels to talk to Adisa. "Go ahead with command sequence?" he asked. There was no answer. He checked his channels and asked again. *Am I getting panicky?* "Thunder?" Nothing.

A strange chill ran down his spine. Awkwardly, Beezan stepped around, just enough to see if Thunder was signaling him.

Gone! Beezan turned 360 degrees. "Thunder? Where are you? Adisa? *81*?" No response. He turned back to #9 and switched back to that channel. "#9, do you hear me?"

"Affirmative." *Okay. Okay. Don't panic.* Thunder must have gone to check on the communication problem. Not being able to see behind him was creeping him out though.

"Suit, rear camera to inset 1." But on his little inset, the screen was black. Again he ploddingly turned around. There was a big black shape just above the hull. His veins went cold. A shuttle! A big shuttle with all lights off was stationkeeping only a few meters from the hull. "#9! Is that a Chike shuttle?"

"Negative."

Calm down. Breathe. "What is it?"

"It is the *Edelweiss*."

And then Thunder was walking toward him. Except he was not tethered. And walked a little awkwardly. "Thunder?"

"Greetings, Honor Beezan." Beezan's stomach seized.

Ulf! On the hub. No! With a shuttle. Heaven help us. Beezan tried to put on his captain voice. "What are you doing up here?"

Ulf's hands went up to appease. "Honor. I'm here to help. These bots and their AIs are my area of expertise."

"Where's Thunder?"

"He's fine."

"Ulf!" All kinds of crazy thoughts ran through Beezan's head, but the overwhelming one was to get back inside the ship. He took a step toward the hatch.

"Sorry, Honor. You won't be able to get in. I have the crew somewhat distracted."

"What do you want?" Beezan demanded.

"The same thing that you want."

"I want to go inside."

"I want to go home," Ulf said. "And so do you."

Beezan was truly confused, but knew Ulf was overly attached to his former AI. "Tundra? Why would I want to go there?"

"Really, Honor. It's so easy," Ulf explained. "You and I jump to the *Drumheller* in this shuttle. Then you take me to Tundra. Win win."

He's lost his mind. But he's in control of the bots and the shuttle. Don't panic! 81 and Iricana will figure it out. Teeve will be through that hatch. Thunder, God, what's he done with him? Stall.

"Ulf, even if I wanted to go, we can't jump in a shuttle."

"Of course you can. You could probably jump in your suit."

"Ulf, there's not enough room for supplies. We'd starve. I've run these numbers before! It's crazy." *Don't say crazy!*

"Supplies are loaded. You will come in close. You will be reunited. I understand how hard it is. You can have the *Drumheller* back."

Beezan told himself he would never consider a rogue jump, but just the thought sent pain through his whole system. "I'm not taking you to the *Drumheller*! I can't leave. I can't leave Jarvie. I can't leave Sky," and he realized he was starting to cry. And then he was angry. *Look what this Ulf has done to me!*

"You'll be back to them in a few days. With the *Drumheller*. You're not leaving anyone. You'll all be together again!"

"#9! #9, I order you to restrain Ulf!"

"#9 is under my control now. And it will be several hours before the quite innocent *81* can recover from my work. We'll be gone. I've heard how you can jump. We'll be at the *Drumheller* today. All you have to do is come aboard the shuttle."

Desperately, Beezan tried to reroute his s'link. *Why can't they hear me?* "#9! Forward my signal." Nothing. Beezan took another step toward the hatch. *I can beat him there. He's a novice in the suit.*

Jarvie sat in the back of the Command Bay with Terina as Iricana, Katie, Ra'Tama, Adisa, and Sho monitored Beezan and Thunder on the hub. Teeve stood by inside the hub hatch and Sequoia and a shuttle crew were in the hangar.

Beezan seemed to be arguing with #9 for a long time. Every once in awhile, Thunder would say, "Negotiations proceeding." Iricana shook her head, "What's with that?"

Adisa had a private channel to Beezan, "Go to Plan B," she

said. But instead of starting on the Zann angle, Beezan started on Plan C, with no change of inflection.

"It doesn't even sound like him," Jarvie whispered. He'd never known Beezan to spend more than thirty seconds arguing.

"He knew it would take time," Terina said.

"Suit feeds are fine," Katie added.

Adisa tried again. "Beezan, acknowledge, Plan B, the Zann approach."

Iricana opened a channel on her panel. "Thunder, acknowledge you can hear me."

"I acknowledge I can hear you," he answered. She frowned.

Adisa tried. "Beezan, can you hear me?"

"I can hear you."

Adisa and Sho looked at each other in alarm. "Beezan!" Adisa said with fake urgency. "Come inside now. Jarvie's been hurt!"

"Stand by."

Both Adisa and Sho gasped. "It's not them, Captain," Sho said. "It's an AI, and not a very good one."

"*81!*" Iricana asked, "Where is Beezan's feed coming from?"

"S'link router on the hub."

Sho looked suspicious. "*81*, what's happening on the hull?"

"Negotiations are—attempting to trace—"

Oh my God, Jarvie thought. *There's something wrong with 81.*

Sho leaped out of his seat. "*81!* Command sort override! Captain, your override code!"

While Iricana gave the code, Adisa turned to Katie, "Where is Ulf?"

"Ulf? In his cabin, A24." And Adisa was sprinting out the door, with Katie right behind her.

Jarvie got on the s'link. "Teeve, can you hear me?"

"I can hear you."

"Sequoia, can you hear me?"

"I can hear you."

"Jarvie!" Iricana said, running for an equipment cabinet and pulling out three captain's radios, handing one to him and the other to Terina. "Jarvie, get up to Teeve and tell him to find out what's happening on the hub. Terina, get to the hangar and have Sequoia do a flyover. Ra'Tama, get your crew and go with Terina to stand by in the hangar."

As they sped down the rimway, they met Katie coming back. "Ulf's not in his cabin!"

Terina and Ra'Tama went for the tram station elevator, but Jarvie decided to climb for the hub, in case the *81* got any ideas. Up the stairs to rimway 2, more stairs to rimway 3. He grabbed a manual door opener and a breather at level 4, where there was no more rimway, just an access strut. Gravity was less at every level, but he was already tired. Just ladders now. He hooked his stuff on him to be hands free, and tried to pace his breathing. *What could possibly have happened?*

And then, at the hatch where they went out to the hub, he found Teeve floating unconscious.

Beezan committed himself to a race for the hatch. He turned his back on Ulf and released his grips, jumping toward the hatch with his tether in hand. He was just about to blast his thruster, when a mass of bots rolled over the hull and transformed into a robot arm. It grabbed him, clanking against his helmet. "Ulf! Let me go! You can't force me to jump!"

Rather than just taking him, the arm roughly shoved him toward the shuttle—*too fast!* He grabbed for his tether, but the suit ejected it. *Oh my God. I'm loose!* A terrifying panic set in. He tried to slow himself with his thrusters so he wouldn't be injured hitting the shuttle. But something hit him hard from behind, pushing him toward the shuttle again, thrusting dangerously close to him. "Ulf! Be careful!"

"You will cooperate! We will both win!" Ulf shouted.

"Let me go!"

"What's wrong with you? I'm offering you your heart's desire!"

"No! I have no desire to leave the *81*! I order—"

Suddenly, Ulf was spinning him. "Stop thrusting!" Ulf commanded. Beezan stopped before he made the spinning worse.

"You're making me sick. Stop the spinning!" Beezan said.

"Promise you'll help me," Ulf demanded.

"We'll talk about it."

"This is for our own good. And Tundra . . . needs me."

Normally, Beezan would be sympathetic and concerned to hear such a breakdown, but the spinning and increasing danger were making him angry. A surge of mad primitive energy overcame him, focusing his mind against . . . his enemy. "Suit! Auto-stabilize."

"The suit is under my control. You're coming with me!" Ulf said.

On his next rotation, Beezan could see the hatch of the shuttle coming up fast. "#9! I order you to help me!" He pulled his hands and feet in, hoping to enter the hatch, but no. His shoulder hit the edge painfully and he bounced back out. But Ulf crashed into him again, pushing him into the shuttle, Ulf's thrusters firing millimeters from Beezan—melting part of his suit. "My suit!" He felt a decompression and saw his red light go on. "#9! I'm losing air!"

The shuttle was his only hope now. He grabbed a hold bar to

keep from bouncing too far out, and with Ulf pushing they both entered the lock. But he was losing air faster than his suit could compensate. He wasn't going to be conscious much longer. *Close. Close. Close*, he willed the door. But it stopped halfway. *No!*

A metallic hand pushed the door open. *It must be Teeve or Thunder.* "No! Let the door close!" But it wasn't either of them. A mass of bots flooded into the airlock. *Oh no.* "#9! Close the door! I need air!" But it didn't shut the door. In one massive shove, Ulf was propelled out the hatch. The door shut and a swarm of nanos converged on Beezan's suit where it was damaged.

Beezan was heaving for air, vision going, trying to think straight. But his oxygen levels started to go up again. Slowly. *Breathe. Just breathe. Ulf is loose. Thunder is missing. I'm stuck in the shuttle. Breathe and think.* "#9. Is that you?"

"Protect. Protect the Zann."

"Yes. Yes. Thank you," he said, between gasps of air. "Can you fix my link to *81*?"

"Link restored."

"*81! 81*, what's happening?"

"Beezan!" a near panicked Adisa answered. "We have a red on your suit!"

"It's temporarily repaired. I can breathe for now. I'm in a shuttle near the hub. Ulf is off tether and loose."

"Ulf!"

"God Almighty," he heard Sho whisper.

"Jarvie!" Iricana ordered. "Wait for backup before you open that door! Ra'Tama, take a shuttle to get Ulf!"

"I don't know where Thunder is!" Beezan warned her.

"We'll look," Iricana said tightly.

"#9, where is Thunder?"

"On the hub. He is unharmed."

"Restore his beacon."

"Restored."

"Create a beacon for Ulf," Beezan ordered.

"Ulf is the enemy."

"Careful," Sho breathed.

"Ulf is human. We must save him. #9. You must obey *81*. For all our sakes."

"I obey the Zann."

"Acknowledge: I am the last of the Zann. That's why you saved me." There was a pause.

"Affirmative."

"*81* obeys me. You will obey me and *81*."

"Concur. I will obey you and the *81-Petals*."

"Always and completely," Beezan said. "Turn over your codes."

Another pause. "Always and completely."

"Transfer complete," *81* reported. "Loyalty lock confirmed."

"Thank you #9, for saving me. Now please fly this shuttle back to the hangar." On their way, they saw Ra'Tama going after Ulf.

"Thunder rescued, Honor," Iricana told him quietly.

"Thank God. I'm just going to rest a minute, Captain," Beezan said, as he pulled off his helmet and wiped his face.

"See you in a bit," she answered.

And he strapped into the shuttle, but couldn't help looking over his shoulder. *That way. That's where the Drumheller is. Maybe only one jump away.*

3 / THE CRUX

81-Petals, near OSRI in Harbor System

Beezan woke up early with Sky whining in her sleep. "It's okay," he whispered and patted her. He was tired and sore, but happy to be alive and feeling a bit "older but wiser," as Kelson would say. Yesterday, after his frightening foray on the hub, the discovery of the unconscious Teeve and Sequoia, and Ra'Tama's masterful rescue of Ulf, he didn't think he'd be able to sleep, but he had.

Concerned that the *81-Petals* had been so easily misled, he talked to Iricana privately at breakfast. "We need to add more exemplars. People with more . . ." He didn't want to say cunning, or suspicions.

"Savvy," Iricana supplied.

"Yes, like you." Beezan agreed.

"Not nearly enough, apparently. And I'm an exemplar already, although we really haven't been here long enough for *81* to collect a lot of data."

"What about Jarvie?" Beezan suggested.

"Tendency to avoid the rules?"

"Well, tendency to consider all the angles," Beezan said, and then sighed. "No, you're right. He's a little too flexible with the rules."

"Let's think about it," she said. "Meanwhile, they're going to test the shimmer shield concept. Let's head down to the hangar."

Jarvie headed for the lift, suited up and carrying his helmet. Things were moving so fast! With #9's cooperation, the *81-Petals* was able to take charge of the Chike nanos. It even generated a special class of nano guards to keep the Chike nanos on their good behavior. Bringing the rogue nanos under control was almost too easy, according to Sho, but it meant they could work directly with Jamez and the OSRI people. They were cleared to dock, but instead, they went out to a safe location where Jamez had a spare gravity ball.

Iricana had shared Veez's plans for the shimmer shield that would hide a ship from the Chike so they could check on the colony planet. In a stunningly short time, Jamez had gone from "you're dreaming" to dismantling the extra gravity ball to get the special non-reflective material. Now a believer, Jamez was running them around, insisting on immediate tests of the proto-type. Jarvie was on his way to the hangar to help.

Jarvie caught up to Thunder, Chip, and Kente in the lift. Chip hugged the wall behind Kente, eyes down. *Am I that scary?* But then he realized that the two shy Tektite kids, unfamiliar with strangers, were stuck in the lift with the two biggest people on *81*.

Jarvie put on his most mild expression as he glanced at Kente's digital slogan on the front of ziz makeshift uniform. It read *CONSIDER IT DONE,* but when Kente saw Jarvie looking, it changed to *WHAT?*

With a flash of his miserable school days on Hamada, so far behind him now, Jarvie laughed out loud. Thunder gave him a raised eyebrow, and Kente scowled, but Jarvie just smiled at them all. *Anywhere is better than there.*

Jarvie, Chip, and Kente suited up together. Kente got up the nerve to side comment, "I thought ya were the Captain's *Diplomat.*"

Jarvie smiled. "I am."

"So what ya doin' here?"

"Supervising the tubeway and Entry Lounge hatch. Also cross-checking."

"We crosscheck each other."

"Not just you two. Everyone."

"So ya don't actually fix things."

"Sure I do," he said in his friendliest voice.

As the two of them helped each other with gloves, Jarvie waited patiently for one of them to help him. Finally, Chip tilted ziz head to Jarvie and Kente floated over. As Jarvie braced against the wall, Kente helped push the glove on. "So how old are you?" ze whispered.

"I'm 16." Their eyes bugged out.

"Why aren't—" Chip started to ask and then froze.

"Why aren't ya in a test group?" Kente followed up.

Patience, Jarvie reminded himself. *Fix things.* "Because . . . I don't have a partner, my parent wouldn't like it, and I'm not that experienced in EVA," he answered honestly.

"We're experts!" Kente said. "But all we get to do is help. We could drive that shimmer thing! No prob." Chip nodded. They finished their crosschecks and grabbed their helmets.

"Well," Jarvie suggested, "Let's do the best job helping we can do today, and see what happens."

Chip rolled ziz eyes. Kente gave a grudging laugh. "Yeah, we get it. You're diplomatin'."

Jarvie smiled. *Yeah. Fixing things.*

Terina parked herself at the observation window where she had a good view of the hangar deck. Ra'Tama and the Kays waited in the other hangar in the shuttle *Lotus*, the one they would use for the landing.

Jarvie, hovering right near her at the hatch, had already processed everyone through to the hangar. All eight Tektites, plus Taj and Hisoka were out there. The two younger kids, Chip and Kente seemed very competent, helping the others with various exosuits, jetpacks, and scooters. They never even got their tethers tangled. The Tektites had their own sign language, and she saw Chip squeeze Sunny's arm.

Terina brought up the "score card" that Jarvie made:

Sibs: Maura and Cooper, Teeve and Mika, Sunny and Chip, Danny and Kente.
Couples: Maura and Teeve, Mika and Cooper, Sunny and Danny
Friends: Chip and Kente

Iricana and a stressed Beezan came in with Kelson and Sky. They joined Thunder, who was in charge from the control panel in the Entry Lounge. Of course, the captain was fully up to date, but Terina smiled as Thunder explained from the start.

"Jamez, his OSRI people, and Sho have been working nonstop on Veez's shimmer shield. They've been able to dissemble one of the extra gravity balls—"

"One of them?" Kelson asked.

"Apparently, Thayne accidently called a bunch of them. Luckily Jamez stopped them before they came careening into the station."

Beezan closed his eyes as if in pain.

"Using the same Ramian control panel that they used to stop the gravity balls, they were able to turn off this particular gravity ball, and the Chike nanos dismantled it.

The Tektites built this shield-shaped frame that rolls up. Once we unroll it, the Chike nanos and gravity ball materials can be released from their protective boxes.

The Chike nanos will cover the framework of the shield in this gravity ball material."

"How does this all work for us?" Iricana asked.

"The idea is that we jump, and get the *81* behind a planet or moon right away. We roll out the shield and turn it on. Then we can launch the shuttle Lotus. It gets on the inner side of the shimmer shield. Then the gravity ball material does the same thing it does with the gravity ball, absorbs energy and sends it into this central point. We're calling it a crux. The shuttle will be hidden."

"What happens to the energy?" Beezan asked.

Thunder hesitated. "We don't know. Veez said it goes to 'another place'. But he was adamant that nothing can get between the shield and the crux."

"Or . . ." Kelson said.

"Well, of course, Jamez had to try it. He put a beacon between. It flowed along this line to the crux. It was destroyed before it disappeared."

Iricana bit her lip. "We're playing with other dimensions here?"

Thunder nodded. "Same as every time we use a gravity ball. The big difference is that the ball shape protects us from the crux and from these lines of energy between the shield and the crux. We won't have that protection. Anything that gets in there . . . will be lost."

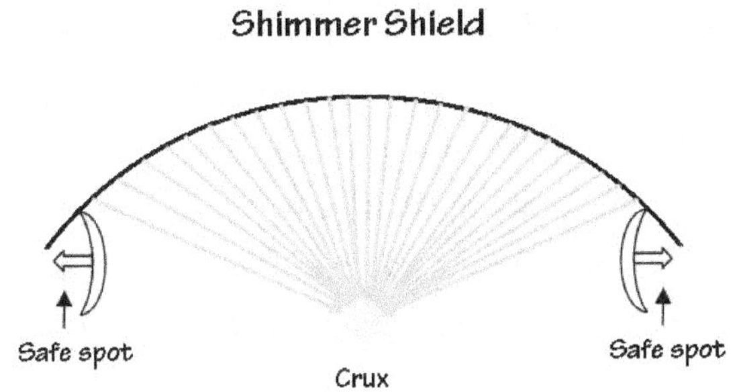

"Once the shield is up and the shuttle *Lotus* is behind it, at a safe distance, they will have to travel together, maintaining stationkeeping, to the planet. If there are no Chike, the *Lotus* can leave the shield and land. The total mission has to be completed in 20 hours, the maximum time for the suits. We need to get the *81* in close."

Terina studied the diagram. "Where does it attach to the shuttle?"

"It doesn't. That's the hard part. The shield has to be piloted by hand, by two people who can work very well together as communication will be minimal. There are only two safe spots, at the edges, where they can attach a jetpack or scooter. They have to keep their thrusting behind the screen. And we won't be able to communicate with them, or our signal would be detected."

"So two people have to work together . . . one pushes one way, the other pushes the other way," Beezan clarified.

"They'll each have a range of motion, but basically, yes."

"It's so dangerous," Beezan said.

"That's why we're testing today," Thunder said.

Iricana and Beezan looked alarmed.

"It's a fake crux," Thunder said. "No Chike nanos either. They just have to practice flying the frame. We want to know if it's even doable." He took a big breath and signaled the hangar. "Send team 1." He didn't look very hopeful. "We're giving each team ten tries."

Terina wrote in her notes: First up: Maura and Cooper.

She wasn't sure about sending sibs. But they had worked together all their lives. *What would that be like?* Her brother was only 7 when her dad took him away.

Maura and Cooper, in 20-hour jetpacks, positioned themselves in the safe spots at each end of the shield. As Ra'Tama came around in *Lotus*, Maura gradually fired up. Her thruster would be hidden from outside observers by the shield. They shakily got in sync with Ra'Tama, but it was obviously going to take practice. As Ra'Tama slowed down, Cooper had to thrust.

"Oops," Thunder muttered. Cooper had overdone it, jerking the shield and pulling the framework apart. Robot #9 sent the Human nanos to put it back together and they set up for their second try.

Beezan was the first to leave, holding the sides of his head like he couldn't watch. He didn't miss anything. Maura and Cooper just got worse as they got frustrated and decided that eight failures were enough.

Terina eavesdropped on the Tektites channel as Maura and Cooper came in and they prepped Teeve and Mika for their try.

"It's harder than it looks," Cooper said. He didn't sound

mad, just frustrated. "Just staying attached to the shield is one thing, then I can't see Maura and the shuttle at the same time."

"Let's set up some helmet cams," Danny suggested.

"No time for us," Mika answered. "You guys try that."

Mika and Teeve couldn't stay with the shuttle as it got up to speed. On their third try, they somehow got the shield vibrating. Thunder almost talked to them, but Iricana grabbed his hand. "Comm silence."

The shield started to flex back and forth and threw both of them out of their safe spots. Teeve went flying forward, but Mika was sent into the crux. If it had been real, she would be gone. "Oh my God," Sunny said. "I'm not sure this is possible."

"Be careful," Chip whispered.

But with the added cameras and ten times practicing, Sunny and Danny were able to make a system. They kept up with the shuttle and stopped and started without disaster.

"Good work!" Thunder said. "All of you." He turned to Iricana. "Doable?"

"God help us," Iricana answered. "Danny and Sunny. Give Taj and Hisoka a try and if they have any hope, make them the backup."

"What if they're better?"

"They don't even know each other."

"Are ya two sure ya can do this?" Teeve was asking Danny and Sunny.

"We can!" Sunny answered.

"Twenty hours. No nappin'. No eatin'. No nothin'."

"They put their helmets together for a minute. "Yeah. We can. Big job, but we can do it."

4 / THE MUSIC OF THE SPHERES

81-Petals, near OSRI

Again, Beezan found himself at a command crew meeting with a whining Sky, again, trying to solve impossible problems.

"Captain," Falcon reported, "Harbor Council is anxious to evacuate before the Chike show up. Jamez is holding his people for now and has a dedicated ship. All other ships are now assigned, but they are short 412 spots. For example, the 351 people on ARA2, the pilot retirement station, are unassigned."

"It's been suggested," Kelson added, "that we jump to Atik and then come back for them."

"That's assuming we can offload people at Atik," Iricana answered.

Falcon nodded. "If they spread out the overage between all ships, we'd each be 12% over. In our case, 12% over emergency capacity."

Teeve shook his head. "Systems are already strained. We're running trams only part-time. But there are plenty more drastic energy-saving measures."

"I think we can assume that all inward stations will be

crowded. Overcrowded," Iricana said. "So anyone we take on may end up being permanent. And we can't be 12% over emergency capacity permanently."

Falcon nodded. "The council prefers that everyone go, but they are considering having either all of OSRI stay, or all of ARA2.

"Abandon them?" Beezan asked, concerned.

"Just hoping someone can come for them," Falcon answered.

"No one else is coming," Iricana said firmly. "We're the last ship."

A strange thought started in the back of Beezan's mind. "Why leave the pilots? We could use them."

"They're not active," Iricana said.

"Because they thought they could jump anywhere," Beezan reminded them. "Which maybe they could . . ." There was a contemplative silence around the table.

"Let's talk to them," Ra'Tama suggested.

"What? Why?" Iricana asked.

"To see if they're dangerous, or if they are just freejumpers."

"It doesn't solve the problem of not enough ships," Iricana reminded them.

Everyone was shaking their heads. Beezan looked at the map of Harbor system, with ARA2 in orbit around the station. He closed his eyes. Threads were everywhere, but thin. *What if .. what . . . swirling threads.* He grabbed the chair, heart pounding. Jarvie put his hand on Beezan's arm as if to hold him in place. Everyone was looking at him in alarm. "What if we jump ARA2?" he whispered.

A commotion of objection erupted in the room, but not from the other pilots. They stared at him in speculation. "Stop! Please stop!" Iricana admonished, giving Beezan a stern look. "How? They have no engines."

Beezan looked to Thunder for help. "They do have thrusters," Thunder said.

"We only have to get them out of Haven's planetary gravity well," Sequoia added. "But we'll need more than those station-keeping thrusters."

"Rock relocators," Thunder suggested, sitting up in excitement. "ARA2 really isn't much bigger than the *81-Petals*."

Falcon shook her head. "It's crazy. Council will never—"

"Falcon," Iricana said, "no one speaks for the Council, except the Council. First, we will study the problem. Then we'll propose a fact-based solution and take it to the Council. NO ONE is to say one word about this to anyone outside this room. Is that understood?"

There was very subdued nodding around the table, especially from Falcon. "Thunder, get the mass and specs of ARA2. Beezan, Jarvie, and Terina, visit the pilots as a humanitarian exercise. Don't ask them about the idea. Just get a feel for their mental states. Sequoia, work on trajectories with me."

1-Sovereignty Eve

ARA2

Beezan crowded into the lift with the other musicians, trying not to bump his violin, slung over one shoulder, or Sky, in his front podpup pocket. That Sky was allowed to visit ARA2 and Star and Rocket were not had boosted her mood for the first time since the jump.

It was Jarvie's idea to visit as musicians. They had recruited Sharlee, a performance-level cello player from Arc 4. She and Beezan, plus a viola player, Zaira, and a bass player, Leon, had formed a quartet and practiced almost non-stop. Leon was young and strong and could heft his metallic bass in a hardcase with one hand. Zaira, approaching 70, had a severe limp, which didn't matter in nogee. Sharlee, breezy and professional, led them on with an air of stardom. Sky, head poking out of the pocket to watch, nodded in approval. Meanwhile, they all crossed their fingers that the Chike would not come, not yet.

Terina accompanied as journalist and Jarvie served as pilot. They flew over in the *Bird of Paradise*, Beezan more nervous about playing in public than their mission of feeling out the pilots. The practices had been good for Sky, who would even abandon Beezan to sit by Sharlee, soaking in those long vibrations. But Beezan noticed something mysterious about the music. He was curious to see how the pilots would react.

As a couple of techs helped them set up in the ARA2 nogee auditorium, a quick and intense coordinator named Khurshi quietly explained what to expect. "The pilots here are those that don't have close families and can't be released into the general population. Some wander all the time. Others who are partially coherent may visit the schools, podpup center, or even help out with teen training. We just don't let them near a vessel."

Sharlee slipped her feet into the deck braces next to her chair and stretched to her full height. "It is about the music," she said. Khurshi scowled.

When they were strapped and ready to play, the auditorium doors opened. A mix of people entered: station workers, doctors, and pilots. Many pilots were old, possibly old enough to be actually retired, but many were young. They seemed to fall into three categories: the intense type, the serene detached type, and some wandering so much they were being led to their seats and strapped in. Not touching the pilots didn't seem to be a rule here. Beezan tried not to stare. In fact, he looked away quickly as pilot after pilot gazed at him, not with jealousy, not envy, but with such yearning it was heartbreaking. Beezan was suddenly worried he shouldn't have come, afraid they'd think he was flaunting his freedom. He glanced up just before they started. So many people had crowded in that he lost track of Jarvie and Sky at the back of the room.

They played their introductory piece, a classic old Earth quartet, followed by an upbeat Martian quartet, and a concerto so difficult that Sharlee played along to a recording.

The last two experimental pieces were written by pilots, one fifty years ago and one only five years ago right here in Harbor. Sharlee had selected the pieces she thought the pilots would like, but Beezan found them a bit unnerving. The first composer used the metaphor of strings trying to reach a chord to represent finding the thread to jump. But she strung out the wait so long that Beezan's hands would shake, wanting to tip into that proper frequency. The pilots winced and heaved a collective sigh of relief when they finally achieved the harmony. Some shook their heads in disapproval and applause was not enthusiastic.

The last piece used a similar approach, but the sequences of finding the harmonies and jumping around were much faster, as if a little ship could flit around the galaxy with no more difficulty than plucking a cello string. The pattern was like an actual map of the outer sectors, except with jumps they would never attempt. The harmonies passed from the bass to the cello to the viola to Beezan and raced back down, as if the stars were not unreachable, but their playground.

Beezan had to concentrate, but he felt the mood in the room shift entirely. The pilots leaned forward. They followed the piece, then anticipated where it was going, turning their heads to watch the strings advance. Beezan realized that the difference between the two compositions was similar to the difference between the threads how they used to be, and the threads now. *Something really has changed.*

As the piece raced toward conclusion, the pilots pushed away from their seats, straining their straps. Some held their hands over imaginary thrusters as if they were jumping. Beezan missed a cue and glued his eyes back to the music—and suddenly saw what they were playing, what the composer must have seen, what he saw in his wandering: A thousand pathways, threads, one note away, a million more in the background, a pulsing galactic web-like harp. And when they reached that final chord, a hundred voices joined them, spooking the non-pilots, but bursting into Beezan's mind and sending him wandering.

Jarvie floated, entranced, at the back of the room, no longer able to see Beezan or the musicians. His heart pounded with the music of the jumping. And then everyone was unstrapping, floating, finishing the piece together, and clapping wildly. Sky was excited and crawled onto his shoulder. He wheeled into the rimway to recover and avoid the crush of cheering people, and found himself carried along with the energized crowd. He tried to maneuver aside to go back, but subtle movements of others prevented him. After several odd bumps, he realized he was being herded. He tried to stop, but an old man gently took him by the arm, "This way." He felt no sense of danger, so although nervous, he decided not to resist. A few more pulls and he was in a cabin—with the arm-holder and two others, all obviously pilots.

"My apologies, friend," the arm-holder said, releasing him.

"My name is Rendra." He wasn't as old as Jarvie first thought. His hair and skin were white, almost translucent, like a ghost. He was probably Beezan's age and had ship pins running down both sleeves. But his startling green eyes twinkled as he introduced the others. "This is Sandra and Melina. We're *patients* here."

Jarvie reached for his p'link, meaning to call Terina, not security. Rendra held up his hand. "We mean you no harassment, just one minute of your time." Jarvie didn't know what to say, but he dropped his hand from the p'link. Rendra nodded. "We have a message for Honor Beezan."

Sky drifted off Jarvie's shoulder to give the man a good look. "Sky!" Jarvie said, grabbing her.

"Check," she insisted. So Jarvie held her so she could look Rendra and the two women in the eyes. Satisfied, she returned to Jarvie's shoulder and said, "Friends."

"Okay," Jarvie said with some relief, even as they smiled at Sky.

"We're ready," Rendra said. "Tell the freejumper we are ready." The others nodded. *Ready? To jump? Do they know the plan?* They all nodded in intense unison. "We just need a leader," he added. Sandra opened the door and gently pushed Jarvie back out of the room into the thinning crowd. *God help us. Beezan is going to jump the ARA2.*

Terina looked back and forth between the musicians and the audience. She wanted to record the end of the piece with the camera on the musicians, but the audience was a bigger story. Finally, she used her backup camera, just in time to record the pilots joining in. Terina thought it was wonderful, but the station commander, Altan, was rattled. He signaled a couple of doctors to settle the pilots down.

Before the doctors could do anything, the pilots surged forward. Sharlee and Leon floated down from the stage to shake hands and work the crowd. Some pilots remained strapped to their seats, staring off into space, but with peaceful happy looks on their faces. Terina turned back to the stage—where Beezan drifted, violin still on his shoulder, clearly wandering, and in full view of the whole crowd. *Yikes. I need to get Honor down from there.* Terina, camera still in hand, looked for Jarvie, but he was gone. The doctors seemed to be in a hurry to clear the room, as if something bad had happened. She tossed her other gear in her bag, quickly put it over her shoulder, and pulled along the tops of the chairs toward the stage.

Zaira had gently taken Beezan's violin and bow and packed them up, talking to him quietly. "We need to go now, Beezan." She put the two instruments over her shoulders.

Just then Khurshi dove onto the stage and looked at Beezan. "Hey. He should stay here. He should be retired."

"He's fine," Zaire said smoothly, moving towards the door. "You can move the chairs now."

"I'm not a stagehand. I'm the audio tech—and a medical assistant. And I'm telling you, this one belongs here, not out flying!"

By now, Sharlee and Leon were back, packing up their big instruments. "My friend," Sharlee breezed, "there is no cause for concern." She looked up dramatically. "The music. It is so powerful and yet draining."

Khurshi rolled his eyes. "We'll see," and took off to get a doctor, no doubt.

"Honor, we must go quickly," Zaira whispered. "Please hold my arm."

They got out the door of the auditorium before Khurshi and Commander Altan cornered them, two doctors actually grabbing Beezan by the arms. Beezan frowned and pulled away slightly, but shockingly, they did not release him. *Where is Jarvie? Should I call Iricana?* But Leon was doing that. *What we need is a distraction.* Her camera was still in her hand. Taking a huge breath, she flicked it on and braced in front of the commander.

"Such a privilege to host the renowned Sharlee, commander. Wasn't she spectacular?" Caught off guard by her leading question, and not wanting to be rude, the polished administrator straightened, faced the camera, and started to give his answer. *I need another question when this is done. Blah blah blah honor to host . . . Where is Jarvie?* "And wouldn't you say it went well, Honor?" Facing the commander, she couldn't see what was happening behind her.

Back in the rimway, Jarvie's p'link buzzed emergency. He grabbed it. "Leon, what's happening?"

"The docs are trying to hold Beezan. Left stage door, where we came in. Terina's distracting the commander but we don't have much time!"

"You and Sharlee get your gear to the shuttle and start the preflight."

"Got it."

Jarvie glanced up at Rendra and the others, who heard the whole thing. "This way," Rendra said and sped up. Jarvie put Sky in his pouch.

Sandra and Melina pulled in front of Jarvie. "Just stay behind them," Rendra said. Jarvie got a glimpse of Beezan being held by the arms, trying to shrink away from the doctors. A surge of anger went through him, which alerted Sky. She started to crawl out.

"No Sky, stay with me. There's a plan." *I hope.* Jarvie approached as if he cared nothing for the scene. Sandra and Melina altered their pulling to a clumsy yanking, knocking straight into Beezan and the doctors, breaking their hold on Beezan.

"Sandra, watch out!" one doctor complained.

Jarvie then took Beezan's arm. "It's me." Rendra behind, joined by some other pilots, created enough buffer for them to speed up and break free, all without creating a big scene.

They got around a curve, but Zaira fell behind to block them. "Go!" she said.

"Yes, go!" Rendra agreed.

"But Terina—" Jarvie objected.

"They don't want her. I'll take care of her," Zaira said. "Go!"

Jarvie didn't have to urge Beezan. They pulled up the rimway to the hangar lift. As the doors closed Jarvie saw the rimway filling up with pilots.

At the shuttle, Leon had the instruments stowed and the shuttle started, while Sharlee sat as regally as always. "Strap!" Leon ordered. "The monitor is a pilot," he whispered to Jarvie. "We're cleared for launch."

"They're running the station!"

"Good thing, but I hope they won't consider it mutiny."

"Check door!" Jarvie ordered.

Beezan, now fully alert, checked the door. "Door secure. Lock released."

And Jarvie boosted away, already dreading what Sequoia would say when she heard he left Terina behind.

5 / CHANGING PLACES

1-Sovereignty

ARA2

Another call from her mom. Terina was tempted not to answer, but understood that her mom was anxious—furious actually—about her being left behind on ARA2.

"What's happening?"

"We're fine, Mom. Really. Zaira is helping me get a lot of good stories from the retired pilots."

"Okay. You're okay."

"Yes, mom. We have free reign of the place, and all the food we can eat. But I'm in an interview."

"Okay. Thunder is coming for you in the morning."

"Got it. Don't worry, Mom!"

Terina smiled at Rendra. "Sorry."

"It was a pleasure to hear the voice of another pilot."

"So you were saying you've heard that composition before? The last one," she reminded Rendra.

"Yes," he answered. "The pilot that wrote it lived here. About four years ago they played it. But it caused such a ruckus the doctors wouldn't let us play it again. And there was no recording. We were sad. It gave us so many ideas."

Terina scanned through her notes. "Who was the composer? —oh A.E. Indigo. You knew her?

"Oh, yes. Quite a character that Alesta Eve. We do miss her."

2-Sovereignty

Terina and Zaira waited quietly, strapped in side chairs in the commander's office. There was no question of their release. They had never been held; they only waited for enough people to settle down to run a docking crew.

The idea to jump ARA2 had come to Commander Altan, and he wasn't happy about it. He scowled at Terina occasionally, for her stalling tactic, even though she'd posted his interview and made him look good. Thunder knocked and came in, followed by Iricana.

After all the greetings and formal stuff, they strapped loosely to some chairs. "Thank you, Commander," Iricana said. "I'm taking advantage of this trip to review operations with you."

He didn't even try to be friendly. "Council has not directed me to turn this facility over to you, Captain."

"I understand, but there won't be much time if they do approve the plan. We'll have to act fast for a favorable orbital position." He nodded grimly, agreeing. "And we don't plan to take command, Honor. You'd still be—"

"No. I won't be jumping with ARA2 or any other retired, or should-be-retired pilot." Iricana leaned back. Terina put her mind into record mode during the long awkward pause.

"There's nowhere else to go, Commander," Thunder said.

"We'll stay at Harbor station, or at OSRI. Wherever. Captain, you seem to have confidence in your pilot. But I've lived and worked with these reckless wanderers for nearly two decades. They think they can jump anywhere, but they are delusional."

"Beezan is not delusional. And he has completed several extraordinary jumps."

"So did many people here, until they made the one jump that killed off their whole crew—as I believe your pilot did once." Iricana couldn't deny that. "There are probably 100 staff here who won't go," he continued. "And I don't think even the Council would force them."

"Commander, this sector is evacuating. OSRI has a ship on standby. Harbor station will be empty. *81* is full."

Terina scowled. There were 4000 people on the *81* who had faith in Beezan. She did. "I'll trade," she said impulsively. They all turned to look at her. "I believe in Honor Beezan. I'll trade my spot on *81* to someone from here. And 100 other people will too!"

"Very sensible." Zaira nodded.

They all looked stunned. But the commander's brows lowered. "Yes. We jump on a ship with a normal pilot. You take a risk with your pilot. Only fair." He turned back to Iricana. "I'll make a list, Captain. Find yourself a new station commander."

Altan rose out of his place abruptly.

Everyone else unstrapped. But Zaira turned and handed Terina Beezan's violin. "Please give this to Honor Beezan. I'm not returning with you." There were gasps all around. "Well, why bother," she responded. "I'll just be coming back in the trade."

"But your things?" Terina asked.

She hugged her viola. "I have everything I need."

. . .

81-Petals, near ARA2

While they waited for the Council's decision, the *81* command crew finalized the plans to refit and jump ARA2, and to swap personnel as necessary. Terina was trying to follow their talk and keep up with all the ArcCom newsfeeds. "We shouldn't underestimate the risk," her mom was saying. "We all have total confidence in Beezan, but jumping a whole station has never been done. And there are no jump chairs."

"Harbor to Atik is a standard jump," Ra'Tama said. "Ship size should not matter."

"The hazard is the thrusting," Iricana explained. "Can the station hold together and get enough boost from their makeshift thrusters? If they can't, no one will be left here to save them. The OSRI ship is leaving. And there's nowhere to put them anyway."

"If they fail," Thunder elaborated, "they'll deorbit into the star in a week. Maybe less. But if they don't show up at Atik, *81* may be able to organize a rescue."

Falcon tapped a screen. "Here's Commander Altan's list. Only 73 additional people need to trade."

"Good," Iricana said. "Taj has already agreed to command. So we need 72 more. We need these volunteers today or the deal will be off."

"I volunteer," Thunder said. Iricana's shoulders sagged and she sighed. "I really need you here. You can do all the work with the thrusters and rock relocators and come back. Others will volunteer."

"Is there no circumstance where you would allow me to go, Captain?"

She bit her lip and nodded. "If there are only 71 volunteers."

. . .

Beezan and the pilots were in the prayer room when the news came through. Harbor Council had approved the ARA2 jump. Beezan knew it from the pounding in the rimway as people ran around, and from the surge of emotion and excitement that seemed to stream through the walls. They stood. "I must go to ARA2." He didn't want to say goodbye. "God bless you all."

Sequoia and Ra'Tama shook his hand and hurried down the stairs. Jarvie turned to him. "You'll pilot me over in the *Bird of Paradise*," Beezan told him.

"I know. With a full load of people." Jarvie hugged him. "I wish I could come."

"I know. But it may be helpful to me, to have you jump first, on the *81*—a stronger tie." He squeezed Jarvie's arm again and they went down the stairs into the crowded rimway. Thank heavens, Iricana had sent an escort for him, and they headed for the hangar.

The volunteer message had gone out. People aboard the *81* willing to jump on ARA2 were to pack their belongings immediately and meet at Entry Lounge 4. No one under 21. No pregnant people. No one not of sound mind. No one who could not choose for themselves. The captain and Taj reserved the right to reject anyone for any other reason.

Of course, Terina wasn't allowed to go. Even though it was her idea. But she packed a camera and went down to record the volunteer line. It was a relief to get out of Arc 1 where it was so crazy in the rimway. Cabins were being swapped and prepped and the volunteers were rushing around saying goodbye.

Down in nogee, Iricana and Taj hung at the Entry Lounge door with two security people. Beezan had gone with Jarvie on the *Bird of Paradise*. It was Jarvie's job to bring it home. All extra shuttles and excess mass was being removed from ARA2. Iricana held a stack of 72 numbered markers, showing them to security. "No one without a marker gets through this door." The security people nodded.

There was a line of volunteers. Terina had expected hundreds, but there were not nearly that many. After the restrictions, and people who didn't want to leave their friends, there was a relatively small group left. But her quick count revealed over 90 people. Terina turned on a discreet cam at the front of the line, and followed the progress.

#1 was Falcon, always first in line with drama. She smiled at Terina and pulled past the security people, flashing her marker. Iricana and Taj worked through the line. Some people had obviously come just to show symbolic support for Beezan. Iricana sent the life support manager and top garden tech back. Ulf, waiting with a guard, was sent back. Clearly, he believed in Beezan. A very elderly man pulled along smoothly. He had a dockworker jacket on. "Is this the shuttle to Firelight? And then to Earth?" Iricana's eyes filled with tears. "No Honor, let's get you to the right place," and she turned him back.

A hooded youth with no armband came to the front. "Cooper!" Taj objected. "You're not old enough!"

"Three weeks! I'll be 21 in three weeks!" Taj sent him back.

So many faces from Arc 1, the people who actually knew Beezan and the other pilots. The tram supervisor—Iricana sent her back. They reached the end of the line. Taj put #71 in his jacket pocket, "That's for Teeve, on the rock relocator." He hung there, holding #72. They all looked up toward the lift, but the deadline was well past. No one else was coming.

Iricana took several deep breaths and touched her p'link. "Iricana to Thunder."

"Thunder."

"You are #72. Goodbye, for now."

"I'll see you on the other side. Love you."

"Love you too," she whispered.

Taj nodded to Iricana. "Godspeed to us all." He grabbed his bag off a hook and shoved for the lock, the security people pushing it shut behind him. On the Entry Lounge screen, the *Bird of Paradise* was already on its way back.

5-Sovereignty

The Western Coast

After two weeks of walking with Ellant, Melawn wondered if his brain or his body would shrivel up first. Twelve hours a day they walked, and yet, seemed to go nowhere. It was so far. How could a person walk for weeks and cover only a miniscule part of the planet?

He thought back to humanity, walking across continents. About his hero, Mullá Husayn, walking across the Persian desert on his quest for the Promised One.

It was boring, yet amazing at the same time. Melawn tried to walk with different people, tried to get to know them, but Ellant kept a fast pace and he needed his energy just to keep up. He'd start out up front every day and straggle in at the end, usually with DeeZann keeping him silent company.

Not long before lunch, the scout Fez came running back.

"Is he expected?" Melawn asked.

"No," Ellant answered, but kept going in his normal stride, not raising his hand for a halt or to hurry. Melawn moved aside to give the boy room next to Ellant.

"It's a house!" Fez reported breathlessly. "We found a house! It's broken."

"Where?" Ellant asked.

"Almost to the main river."

Other aliens? Another group of humans? The coastal outpost moved? Melawn wondered.

"Just one house?" Ellant asked.

"Yes. Made of planks of dark wood. Strange. Kind of like a cart house. Tepperzann is guarding. I came alone."

Ellant allowed a small smile. "You've done well. How long for us to walk there?"

"Three hours."

Ellant turned to Halim. "Announce lunch on the walk. Keep going." As they always packed their lunches, people pulled out their food and continued on, Fez falling in with them. Melawn saw that Fez had no food and gave him his dried fruit. Tenshi gave him her bread and they carried on.

As they came over the latest ridge, the scientist Benjai, holding his homemade spy glass, shouted, "I see it!"

They half slid down the sandy ridge, and discovered three sets of footprints at the bottom, two going forward and one returning, Fez on his way back. "Look, the ground is crunchy," Zonta said.

"It's so smooth, except where they walked," DeeZann said.

Tenshi stopped and picked something up, holding it for them to see. "A seashell. Look. Other debris too. The tsunami."

"That can't be. We're too far inland," Halim objected.

Tenshi shook her head. "We're near the river. Just like in Paradise. It's just sandier here."

Melawn squinted at the brown wreckage. As they got closer, he thought it did look like an old wooden house that had fallen down. There was no talk of stopping or resting. They were stepping on small stones, shells and dried seaweed now it was so thick. And then Tenshi gasped.

"Not a house!" She took off running. Melawn bolted after her, followed by the other scientists. They jog-ran about five minutes, until it became clear, and then they stood gasping for breath.

"A boat," Melawn said.

"A ship. An ocean-faring ship, or half of one," Tenshi said and pointed to two long poles, draped in huge green rags. "Two masts. A sailing ship. Wind powered."

"Thrown this far?" Benjai asked.

"I've seen old newsreels," Tenshi said. "Yes." Melawn could see the river was not far, sparkling in the late afternoon sun.

Then Tep waved them over to a big pile of debris, not fifty meters from the broken-up ship. She signaled for them to be careful; the debris was a fire pit and scattered bones.

"People were on that ship!" Benjai said, removing his hat.

DeeZann actually picked up a bone and studied it. "Birds cleaned off these bones. I hope the people were already dead."

Melawn backed away, scanning the sky. Tenshi was on her knees carefully examining a skull. "Yes, people," she said. "But not humans."

Ellant turned to her sharply. "Ramians?"

Tenshi nodded, tracing her finger across the brow ridge of the skull. She stood and pointed out two small bumps on each side, "These must be where the light band attaches. We don't have that."

Ellant tipped his head back with dismay. "Ramians. They crossed the ocean and had the bad luck to get caught in the tsunami. And that must mean . . . our people on the coast . . ."

Tenshi shook her head. "I would have very little hope for them."

"We were in the right place after all," Yuki, one of Thayne's scientists said.

"You were waiting for them?" Melawn asked.

"Yes. We calculated where the currents would bring a ship if they crossed, and decided on this latitude. We were right, but the ship got caught in the tsunami and washed up here, and they died."

"They did not know how to survive?" Fez asked.

"Maybe they were better sailors than hunters," Tenshi said sadly.

"But I don't understand," Melawn was still stunned by the turn of events. "You know we're not allowed to cross the water."

"And yet, here they are," Ellant said.

"But how could you know they would try?" Melawn asked.

"After reading the Ramian information in the *Cheetah* data and then talking to Thayne, we took into consideration their culture of boldness."

"Or recklessness," Tenshi said, setting the skull down carefully. "We need to bury them."

"Over there," Ellant pointed, just as the cart came over the ridge. "Tomorrow, we'll search the ship for anything useful."

Melawn's stomach seized with fear as he stared across the sands at the broken thing. He whispered to Tenshi, "This will be three times for me, searching a wrecked Ramian vessel."

"Foolhardy," Tenshi whispered back to Melawn. "Their actions could bring the Chike down on us all."

6-Sovereignty Eve

During the night, when he was supposed to be sleeping, Melawn was busy reliving the nightmarish details of his two previous explorations of destroyed Ramian vessels. Images of bodies floating out of the dark rimways gave him chills even now.

Lying awake only made it easier to hear the local rodents nosing into their camp. Tep would shoo them if they got too close. But Melawn imagined whole tribes of them nesting in the wooden ship.

By morning he was a wreck, but Ellant had given him an order. He was to go, along with Tenshi, DeeZann, Tep, Fez, and a few others.

"What about light?" Melawn asked as the others ate breakfast.

"Torches," Tep answered, pointing to a stack she must have made during the night.

"Hey," one of Ellant's people, Cypress, said. "Maybe I could chop a hole in the wall for light." He sauntered over and swung his big axe against the hull. It bounced back so hard it knocked him flat. "Whoa!" He said, dusting off the sand and collecting his axe as the other Dragons laughed uproariously. Tenshi just shook her head.

"Torches it is," Melawn muttered, looking down at his hand where he'd burned it during Chike training.

Tep led them to a series of boards on the side of the ship that made a kind of ladder. She scrambled up first, carrying the torches on her back. It was a six-meter drop to the sand, so Melawn went carefully, sighing in relief as he clamored over to the tilted deck.

There was nothing there except rodent droppings. He pulled his shirt collar up over his face. Tep pointed to a hatch. She lit the torches and started passing them out, but scowled at Melawn's shaking hands and didn't give him one. "Stay with me," Tenshi whispered, taking one.

Carefully, they dropped below, spreading out on the lower deck. No bodies. Melawn was just about to relax slightly when he saw the glint of a knife in the axe man's hand.

"Cypress, what is that for?" Tenshi hissed.

He gave a wicked smile and held a finger to his lips. "Tasty rodents."

"Oh my God," Melawn whispered and turned the other way. "Where's the Command Bay?"

Tenshi answered from right behind him. "Near the front, where they could see out."

They worked their way forward while the others explored a deck below. Melawn and Tenshi overheard various exclamations, as well as the occasional thunk of a thrown knife. Tenshi gripped his arm. "It's okay. No matter what, we're not going to depressurize, get blown up by a gravity ball, or even drown. And any bodies will be long gone from the rodents."

"Okay. That makes me feel better."

Tenshi passed in front of Melawn with the torch, glancing into empty spaces until she got to a small room and gasped, stepping back. She shook her head at herself, recovering quickly. "Bones. That's all."

Melawn took some deep breaths through his shirt and joined her. The bones were scattered, but the skulls seemed to catch the torchlight and glow menacingly. "May their souls rest in peace," he said.

Tenshi cast the torch around. "They congregated here in their last moments, rather than outside." She leaned over and picked up a bracelet. "Tokens."

Melawn couldn't speak, it was so sad. He wondered if he'd met any of these people on the Chike ship.

"We should collect the tokens," Tenshi said. "The families might value them." Melawn didn't see how they would ever return them. But then Tenshi's torchlight flashed by something half buried under bones. Paper.

Melawn gingerly pulled it out—a notebook. He flapped the dust off as best he could. "It's in Ramian."

"Can you read it?"

"No," he admitted, disappointed with himself. "I only learned to speak a little."

"We might be able to decipher it though."

"Yes." Melawn paged through it while Tenshi carefully gathered the tokens.

"Only five skulls here," she counted. "Twelve outside. A ship like this would require more. Maybe some survived."

And then Melawn turned to the last page. He gasped. Tenshi brought the light closer. "What?"

"The last entry. It's in Alkulu."

After several stunned seconds, Melawn whipped off his pack and sat down, pulling out his own notebook. Tenshi stood over him while he quickly copied maps, star charts, the Alkulu section, and several other sections in Ramian, including the beginning and some underlined parts. "They're coming," Tenshi whispered. Melawn hurriedly put his notebook away, and they emerged, excitedly showing their find to the others and turning the book over to Ellant when they returned to the camp.

Tenshi showed Ellant the tokens and explained what they were, as well as the humans knew. They searched around the fire pit for more and found a few. Tenshi then stored them all on one of the carts.

At dinner, standing in the glow of the fire, Ellant read the last page of the logbook for everyone.

"To our human friends
Although, after long struggle, we have finally reached your shores, sadly, we will soon pass to another sea. It was our desire to connect with you, bring our colony here, and try to build a better civilization together. We have tried to ride the top of the sea and not bother those below and that seemed to work. We were just approaching your harbor, we even saw your outpost, when the wave struck. We are injured. We cannot find enough food here and don't know which way to go. We sent people north and south in hopes of finding you. God willing the second ship will arrive safely. Please relay to all our blessings."

There was a long silence. Then Fez chanted a prayer.

Ellant looked them over. "Tomorrow. All speed for the coast."

8-Sovereignty

Two afternoons later, it was overcast and bright when they approached the coast. The sound of the ocean and the smell of the water set off something elemental in all of them, and stirred up a great nostalgia in the Earthborn. They hurried along, leaving trees behind and scrambling over hard-packed sand sprouting low bushes. They could now see the horizon of water under a low sun, with birds, smaller than the desert attackers, reeling and screeching.

"My God," Tenshi marveled, "even the birds sound just like the gulls of Earth."

They trampled over one last ridge of hard sand, which dropped sharply off to a beach of soft sand. It was so different than the small, calm bay at Yosemite. Here was the power of the full ocean straight on. The wind blasted them. The waves crashed onto the beach and made a strange fizzing sound as they retreated. Melawn had never seen anything like this. "Wow," he whispered. Then louder, "I can feel it inside. It's like the planet is alive."

"A live and powerful thing," Tenshi agreed, almost shouting over the wind.

DeeZann had to get help to hold her map against the wind. "The river exit has changed," she said. "But the outpost should be north, about half a kilometer."

So they started up the coast, with the Earthborn walking along the beach, raising their arms in the wind for the thrill of it, and the spacers going no closer, nervous of the overwhelming power of the ocean.

The beach had small crescents that Tenshi called coves where the waves were less intense. At a larger one of these, DeeZann stopped. "Here." She pointed out where another small river drained into the ocean near some rocks on the right. "Don't go there. The undertow is strong. But this side is calm." Melawn had no intention of going near the water, period.

DeeZann turned and pointed out some rock formations up on the ridge. "The outpost was there. The rocks were bigger." Some people spread out to look around. Benjai climbed onto the ridge to scan with his scope. He looked north and south and inland. "I don't see any sign of survivors, or any other wrecked ships," he shouted down to Ellant on the beach. Melawn agreed. It looked like the tsunami had wiped the whole coast clean.

Tenshi pointed to the trees further back from the ridge. "Dried seaweed, hanging from the trees. That's how bad it got here."

They could see the cart coming up, angling over to meet them. Melawn looked again at the birds, which all seemed to be circling over something out at sea. Benjai had his scope pointed that way. "Look!" Benjai shouted, pointing. "Something is out there!" Everyone turned. "It's the ship. The second ship!"

Ellant squinted. "Is it wrecked?"

"No!" Benjai literally jumped up and down with excitement.

"Its sails are up! It's coming this way! It's amazing!" Tenshi shaded her eyes from the sun and gave the natural harbor a more critical look. "Do we know how deep the water is? Are there rocks? Can they even get in here?"

But the others didn't understand what was required or were so excited to see a sailing ship, they didn't care.

The wind was blowing hard; within an hour they could see the ship clearly in the setting sun. Tep, Fez, and the natives, even the spacers, marveled at the sight of the two emerald green triangular sails billowing out. They could hear the creaking and groaning of the wood. "Get some brush together and prepare a bonfire," Ellant ordered the cart people. They all scurried around in excitement, except Ellant and Tenshi, who stood on the shore in concern.

Soon enough, they could see people on the deck. They waved to each other. First contact, Melawn thought and estimated the time. The rear sail was pulled down and the ship slowed. Just as they entered the small cove, they dropped the forward sail. "They may have to anchor out there," Tenshi said.

They lowered a small boat over the side and seemed to be gathering people to board when a strange churning started around the ship. "What is that?" Tenshi asked in alarm.

And then Benjai shouted, "Crabs!"

From out of the churning foam, orange and pale crabs climbed up the sides of the ship, multi-legged, each one holding a coral spike in one of its claws.

Screaming started immediately. "Are they attacking the Ramians?" Ellant asked.

"No," Benjai said. "They're breaking the wood. Chopping it with those spikes."

"Are the people fighting them off?"

"A couple did, or got in the way. They were pushed aside, but they may be injured."

A chill went down Melawn's spine. Another case of misunderstood assumptions, that one civilized race would not hurt another. The ship began to rock. Ramians jumped over the side. "They're going to swim for shore!" Tenshi shouted.

"Start the fire!" Ellant ordered, running to the edge of the water with Tenshi.

The ship was already listing to one side. Some people were in the little boat, but the crabs attacked that too. Melawn stood in horrified paralysis. Tenshi was cursing. He'd never heard her so mad. She pulled off her shoes, her jacket, and outer clothes. "You're not going in!" he shouted.

"There are children!"

The other Earthborn did the same, and even a couple of spacers. "I can swim!" one assured Ellant. But no spacer had ever swum in an ocean.

Tenshi ran into the surf until it picked her feet up and then she swam in a way that kept her head out of the water. The Ramians were desperately bobbing up and down in the water, sometimes disappearing.

Melawn threw his pack down far from the water, took off his coat and boots, and ran back to the edge. *I'll just walk in a little ways and help.* After only a few steps he stopped. It was freezing. They would be numb in minutes. He doubted even good swimmers could make it. The sand disappeared under his feet as if the waves were trying to suck him out. He staggered a few more steps until the water was to his knees, but he would go no farther. An exhausted Ramian made it that far though. Melawn grabbed her and helped her walk up the beach. She was shivering hard.

Spacers on the beach took her from Melawn and headed for

the fire. Melawn forced himself to go back for more. "More fires!" Ellant was yelling. "Get their clothes off! Bring blankets!" The carts had just arrived, and those people jumped into action, not even freaking out over grayish-blue aliens.

Melawn glanced at the sun. Thirty minutes max. But it would be over by then. Melawn and the others went into the water as far as they dared, helping the others up the beach. His own teeth chattered so hard it hurt.

On his fourth person, Melawn's organizational mind kicked in. "How many?" He asked. Amazingly, the Ramian spoke Alkulu. "Thirty-two!"

"Thirty-two!" Melawn shouted and heard people relay. He set the terrified Fez by the fire. "Keep count!"

Some were able to crawl up the beach under their own power, looking back over their shoulders for friends or crabs. Tenshi came in with a small child and went right back out.

The crabs didn't pursue them up the beach, but they continued to attack the ship. "There's nothing left but planks!" Benjai shouted. Tenshi dragged a screaming woman up next. Two other humans came to help her, as the woman kept trying to go back.

"Baby!" she cried and pointed back. "My baby!"

Oh my God, no. Melawn thought. It was getting dark. Tenshi turned to go, but Ellant was there. "No!" And three people grabbed Tenshi to stop her.

"I'm sorry," Melawn whispered and pulled Tenshi to the fire.

"Thirty!" Fez reported.

"The baby is thirty-one," Melawn said. "There's one more."

Tenshi dropped to her knees and someone threw a blanket around her. Melawn turned back and scanned the water, looking for disturbances in the sun's reflection. *There!* He was holding a plank and kicking his way to shore. Melawn ran back into the surf to his knees, but the man kept getting washed back. Melawn carefully went to his hips, bracing himself with each step. He felt the ocean trying to lift his body.

The man was so close, Melawn lunged for the plank. His feet left the sand. For a moment it was just like nogee, and then he went down under the water. Terrified, he tried to grab the plank but his cold hand slipped off. In a surge of panic and instinct, he tried not to breathe and flailed around for the plank. His arm hit it and the Ramian grabbed his arm, barely. Melawn threw his other arm onto the plank, gasping. They were now both on the plank, and it was under the water, but Melawn felt himself being pulled from behind as the axeman towed them both in. When his feet hit the sand again, it was the most glorious feeling in life.

Melawn staggered to the fire with the rest, coughing. The poor mother of the baby was flanked by two men, and all were sobbing uncontrollably, their colors running dark gray. Blankets and dry clothes were being distributed. Incredibly, the cooks even passed out tea.

"Why?" Fez asked. "Why let them get all the way across and then attack here?"

Ellant and Benjai stood at the edge of the water looking out into the dark waves. And then a crab crawled out of the surf, and another and another, in a solid line across the beach. Benjai ran backwards, not taking his eyes off them. Everyone on the beach tensed or backed up. But Ellant stood his ground. A frothing of water on the left side roiled over and three crabs appeared, tipping a blue baby out of their claws into the beach.

Tenshi was on her feet and running, blanket thrown aside. The mother screamed in anguish and broke free, following her. Not half a meter from the nearest crab, Tenshi reached the baby, checked it, and started CPR.

Melawn went to his mat and pulled out the rolled-up blanket. He ran down to the beach as Tenshi worked on the baby, pressing the water out and giving mouth to mouth. Suddenly she stopped, as a weak wail escaped the baby. Ze was breathing! Tenshi folded the baby into the mom's arms and wrapped them both in the blanket, getting the two men to hold on to them. In a shivering stupor, Melawn gazed down at them. The woman and one of the men. *I know them.* A memory popped into his mind: Danulell and Zhenumae. Walking down the steps with Quay. *Small galaxy.* And then Danulell turned to the crab, a crab holding a spike aloft, and gently reached out his hand and tapped the small empty claw. "Thank you," he whispered.

Melawn slowly turned to look. A long row of crabs stood along the beach, all holding their spikes aloft, like torches. Ellant looked over his shoulder at the axeman and the knife throwers, behind him. "Stand down." They immediately lowered their weapons.

"Let's move back," Melawn said and helped the Ramians back to the fire. Ellant now stood alone on the beach facing down the crabs. Right in front of him, foam bubbled up, and from it emerged a giant orange crab. Everyone on the beach backed up again, except Ellant.

The crab's body was at least a meter wide. Dark markings covered ziz carapace as if the story of ziz life was written there. Ze had one large claw and one small, but the large was the size of a dinner plate. On solid stalks, ziz eyes glared at Ellant.

Ellant, with no semblance of surrender or humility, got down on one knee to look the creature in the eye. For a long moment they gazed at each other in obvious anger. Then the crab raised ziz big claw and jabbed over Ellant's shoulder, pointing to the land behind. Ze jabbed again, and a third time.

Ellant turned to Tenshi. "The baby lives," she reported through chattering teeth. "All crew accounted for."

Ellant looked back at the crab again and nodded once. Without turning his back Ellant ordered, "Move the fires. Fall back to the trees!" And he stood.

And the giant crab made a swish with ziz claw and all the little crabs slammed their spikes into the sand and submerged back into the ocean, leaving a spiky fence behind.

9-Sovereignty

The Coast

Melawn slept like the dead, not waking until he felt a gentle tap on his shoulder. *What's Nkiroo doing here?* But it was Cypress, the axeman. "Ellant wants you," was all he said.

Melawn dragged himself up. His muscles were cold and tight. He'd given away his extra dry clothes, mat, and blanket. He clutched his coat around him and joined Ellant, DeeZann, Fez, Tep, and Cypress. Ellant looked like he hadn't slept at all.

"Here's the situation. We have injured and some sick. More will be sick soon. We have to put them on the carts. It's going to be slow going. I need you, Melawn, to lead a team ahead and bring back more food and carts. I'm sending DeeZann, Cypress, Fez, and one beast. Go as fast as you can."

Melawn was about to stupidly ask *Why me?* when he remembered Ellant was in charge, *like a captain*. "Yes, Honor."

Danulell, dressed only in a blanket and a few tokens, came up to them. "I'm going."

Ellant shook his head. "There's no need."

"There is. I will represent my people. My captain, Getti Mezt, is sending me."

Ellant gave him a long look before turning to the cart

people. "Pack five sets of food and water. Find Danulell some clothes and shoes." He turned back to them. "You leave in an hour. I estimate we'll be out of food in six days. Godspeed to you." And he strode off to the next task.

Melawn had no time to say goodbye to Tenshi. Tep reviewed the route with Fez, DeeZann gathered her maps, and they grabbed a snack for breakfast. Shouldering the packs, they turned to Melawn. "Okay," he said, shakily. "Fez, lead the way, please." And they quietly slipped out of the camp, rounding up their beast on the way. Melawn turned back to see Tenshi wave to him, grave concern in her eyes.

ARA2

Beezan sat at a small table in the operations room of ARA2 as a special guest, the friendly and easy-going Taj commanding with a smile. He tried to sit more comfortably, but they were at 1.2g playing catch-up to their jump point. They would be the last people out of Harbor as all other ships were in the a-rings now.

On the main screen, Beezan watched the seven ships circling through the a-rings while Sky slept fitfully in her podpup pocket. After about an hour, Rendra and Thunder came in. "Are we disturbing you, honor?" Rendra asked.

"No." Beezan patted the chairs next to him. "Please call me Beezan." Sky popped out of the podpup pocket, gave them both a look and decided things were sociable enough to come out and sit on the table.

"So," Thunder said, looking at the screen, "What have we got?"

Taj explained, "Sequoia, in *Horizon*, the OSRI ship, carrying three sets of collapsible a-rings, is in front. Then Ra'Tama, in the

81, carrying five a-rings, four extra shuttles from ARA2, and 110% capacity." Both pilots sucked in their breath at that. "Next are the final five ships from Harbor Station, including the tug with Swooper in command. All Harbor souls are aboard those ships—except us."

"Last ship out of Dodge." Rendra said.

Huh? Beezan thought, but Thunder laughed. "Do you know Kelson McNelson?" he asked.

"Of course," Rendra answered. "Who doesn't?"

"I didn't," Beezan said quietly. *But I guess I do now.* And he sent a little prayer for Kelson, staying on the *81* with Terina, while her mom jumped the *Horizon* to demonstrate the prejumping.

They alternated quiet talk and prayers for a couple of hours. Beezan was about to suggest a snack when he felt a little rattling in his implants. "Resonance," he whispered, and everyone looked to the screen.

"*Horizon* jumped," Falcon reported. "Atik direction. Three hours early. Other ships reporting that all is well." On the very next lap, Beezan felt a painful surge of resonance—Ra'Tama jumping the *81*. He leaned over the table and grabbed his head. "*81* away. Atik direction," Falcon announced. Rendra was also holding his head.

"You have implants," Beezan said, surprised.

"Most of us do. They can't force you to remove them," Rendra said.

Sky crawled back into Beezan's lap, sad. "Star gone. Zharvie gone. Terina gone."

She dropped her head on his chest as he hugged her. "I know. They're at Atik. We'll be there soon." But he gave a little laugh and whispered, "No lament of Rocket gone?" She humphed and Thunder cracked up.

· · ·

12-Sovereignty

ARA2

Beezan had spent hours praying with the other pilots, subtly letting Rendra know which ones would have to be put under for the jump. He had endured days of trying to eat and sleep in 1.2g and scolded himself for his disgruntlement. Most people here were much older. He had tolerated walking around the station so everyone could see him to build up their confidence.

And the entire time he felt less and less sure of the whole idea. ARA2 made some frightening noises as if the stress of thrusting was slowly cracking it apart, although Thunder and Teeve reassured everyone that they were well within tolerances.

Thunder and Teeve had taken #9 from the *81*, along with a contingent of nanos, which they used to carve apart the small ARA2 station, reducing its mass. They attached boosters and rock relocators. As those became unnecessary, nanos would seal the area and cut them off.

I'm jumping a whole station. With alien nanos, jury-rigged jump chairs, and risk-taking pilots. But worst of all, Sky just wasn't herself. And now, this morning, when he most needed calm and confidence for the jump, she started whining during prayers. He tried to talk to her and she started saying "Wrong way." He rushed her out so no one could hear her.

"Sky, what do you mean?"

"Wrong way."

"What's the wrong way?"

And she whined some more. "No."

I won't be able to jump like this. He had just enough time to stop at the Med Bay. He wanted to get into his jump chair in the auditorium before everyone else came in.

"We don't have a podpup doctor, but I'd be happy to look at her," a calm and patient young woman said, but Sky would not leave Beezan's podpup pocket, fussing even more now.

"I hate to do it, but I think we better sedate her for the jump," he whispered.

"Nononono,"

"I'm so sorry Sky."

"Bee bad . . . wrong . . . bad."

As the sedative took effect, she relaxed. "I don't think there's anything physically wrong," the doctor said. "I'll do some research after the jump."

"Thank you." He was going to be late, so he turned to go.

"Oh, honor. Sorry. You have to leave her here."

"No. I . . ."

"It's safer if I monitor her." Beezan reluctantly handed Sky over. "I'll take good care of her, personally. I promise."

Now he was late. And flustered. And his mind felt incomplete with Sky unconscious. What if he couldn't jump without her? What if this whole freejumping thing depended on podpups?

When he got to the auditorium, where they'd converted the chairs for jumping, building him one on the stage, he was late. He had to walk up there in front of everyone. People clapped and said his name. He hadn't planned to make a grand entrance. He was embarrassed and his nerves were rattled. Somewhere on the rebuilt edges of the station, Thunder and Teeve and the rest of the mechanics, in spacesuits, tried to be ready for any mechanical emergency. They would be *up* during the jump. A severe chill ran up his spine. He got to his command chair, between Falcon's and Rendra's, facing a big screen at the back of the stage. There was a smaller screen showing ops, with Taj and a couple others. And an auditorium full of passengers. No suits. No cocoons. No recess packs. This was really do or die.

Once everyone was secure, they began to simulate a jump sequence, accelerating in kicks every few minutes, as if they were passing through a-ring segments, until they intersected the Atik best path at just the right moment—all programmed by Iricana.

The first hour passed, with the usual amount of discomfort, but Beezan could not settle into the pattern. His mind kept going back to Sky. What if she really was the key to freejumping? He should not have put her under. He tried to mentally locate her in the Med Bay, but he couldn't even clearly visualize the whole station. "ARA2, display schematic of the station." A screen popped up from his chair with "New alterations in yellow." *I shouldn't look at this*, he thought. Only the path. No distractions. He tried to put Atik and its thread back in his mind. *Nononono, wrong way*, Sky's plaintive voice kept popping into his mind.

Beezan knew that some people expected him to jump early, but that wasn't possible for this trajectory. They had to wait until the arc of their path turned just enough to go "with the wind" to Atik.

"Relocator separation in five," Falcon said. Thank heavens for the warning because the banging made Beezan's skin crawl. It was so strange not to be in the brackets. He could look down at his hands. He had thrusters, but wasn't in complete control. Teeve and Thunder had to switch different sorts of thrust to him, and some they controlled themselves.

I need more prayers. **"The steed of this Valley is patience; without patience the wayfarer on this journey will reach nowhere and attain no goal."**[1]

He repeated it over and over. A steed was a horse; he had

looked it up. But for him, it was the station. And if he could not bring it into the path they would literally go nowhere.

Finally, Beezan thought they were going fast enough to start looking for the path. Immediately he saw the fireball. Still there. And it was so bright it made the other threads hard to see. *Patience.*

Slowly, the threads became more substantial, to Beezan's immense relief. *That one. Almost there.* He reached for his thrusters. "Last relocator separation in five."

Okay, okay. He'd have to wait. BANG! And the room slowly started spinning, like a dream. *No!* There were gasps in the auditorium. "Malfunction on the separation!" Falcon shouted.

"ARA2, cancel the spin!" he ordered.

"Flight ops are on manual," the AI calmly reported.

"Taj?"

"All thrust is under your control, or Thunder's," Taj answered.

"Thunder!"

"Working on it. We don't have jets in all directions."

Panicked, Beezan looked back to the thread. "We'll miss the thread if it's more than 20 seconds!"

Another jolt rocked the station, which made an unnerving metallic rumbling. Some of the spin canceled. But was it enough? Pilots knew that spinning would knock you out of the path, but *how much spin?* No choice. They were out of time. Beezan focused on that thread, their lifeline to Atik, and thrusted into it. *We're in!* And then, in a horrible, sickening lurch, they were out. Dumped into normal space. "Location!" he demanded.

"Harbor!" Falcon answered. "Still have Harbor beacon."

"Honor," Rendra said quietly, "our position is sunward of where we were, but we still have JV."

Beezan, head spinning as Thunder and Teeve were still making corrections, tried to focus on the orbital plot. He gasped. *No! They were far inward. Too far.* Not weeks from a death spiral, maybe only days or hours. And it was heating up. "Thunder? What's the situation?"

"We're going to get the spin canceled, but we are almost out of thruster fuel."

Beezan tried to stay calm, but his hands trembled on the thrusters. Taking a deep breath, he tried to see again, all those paths. Atik was gone. They'd missed their window.

For a moment, Beezan battled despair. But a well of determination rose up inside. There were other threads. *Where do all those threads go? I need one that's very close. Calm. Calm. The steed of patience.* There were two. One weak, but close, and one stronger, but a little harder to reach. "Rendra, do you see it? Strong and red?"

"Yes."

"We're going to take it. Thunder, I need more thrust."

"We don't have any."

"Get some! Vent the ship. Do whatever you have to do!"

He could hear Thunder and Teeve shouting to each other now, and to #9. "Spin canceled. Give us a direction!"

Thank God, Beezan thought, and used what little thrust he had to turn the station the way he wanted to go. "Ahead!"

Beezan could see on the schematic as the nanos tore apart the station, venting in as controlled a manner as possible. "More!"

"No thrust remains," ARA2 reported.

"We've vented all vacant areas!" Teeve reported. That's everything but Ops, the Med Bay, and the Auditorium. Taj could order venting of the Med Bay or ops to save the others. But Beezan wouldn't do that. He looked at the thread again. Just a little more, maybe they could reach it without more thrust. But in the back of his mind, he thought it was wishful thinking and that they were done.

"WATER!" Thunder shouted and got the nanos going. "And dump sections of the station!"

Trickles of power came to Beezan's thrusters. It was going to be a reach. "Help me," he whispered to Rendra and the pilots. Straining with everything in his mind and body, Beezan reached for the last elusive thread, the only thing that would save them from a certain death spiral. He could feel the strength of the others. *Yes. Focus.* He pressed the thrusters. A little burst. He tried to pull the station closer, all the pilots joining him. Sentries began to appear. *No!* All they needed was another 20 seconds.

The huge wrenching and banging as ARA2 came apart was barely in his consciousness. His heart and soul were pushing into that path. Just 15 more seconds of thrust. He pressed on the thrusters. 13 . . . 12 . . . 11 . . . 10 . . . 9 . . . 8 . . . 7—it cut off. *REACH!*

Beezan tried to throw his own soul forward into the path and pull the station after him. He burst through a veil of sentries and slipped into the path. *In! I'm in!* But his moment of victory was short. He could not hear or sense the pilots around him. He had no idea where they were going, if they had air, or water, or nanos. He wasn't sure if he was alone, or if the station was with him, or if anyone still lived. It was utterly silent. And the sentries surrounded him in a familiar way. He was going to die, but there was no recess pack this time. And his greatest fear was that he would not be able to tip them out of the path close enough to be saved on the other side.

13-Sovereignty

    81-Petals, at Atikameq

. . .

"Atikameq beacon," Kay Ling, Ra'Tama's monitor announced, just after he tipped them into normal space.

Jarvie mentally cheered and sent a prayer up for Beezan and the ARA2, soon to follow.

"No red lights," Katie reported. That inspired another cheer from everyone. Jarvie clamored out of his cocoon and assisted with recovery—podpup duty—his job when he wasn't monitor. By the time he got them fed and situated and helped reset the recess packs in the Passenger Lounge, three hours had passed. He was tired, but he put on his uniform and went to Ops to wait for the ARA2 to come in. As he passed the other bays and cabins, he could see there was only one thing on all the screens—the incoming Ship Tracker.

Jarvie joined Terina in the crowded room, checking out the big screen. All seven ships from Harbor were incoming, spread out with ETAs of four days to four weeks, with *81* in the lead. Sequoia in *Horizon* was close behind, with Swooper, surprisingly, only seven days out.

He leaned over Terina's pad to spy on her notes.

- Atik Incoming Authority—all business, rerouting Swooper and a couple other tugs to the outer system when they heard that ARA2 was coming on a high-risk jump.

- Mom will return to the *81* in her shuttle once *81* and *Horizon* trajectories converge.

- Atik was visited by the Chike, but they didn't seem to attract much attention. Must evacuate by 18-Loftiness, 7 weeks away.

- Atik station crowded, but not panicked. Sending people through in small batches to give Firelight time to assimilate them.

"Thanks," he whispered to Terina, as he strained to hear what Iricana was talking about with a stern man at Atik Incoming Authority.

"So Firelight is open?" Iricana asked.

"A ship came in from Firelight," the A.I.A. man was saying. "They received rebuilt a-rings and a new gravity ball from Jamez at Harbor and got it up and running a few days ago. They sent a ship to Athabasca, but so far, no news from Sector 4. We don't know what's going on in the inner sectors. Firelight might be the end of the line."

"There's no room for the entire population of the outer sectors at Firelight."

"That's what we're telling the Chike, but until I hear otherwise, I'm following Council's orders to send people through. Besides, if you've caused trouble with the Chike, you can't stay here."

Iricana got off the call, turned, and seemed surprised at how many people were there. "Thank you for coming. Realistically we should hear from them in seven hours at the most." Atik was a small system, less than 40 AU across, although it was always possible to come in way out in the k-belt, as Jarvie well knew.

Kelson came by and told the captain that other ARCs were also gathering, especially Arc 4, where many of the ARA2 people ended up. Terina seemed expectant and excited, but Jarvie just wanted it to be over. He just wanted to hear that signal, see ARA2 on that screen, and know that Beezan was okay—even if he was 17 weeks out again. *Just be okay.*

"Jump time plus 1 hour," Kay Ling said quietly.

Jarvie exchanged glances with Iricana. She seemed as grim

and impatient as he was, sitting in the remotest part of the room as if she'd rather endure this in private.

There was a slight commotion when the former ARA2 commander, Altan, came to the door, but he was admitted. A couple of people scowled, but Jarvie supposed Altan still felt responsible for his station. And it had taken some courage to come here. They started a round of prayers, but people quieted after an hour or so.

No one really expected to sit for hours. If Beezan came in with his usual accuracy, it wouldn't be long. But everyone stayed put for a solid two hours. As excitement waned, and it got late, a few people started nodding off and slipped out. After four hours, some people patted Jarvie encouragingly on the back as they left.

At six hours, the screen showed an expanding ring of possible appearance. It was now past the last major planet of the Atik system. Those few who were left said another desperate round of prayers. After 12 hours, Iricana put her head down on a panel. Sleeping or not, no one disturbed her.

Jarvie took several breaks, fed himself and the podpups, who seemed completely normal, wandered around to find someone to watch them, and found the remaining Tektites huddled together in the Social Arts Room, distraught about Teeve. He nodded to them and finally left the pups with Roza.

When he got back to Ops, only Terina, Ra'Tama and his silent crew, Iricana, Altan, and Kelson were left. At 15 hours, Iricana couldn't hold back the tears. Altan was dazed, finally getting up to leave, muttering, "I should have stayed." He turned in Iricana's direction and said formally, "I'm sorry, Captain."

At 16 hours, they received an official notice of condolence from Sector 6 Council. Kelson said a short prayer for the departed. Jarvie refused to accept it. He left in a rush, rudely saying nothing to Iricana, and ran to his cabin. *Beezan is alive! Somewhere! Or they jumped late. Or they're out there at 17 weeks. And heaven knows where they might have ended up with all those extra pilots. Beezan is still alive!* But he didn't understand why he couldn't stop crying.

14-Sovereignty

"That man is not dead!" Sequoia insisted as Kelson and Terina accompanied her up the lift and back to Arc 1. "He's too stubborn a pilot. Besides, I would know."

"Don't you think Jarvie would know?" Terina asked.

"What does Jarvie say?"

Kelson looked at Terina, who answered, "Actually, he seems to be in what the doctor called denial. But please don't get their hopes up, Mom."

"Well, first we need to go back to check. If they didn't leave, we might still rescue them."

"We have orders to go to Firelight—" Kelson started to say.

"Why? Someone needs to go back!"

Kelson put a calming hand out. "Iricana's mission is to deliver the *81* and GenThree info to Firelight. Then she's done. She hopes to locate a ship to take a few of us back to Harbor."

"*Wheel!*" Sequoia said. "Is that Tiati here?"

"No," Kelson said. "But they're supposed to be at Firelight."

Sequoia stopped in the rimway. "Firelight it is then. When do we jump?"

"Tomorrow," Terina said quietly. Calmer now, her mom looked at her and suddenly pulled both of them into a hug.

. . .

15-Sovereignty

Jarvie couldn't help it. Even in the Atik a-rings, when he should have been focusing on the jump, on the thread that would take them to Firelight, on being in sync with Ra'Tama, he secretly had the Ship Tracker on. Just in case.

After two hours, Jarvie thought Ra'Tama might start feeling out the way, so he reluctantly reached to shut off the ship tracker, when it beeped. He gasped, and everyone heard him. "What?" Ra'Tama insisted.

"Incoming ship!" Jarvie said, hope surging through him. And then the ID popped up. "Chike," he said in despair, sorry and mad at himself.

"Ra'Tama," Sequoia said, "Get us out of here."

And on the very next lap, Jarvie felt Ra'Tama's head-slamming resonance and they were in the path.

Whoa, Ra'Tama, Jarvie thought, as they heaved into normal space. How can such a quiet person be such a forceful pilot? But the Firelight beacon flashed and everyone breathed a sigh of relief. More than a sigh. Not long ago, they never thought they'd see Firelight again.

Kay Ling reported they were 7 days out, and Katie reported no red lights. Jarvie yanked off his helmet and pulled up the Ship Tracker. Wow! There were at least a hundred beacons. "We're receiving an automated message," Kay Ling said, reading it out: "Welcome to Firelight, hub of Sector 5 and future gateway to the inner sectors. All traffic is currently restricted. Submit jump requests to F.O.A. Maintain Firelight traffic patterns. A monitor will contact you shortly."

Jarvie half-listened while he scanned the ship names. "*Wheel!*" he announced. "Incoming from Redrock!"

Iricana, slowly coming alert, asked, "What's our lag time to Tiati on the *Wheel*?"

"18 minutes," Kay Ling answered.

"Send him a tight beam message for any news from Redrock . . . and . . . never mind. I'll have to talk to him myself. Let's do the spin-up right away."

The jump had been more gut-wrenching than depressing, and the pups wobbled on to the kitchen, where Jarvie left them with Roza. At 36 minutes, he checked back in at Ops to wait for *Wheel's* answer. "It's a recording," Kay Ling warned.

Tiati's face popped on screen smiling like a maniac. "Beezan's alive!"

Iricana dropped her head in her hand, like even Tiati was in denial. But Sequoia nodded and Tiati's recording went on. "Okay, he's not in the best shape, but he'll be fine. You know him. I hope F.I.A. told you! Check the clump of tugger ships incoming to Firelight Station. They're bringing in what's left of ARA2. It should be ARA point-two now."

As Tiati talked, everyone in the room held their breath in excitement and dread. Kay Ling frantically tried to sort out the tug beacons. Iricana covered her mouth with her hand. If it was such a wreck, maybe Thunder had not survived. "Tiati! Tell them the whole thing!" Hana scolded from off-screen.

"Oh, right. Beezan will be fine. Everyone will be fine. All souls alive." A huge cheer went up in Ops, drowning out the rest of Tiati's message.

"Kay Ling," a tearful Kelson said, "We would most appreciate if you could get a message to one of those tugs to confirm."

But they didn't need to. The tugs had spotted *81* on the Ship

Tracker. An urgent message came through and Thunder's smiling, but tired, face appeared on the screen.

They heard nothing. Iricana and Altan collapsed in tears. It was a riot in Ops that spilled out into the rimway and circled the ship.

Jarvie ran to get Star, accepting hugs, handshakes, and back-slaps the whole way. "Star, they're okay!" He picked Star up and swooped him around. "Sky is okay!"

Star, although enjoying the wild attention, looked at Jarvie, puzzled. "Star know."

"What?" Jarvie brought him down so they were nose to nose.

"Sky okay," Star said nonchalantly.

"You knew since the jump, that Sky was okay?"

Star practically shrugged. "Sky here." He looked in the direction of the tug. "There here. Here there."

"You didn't tell me!"

"Why tell?"

Jarvie hugged the abstruse pup and cried for joy. Then he continued on to the Med Bay, giving Katie a hug. The party atmosphere sobered considerably once pictures of ARA2 came in. Only about a third of the station that left orbit at Harbor had arrived at Firelight. There was almost nothing left. No water, no fuel, barely any air. But the crowded Firelight system had been a blessing, and ships had rescued them immediately. Only one person had recessed, Beezan, who was saved by Rendra, the old-fashioned way.

Beezan had jumped a station. It might have been the size of a ship by the time it arrived, but Beezan had done the unthinkable.

8 / THE BIRD IN THE BACK

16-Sovereignty

The Western Coast

After eight days of walking, Melawn, DeeZann, Cypress, Danulell, and Fez were tired, but still kept a fast pace. They started at dawn each day, paused for a short lunch, and stopped one hour before sunset. The trail was clear, and only the beast showed any reluctance to follow Melawn's orders.

Although the days were lengthening and warm, nights were still cold. They slept together on two mats, with only two blankets. Danulell was especially cold and huddled between them, extending the unity in diversity of humanity into an alien realm.

As they trudged along, Melawn dropped back with Danulell. "We're not supposed to talk about space with the natives," he said, pointing with his chin to the others, ahead.

"Really?"

"So say the Chike."

"Oh. We have not much bothered with their rules."

"So I see."

"Results have been mixed," Danulell said.

Melawn started to laugh, but sobered quickly. "Your people may be stranded with us. I hope you can adjust to our ways."

"I can. But there are those who will risk everything to protest the Chike."

"We have those too." Melawn feared Danulell would meet those people soon. "You must have a huge colony, to build those ships."

"About five thousand. But many people know how to sail and build. It's part of our culture. And we have five water planets to keep the tradition alive."

Five! And humanity had not found one good planet.

"But you were raised on a ship? A spaceship, I mean."

"I was born on a planet, the one you call Three. We joined a finder ship when I was thirteen. But I guess you could say I grew up in that place where you rescued us. There's something about sailing on the ocean, something so powerful. In space, you're disconnected. But here . . . it was heartbreaking to see the ship go down."

"You've seen a few ships go down."

"Yes," Danulell said sadly. "But nothing compares to my brother being taken."

"I'm sure he still lives. He may even end up here. We just don't know."

Danulell fingered a necklace token that Melawn suspected was Quay's. "It's my mission to find him."

17-Sovereignty

"Melawn!" DeeZann was hissing at him in his sleep. "He's sick!"

"What? Who?" Melawn crawled out of the blanket pile, trying not to disturb Danulell and Cypress. It was just light.

DeeZann was kneeling by Fez. Melawn felt Fez's head. Hot. And when Fez turned towards Melawn, the unmistakable sign.

"Oh no," Melawn whispered. "It's called the Mershla—a Ramian disease."

Danulell's eyes peeked open. "Mershla?" he mumbled. "Nothing to worry about."

"For you, maybe," Melawn replied. "Move back," he warned DeeZann.

"What about you?"

"I'm vaccinated."

"It's just a little cold," Danulell said, sitting up. "You get a rash."

"For us, it's two weeks of high fever. Fatalities are low, but that's in the Med Bays, not out here."

"We can go for the Dragon's Den today. Maybe 10 hour's walk," DeeZann said. "There's a stash of meds, maybe not for this, though."

"The hospital will have the formula," Melawn said, shaking Cypress awake. "But you and Cypress need to stay back. We'll have to figure out how to carry him. I don't think he can ride."

But DeeZann didn't need to stand around figuring. She wove Fez's spear and her unstrung bow through the sides of a folded mat, creating a makeshift, if uneven, stretcher. They set a hat over Fez's face, piled their packs on Stubby, and walked, rotating positions at the corners of the stretcher.

On one of their rotations, DeeZann suddenly dropped her hold on the stretcher and shouted, "Birds!" Cypress pulled the stretcher free from Melawn and lowered it, kneeling on the ground over Fez's face. DeeZann knelt with her head on her knees and covered the back of her neck with her arms. Danulell instantly followed her example while Melawn stood staring at the approaching V formation. He didn't remember ever seeing more than one of the big birds at a time.

"Get down!" DeeZann shouted at him. Melawn dropped down just in time. In a flurry of feathers and sand, the birds dive-bombed them, one hitting Fez in the leg. A wing caught Melawn in the side of the head as they took off again. It was like being hit with a flying wrench. Melawn had a moment of white-out. *This should have been in the Chike orientation.*

DeeZann was yelling at him as his head cleared. "You have to get down! They can kill you!"

"How?"

"They stab you through your eye to your brain. Cover your face and protect your neck!"

"I've never seen them attack before."

"Weakness." She pointed to Fez. "They smell it. We have to move faster. They've combined their territories to hunt us, so we may have to go a ways to lose them."

Stubby was standing there looking innocent. "Can he help us?" Melawn asked.

"More likely to step on us," DeeZann said, looking at Melawn as if expecting something. *Direction.*

"What do you recommend?"

"You hold Stubby, I'll watch for birds. They like to hunt in the heat of the day when no one is looking up." She pulled her hat down and grabbed the stretcher facing the way they came, so she had to walk backward.

They proceeded more slowly, and it was Fez, peeking out from under his hat, who gave the next warning. "There!"

They all dropped again. This time, the birds hit them harder, bruising their backs and legs. "They're trying to cripple us," Cypress complained. "We should shoot them."

"The meat's no good, so it would be a waste," DeeZann said.

"And they usually give up after the third try." They pulled out the other mat, hoping to have time to throw it over themselves for the third and probably most aggressive attack. As the birds were attacking from behind, Melawn persuaded Stubby to walk behind them, hoping to disrupt their angle of attack.

Only a few minutes later, DeeZann shouted a warning, they took their positions, and Melawn quickly turned Stubby sideways, standing right against him. The lead bird actually hit Stubby. The others veered off. They all went around to look at the bird that hit the beast. Its neck was broken. It was big.

"Doesn't look starving," Cypress commented. "Don't know why they're trying so hard."

They looked up again—just in time to see another wave coming in. "Fez!" DeeZann shouted and sprinted for him. They barely had time to take cover when they were hit again, this time cut and bruised.

"That's four times!" Cypress said. "They think they can wear us down."

"They can if we don't fight back," Danulell agreed. Melawn merely nodded at the logic, not really meaning to give an order. But DeeZann got her bow out of the stretcher, Cypress had a knife and Danulell found a couple of rocks. "Strike down the leader," Danulell advised.

"Why?" Cypress asked.

"If we attack randomly, each bird will think he can survive and they'll keep coming. If we always attack the leader, then soon, no bird will want to lead."

That is a stunning bit of strategy for a supposedly peaceful people, Melawn thought. They packed up again. Leaning on his spear, Fez was able to walk slowly. "If we can just get to a protected area, we can stop until it's dark," DeeZann said. But they barely got started when the birds attacked again.

"That way!" Cypress shouted. The birds were no longer trying to sneak up. The beast was their only cover, and it took all Melawn's attention to hold him steady. He didn't even hear the bow and arrow, but suddenly, a bird dropped from the sky.

"Was that the leader?" He asked.

"Yes. Two leaders down now."

"The attack has been going on for over two hours. And their tactics are changing," Cypress said.

"I'm wondering if this planet is as benign as the Chike claim," Melawn said. "The wildlife seems awfully intelligent."

They just started out when the birds came again. This time, DeeZann missed, but Cypress's knife didn't. Melawn didn't watch, but the bird landed so close they were splattered with blood. He started to shake. "DeeZann, take over," he whispered.

"Five left," she said.

"I have some trail meat," Cypress whispered to DeeZann. "We could leave it out. They love lizards."

"Let's try," she said, but Melawn could tell she and Danulell were skeptical. This time they put Fez on Stubby, with Melawn by his side, ready to pull him off. But this made Fez a big target for the birds, as they immediately came back, completely ignoring the lizard meat.

"Down again!" DeeZann called. Melawn pulled Fez down and made sure Stubby didn't step on him, but Stubby was getting the hang of it, turning sideways and bellowing at the birds. DeeZann winged the lead bird, but before she could even get her arrow back, they were circling around.

"What do they want?" Fez asked.

"They don't want anything except to win," Danulell said, his colors shouting danger. "We have a word for it. *Turjikta*: boldness beyond reason or compassion."

DeeZann regarded him. "Okay. Then we fight." The four

remaining birds circled back. "I'll take the lead, Danulell the left, Cy, the right." That will leave one on the far right, Melawn thought and looked at Fez, on the ground with his spear. *Well, I couldn't throw that anyway.*

Melawn pressed his face against Stubby, holding the beast with both arms. He peeked out just enough to see the lead bird fall to an arrow. The others came on, screeching this time. It was terrifying. Just when they were almost on them, the left bird dropped with a knife wound, and the right bird veered off, winged by a rock. But the last bird came on. *Is that one bigger?* It was too late for the bow, and Cypress was out of knives. It was going to skim right over the top of the beast. *Fez!*

Melawn turned in alarm in time to see the last bird dive for Fez and impale itself on the perfectly-timed lift of Fez's spear. It still tried for Fez's face, but Cypress and DeeZann grabbed its wings and held on until it went limp.

Melawn quickly checked the sky, but the one injured bird was winging its way west. *Don't throw up. Don't throw up. We can't spare the water.*

"What is that?" Cypress asked.

Melawn and Danulell joined him. Around the big bird's neck was a metal bracelet. They gasped. Danulell gently removed it. "A Ramian token," he said sadly.

"You mean those people by the wrecked ship were killed by these birds?" Cypress asked.

"If they were already injured, that's possible," DeeZann said. And the birds are hunting outside their territory," she added, concerned.

"This was the leader," Danulell said. "Not the one in front." They all sagged in realization. They'd killed the others in their ignorance.

"It pushed the others forward, in its bold craziness. Or they were afraid of it," DeeZann said. They all nodded grimly.

"Short rest," Melawn said, and they all nodded. He chanted a prayer for forgiveness as the blood dried on their clothes.

Melawn staggered along, no longer bothering to call for rotations. His arms and back ached, his legs hurt from the bird attacks, and his head was pounding. He so missed the med patches of his previous life. The others were no better off. The only relief was the blazing sun was finally setting.

"Stubby," he complained. "Stop pulling."

"Wait," DeeZann said, and they gently set the stretcher down. They tried to stifle the groans for Fez's sake. "We're at the last ridge. We need to let Stubby go. He smells the herd." Melawn had no objection. He helped Fez sit up for some water while the others got the packs from Stubby.

"I'm going to leave the cooking gear," DeeZann said. One of the herders can return it." Melawn gave a vague hand sign that was somewhere between *yes* and *I don't care*. But then he wrote a note from his journal, asking them to send beasts and carts in the morning, and telling them they had Fez. DeeZann tucked the note under the harness and gave the beast a shove. "Off you go, Stubby."

"Bye, Stubby," they all added. He tossed his head and trotted off, faster than he'd ever walked for them.

"Only an hour to go," Melawn said, trying to encourage them.

In the canyon

An hour and a half later, they were lost in a dark maze of

rock near the entrance of the Dragon's Den. "I'm sure we've come far enough," DeeZann said, whistling again.

"Let's just sit," Melawn suggested. "Heartless will be rising soon." No one argued. They set their gear carefully where they could find it in the dark and wrapped the blankets around them while they rested against some rock, quietly sipping their water.

Melawn watched the stars for the first time in days. "Look, there's a ship—a big one."

"More people," Cypress said.

Melawn was nodding off when DeeZann jumped up. Voices.

"Here, over here," DeeZann whispered.

"Who's there?" A man's voice answered, not demanding like a guard, more hesitant.

"It's DeeZann, and Cypress, from the expedition."

A man and his family came out of the shadows. They had packs on their backs and one small torch.

"Sorry," DeeZann said. "We don't have a light. Can you take us to the entrance?"

They looked at each other in alarm. And then Melawn finally grasped the situation. They were packed to leave. They were sneaking out.

"What's happening?" Melawn whispered.

"We're going. The entrance is back that way," he pointed, "about 100 meters."

"Why are you leaving?" Melawn asked.

His wife grabbed his arm and pulled. "You'll see," she said and they started to go.

"Thayne?" Melawn asked. "Is he here?"

"Him?" The wife answered. "Not like he could walk out alone." And they hustled away.

"Should we wait until morning?" Danulell asked, no doubt wondering what he was in for now.

"No," all three of them answered, picking up their gear and the stretcher.

They walked back about 100 meters, practically tripping over a guard. "Hey! You didn't whistle!" he complained.

"We did!" DeeZann answered. "You didn't answer! What's going on here?"

"Nothing—Cypress! You're back."

"Yes, but we need help. Tell us what's going on."

"Just the usual after-dinner drama." And he stepped aside to let them go by.

DeeZann and Melawn took the lead maneuvering Fez's stretcher through the last twists and turns to the Dragon's Den.

"Where is everyone?" DeeZann whispered. The usual echo and bustle was gone. "Hello?" she said louder. They reached the main cavern and the few people sitting around the fire jumped up.

"We need to go to the medical cave," Melawn said, starting to the left.

"There's no one there," someone said.

"Where's the new medtech?" Melawn asked.

"She left."

"Melawn!" AnnaLee scolded as she came in with her family and assistants. "Why are you back so soon?"

From her angle, AnnaLee couldn't see Cypress or Danulell, but she could clearly see they were carrying a stretcher. "Greetings Honor," Melawn said carefully. "We need medical care for our scout. And we need to organize a rescue team right away."

Thayne came around the corner. He headed for Melawn, but AnnaLee put an arm out to stop him. "What happened?" she asked. "Where's Ellant?"

"The Ramians were shipwrecked. They're injured. The humans are sick. There's not enough food. We need to send help. Beasts. Carts. Food."

AnnaLee frowned. "We have no food to spare." The others looked down, embarrassed.

"You can be resupplied in a day from Paradise," Melawn said.

"We're not asking them for food! Go there directly if you want to." Melawn realized that's what he should have done anyway. There was no medical care and no help here.

Melawn moved forward until all of them were in view. There was a tremendous gasp in the room as people saw Danulell. Hearing about Ramians was obviously different than seeing one.

"Please help us," Danulell said, in perfect outer sector Alkulu. "I'm asking on behalf of our people."

Thayne swooped around AnnaLee's arm and came forward, reminding Melawn of something, but he was too tired to think of it. Thayne grasped Melawn's hand, then DeeZann's, then greeted "Danulell, my friend," and nodded to Cypress. "Bring this child to my cave."

That Thayne ignored her, and that he *knew* the alien, was just enough of a shock for them to get by and into Thayne's space, where his other student, Patrick, took up a position by the door.

"What's happening here?" DeeZann asked.

"Long story. The Mershla, I see. Patrick, the med kit." Thayne took a long look at them in their dirty, bloody clothes and shook his head. "AnnaLee has become unmanageable. She's refusing supplies from Paradise." Thayne's eyes flickered to the door. "Everyone is leaving."

"Why didn't you leave?"

Thayne glanced at the returning Patrick, who handed him the med kit. "We're waiting for the Ramians."

"You've been expecting them?"

Thayne lowered his voice. "Plan A: Sail across the ocean, combine technologies, build a transmitter, and send a message."

Melawn was stunned. "All that bragging? With the Ramians? You were actually making plans?"

Thayne rolled his eyes, "Yesss."

Melawn just couldn't fathom the level of scheming. "But how can we send a message? We don't even know where the sectors are."

"Once we build a telescope we will know."

"How?"

"Patrick was doing research on nearby galaxies. He has positions memorized."

"That won't tell us much."

"Depends how far we are. If it doesn't seem too far, then we'll use the second method. He had a personal notebook with a list of hub stars and their spectra."

"You should give this data to the Council."

"We did. But they won't do anything."

Melawn scowled. He didn't like Thayne's disrespect of the Council, and he wasn't sure they would disallow a telescope anyway. But he was too tired and worried to argue.

18-Sovereignty

Despite everything, despite worry, hunger, and being dressed in filthy, itchy rags, Melawn slept a few hours by Thayne's fireplace. Before dawn, Melawn groggily listened to Thayne grilling the still half asleep DeeZann and Danulell.

Thayne was asking everything about the surviving Ramians, what their specialties were, if they still thought they could combine technologies to build a transmitter, about the drops, the crabs, and how long to build another sailing ship.

That woke Melawn up. "Are you crazy?" he asked before thinking. Thayne looked over at him, astonished. Apparently, in the ten years they'd been together, Melawn had never actually vocalized that question. "There won't be any more ships. They sent a clear message." DeeZann and Danulell nodded in agreement.

"Dee said the crabs stood on the beach in a line," Thayne said and shrugged. Shaking her head in exasperation, DeeZann got her sketchpad out of her pack and flipped it open, handing it to Thayne. As he studied it, his expression changed from annoyance to understanding to disappointment. Melawn dragged himself over to look.

It was a drawing of the crabs lined up on the beach, holding their spikes aloft, with the giant crab staring down the defiant Ellant. In one corner was a small sketch of the huddled Ramians, one bunch clinging to a baby. Another inset showed the empty beach, with the waves receding from the row of embedded spikes. Even though it was just a pencil sketch, it somehow captured the emotion and finality of the moment.

Thayne deflated a bit and closed his eyes in acceptance. "The crabs are a formidable enemy and we won't be able to sail."

"Agreed," the three of them whispered.

Thayne handed back the sketch. "Thank you. This does make things much more difficult. We'll have to go to plan B."

DeeZann and Melawn snapped their necks turning to look at each other in alarm. "What is plan B?" Melawn demanded in a whisper.

Thayne turned to Danulell. "Do your people have methods to extract hydrogen and helium?"

"I have no idea," Danulell answered.

"Why?" DeeZann asked, puzzled.

The pieces clicked into place and Melawn thought he would scream. *"Airships!"*

DeeZann looked at them in terror. "Fly? Over the whole ocean?"

"In a giant balloon! Basically," Melawn added.

"Impossible!" Danulell said.

"Possible," Thayne said calmly. "It's been done. On Earth."

"Incredible. Humans. No shortage of the bold," Danulell said.

Or the crazy.

Melawn checked on Fez, who was doing better, and found Cypress, who reported that the rescue party would leave in an hour. He'd arranged for the herders to meet them at the canyon exit.

"No one is vaccinated though, for the Mershla."

"No. They all agree to take their chances."

So Melawn prepared to head back out—with DeeZann and Danulell. Leaving Thayne wouldn't matter. He wanted nothing to do with these schemes.

9 / THE MARKERS

4-Dominion

Watcher

Luckily, Lanezi shooed the birdcams away before he entered their cabin, because Io and Euro were facing off in the main room. *Arguing?* Never in the years he had known them. They quickly went silent and tried to hide it, but it was pointless. "What's wrong?" Lanezi asked as mildly as possible. Io shook his head and sat down, almost missing the chair. "Are you alright?"

"Fine."

Euro tentatively came closer. "He's been dizzy."

"Euro!"

"You can't hide it anymore. I might as well tell."

"How long?" Lanezi asked.

"A few weeks," Euro answered.

"Weeks! Have you gone to the doctor?"

"No. It's probably just being cooped up in the heat with Raykatoo all day," Io said. Lanezi scowled and took a closer look. Io was flushed and his hair hung limp. He was thin and his dark skin had a gray tinge. Euro was thin too. Not as bad as when they were starving, but it didn't look like they'd returned to normal weight.

"Are you getting taller?" Lanezi asked, alarmed. Neither had grown for years, not since the adolescent inhibitors. And if they were growing again, that meant their mutation might soon kill them.

"A little," Euro admitted.

Stay calm. Just talk to them. "Are you eating?"

Euro nodded yes, but Io said, "The food is gross."

"You're eating Chike food?"

"No! The Ramian food."

Lanezi didn't understand. He liked the Ramian food. Or was he still food obsessed since almost starving?

"It is pretty tasteless," Euro agreed.

"You've had the cortay?" Lanezi asked, wondering how anyone could dislike the sweet, almost chocolaty pudding.

They both made ick faces. "Okay, that's it. To the doctor. Let's go."

Euro rolled his eyes. "Because we don't like cortay?"

"Yes. It's obviously an emergency."

5-Dominion

81-Petals, at Firelight

The 72 volunteers that had gone to ARA2 and had been rescued by various ships were now all together on an outer docking ring at Firelight. Extra pilots and monitors and a few medical people from *81* had flown over to collect them. Terina held the holdbar by the big observation window in the big Entry Lounge of the big *81-Petals*, waiting for the shuttles to return. In her other hand, she held the cords of a fancy blue velvet bag that her mom had mysteriously instructed her to bring.

The captain wouldn't let her record the return and reunions but she was allowed to help expedite their passage through the Entry Lounge and to the lift.

The big hangar door was already open, and she could see a string of shuttle lights in the distance. Behind her, at the big three-person control panel, Vante Kay acted as monitor for Iricana and Kelson, who were overseeing the whole operation.

"What's the bag for?" Kelson asked her.

"I don't know. Mom told me to bring it." Kelson and Iricana looked at each other, mystified.

Just then, Adisa, Jarvie's monitor, reported in. "*81, Bird of Paradise*, ETA: 3 minutes. No injured aboard."

"Parking spot 1," Vante answered. The hangar deck crew stood back, ready with the tubeway.

Vante spoke again, his Earthborn accent going very formal. "Priority message for the captain, from Firelight Council."

Iricana gave Terina a look, like *this is not for your feed*. "Yes, Captain," she whispered and Vante played the message.

"Captain Iricana," a voice said, "please be advised. We are receiving relay reports from ships that have jumped out of Redrock." They all gasped. "In the words of one captain: The nanos have hijacked and assimilated every Chike gravity ball in Redrock system. Only the big gravity ball at the a-rings is intact. A loose sphere of nanos surrounds it, only letting the Human ships through. Every time a new Chike ship enters the system, the nanos rocket out to intercept it and transform its gravity ball. They've also disabled the Chike comm systems somehow, so they can't warn just-arriving ships. But the Chike are figuring it out. Redrock estimates they'll get a ship out in the next six days. Otherwise, Redrock is unharmed and continues to evacuate to Petrichor, unhindered by the Chike."

They sagged with relief. "Please send our thanks," Iricana told Vante.

Wow. What a story. Too bad I won't get to write it. I wonder what ships—

"*Bird of Paradise* on auto dock," *81* announced. *Bird* came in and touched down perfectly on the paint, auto anchors attaching. "Clear for tubeway," Adisa announced.

The first person to pull through the hatch was Falcon. "Captain, Honors," she said, "on behalf of the 72, requesting permission to board."

"Permission granted," Iricana said, a bit surprised at the formality. After all, they were their own crew returning. Then Falcon pulled a small bamboo slat out of her pocket. She flashed it dramatically, showing the #1 on one side and a drawing of a falcon on the other. *Her marker, from when they handed out 72 markers to the line of volunteers. They kept their markers.* Falcon handed it to Terina. *That's what the bag is for!*

So as each shuttle came in, the returnees handed over their markers, all signed on the back. Some had drawings, prayers, or additional messages. By the last shuttle the rattling bag was almost full, floating at Terina's side.

Chip and Kente, monitors for their sibs, pulled through, but stalled in the Entry Lounge waiting for the last people. Her mom, the pilot, came in, followed by Thunder, Teeve, and a downcast Beezan carrying a limp Sky, escorted by Katie.

Thunder handed over his marker and shared a tearful hug with Iricana. Teeve gave Terina his marker and hugged the young Tektites, but the three of them slowly turned to watch. Beezan wasn't wandering, but he was puzzled and unnerved by everyone looking at him. He didn't have a marker to hand over.

No one had told him. And suddenly Terina understood. She smiled at her mom, who nodded, then cinched up the cords on the bag of markers.

"For you, Honor Beezan. These are the markers of a few of the people that believe in you."

Katie steadied him as he slowly took the bag. He looked at Terina and then the others, who broke into a big round of applause. His eyes filled with tears and he clutched the bag to his chest next to Sky. "Thank you."

6-Dominion

Watcher

It only took a day for the Ramian doctor to study the test results of Io and Euro and call Lanezi to their med center. Anitoran, the medical aid, or his tan, whichever she was, let Lanezi in. "This is doctor Pranakeen, in case you don't remember."

"Thank you," Lanezi said, wincing a little, as he didn't remember.

"Lanezi," the doctor said, colors hidden under a hood, "please sit."

"Ah, thank you." He sat down in front of the desk, opposite the doctor.

"I have studied everything in your database about this rare condition, as well as the treatment Io and Euro were receiving, and the experiments of your Dr. Tenshi.

"When you first came aboard, you were all treated for severe radiation, and health was restored. We knew at the time of Euro and Io's genetic resistance to radiation poisoning. However, I now understand that this resistance is tied to late adolescence.

Once adolescence is complete, a short period of degeneration is followed by death."

It pained and panicked Lanezi to even think about it. He nodded.

"I've studied the research thoroughly, and sadly, I believe your doctor made a mistake."

Oh, no.

"She was distracted, or went off on a tangent, due to one outlier."

"That doesn't sound like Tenshi. She would have known better."

"But this was a very compelling outlier. Just one rat. It *did* survive better than the others. Even better than normal rats. The survival was real. It's just that, in my opinion, it didn't have anything to do with her treatment.

"And now, sadly, adolescence is upon them. They will show conflicting signs, both the growth of coming adulthood and a wasting of the disorder. Normally, a functional system would prevent growth to conserve energy, but that's not happening here. The system is broken and conflicting signals will overwhelm the body."

"What can we do?"

"Of course, my entire team is on this problem already. Meanwhile, we will start a feeding and support program. We may be able to save them if we act quickly. The most helpful thing would be a healthy genetic sample. And you are the only possible donor."

"Of course. Whatever you need."

"And . . . your advice, about what I should tell them."

"The truth. Always."

The doctor nodded with satisfaction.

. . .

Lanezi, now that he had taken over Io's afternoon shift with Raykatoo, was learning more about the Chike and GenTwo than he had ever wanted to. It sounded like they were the geniuses of the galaxy and could do anything. So he brought a datafile of all the doctor's research with him. And after scrubbing Raykatoo's back with sand, and feeling ashamed that he'd let Io do all this hard work himself, he gave it to her.

"What is this?"

"All the data on Io and Euro's disorder. I thought you might want to look it over."

"I am not a doctor."

"I thought your people might have a cure."

"We do not dabble in primate medicine."

"But you could probably find a cure."

"The Chike's expertise is with machines."

"But one of the GenTwo . . ."

She hissed. "Absolutely, the GenTwo could find a cure!" She swung around to her large side eye. "But we would not give it to you!"

"Why not?"

"Have you forgotten the taboo?"

"You're exempt."

"Only to *talk* to lessers! This one would never hand over technology."

"Medicine."

"No different. It would be like giving you Chike nanos. The Creator only knows what you would do with them."

"You can stand by and let them die?"

"We let the GenFive die all the time." A chill went down Lanezi's spine. "But we don't kill them! As you did our eggs."

"An accident!" Lanezi protested.

"Ignorance! This collapse of the ways, it's probably the Ramians' fault! Out there doing art with stars or something."

"No. I was there. It was an accident."

"The Ramians! One accident after another! Ignorance!"

He played his final card, "Euro and Io are not Ramians."

7-Dominion

81-Petals, at Firelight

Jarvie rode the tram with Terina after their class in Arc 7. "We could have walked," she said. "We're getting lazy."

"I miss skating," Jarvie responded, "but it's too crowded."

"Yeah. Wouldn't that be awful to smash into someone, like the captain."

Jarvie shuddered. "I did that once, you know. On the *Drumheller*."

"What?"

"Shhh!"

"On a ship with six people, you crashed?"

"Actually, there were just the two of us at the time." Terina's eyes went wide. "I hurt him. I felt so bad. And he was so patient with me."

"He's *still* patient with you."

"Hey. He has bigger worries now. Especially with Sky acting strange."

Terina lowered her voice even more, even though the car was mostly empty. She was looking at her p'link. "What do you think? Will the Council send the *81* to the colony?"

Jarvie shook his head. "No. They're not going to send 4,000 people on a high-risk assignment."

"But they might send some of us." She looked worried.

"Don't worry," he reassured her. "I'm sure they won't separate you and your mom." His s'link beeped. "I'm being summoned to a meeting with the captain in 15 minutes." He glanced up at the destination sign—Arc 3. He was just going to make it.

"See," she said, slumping in her seat. "You're going to go and I'm not."

Jarvie had a pang of sadness. Although he and Terina had no romantic interest in each other, they had been through a lot together and were good friends. "I hope they keep the *Drumheller* crew together."

When they got to Arc 1, they hurried down the stairs. At the rimway, Terina grabbed his arm. "If they don't," she said, "if you have to go . . . thank you. For being my friend." Impulsively, he hugged her.

"Let's not give up hope," he whispered. But his stomach churned as he jogged to the Operations Bay. *Would they split us up? Would they separate me from Beezan?* Anything could happen. The message was only addressed to Jarvie. He had no idea who else would be going.

He ducked in the door of Ops out of breath and with only a few seconds to spare. Bad diplomatic form, he scolded himself. But he saw Beezan sigh with relief. *Beezan's going. Thank you, thank you.* He sat with his head down during the prayer and then quickly looked around. And surprise—a Firelight council member was with them, sitting right next to Iricana. Jarvie tried not to be too obvious as he took inventory. Sequoia, but not Terina. Thunder, Taj, Katie, and her new assistant Roza, Falcon, and Ra'Tama. And Rendra, who must have come over with the council member. No Kelson.

"Honor," Iricana prompted the council member. "Thank you for coming."

"Honors," he nodded, making eye contact with each person.

It was likely that he knew everything about all of them. "We're all busy. I'll make this brief." He turned to Iricana. "Tomorrow at 13:00, we'll be transferring command of the *81-Petals* to Captain Bozenka, formerly of the *Midnight*." The room went completely still, as if no one dared to breathe. "She'll be boarding with her command crew." They nodded, barely. "Captain Iricana will transfer to the *Midnight* . . ."

Midnight! A small ship. Newer. And entirely painted black, almost invisible. Captain Bozenka must be sad to leave. Jarvie snapped back to attention, but the council member was only saying the names of everyone in the room. *I'm going to Midnight.* Sequoia turned pale with a stricken expression. Ra'Tama barely lifted his fingers from the table, but the council member turned sharply to address him. "Of course, Honor Ra'Tama, you and your crew may join or stay at your discretion."

Ra'Tama nodded formally. "We will transfer to the *Midnight*."

"Additionally, Kelson and the Tektite crew may come of their own choice. And any attached minors may come at their guardians' discretion." Sequoia's gasp of relief did not even make the council member blink. *Yesss!* Jarvie smiled to himself.

"The tests with the so-called shimmer shield were successful, although we estimate the failure rate too high for everyday use. Your mission on the *Midnight* will be to jump to the colony location and determine if Humans are being held there. If the system is crowded, jump right back to report. If there is good chance of reaching the colony undetected, we'd like any kind of report on their condition. At this time, we do not want to attempt a rescue."

"Yes, Honor," Iricana answered.

"If the Chike were to arrive here in Firelight while ships were jumping, and they witnessed your ship going in the direction of the colony, they might be suspicious. Therefore, we are planning a mass jump. Eleven ships will load the a-rings and jump in multiple directions. *Midnight* will be 4th."

Eleven in the rings at the same time! Wow.

The council member turned to look at Iricana. "Please send your crew to the *Midnight* at 10:00 with nine of *81*'s planet-landing shuttles. You'll wait here for Captain Bozenka and then transfer over. Thunder can be in command until you get there."

"Yes, Honor."

The council member nodded curtly, stood abruptly, and strode out of the room as they scrambled to their feet. "Jarvie," Iricana whispered, nodding her head towards the stairs. Jarvie scurried down the stairs after, to escort the council member back to his ship. But it was a mere formality as people in the rimways stood aside and hushed as he walked by, determined and distant.

9-Dominion

Bird of Paradise, in Firelight System, transferring to the *Midnight*

Despite 200 years of cleanup, Firelight System was still a messy place, with a wide asteroid belt between 3 and 9 AU, many crossing asteroids, and a smaller belt inward of the station at .9 AU. Add three Human stations and hundreds of ships and it started to look like Veez's home system.

Beezan, sitting in the monitor position aboard *Bird of Paradise*, checked the list of shuttles in the Convoy. *Paradise* was third in line of ten, now that *Pinecone* had been added at the last minute. Chip and Kente somehow provided evidence that the little shuttle was their personal property, despite the fact that neither of them even had a birth certificate, any medical records, or legal evidence of their *own* existence. So *Pinecone* was added to the nine landing shuttles now headed to *Midnight*.

Convoy to *Midnight* — Assignments
Shuttle / Pilot / P&P
Sonata / Ra'Tama / Kay Ling, Cookie
Thunder Bay / Thunder / Katie
Bird of Paradise / Jarvie / Beezan, Star, Sky
Star of Bethlehem / Teeve / Maura, Roza
Larkspur / Cooper / Falcon
Snapdragon / Mika / Vante Kay
Lotus / Taj / Kelson
Hyacinth / Sequoia / Terina, Rocket
Edelweiss / Rendra / Iricana
Pinecone / Chip / Danny, Sunny, Kente

Neither *81-Petals* nor *Midnight* was actually docked. In fact, they were an hour apart. There were so many ships at Firelight that they were assigned to various strictly-observed parking orbits. Their convoy's trajectory was carefully plotted, approved, and posted. Since it was a short trip, and very low gee, Beezan kept the whining Sky with him, in his podpup pocket.

Jarvie was piloting, but they were both gawking at all the activity. "Kelson said it was Grand Central Station here, whatever that means," Jarvie said.

Beezan smiled. "A train station. Next to Earthport NYC. My parents sent me a picture when they went through. They just couldn't comprehend the kind of crowds they have on Earth."

Sky suddenly cried out and jerked in his podpup pocket. "What's wrong?" Beezan asked softly. She looked at him and her eyes glazed over. Her head fell back and she started a horrible keening. At the same time, their comm went on with a message from Firelight.

"Alert: Chike detected in system!" That message was overblasted by a Chike message.

"Attention lesser ones! All vessels will hold position until further notice!" There was more unintelligible noise.

"Alert: All ships hold position," the Firelight monitor repeated.

Beezan tried to turn it down, but the most painful thing was Sky's keening. Beezan couldn't think straight. The keening seared up his nerves to his brain and set it on fire. "Sky, stop, stop. No, please, you're hurting us."

"Alert: *Bird of Paradise*. All stop. Hold your position!"

Beezan could barely open his eyes, but he could see Jarvie spastically trying to control the shuttle. "*Paradise!*" Beezan tried to say, but it came out in a groan. "Hold position on *Midnight*." He could hear himself panting in pain. *Focus!*

"Jarvie! We need to get you two in the scanner!" Thank heavens Katie had insisted they install one. But Jarvie was just collapsed, hanging in nogee now that the shuttle was station-keeping. *I can't think straight with her.* Beezan unstrapped and pushed off the panel with his legs, zooming to the back of the shuttle. He caught a hanging strap, wheeled over to the scanner, and opened the lid. Then he had to pry Sky out of his pocket and hold her in while he shut the lid.

Relief. "Oh my God. It's the Chike. Whatever is bothering her, it's caused by the Chike."

"Alert: Chike have jumped inbound two times. Prepare for Chike ships in the vicinity! Hold positions! Comm silence!"

All their nanos and alien tech were carefully hidden in scanner boxes, but Beezan had to get Jarvie into the scanner, or he didn't know what would happen. He didn't want Chike boarding this little shuttle or taking Jarvie. Jarvie was just as panicked. He unstrapped and dove for the scanner. But when Beezan opened the lid, they nearly doubled over in pain from Sky's keening. "I can't go in there with her!"

Jarvie slammed the lid shut, barely holding onto the holdbar.

"I'll get her a sedative. Get in!"

"I'll wait."

"We don't know where the Chike are! I'll get it. I promise!"

Beezan opened the lid again. "Ahhh! Sky please!" She tried to come out, but Jarvie grabbed her and pulled her in with him. Beezan carefully shut the lid. He took a few breaths, but Jarvie was wincing in pain.

Ignoring more alerts from the Firelight monitors, he swung over to the med cabinet and fumbled around for the sedative. Back at the scanner, he tore it open with his teeth, braced himself, and opened the lid again, wincing. Jarvie was gasping for breath. Beezan slapped the patch on Sky. She shot him a terrible look that tore into his soul. "I'm sorry. I'm sorry." But she went limp and the horrid keening stopped. He shut the lid and hung there, shaking, head pounding, eyes watering.

"Alert: Prepare for some Chike operation. We don't know what."

"*Paradise*, turn our exterior lights off." *Maybe they'll skip us.* He gingerly pushed back to his seat and checked on Star, in his box. He looked a little strained but was conscious. "Bee. Ow."

"I know. Good Star." His own voice seemed too loud in his aching head. He strapped back in and toggled the intercom. "Jarvie? Can you hear me?"

"Yes. Better. She's out. What's happening?"

Beezan wiped his eyes and blinked at the screen. "I don't know. It doesn't seem like an inspection. All the Chike beacons are in one place." He tapped the screen and said, "Enlarge." In the center of the circled Chike ships was one Human beacon, the *81-Petals.*

"Oh, no," Beezan said. "They've surrounded the *81*."

"*Paradise*," Beezan asked, "Status of *Edelweiss*."

"Holding position near traffic beacon 32." He clutched his chest with relief. Iricana and Rendra were off the *81*.

"Status of *Pinecone*?"

"Still aboard the *81-Petals*."

Suddenly, the combined Chike ships and the *81-Petals* blinked out of existence—and back in, further from Firelight— like a mini jump. "They've got the *81*!" he told Jarvie.

The Firelight monitor broke the silence: "Alert: *Snapdragon*! Hold position!"

Mika shouted over the comm, "We have to go back! Our people are on the *81*!"

"HOLD POSITION!"

"We can't just—" and Beezan knew that Vante had cut Mika off.

The Chike and *81* blinked again, doing another mini jump. It took thirty seconds to get a signal. Now they were just inside the asteroid belt.

"Oh no!" Jarvie said. "The *Pinecone*?"

"They're still aboard *81*," Beezan told him.

And then, without any acceleration, the Chike ships and the *81-Petals* blinked out. Beezan knew they would scan the outer system for hours, but it would be useless. "They're gone."

Jarvie gasped. "They took them! The Tektites are separated."

"Everybody's separated. And all those thousands of people, going to the colony now. We got off just in time." But not really. Their shimmer shield pilots, Sunny and Danny, were still on the *81*.

Hyacinth, approaching *Midnight*

"*Thunder Bay* to Convoy: Proceed to *Midnight*."

Terina tried to calm her breathing after the *81* disappeared. Her mom was piloting the *Hyacinth*, which sounded like the name of a relative, and they were last in line of this part of the convoy. The *Edelweiss*, with Rendra and the captain were much farther behind. And *Pinecone* didn't make it. Those two kids her age were going to the colony.

"*Midnight*," came Beezan's shaky voice, "Request autodock."

A new voice, calm and melodious, came on. "Convoy, this is *Midnight* hangar control monitor Magadi. *Bird of Paradise*, autodock will engage when *Thunder Bay* is clear."

"Convoy," Thunder ordered, "*Sonata* crew and Katie assist *Paradise*. Roza, get to the Med Bay ASAP."

Terina's mom gently thrusted the *Hyacinth* back onto its trajectory, and then slowed down again. "Okay," her mom muttered. "What's the problem? Why is *Lotus* slowing down?"

Her mom was following the *Lotus*, but on the tactical display, Terina saw the problem. "*Snapdragon* isn't moving. Now *Larkspur* is turning around."

"The Tektites," her mom said. "I get it; their family is gone, but where do they think they're going?"

"Convoy—proceed to *Midnight*!" Thunder repeated.

Terina sent the tactical to the big screen so her mom could see the whole scene.

"*Snapdragon*, Vante Kay, report," Thunder ordered.

When no one answered, Terina glanced at her mom, who frowned with concern.

"Maybe Mika's too distraught to fly," Terina said.

"But Vante's not, so why doesn't he answer?"

"*Thunder Bay* to *Larkspur*, Cooper, continue to *Midnight*!" Thunder's usually easy-going voice was crisp and demanding. *Larkspur* slowed down, but didn't turn back to the *Midnight*.

"*Sonata* to *Thunder Bay*, request permission to assist *Snapdragon*."

"*Sonata*, proceed to *Midnight!*" Thunder ordered.

"Acknowledged," Ra'Tama answered immediately.

"*Star of Bethlehem*, Teeve, Maura, proceed."

There was a delay, but *Star of Bethlehem* finally moved, and then Maura came on, "Yeah, convoy leader. The rest of you, get with it!"

Larkspur finally turned for *Midnight*, and Falcon announced, "Proceeding." Taj, in the *Lotus*, began to circle around the *Snapdragon*.

"Mom, if we go out of order, the hangar parking will be messed up."

"It's already messed up if Beezan is on autodock, so I'm going around. Besides," she frowned and dropped her voice to a whisper, "it won't matter. There will be plenty of room without the *Pinecone*."

Terina nodded, feeling bad for the Tektites. "I hope Chip and Kente will be okay. At least they're with their sibs." *Unlike me . . . but I have my mom and grandpa.*

Hyacinth was just touching down in the hangar when Vante finally reported from the *Snapdragon*. "Proceeding, convoy leader. ETA 12 minutes." He sounded as business-like as always. But no time to speculate; Terina had to scramble, hauling out Rocket in his box, and going around to Beezan's shuttle to help with the other podpups. Kay Ling and Ra'Tama were helping Beezan and Jarvie out, so Terina grabbed Star. She waited to give them all space in the lift, and then couldn't help her curiosity. Hauling the box with Rocket in one hand, and stuffing Star in her podpup pocket, she pulled back to the Entry Lounge, where Thunder and the *Midnight* monitor Magadi were still at the panel, and the last people were coming off the shuttles.

When Vante came in without Mika, Thunder asked, "What's happening?"

"My agreement with Mika is complete. I insisted she bring me to the *Midnight*. In return, I agreed not to personally haul her off the shuttle. Someone else will have to do that."

Cooper, already upset, went wide-eyed. "Not me."

"You're her husband," Thunder said.

"Yeah. I know better."

"Teeve's the only one, but he's gone to help the *Bird of Paradise*," Maura said.

"This is *Snapdragon*. I'm going back to Firelight. Release my auto anchors before *Edelweiss* gets here."

"I'm sorry Mika. You need to stay here," Thunder told her, more mildly than Terina expected.

Maura floated to the panel and pressed the button. "Heya, it's tragedy, yeah, but no more splitting up the family. We're here now. And goin' back to Firelight won't help. They took the kids to the colony. Get yourself out here so we can follow them!"

"Serious doubt. They could still be here in the outer sectors."

"No doubt. They're gone. Hey, you, podpup girl, ask them."

"Oh, ah," caught off guard, Terina had to think a second to come up with podpup names. "Star, sweetie, where's Tiger? Where Tiger?"

Star looked up, unconcerned. "Gone." The others nodded, pained.

"Where Peeps?"

"Gone. All gone."

"Hear that Meek? Pup says gone. They're gone," Maura told her, wiping a tear from her face.

There was a long sigh. Magadi pointed to the panel and whispered, "Engines powering down."

"Alright you lot," Thunder said, mainly to Terina, "let's clear out and give some privacy."

"Yes, Honor," Terina said, and pulled to the lift. As she got in, Star started chanting.

"Tiger gone. Peeps gone. Chilly gone. Coco gone. Juju gone."

"Rocket here!" Rocket said, banging against the side of his box and nearly knocking Terina into the lift wall.

"Rocket here!" Star repeated. "Cookie here! Sky—"

Terina looked down in alarm. "Sky?"

Star shrugged. "Sky . . . fuzzy."

"It's just the sedative." *I hope.*

10-Dominion Eve

Midnight, in Firelight System

Terina, still shaky from the capture of the *81-Petals*, worked her way to the *Midnight* Med Bay and was about to go up the stairs, but jumped aside as Ra'Tama came bounding down. He handed Cookie to her without a second glance. As much as she wanted to follow him, she was now juggling three pups. She peeked inside and saw Beezan on an exam table, Jarvie holding his head, and Vante holding his arm. Katie was frowning over Sky, but said, "There's a lot of brain activity. I don't think there's any damage."

Two other *Midnight* med techs were getting Jarvie and Vante settled, so Terina figured she wasn't needed and headed for the only logical place—the kitchen. When she got there, she discovered that the *Midnight* crew had left them a welcome snack. Untangling herself from two podpups, she let Rocket out of the box. They ran around crazy until she took a few pieces of fruit and crackers and handed them out.

"Why, who do we have here?"

Startled, Terina looked up. She hadn't even noticed the young woman in the prep area. And she looked just like Magadi from the hangar. "Oh, hi, I mean, God is Most Glorious."

With a flutter of hands rolling over her heart, slight bow, and tinkling bracelets, she replied with a low melodious voice, "God is Most Glorious. Welcome to *Midnight*. I am Pongola."

Terina blurted out the first thought that came to her mind, "Are you and Magadi singers?"

"We sing. We chant. We dance." Pongola said. "And we will welcome you all tonight during jump prayers," she added. "But you are troubled."

"Things didn't go as planned," Terina explained.

Pongola nodded sympathetically. "People have plans, but God has bigger plans." She fluttered past Terina to help put more food down for the pups. "We will be flexible. We will trust. We will have hope."

Does she even know where we're going? Hope is all we have.

As Jarvie sat on the exam bed in Med Bay, Katie asked Vante what happened to his arm. He didn't exactly say, only indicating where it hurt. But then Mika stormed in, blurting out, "Where's Maura?—Oh you again," she said when she saw Vante.

Katie narrowed her eyes and said, "If you're not injured you need to go to Ops, now." Mika scowled at Vante, unmoving.

Roza had just finished refilling his med patch, so Jarvie had no excuse to ignore his diplomatic duties. "Come on," he told Mika, "I'll go with you."

"Pfft. Don't need a babysitter." But she came downstairs with him.

"Hey," Jarvie said, "We all want to get to the colony, but the more fuss you make, the longer it will take. We need calm for the jump."

"What, pilot can't jump cuz his pup is whinin'?"

A surge of anger went through Jarvie, but he tried to channel his brother and gather some patience. "What happened with Vante?"

"Who?"

"Your monitor? The hurt arm?"

"Oh, you know."

"What? You hurt him?"

"Naw. Barely touched him. Shouldn't be messin' with my panel."

"He seemed injured."

"Is everyone here a lightweight?"

Jarvie stopped dead in the rimway and turned to face her. "*Everyone here* respects the captain. *Everyone here* respects their crew mates. *Everyone here* is careful not to hurt people smaller or gentler than themselves. And if *you* want to stay *here* you better take my advice and apologize to the Captain and Vante right away!"

"Hey! Just cuz yer a pilot, you can't tell me what to do."

"No! I advise you because it's my job! And I'm advising you to step back and start over with a big dose of respect!"

"I got no respect if yer not goin after that ship right—"

"MEEK!" A very stern voice rang out. Maura, with Teeve at her shoulder and Cooper behind, shaking his head. Maura looked at Jarvie. "Where's the cap?"

"In Ops, where we're all supposed to be."

"You go on. We need a *word*," Teeve said.

Jarvie didn't argue, escaping to Ops.

Inside, Iricana had come straight from the hangar. Kay Ling was already there, along with Sequoia, Kelson, Thunder, and

Falcon monitoring a panel. Terina came in, free of pups. Iricana was talking with a Firelight council member, so everyone was very quiet. "Yes, thank you. We'll await word." She signed off and sank into a chair.

Thunder sat next to her and put an arm around her. "Thank heavens you got away."

"Four thousand people," she said, shaking her head. "There was no way we could have gotten them off in time. I hope it's a big colony."

The four Tektites came in quietly and tried to sneak into the back row, but Ra'Tama, captain's jacket on, came in right behind them with a stormy expression. He headed for Iricana, but Jarvie jumped up and beat Ra'Tama to her. Standing in front of Iricana, he said, "Captain, I would like to formally apologize for our delay in responding to orders. It was not our intention to disobey." He hung his head meekly as Iricana blinked at him in confusion.

Jarvie peered at Mika out of the corner of his eye. And Iricana nodded with understanding. She stood and said, "Crew Jarvie, you performed admirably under difficult circumstances and did your best to comply." Then, very informally, she hugged him.

"Thank you, Captain," he whispered, touched.

As Jarvie sat down, Teeve hauled Mika out of her seat by the back of her coveralls. She shrugged him off and sauntered up to the Captain. "I, ah, well, didn't mean to make trouble. Sorry."

Before Iricana could answer, Ra'Tama stepped forward. "Captain, under the circumstances, I . . . request . . . that my crew be returned to my command."

Everyone's head snapped toward Ra'Tama. Was he going to leave? Iricana looked between Mika and Ra'Tama and held up her hand to pause any more discussion. "Maura, I can forgive a momentary lapse under emotional stress, but I need you and your team to decide if you are part of this crew or not. And if you're not, you'll stay on station."

"No!" Mika said, and everyone turned to shush her.

"If you stay with us, it's with the understanding that you will all follow orders. Go decide." And she dismissed them with a toss of her head.

The four of them left, but Ra'Tama stood his ground. Iricana turned to him. "Captain Ra'Tama," she said firmly, "request granted." There were small gasps of surprise from all, but they were quickly covered up.

Ra'Tama took a big breath. "Thank you, Captain. In that case, I volunteer my crew to be the replacement shimmer crew."

"What? They never even trained."

"I'm told that Vante Kay is not seriously injured. They could test it tonight." Kay Ling gave a sharp nod.

Iricana's eyes went wide. Then she pulled out her s'link. "Taj, when you're done with the shuttles, get a snack and set up the shimmer test again."

Wow, Jarvie thought. *Maybe we can still do this.*

After news of the successful test of the Kays and the shimmer shield, and confirmation that they would be jumping, Beezan had set his p'link to wake him up in the middle of the night, which seemed like a good idea at the time. Now, in the dark, on an exam bed, he struggled with the reasoning. *Am I really supposed to jump tomorrow? Today actually.*

Midnight on the *Midnight.* The splitting pain in his head was blissfully gone. Sky was on his chest, sleeping soundly. *No apparent damage.* That's what Katie had said.

Quietly, he got up, sliding Sky into his podpup pocket.

Beezan looked at his p'link, pleased that he could see again. He tapped it to the panel and got a connect. "Med files, Sky, display," he whispered. A short, but unhelpful report came up.

Keening similar to abandonment, but was not abandoned. Ongoing signs of distress or pain. Complaining of going the wrong way. Keening correlates to audio Chike messages.

Beezan slipped into the dark rimway, which was empty. No more noise and crowds of the busy *81-Petals*. He sighed. All that work. All that community building. And now everyone was gone. Although maybe on the colony they could use that training.

Beezan didn't want to go to his cabin. He didn't even know where it was. He swiped a wall panel for the location of an unused Observation Bay. He worked his way there in the slightly lower gee of *Midnight*, being careful on the stairs. He sank into a viewing couch. Way more comfortable than the exam bed. Sky stirred. "Bee," she said, sounding regretful.

"You okay?" She burrowed into his shirt as if shaking her head no. "Sky, please tell me. What's wrong? Why do you cry?"

"Wrong way."

This isn't helpful. I'll just get her agitated again. Wait. He got up and slipped his s'link in the main screen slot. A second later, a huge, wall-size secret map came up. "I'll show you where we've been and where we're going next."

Surprisingly, Sky sat up, alert. Beezan held her up to the map and pointed out every stop since she was born. Then he pulled in a close-up of where they were going. She looked at it as if she understood, as if she felt better. But she couldn't possibly really understand it. Then he remembered her looking at the Ramian map. Maybe she just liked maps. He stroked her head until she looked at him. "Jump tomorrow. No whining. No keening."

"No."

"Promise?" he asked. She cocked her head at him.

"Bee promise," she demanded.

"You want me to promise something?" Did she even understand the concept? But she pointed to the map.

Beezan brought her closer, and she pointed up. He scrolled the map down and moved it back and forth until she was pointing right at a star, seemingly ordinary. "Take Sky."

It was out of the sectors. Very far out. The podpup homeworld? He swallowed. "You want me to take you to this system?"

"Good Bee. Take Sky."

"Here?" He pointed to the star.

"Here." She pointed.

"Save location," Beezan said, touching the star. "I don't know how, or on what ship, but I'll try, Sky." She turned and looked intently into his eyes; he could feel the burning starting up. "Yes! Yes, I'll take you, somehow."

"Promise."

I could be throwing my life away. And I have Jarvie to think of. But a strange sense of destiny came over him, reminding him of Oatah. "I promise."

10-Dominion

In the morning, Jarvie tracked down Beezan and Sky in the Observation Bay. Beezan was asleep, slumped in a reclined chair, with crumbs all over him and Sky's bottle on the floor. Sky, calm as ever, was sitting on the table gazing up at an off kilter—and secret—sector map. Jarvie pulled Beezan's s'link out of the slot, making the map disappear, and set it on Beezan's chest.

"Come on, Sky. Breakfast!" And she ran to the edge of the table and leaped into his arms.

"Good Zharvee!"

Beezan went to the Command Bay while the others were still in the prayer room or securing the ship. Iricana had reminded him that the *Midnight* AI was not an unleashed entity like the *Drumheller* or a novice like the *81*, but a modern, highly interactive, supposedly sophisticated intelligence, with minimal interface. *How savvy is it really? And how cooperative?*

"Greetings *Midnight*."

"Welcome, Honor Beezan."

"*Midnight*, how old are you?

"I am 57."

"Who are your living exemplars?"

"Captain Iricana, Honor Kelson, Honor Thunder, Honor Beezan, Honor Ra'Tama, Doctor Katie, and Captain Bozenka, provided that she is still living."

"We will be taking a very long, unusual jump."

"Understood."

"Our destination is not on the regular sector map."

"Understood."

"You will not intervene unless all command crew lights are yellow or red."

"Understood."

"*Midnight*, we're going to find Captain Bozenka."

There was a long pause. "Understood."

Beezan breathed a sigh of relief when Sky went into the podpup box without a fuss. He started getting his brackets on as the other pilots came in. Ra'Tama set Cookie right next to Sky and they pressed together, humming softly.

A familiar hand came down on Beezan's right arm and squeezed as Jarvie slid into his seat on Beezan's right. Then a strong, but gentle grip on his left shoulder. He looked up to see Ra'Tama smiling at him. As Ra'Tama sat to his left, Beezan caught Sequoia's eye on the far left as she nodded with solidarity.

Beezan had a surge of confidence. This wasn't just him. All of Firelight was praying, and all the ships, and there were four unified pilots. Terina was sitting behind Sequoia, then Falcon, then the captain right behind him and Kelson behind Jarvie. His people surrounded and supported him. His heart filled with affection for all of them.

Falcon held up her hand "We're number four for jump. Relay ships have come in saying that Chike are leaving all systems."

"Let's hope they're not all on their way to the colony," Jarvie whispered.

"Passenger monitor to Captain, P&P is 45 and 9. Ready for jump."

"Thank you, Doctor."

"Settle in," Iricana said, "we're doing this the old-fashioned way."

Ra'Tama did the roll call and they started into the rings, following *Venus Vagabond*, *Hummingbird*, and *Waxing Moon*, all bound for Cove. The other ships were making various decoy jumps, just in case there were undetected Chike in the system. The colony was far out of the sectors.

As they made their early a-ring laps, Beezan put everything out of his mind: the new ship, the fact that the sectors would soon be open, the possibility of capture at the colony, and the insane promise he had made to Sky.

Such a man will, with his inner eye, readily recognize how altogether vain and fleeting are the things of this world, and will set his affections on things above.[1]

Beezan barely listened to the crew.

Sequoia: "Beacon off. Lights off."

Falcon: "Incoming Human ship from Sector 4!"

Iricana: "Stay on."

Ra'Tama: "To you, Honor Beezan."

Beezan opened his inner eyes to the pathways. He had the coordinates, the direction, but the ways were still jumbled, the distances immeasurable in Human terms. Thankfully, the fireball would be left behind. He put his trust in God, in prayer, and cast his hope upon the heavens.

A very strong pathway appeared in the right direction, and with a small correction and a burst of thrust, they were in. He felt the thrill of the other pilots with him, and a relief from all the correction thrusts in the a-rings. All the pilots focused on keeping them in the path, and after an especially long and hazy interval, Sequoia tipped them out at the first sign of mass. Still, they were rocketing into the system at high speed. *Tired. So tired.* Beezan closed his eyes for just a minute.

Jarvie wrenched his brain out of jumpspace. *Check for the beacon. No. Falcon is monitor.* He scanned the chair lights instead. All green in the Command Bay.

"Beacons," Falcon reported. "Dozens of Chike beacons. Locations up on screen."

"Those are buoys, except the four by the planet. Those are ship beacons," Thunder said.

"Human beacon!" Falcon said. "It's the *Drumheller* beacon!"

For a second Jarvie was confused, then remembered the *81*

was still running with the *Drumheller* beacon. They pulled their helmets off trying to focus on the screen better.

"*81-Petals* is in orbit around the fourth planet at .7AU. It's in the habitable zone," Ra'Tama reported.

"That's got to be the Colony!" Kelson said.

"Also, there are a-rings here," Sequoia added.

"Captain, 45 and 9, alive and well," Katie reported.

"Good jump," Iricana said, smiling at Beezan and nodding at them all.

"*Midnight*," Iricana ordered, "Take us around to the back of the moon of the fourth planet, with minimal burns and keeping our distance from all buoys."

"Understood. Stand by for burns."

As soon as they spun up, Mika was in the Command Bay arguing with Iricana. "Captain, please. Hear me out. We could send our shuttles to get people off the *81* before they take them down to the planet."

"Mika, I understand your desire to rescue the *81* crew, but that is not our mission. We must not give ourselves away."

"It's too late," Ra'Tama said quietly. "We can't see *81* from here, but the short scan we got showed that the fields are not running."

"Maybe they just turned them off!" Mika insisted.

Iricana shook her head sadly. "I'm sorry Mika."

Maura pulled her away. "They're already downside. And we agreed. Follow orders." Mika hung her head.

"Captain," Falcon looked up, even more excited than usual. "We have packets from Sector 4! We just had time to receive one condensed packet with the top 1000 official messages. Some are from Earth!"

12 / THE CONFIRMATION

Dragon's Den

Almost home, Melawn thought, and then reprimanded himself. *I must be exhausted if I'm thinking of Dragon's Den as home. As if I have a home.* But he was relieved to be back.

When their hurried rescue mission had first encountered the expedition party, with people pulling makeshift sleds, Melawn had feared the worst. But the sleds were loaded with patients, not bodies. To everyone's great joy, the rescuers and food had reached them in time.

And now their struggling party made the last turn into the canyons. Melawn was beginning to understand Ramian social structure, and knew that Danulell had shown uncommon boldness and conviction during the rescue. Melawn urged Danulell to the front of the party as they neared the Dragon's Den. He deserved to be walking shoulder to shoulder with Getti Mezt and Ellant.

Meanwhile, Melawn and Tep took up the rear, making sure no one was left behind. At the entrance to the canyons, they sent as many beasts as possible, and a few of the herders who had braved the trip, back to the herder camp.

Tenshi walked beside the sickest person, a Ramian who had something like pneumonia. But Tenshi was determined that this person would live, and that meant that everyone off the second ship had survived.

After the beasts and herders had turned off, Melawn scrambled up one of the rock pillars and surveyed their caravan, winding up the canyon. He was tired, dirty, and worried about Thayne and his schemes, and he had a permanent headache from scanning the sky for birds, which never appeared. The Ramians and Humans walked mixed together, helping and befriending each other. Melawn spotted Zhenulor, the baby, looking back over the shoulder of zir mom. Some primitive parental instinct took over and he smiled and waved at the baby. The baby's colors blazed to a beautiful sunset orange. The whole group of Ramians, somehow sensing ziz flash of color, turned to look up at Melawn, and they all flashed the same color. Melawn had a surge of joy and waved at them all with both hands. Then he laughed at himself and scrambled back down, embarrassed, but deeply satisfied. And then they started to sing.

The Ramians were in the other caves, getting settled, and Thayne had gone to greet his contacts. Melawn found himself back in Thayne's cave drinking a cup of tea. At least this time, he'd had a bucket bath and a change of clothes.

A small blackboard was propped against the cave wall. It was a metal ship panel coated with black grit. A clumsy piece of chalk sat next to it. Thayne's three-part *Plan B* was written on the blackboard: *1) Open a joint Human / Ramian engineering school, 2) Build a telescope, transmitter, and receiver, 3) Get off the planet.*

Melawn was too tired to even get worked up about it. He'd heard that Nkiroo was around, but was too tired to look for him. He'd show up here eventually. Melawn curled up on the cave floor and slept.

11-Dominion

In the morning, Melawn took his gear and tried to look nonchalant as he searched for another place to sleep. He was fed up with all the talk, the scheming, the arguing and outright power struggle that tried to pass for consultation in Thayne's cave. Cypress saw him and motioned for him to follow. Cypress brought Melawn to his own cave.

At first, Melawn thought he was going to offer him a place to stay, but Cypress held his finger to his lips. They set down their stuff and continued further into a narrow passage of the cave. Melawn didn't like it and stopped, but Cypress gently took his arm and urged him along in the dark.

"Very quiet," Cypress whispered, and they moved a last few meters. Cypress got down on his hands and knees and then lay all the way down on the rock. There was a tiny crack of flickering light near the floor. *Voices!* Melawn got down and looked.

By the light of a few candles, the Ramian leaders and Nkiroo were hunched on the floor of an adjoining and slightly lower cave. The Ramians' colors were subdued. Getti Mezt was talking to Nkiroo in Alkulu. "Danulell is telling us this Dragon outpost is unauthorized."

Nkiroo nodded. "Yes, these Dragon Den people are rebels. They want to separate from the main Human colony."

"And this is not your way?" Getti Mezt asked, sounding truly puzzled.

"No. If AnnaLee actually declares separation, she'll be in mutiny. It's a crime. And a sin. As if someone overthrew your Getti."

They looked at each other. "That happens," Mezt said.

Danulell put his hand out to explain. "We have different societies. With us, it's not betrayal to have another person rise to the top. People will align one way or the other. A transition occurs."

"It must be chaos," Nkiroo said.

"It makes sense," Danulell said and everyone turned to him. "Your society is full of the bold. There's a strong tendency toward independence. So your core value is unity. You work in groups to counteract and focus the bold. Our society was timid. We came to value boldness, independent action."

"But doesn't that boldness have to be in the service of the common good?" Nkiroo asked.

"Yes," Mezt said. "And that's not what's happening here. Even we can tell that this AnnaLee is jikking for her own power. It makes no sense to have a colony of a hundred, when you could be in a colony of—"

"Sixteen thousand," Nkiroo said.

They all flashed amazement. "AnnaLee claims the main colony won't help us get off the planet. That only the Dragon's Den will cooperate," Mezt said.

"Humans have been here 500 years. This is home to them. Anything we do affects everyone," Nkiroo argued. "The council has to decide what is best for all."

Danulell continued. "This group here—they are in mutiny, like a betraying tan." That was something the Ramians understood, and they scowled. "Sixty crabs put us in our place.

Imagine what sixteen thousand Humans could do. We need to be on the same side with them."

"Humans?" scoffed one of the Ramians. "They're a muddling society of groupthink." Nkiroo frowned, but was seemingly forgotten.

"No," another answered. "I read Neah's reports. They're a powerful society with so many bold people they are tasked to work together to avoid chaos. Ill-considered independent action is frowned upon, forbidden even."

"And what do they have to show for it? We have ships!"

"Our people are decimated. Theirs live!"

"We're a sailing people," Danulell interrupted, "but they have a saying we don't have." He glanced at Nkiroo. "A rising tide lifts all boats."

There was a long pause. Then Getti Mazt nodded. "Yes, we are in this together. We must convince this Human council. Tomorrow, I will go."

"Getti," Danulell suggested. "They put so much value in groups. What if we all go?"

There was a clap of hands, a flash of yellow, and the group quietly dispersed. Cypress and Melawn hurried back to pick up his gear. "I'm going with them, tomorrow," Melawn told Cypress.

"I'm coming too, then."

"I'll find Tenshi and let her know. Thanks Cypress."

But as Melawn wandered around the caves, a panicked Nkiroo found him. "Melawn!" Nkiroo turned Melawn around and looked at the gear he was carrying. "Do you have my bag?"

"No. Why?"

"O my God. I have to find it!" Nkiroo leaned close to Melawn and whispered. "My power tool! Someone's taken it!"

"Oh, no." No wonder he was so panicked. "Searching won't help. We need Thayne to find out who took it and get it back."

In Thayne's cave, Thayne, DeeZann, and Danulell listened with growing concern. "What kind of tool?" DeeZann asked.

"It's a combination metal cutter and welder. If I don't have it, they'll throw me off the salvage team. Maybe worse."

"What use is it to anyone here?" Melawn asked. "They don't know where the ships are dropped."

"Yes, they do," DeeZann answered. "The birds always circle when the teams are out there—waiting for an accident."

"Yes," Nkiroo agreed. "We have to watch out for them."

"So the scouts note their location and know you're gone after the birds leave."

Nkiroo covered his face with his hands. "I have to get it back."

"Come on. Let's go look while Thayne does his thing." And Melawn dragged Nkiroo out.

Had it only been minutes ago that Melawn had left Thayne's den? And here he was, as usual, back again. But there was no help for Nkiroo, as Thayne was obviously just recovering from a minor mindstorm. He was sitting at his table with DeeZann hovering over him. Before Melawn could say anything, AnnaLee came in, pushed past him, and confronted Thayne.

"That Ramian Captain, Mess—"

"Getti Mezt," Thayne corrected wearily.

"Mezt! He's taking all the Ramians to Paradise tomorrow!"

Thayne's eyes came to full focus as he got out of his chair, "No! I need them. Don't give them a guide."

"Cypress has already agreed. You have to stop them," AnnaLee ordered Thayne, and then thought better of it and pointed to Melawn. "He should stop them."

"How could I?" Melawn whispered.

Exasperated, but cautious, she lowered her voice to a conspirational level. "Offer them whatever they want. Make their lives easy if they cooperate."

Melawn was incredulous. "You live in *caves*! You have *nothing* to offer. And they're not like that anyway."

"You could convince Danulell."

"Manipulate my friend?"

"Persuade."

"Actually, I was thinking I'd go back tomorrow too."

"You're such a—" AnnaLee cut off as Thayne grabbed his head. Another wave of mindstorming was taking over. DeeZann, his remaining faithful student, saved him from falling and helped him into his desk chair.

"Fine," Thayne whispered, "because I'm going too."

"No!" AnnaLee took a step toward Thayne. "You have to stay. We had an agreement!"

Thayne shook his head, still holding it in both hands. "Melawn is right. It isn't our destiny to live in caves."

"Your destiny?" AnnaLee scoffed.

"It is not MY destiny."

"How do you know?"

"I know! I've had visions! Confirmations! Signs!" Irrationally, or maybe because Thayne was sounding like the Chike, Melawn found himself taking AnnaLee's side. "How are the destruction of the *Cheetah*, capture by the Chike, and being stranded on a colony *confirmations*?"

Thayne got up and swooped around AnnaLee to reach Melawn—and DeeZann gasped. Melawn understood why.

Thayne is the bird in the back. He was the real danger, not Anna-Lee. The last veil dropped from Melawn's vision. The truth was hard, but now Thayne had come forward. Thayne came right up to Melawn and hissed, "I have seen the future! And my destiny is not here!"

"You can't know the future," Melawn said, unnerved to see Thayne like this.

"I can! Tomorrow!" Thayne's gaze swept up everyone in the room. "Tomorrow, we will all go to Paradise. And you will see! You will witness the confirmation!"

12-Dominion

They hiked along the canyon, already hot, since it had taken until mid-morning to get their crews on the way. Tenshi had finally given up and started out. Melawn, Thayne, Nkiroo, and DeeZann went with her, and Danulell caught up with them a half hour later. "AnnaLee is leading the Ramians, although Cypress is there too," Danulell reported. "And a couple of Anna-Lee's people are with her, the ones named Zonta and Halim."

If not for all the anger and fussing right behind them, and Nkiroo's agitation over his stolen power tool, it would have been fun. Melawn was with his people. He was starting to appreciate the "outdoors," the actual living on a planet. It changed every day, every hour. There was always something new to look at. The wind, when it was gentle, no longer made him reach for a breathing mask. And the sun, as long as he had his hat and sunglasses, shed some great natural power over them. Thayne was keeping up well enough, but that wouldn't last. Eventually, the others would catch up and ruin what little peace they had.

The sound didn't even register at first, not with the spacers.

But DeeZann suddenly stopped in alarm. "What's that noise?" And then it slammed home to Melawn—a sound they hadn't heard for ages, not since the Earth days. A shuttle was landing.

Then a rectangular shadow passed over them and DeeZann screamed. "Too close!" Tenshi shouted, grabbed DeeZann's arm, and sprinted toward the rock pillars. Melawn grabbed Thayne's arm and took off after her, leaving Nkiroo and Danulell to follow.

They huddled behind a wider rock pillar and covered their faces with their shirts as the dust blasted past. Before the noise had completely died down, Thayne circled the pillar to look. Melawn went to follow, but a terrified DeeZann held him back. "It's okay! It's Human!" he reassured her and they all peered through the settling dust.

As the side hatch opened and steps folded out, Nkiroo ran to it, spreading his arms wide in welcome. "The shuttle *Lotus*," he shouted in glee. "A 40-passenger hybrid!"

They gathered around in shock, gawking, until a man ducked out and gasped. "I'm so sorry! We didn't expect you down here. Is everyone okay?"

"YES!" They shouted, surging forward. The man started to talk, but was drowned in a barrage of questions.

"Please, friends!" He held his hands out. "My name is Taj. I'm on a strict timeline to get in and out of here before Chike detection." The back hatch started to open. "We have supplies to offload. Then we can take a limited number of people with us." Thayne stepped forward, but Taj held his hands out again. "Friends, it's a one-way trip. And we're not likely to be back for years—or ever."

One way. Melawn's mind reeled. *Rescue, not rescue, escape, no return, Chike not gone.* Thayne stepped forward again, but Taj blocked the door. "Friends, I need the supplies offloaded."

Melawn ran to the back of the shuttle. It was filled with metal cases, some large ones. A purple-banded girl helped hand over small cases. He and Nkiroo passed them off to the others, and grabbed a large case together, putting to good use the muscles they'd earned planetside. They took the cases back behind the pillar.

As they unloaded in a frenzy, the Ramians and AnnaLee arrived at a full run. They must have seen or heard the shuttle. They actually cheered. Taj was repeating, just short of shouting, that they couldn't take everyone.

Some of the Ramians helped unload as the standoff at the hatch escalated. "You're taking me!" AnnaLee ordered Taj.

"I am going," Thayne said calmly.

But Tenshi's cold clear logic cut through the ruckus. "The Ramians are stranded here. Can you take them back to their colony on the other continent in your window of time? Do you know where it is?"

Taj turned to confer with the pilot and navigator, still not moving from the hatch. "I am going!" Thayne said, this time to Tenshi.

"They have no other way to get back to their people!"

"How many Ramians?" Taj asked.

"Thirty-one, and a baby," Danulell answered.

Taj closed his eyes for a moment. Then opened them and answered decisively. "No, we can't take them to their colony. But we can take them back to the ship and hope to return them to Ramian Space."

"No!" AnnaLee objected. "Humans should have priority!"

"There's no time for discussion!" Taj pointed to Zhenumae and the baby and husband, and started counting. They scrambled onboard.

Thayne and AnnaLee barely moved, forcing the Ramians

to push past them to board. Danulell got the parents to carry the children aboard and Taj counted those pairs as one.

Meanwhile, the unloading was finished. Melawn could have jumped in the back, before he shut the hatch, but he wasn't that kind of person. And in the back of his mind, he remembered he'd promised Jadee that he'd bring his daughter home. Surely Jadee wouldn't mind if DeeZann came back without him. Brushing dirt out of the hatchway, he signaled them to close it and went back around to the line, the swirling panic still going on in his mind.

"Five more," Taj announced when they were done boarding the Ramians.

"I'm next," AnnaLee said. Taj gave her a hard look. "I'm AnnaLee, Captain of the *Dragonfly Dream* and I outrank you!"

Taj didn't flinch. "I'm looking for people with full knowledge of the colony," he answered.

"My people and I have been here fifteen years!"

Taj nodded and signaled AnnaLee, Halim, and Zonta aboard and counted off three more. Tenshi stepped back. "My place is here," she whispered to Melawn and Nkiroo. "I'll take DeeZann home."

"Two more!"

"Three!" Thayne tried to negotiate.

"We're already over!"

Both Melawn and Nkiroo went to push Thayne forward, but there was no need. He sprung up the stairs without looking back. And then a sinking feeling came over Melawn. It was him or Nkiroo, his dearest friend in the sectors. The panic in his mind cleared. "Go!" he said, before Nkiroo could make the same offer. Nkiroo shook his head. "There's nothing for you here!" Melawn insisted.

Nkiroo's eyes filled with tears. "Let's go!" Taj ordered and turned away.

"Go Nkiroo!" Both he and Tenshi shouted. And instead of a hug, Melawn gave Nkiroo a shove. He vaulted up the already folding stairs.

"Clear the area!" Taj shouted as the hatch swung shut.

"Oh my God," Tenshi said, looking down the canyon. The others, everyone left in the caves, were running toward them. If they got too close the shuttle wouldn't be able to take off. But the engines were revving up.

Tenshi ran towards them, arms outstretched. "Cut them off!" Melawn, DeeZann, and Cypress, all that were left of the walkers, shouted and herded the oncoming spacers towards the rock. But they weren't fools. As soon as the shuttle started to lift, they all hit the dirt and covered their eyes.

As the main blast subsided, Melawn sat up, letting the sandy dirt cascade off him. He shielded his eyes and watched the shuttle head toward the ocean. It would fly over the valley. What a scene that would be.

It had been twenty minutes at most since they'd spotted the shuttle. And his whole life had left him. *Don't cry. Don't cry. Maybe they'll be back after all.* He struggled to stand, shaking the grit out of his hat and hair. Danulell, Nkiroo, and Thayne. His people, his closest friends, his brother, were gone from his life.

"What happened?" Ellant demanded.

Tenshi explained. AnnaLee's husband had picked up their young daughter and was standing right there listening. "They're coming back," Ellant said, in shock.

Tenshi looked sadly at the husband, "I'm so sorry. He said it was a one way trip."

Melawn expected the child to cry out for her mother, but her dark eyes just followed the path of the shuttle for a moment before she buried her head in her father's neck, hugging him fiercely. "Thank God you weren't with her," he breathed.

Tenshi pointed out the supplies to Ellant. "We're going on. I expect those supplies to be delivered to Paradise immediately." And she turned on her heel and stalked off.

With nowhere else to turn, Melawn followed her. DeeZann and Cypress tagged along in stunned silence.

Melawn couldn't help it. The tears ran down his face as they walked. Probably sand in his eyes. Cypress squeezed his shoulder and DeeZann moved close to his side. And then Melawn stopped in his tracks.

"What?" DeeZann asked.

"He was right." They looked at Melawn blankly. "Thayne. He said he'd have his confirmation today. And he did."

Tenshi tossed her head and resumed her march. "He better use that mindstorming brain of his to save the sectors!"

"That *is* his destiny," Melawn said softly.

Lotus, leaving the colony planet's orbit

Terina barely got her cameras reset after scrambling into the empty aft cargo hold with Roza to make room for the colonists. They hastily strapped into two emergency restraints as the shuttle lifted off and skimmed over the tall rocks.

Although Terina had heard a lot about the Ramians from Jarvie, to see them clamor aboard the shuttle and sit down like tired dock workers was mind-bending. The air filled with the strange hot smell of desert dust and the filter fans went to high gear. Terina panned one camera across the shuttle and watched the feed on her pad. Everyone had a seat or restraint except Taj, who braced himself behind Ra'Tama and Gadi in the pilot and monitor chairs.

Everyone was stunned at the turn of events. The Ramians' colors were a mix of red, or gray with orange streaks. The observation screens went on just as they entered the valley. "A Temple!" Roza gasped. They passed quickly and then followed a river past villages and farms. There were carts and animals.

Some people jumped up and down and waved; others stood in shock.

"There are five main villages," the bossy woman was explaining.

"Look at the tsunami damage," her assistant said. "This far from the coast."

Suddenly, the man who was last to board actually grabbed Taj's arm. "Turn around! We can't go near the coast. The crab people will see us and tell the Chike!"

There was a panicked chorus of agreement from the others. Taj turned to the pilot. "Ra'Tama!" And they banked so hard to port that Taj ended up on the deck against the wall.

"Sorry, Taj!"

"What's your name," Taj asked, not bothering to get up.

"Sorry, Honor. I'm Nkiroo. The crab people are a sentient species—part of the GenTwo if that means anything to you." Taj nodded grimly. "It's their planet. We can't go in the oceans. But if they see us, they could tell the Chike you were here."

"And that would ruin everything. Thank you. Do you know if they have telescopes?"

"No idea," a small angry man answered. "But I think it's safe to say they have no particular reason to be looking."

Taj waited until they'd battled some turbulence and gained altitude. "Okay, Ra'Tama, turn back when you're ready and get us back on schedule."

"Yes, Taj."

Only after they had banked again, thousands of meters higher, did Taj get up, going back to his brace position facing the passengers. "Friends, can everyone understand me?" Shockingly, most of the Ramians nodded yes, as well as sending a flash of yellow that Taj seemed to grasp immediately.

"We'll translate for those who can't," the Ramian leader answered.

"Thank you. Friends, you're aboard the shuttle *Lotus*, parentship *Midnight*, currently on a mission to confirm the location of a suspected Human colony."

"Mission accomplished," the haughty Human woman said dryly.

"But we need to get that information back to Firelight Council, and we only have a short time to get to the *Midnight*. For some reason, the Chike have abandoned all sectors, but we fear they'll be back any minute." There were frowns all around. "We will share the information with the Ramians, of course, but it may not be possible for anyone to come back for a long time. The Chike are chasing Humans back to the inner sectors."

"Same for us," the Ramian said.

"Ramian friends," Taj hesitated, "could I get your names?"

Terina quickly linked up the camera from the front of the shuttle to get their faces as Taj pointed. "I am Getti Mezt, equivalent to a ship captain." The Getti introduced the rest of the Ramians, indicating family groups. "Most of us are survivors of two previous shipwrecks."

Is that good or bad luck? Terina wondered. They broke orbit and the screens flickered to a black sky and stars. Some of the people started to cry. Taj let them look awhile, setting one screen to show the receding planet. After a few minutes, Taj asked the Humans to introduce themselves.

The haughty one announced, "I am AnnaLee, Captain of the *Dragonfly Dream*." There was a beat of silence. *Wow!* Terina zoomed in. She did look slightly familiar. "These are my aides Halim and Zonta." Terina could see that the determined-looking man had been about to introduce himself, but AnnaLee had taken over, copying the Getti. "And Thayne and Nkiroo, scientists," she said, waving her hand as if they were of little account.

Thayne! She'd heard that name many times on the *Drumheller. Incredible!* Through some stroke of luck, bad or good, they'd picked up key historic people. She would have signaled ahead, but they had to maintain stealth mode.

"Seventeen minutes off our timeline," Ra'Tama announced. Taj nodded.

"Captain Taj," AnnaLee asked. "Who is currently in command of the *Midnight*?"

"Captain Iricana."

Nkiroo clapped his hands together in joy, and then gave Thayne a one-armed side hug. Thayne's face had gone pale, but he smiled. "How interesting."

Another ship came into view on the screens and there was a universal gasp. "The *81-Petals*!" AnnaLee said.

"Yes," Taj answered. "It's empty. It was taken by the Chike."

"It's been in orbit all this time?"

"No. It was caught by a rogue planet in a jump. Someone found it and brought it back to the sectors, but then it was captured again, just recently. We assume the original crew has been here for 15 years." AnnaLee nodded. "The new crew was probably taken down only a couple of days ago."

"Pilot!" AnnaLee ordered Ra'Tama, "Rendezvous with that ship. We're going aboard." Taj blinked in astonishment. Ra'Tama didn't even turn to look at her.

Taj took a second to recover, but then said calmly, "I'm sorry. That's not our mission. And it may not be habitable."

"Stop wasting time!" She sat up and pointed in his face. "I'm the fleet commander and that is my ship! You WILL drop me and my crew off there!" One glance at her crew and Terina knew they were not onboard with that.

"Um, no," Taj said, like he doubted her sanity.

"That's an order!"

"I'm following my orders. You can take it up with the captain."

Finally, Halim put a hand on her shoulder and whispered something. With a deadly look at Taj, AnnaLee subsided, and all the other colonists sat back with relief.

Jarvie, in his space suit, helmet tethered at his side, clutched a holdbar and gazed out the observation window into the small and empty Hangar 3. He was blocking the view of Thunder and Falcon staffing the hangar controls at the panel behind him. But it was just for a minute. *Lotus* only had one side door, so he would have to pull around to the side tubeway.

If all went as planned, the *Lotus*, escorted by the Kays operating the shimmer shield in their personal scooters, would arrive any time. They would be hard to detect until the shimmer shield angle changed to make them visible to the *Midnight*.

A few more people trickled in for the big moment, including the captain and Beezan. Katie came in with a med kit, even though Roza was aboard the shuttle. Jarvie noticed Beezan absentmindedly nodding in approval. "Sequoia," Iricana called over the s'link, "Who's with you in the Command Bay?"

"Mika, Captain. Cooper has podpup duty."

Mika? Sequoia must be keeping an eye on her. Probably the best person for the job.

"Ay! Jarvie, why ya suited up?" Jarvie released the holdbar in surprise at the sudden voice behind him, and Teeve laughed as he put out an arm to let Jarvie grab on and haul himself back.

Jarvie laughed, partly embarrassed at losing his grip, and

partly amused that Teeve was using his Tektite talk on him. "I'm on tube duty. As usual."

"Na, you're a pilot now. No schlep. I got it."

"But you're not suited up."

"For this fancy tube? Press a button and done."

Jarvie tried to hide a frown. Teeve and company were so used to stuff falling apart on Tektite, they were super careful there. But they seemed to think everywhere else was safe. "Well, I'll come with you."

"Great!"

Jarvie cast a glance back at Beezan as he and Teeve pulled around through the safety hatch to the starboard tubeway. Beezan gave a tight-lipped scowl, like he would have sent Teeve for a suit if he were captain. But Iricana was busy and didn't say anything.

"Got a glimmer," Falcon announced. At the tubeway lock, Teeve flipped on a screen so he and Jarvie could watch. "Here they are," Falcon confirmed.

"Thank heavens," Katie murmured as she joined them. They were not far from the control panels, so they could all see each other through the safety hatch. As the *Lotus* slowly nosed into the hangar, the Kays eased to a stop outside, collapsing the shimmer shield and waiting for the nanos to process themselves back into their containers.

"Cancel stealth mode for *Lotus*," Iricana said to Falcon.

"Canceled."

Momentarily, they heard Taj's voice. "*Midnight, Lotus*, we're down and anchored. Ready for the tubeway."

"Welcome back, *Lotus*," Falcon said.

"Captain, are you on?" Taj asked.

"Yes, Taj. Go ahead."

"Captain, prepare to receive 32 Ramians—" Luckily Taj

paused as every person gasped. "Including one baby. Plus five humans, all in good health. Five crew are fine. But Captain," his voice took on a concerned note. "We may have been seen. Apparently, there's a species of crab people who live along the coast. It's unknown if they could see the shuttle in flight."

"Acknowledged," Iricana said. "Let's hope no one is looking for us to start with. Proceed with the tubeway."

Jarvie stood by while Teeve locked the tubeway target onto the *Lotus* hatch and flamboyantly pressed the extend button. They could feel a rhythmic flapping as the folds of the tube extended toward the *Lotus* hatch. With a double airlock on each side, it was very unlikely that anyone would need a spacesuit today.

For all his airiness, Teeve kept a close eye on the controls. After the tubeway latched on though, Teeve frowned. There was a red light flashing on the panel. Teeve ran through the diagnostic. "Problem's on our side," he reported over the s'link. "1% leak on the vacuum door."

Jarvie reached down for his helmet, but before he could even grab it, Taj announced he was coming through. At their hatch, Taj pushed on the seal until the 1% leak alert was cleared. Teeve nodded with approval. *Outer sector people*, Jarvie sighed to himself.

Terina was watching through the forward camera, so she saw Taj pull out his pressure breather and duck through the hatch, saying over his shoulder for Ra'Tama and Gadi to shut down and secure.

"Yes, Taj," they both answered.

"Roza," Ra'Tama said, "Escort the baby and parents through first."

From her spot in the rear cargo area, Terina could see Anna-Lee, the bossy one, who'd been whispering with her aides the whole trip, suddenly became very helpful. She told Roza to go ahead and they would secure the med bay and back of the shuttle. Halim, the man, started on the med bay, and he seemed to know what he was doing.

AnnaLee helped the other Ramians out and kept them in a steady line, feeding toward the front. Terina realized she'd miss the big entrance, so she synced the forward camera on Roza, while unstrapping and folding up her restraint. Everything was being recorded, but she just wanted to watch.

Feeling a tiny bit guilty, Terina ducked down behind the half barrier of the cargo hold, where no one could see her, and watched her pad as the first Ramians came through the hatch.

Taj was in the tubeway just before the *Midnight* lock, helping people through. All hatch doors were open, so it was mostly a matter of maneuvering in nogee. She could see Jarvie and Teeve on the other side as Roza came through. Then the mother. As she passed Jarvie, he gave her a puzzled expression, but looking down at her baby, she didn't notice.

"This way please," Roza said, steering her along. The mother's husband followed. Iricana was now greeting them and trying to move them past the safety lock into the Entry Lounge. Terina congratulated herself for leaving two cameras in there that she could sync up now.

Back at the tubeway hatch, the one named Danulell had just come through. "Jarvie!" he exclaimed. It was suddenly chaos. Danulell had gone to hug Jarvie, suit and all, but Jarvie seemed perplexed, holding him back to look at him. The two of them bounced around in nogee as Teeve tried to steady them. "It's me! Danulell!" His colors blazed bright blue with a line of pink.

Jarvie shook his head. "How can that be?"

"And my sister!" Danulell pointed to the Ramian with the baby who had turned around in amazement. "My parents!" The next people stopped to stare. They reached out, putting their hands on Jarvie's arms, smiling along with their colors. Danulell's mom even patted Jarvie's hair. Danulell seemed like he was about to cry. "You look exactly the same!"

Jarvie looked from one to the other in confusion. "Danulell, he is the same," the father said gently. "Jarvie, we're older. We were caught in a pocket for nine years. It's so good to see you."

Oh, my God, the drama, Terina thought, hoping she had another couple minutes. She could hear people still in the cabin. Jarvie was in tears now. "Quay?" he asked.

"He's your age," the mom said, momentarily flashing gray, "but he's been taken by the Chike."

"He's down on the planet?"

"No, no," she said. "He's a harbinger."

Harbinger! Terina made sure all her cameras were going as Teeve started to politely move people on. "Ah, let's go, crew."

"Yes, forgive us," and they pulled along, with some help, Danulell looking back. Terina was riveted to the screen. It was stunning news. There were Ramians at the same colony and Jarvie knew them and someone was a harbinger, one of the people the Chike were searching for. *Incredible!*

After the Ramians, Thayne and Nkiroo went through. "It's so good to be in nogee," Nkiroo said. "I never thought I'd feel it again." He touched each person on the shoulder as he passed, either some kind of greeting or a quirk. Most people didn't notice, but Jarvie smiled at him.

"Thayne! Nkiroo!" Katie cried out and looked behind them.

"Katie!" Nkiroo embraced her quickly,

"Lanezi?" They both asked at the same time. "He's not with you?" Katie asked, choking up.

"No, but he escaped Friendship in the *Enkindler*. Haven't you heard from him?"

"No," she said, holding back tears.

"Okay people, yeah please," Teeve appealed, "let's keep movin'."

Terina considered sending another camera through, so much was happening in the tubeway, but just as she looked up to see who she could sync to, there was AnnaLee—right in front of her. A half panicked and half scary look passed AnnaLee's face. Suddenly AnnaLee and her two aides hurled themselves into the cargo hold on top of Terina, pressing her down to the floor.

Maybe all those years of reading Earth history allowed Terina to jump to a conclusion of violence and betrayal. So she instantly knew what was happening. They meant to take the shuttle back to the *81-Petals*. And by the look in AnnaLee's eyes, no 13-year-old kid was going to stop them.

Despite the fact that they had not been in nogee for years, they were good. The two underlings braced against the wall and pressed AnnaLee and Terina down. Ra'Tama and Gadi wouldn't be able to hear a few bumps over all the shutdown noise. Terina tried to shout "Ra—" but AnnaLee grabbed her head, turned it sideways so hard her neck cracked alarmingly, and covered her mouth. She was so strong.

Never in Terina's life had anyone tried to hurt her, or even push her around, although she knew these things still occasionally happened. She was frozen in terror. What would they do? How could they take over the shuttle anyway?

"What was that?" Ra'Tama asked. "Gadi, does Terina need help back there?"

"I'll check."

Yes! No!

"Wait!" AnnaLee hissed at Halim. Terina thought it would be the perfect time to struggle, to break free, save the day, but she was paralyzed with fear. "Now!" AnnaLee whispered.

Halim shoved off of them as he tilted up and reached over the barrier. There was a sharp twang. *Oh my God, a trank dart!*

Terina could hear Ra'Tama report, "We have an attacker aboard!" and then the trank dart went off again.

"Got him!" Halim said.

"Get the hatch shut!" AnnaLee ordered.

AnnaLee let Terina go, but her neck hurt and she was dizzy. Nogee didn't help. Zonta peeled out of the hold, pushing off the top of the barrier. AnnaLee pulled Terina up so they could both see, although Terina's vision was blurry and her stomach reeled. Gadi floated peacefully above the seats, out cold. Astonishingly, Ra'Tama was still conscious. He'd unstrapped and was slowly pivoting out of his seat. Halim darted him again and launched for the hatch, slamming it shut.

"Jettison the tube!" AnnaLee ordered.

"No! Someone's in—" Terina shouted, but it was too late. Zonta braced herself and shoved Ra'Tama toward the back and took the pilot's seat.

"Shutdown was incomplete. I have control. Releasing anchors," Zonta reported.

"Strap them in!" AnnaLee ordered Halim, shoving Terina into a seat. "Strap!"

But Terina was gripping her pad in one hand and shaking too hard. AnnaLee snatched the pad and secured it in the seat pocket in front of Terina, not even bothering to turn it off. She pulled Terina's arms through the straps and secured her tightly.

"Stay there!" But she must have thought better of it as she grabbed some medical glue.

"No!" Terina cried, but the evil woman glued her hands together in front of her. Did living on the colony turn them into barbarians?

Looking down the tubeway, Jarvie wondered why no one else was coming. "Did I lose count?"

"No," Teeve said. "There should be more humans." Taj started back down the tube when they heard a shouted warning, both through the tube and over the links. Taj pushed hard for the *Lotus* hatch, but it was too late. Jarvie grabbed his helmet for real this time just as the Lotus hatch slammed shut and someone in the *Lotus* ejected the tubeway.

"Vacuum!" Teeve shouted, popping his breather on in a heartbeat. Jarvie knew they had three seconds before the safety hatch to the Entry Lounge closed. He and Teeve would never make it. He heard Iricana shout for the others; she might be able to hold it open. But it didn't matter. Taj was caught in the partly collapsed accordion of the tubeway, now exposed to vacuum. His breather wasn't on, but at least it hadn't blown out of the tube, it was wrapped around his arm. Still conscious for the moment, Taj was trying desperately to get the breather.

Jarvie dived into the tube. Teeve was right behind him. The blast of the shuttle taking off knocked them all back and buffeted the tube, collapsing it part-way toward them. In the suit, Jarvie was slower than Teeve, but Teeve couldn't pass him, so he pushed through as fast as he could, the folds of the tubeway moving back as he pulled on them.

Finally, he reached Taj's legs. Jarvie tried to brace himself against the folds and push Taj past him towards Teeve, but the folds kept moving. *How many seconds has it been?* He was starting to panic. *Focus!* He finally got the breather and pushed it onto Taj's face. He was now unconscious. Jarvie couldn't secure the breather strap with his suit gloves, so he just held it on. Teeve had gone back and was hand-cranking the tubeway in. When Taj got close enough, Teeve grabbed Taj's legs, squeezed him past Jarvie, and pulled him into the lock. Jarvie made the "close" sign and Teeve pulled the hatch closed.

Thank God, thank God. Thank you. Jarvie just hung there and breathed. Slowly, he realized that there were voices on his s'link asking him what was happening.

"Um, sorry. *Lotus* ejected the tubeway. Taj was caught in the depressurization without a mask. Until maybe 15 seconds ago. He's in the hatch with Teeve."

"Alive?" came Falcon's clinical voice.

"I don't know," Jarvie answered with a sob. *Don't cry in the suit. Don't!*

14 / ABANDONED AGAIN

The *Lotus* was backing out of the hangar. Through the front window, Terina could see the tubeway swinging back and forth, the air still escaping. She hoped that Taj had made it inside. Suddenly, the *Lotus* rocked to the side. Gadi, the dazed Ra'Tama, and AnnaLee, all unstrapped, were thrown across the shuttle. "Hey!"

"Sorry, Captain!" Zonta said. "Two scooters were coming in behind us."

"Get clear! Turn and burn!"

"Yes, Captain." As soon as they cleared the door, Zonta swung them around. AnnaLee and Ra'Tama grabbed on, but poor Gadi smashed into the seats.

"Don't leave! Don't take us!" Terina sobbed.

"Quiet, kid! We're not going to hurt you." Although AnnaLee managed to sound mildly concerned, Terina wanted to scream at her that she'd already hurt them, and she was taking them from their people.

In a break between burns, AnnaLee secured Gadi in a seat.

But when she went to grab Ra'Tama, he pushed away from her. "How can you be conscious? Halim, trank him again!"

"No!" Zonta objected. "Please Captain, it could kill him."

"Fine. Secure him," she told Halim.

Halim zipped the trank gun in his pocket. "Look friend, for your own safety, strap in."

Ra'Tama's eyes were slightly glazed, but he seemed coherent. He slowly pressed back to the row of seats where Terina was sitting and maneuvered into a chair two seats away. He frowned when Halim reached over and pressed him down. Instead of gluing Ra'Tama's hands in front, Halim crossed Ra'Tama's arms over his chest and glued them to opposite shoulders.

Terina considered that neither of them would be able to exit the shuttle in an emergency. Some small part of her mind that wasn't running around in hysterics made a mental note to rip her own hands apart and grab the surgical glue remover for Ra'Tama. When she performed her big rescue.

"I warn you," Ra'Tama said slowly, but sternly. "You are committing a grave crime, and my guards are authorized to use physical force."

Guards?

"Check that ego!" AnnaLee said derisively. "Glue his mouth shut if he talks again!"

Halim looked alarmed at that. Maybe he did have a soul. But Zonta announced 20 seconds to the next burn so he went to the front to strap.

Jarvie watched through the hatch window as the other door swung open and Teeve pushed Taj out, right into Katie's hands. She had stayed behind, her own breather on, when everyone else cleared through the safety door. Teeve helped brace Taj while Katie attached the rescue pump directly to Taj's mask. Teeve turned to shut the hatch again and gave Jarvie the *don't know* sign.

Jarvie was about to cycle through the lock himself when he realized that someone was still talking to him. Thunder. "Jarvie, report please."

"Umm. I'm okay."

"Jarvie, your suit is green. Copy?"

"Yes. I'm just rattled."

"Breathe. Ten big breaths while I tell you what's next."

"Yes, Honor." *You're a trained teen! Pull yourself together.*

"We need that tubeway when we bring back the *Lotus*. It now has three red lights. Are you in condition to fix it if I talk you through it?" He paused. "It's okay if you want to come in. I can send Cooper. He's cooped up with the pups."

Jarvie smiled at the terrible joke. Some of his panic lifted. Thunder was amazing. And he said *when they bring the shuttle back*. Good. "I'm okay. But please, tell me what to do."

Terina watched her pad, sideways, through the netting of the seat pocket. Katie and Teeve flew past Roza to the lift, hauling Taj. "Roza, stay here," Katie said. "I'll take Med Bay."

"Yes, doctor!"

Roza, the camera unnoticed behind her, pushed back to the Entry Lounge where everyone, even the Ramians, were now floating around the controls, holding onto each other like a wall of people, to stabilize and see the screen.

Iricana stood between Falcon and Thunder, with Thayne and Nkiroo slightly behind and above her. "*Midnight*! Control the *Lotus*!" She ordered.

"No link."

Iricana frowned. "Let's risk a message before we go stealth again—*Lotus*! Return to the *Midnight* immediately. That's an order!"

"Captain," Thayne said urgently. "It's AnnaLee, Captain of the *Dragonfly Dream*," he explained. "She wanted to take the *81-Petals*."

"She can't. The Chike will know that we were here and our mission will be compromised."

"No, they can't," Nkiroo agreed. "They can't take the *81* at all." Everyone shifted in their bracing to turn and look at the very shy and shaken Nkiroo. "I was on a salvage team," he told Iricana. "Honor, Captain, they, the Chike, remove the main engine and empty the fuel. They jettison the engine into the star. It's probably already gone."

"Why?"

"They land the ships, for us to salvage." Light dawned in everyone's eyes, and the Ramians colors ran to yellow.

"Captain," Thunder reported, "the Kays are running the shimmer shield again, trying to hide the shuttle from the Chike beacon. The *Lotus* was exposed for about three minutes."

"Captain! Sequoia here. What's going on?" Terina's eyes teared up at the sound of her mom's voice.

"Send the feed shipwide," Iricana told Falcon. "Standby Sequoia. The *Lotus* has been . . . stolen." *Hijacked! That's the word you want! And kidnapped! Hostages!* Old words people wouldn't even know now if they didn't watch ancient movies. "We need a count. Who's still aboard?"

Beezan, who was helping greet people, had a list. His quiet distressed voice was clear though. "Not yet reported: Ra'Tama, Magadi—and Terina."

"I'm coming down there!"

"No! Sequoia, please stay put," Iricana asked. "We may need you up there." Turning to Beezan she said, "So Captain AnnaLee and three of our people?"

"Plus two more of her people," Thayne said. "Halim and Zonta. They're *Dragonfly Dream* command crew. Either could fly a shuttle. Halim is a long jumper. Very loyal to her personally."

"I don't understand why she would do this," Iricana shook her head.

"To get the *81* . . . to get . . . what she wants . . ." Thayne was hunching in on himself and hugging his arms in. He seemed very shaken, even on the small screen. The camera, sensing emotive signs, zoomed in. Nkiroo put a hand on Thayne's shoulder as Thayne continued. "She . . . she thinks she is right. She will never come back willingly."

"The Kays?" Thunder asked. "I don't see them abandoning Ra'Tama."

"What can they do?" Iricana, asked. "What can anyone do without violence?"

Her question hung in the air with the rest of them, but over the com, Sequoia said, "That's my daughter in that shuttle! I already lost one child. I'm not losing another!"

Iricana held a hand up. "Sequoia, stay put. Thayne, can we rely on the other two to be reasonable?"

"I don't know. They've been with her through some trying times, times that would bond people," he whispered, and then he started to shake uncontrollably.

"Mindstorm," Nkiroo said.

"Roza! Nkiroo, get him to the Med Bay."

Iricana covered her face with her hands for a few moments while the rest of the people remained quiet, except Falcon, reading out distances and times. After a few breaths, Iricana dropped her hands to the panel. "Vante, Ling, come back. We're told the ship has no engine."

"Captain," Vante's voice came. "It's our duty to protect Ra'Tama."

"I understand. But we're not going to resort to violence. And there's nothing else you can do. Your scooters are running low. Please return."

There was a drawn-out pause, everyone in the room, concerned, waiting to see if they would obey. Finally Kay Ling's voice whispered over the com. "Yes, Honor. We are returning."

Terina thought about yelling out to AnnaLee that they couldn't go anywhere. That the engine was gone. But one look at the woman convinced Terina that there was no rationality left. Even her two people were starting to act nervous, taking quick glances at her when she wasn't looking.

"AnnaLee—I mean Captain," Zonta turned in the chair. "We need to get the *81* hangar door open."

Nonono Terina prayed. But then she realized that AnnaLee was desperate enough to harddock and that might be scarier. Nothing was going to stop this woman. AnnaLee sat at Gadi's panel. "I'm putting through my fleet commander code. Everyone thinks the *81* captain is a big deal. But I was fleet commander."

Terina remembered reading something about that. The *81-Petals* captain was one who was good with the public. And since the hangar door was opening, it must be true. "Captain, the scooters are slowing."

Ra'Tama closed his eyes looking more relieved than defeated.

. . .

Jarvie got the tube fixed quickly with Thunder's help and pulled back out, sealing the hatches. He'd heard most of what was happening in the background, but when he got to the hangar control, almost everyone was gone.

Teeve came back in, this time in a suit. "Learn if you live, ay?" He slapped Jarvie gently on the back.

"Suit out, Jarvie," Thunder told him. Teeve will bring the Kays in. Help with the Ramians if you can."

"Ramians, right." So many things were happening at once. Poor Terina, she must be terrified. And Ra'Tama, his friend, and Gadi. "Where's Gola?" he asked Teeve quietly.

"Runnin' prayers in Observation," Teeve answered grimly.

Terina lost the feed as soon as they entered the *81* hangar, and then she felt guilty when she realized that she'd broken the stealth mode. Not that she could have shut it off anyway with her hands glued.

They touched down and anchored. "I have computer access," AnnaLee announced triumphantly.

"*81-Petals*, this is Fleet Commander AnnaLee Indigo. Acknowledge."

Terina was about to hold her breath, but the AI answered immediately, almost sounding relieved. **"Acknowledged, Commander. I require assistance."**

AnnaLee blinked in surprise and looked at Halim. "What's wrong?" he asked simply.

"I have been hijacked and disabled."

"What do you mean disabled?" AnnaLee asked with alarm.

"The Chike have shut down the engine."

"Engine! Link us up, *81*," AnnaLee ordered.

Frantically, Zonta ran the diagnostics. "O my God! The main engine is gone!"

"Destroyed?"

A schematic appeared on the screen and they all stared in dismay. "The entire engine has been removed!" Zonta said. "Fuel rods are gone, the converter, everything!" Everywhere on the engine module was red. Ra'Tama and Terina looked at each other, not knowing if this was good news, or if it would make AnnaLee even more irrational.

"I am abandoned. Again. Please help me."

"We can't escape," Halim whispered to AnnaLee and Zonta. "We'll have to go back to the *Midnight*."

"Never," AnnaLee said.

"We can say we lost our minds from all the years on the planet. Apologize. They'll understand," he persisted.

"Never," she hissed.

"What choice do we have?" Zonta asked.

"Stay with me," the *81* said pitifully.

"Voice off, computer!" AnnaLee ordered.

Terina glanced at Ra'Tama again. His eyes were clear now, with no sign of the drug, even though Gadi was still out cold. He seemed angry, calm and calculating, all at the same time. But he didn't seem scared. Terina squirmed up straighter in her seat, even though it was nogee. She wiped her face with her glued hands and determined to be brave.

"There are a-rings," AnnaLee said, switching over to a map of beacon locations.

"Yes," Zonta said, "5.3 days by ship."

"We can't take the ship! How long by shuttle?" AnnaLee asked.

"Captain!" Halim protested. "There's not enough food in the emergency supplies."

"There is no food," Ra'Tama said calmly. "We left everything on the planet."

"Foolishness!" AnnaLee snapped at him.

"Captain," Zonta pleaded. "We can go back to the planet. They won't follow. Back to the Dragon's Den. Turn these three over to Paradise. No harm done."

No harm? Terina wanted to scream. No harm except kidnapping them from their people and stranding them on the planet. As bad as the Chike.

"I'm not going back to that planet!"

Halim got up and checked the water. "We can't survive a jump in the shuttle. Six to seven days in system and two weeks minimum where we arrive. We have 6 people aboard." He stuck his head in the water cabinet. "30 liters. That's it. 1 liter a day split by six people. It's not enough."

"Leave us," Ra'Tama suggested. "Leave us on the *81* and they'll only be three of you."

"Maybe there's food on the *81*!" AnnaLee said. "*81* voice on. Are there food supplies? 60 days for 6 people?"

"The freezers were just turned off two days ago. And two years of preserved food. If you stay here."

"You don't need us!" Ra'Tama insisted. "Leave us here. We'll only testify against you wherever you end up. At least leave Gadi and Terina."

"Maybe we should leave them," Zonta said quietly. "Captain, you only need Halim. I'll stay here and watch them until you're safely away—make sure the *Midnight* doesn't follow."

"Coward!" AnnaLee snarled. "Abandon me now, after all these years?"

Zonta was about to answer, but Ra'Tama overrode her. "As well they should both abandon you."

"I am a fleet commander! This is mutiny!"

"You are irrational and should be removed from duty!" Ra'Tama turned to Halim. "The crew can vote. Just the two of you can legally take over."

"Don't be ridiculous. They're my crew and have been for twenty years. What sort of egomaniac thinks he could turn them against me?"

AnnaLee turned back to Zonta and Halim with a stern look. "No, I think our best course is for the three of you to guarantee our safe escape. Go get the food!" she snapped at Halim and Zonta, "and leave that trank dart with me."

13-Dominion

Paradise Council Chamber

The stone floor of the council chamber was cold. The afternoon was chilly compared to the heat of the Dragon's Den, but there was a fire going against the damp air.

The day after the shuttle landing, Melawn sat in a wooden chair, same as Tenshi, facing the Paradise Council. He had cleaned up overnight and put on his best clothes, although the sand always lingered on this planet. The events of yesterday, part dream and part nightmare, percolated through his mind. That Humans had located the colony was huge, but that they couldn't come back, sobering. And he had lost his people. The anguish of losing Nkiroo rolled over him in waves and his attention to the meeting faded in and out.

Tenshi calmly answered questions about the boxes, the shuttle, the Humans, and who had gone in the shuttle. "You say that Thayne and the Ramians had some prior contact?" Grace asked.

"Yes, they were some of the same Ramians we shared the Chike ship with. They must have made plans. But now, anyone that knows the plan is gone." Melawn shook his head no when they glanced at him. Neither Thayne nor Nkiroo had shared any plans with him.

Just then, there was a disturbance at the door. The clerk opened it, hastily standing aside as Ellant marched in. Ellant was followed by a man bearing the flag of the Dragon's Den—in the council chamber! Melawn cringed. Behind him came the husband of AnnaLee, carrying the daughter. The people behind them formed up, three abreast, and continued to the front, filling the council chamber with rebels. Tenshi and Melawn scrambled to the side, dragging their chairs out of the way.

It looked like the entire Dragon's Den population crowded in. Ellant stopped a couple of paces from the table, eyes locked with the chairperson. Although Tenshi, Melawn, and the clerks were all standing, none of the council moved from their seats. Breathing and the crackling fire were the only sounds.

Slowly, Ellant turned and detached the flag from its pole. He folded it carefully and took a step toward the table as if he meant to hand it over. But then he stopped. No one breathed. Raising his chin, Ellant turned and walked to the fireplace, gracefully setting the flag amid the flames. He stood watching it burn as a breath of sadness and relief wafted over the council chamber.

Ellant returned to the front of the table. "We humbly request to be admitted to your service."

"Is this everyone?" the chair asked with concern.

"All who remained, save the Zann herders. They range as they please." It was a ragged group, dusty and ill-fed. Tenshi was craning her neck to survey the bunch, probably checking for anyone she didn't remember vaccinating.

Slowly, the chairperson scooted his chair back noisily over the stone. He stood formally, put his hands to his heart, and bowed. "Welcome back."

14-Dominion

Midnight, in the colony system

Beezan, clutching the ever-whining Sky, trudged up the stairs into a frantic scene in Ops. The *81* schematic was on the main screen. Iricana, Sequoia, Thunder, Falcon, and the Kays were standing around it, talking shimmer shield, cutting through the hull, disabling doors, reprogramming life support, and all kinds of desperate ideas. Gola was at a side screen running profiles of AnnaLee, Halim, and Zonta, as if knowing them better would solve the problem. Only Kelson sat calmly at the table, praying.

Beezan moved to sit by Kelson, but Iricana saw him, came around, and grabbed his arm gently. "No," she said.

"What?"

"Not you. You can't listen to all this. You need to sleep."

"*Sleep?*"

Guiding him back down the stairs to the rimway she said, "We may need you to jump without them."

With a new surge of panic on top of Sky's whining, he gasped, "We can't!"

"We have to jump right away. The *Cheetah* crew said there's a convocation, somewhere. Not here. The Chike are picking up these harbingers all over the galaxy, and bringing them to this big meeting."

"Why?"

"They make it sound like some kind of judgment day. The fate of different species will be decided."

As far-fetched as it sounded, Beezan felt in his gut that it was the truth. "Chilling."

"The meeting may be why the Chike have left all sectors," Iricana said. "And they could be back any day. We may not solve this AnnaLee problem in time."

"We can't just leave them! You know I can't jump if I know someone will die!"

"They won't die!"

The tromping of the Tektites and Nkiroo alerted Beezan that they were coming up the rimway. "Don't stay!" Nkiroo was telling the Tektites. "I've been there. There's nothing for you there!"

"Our people are there!" Maura said.

"This is our chance to be reunited," Cooper added.

"Have you ever been on a planet?" Nkiroo asked and then the group suddenly noticed the captain and Beezan. They stopped in the rimway, huddled up, and continued whisper-arguing.

"Stay?" Beezan asked. "You're letting *more* people stay?"

"It's just one option. Maybe they can get everyone off the *81* and down to the planet without being detected. Worst case— the Chike find them all and take them down."

"Worst case—they all die on the *81* because we abandoned them! Or the Chike wipe out the whole colony, or—"

"Beezan! We need to think of the big picture! We have to get this info to Firelight. And I need YOU to jump the *Midnight* back there."

"Wrong way!" Sky cried, and the burning started. He shook his head no.

Iricana grabbed him by both shoulders. "I know this is hard! But we have to do this for humanity! If you can't, I'll have to ask Jarvie!"

His heart was pounding out of his chest. His head was burning. "Sky!" Iricana snapped "*STOP IT!*"

Sky was instantly silent and shrunk away from Iricana, leaning into Beezan's chest. "Sky," he choked. *Oh my God, I'm going to have to do this. But I don't know how.*

"*Captain!*" came Thunder's voice from upstairs. They turned and ran back up, the Tektites on their heels.

"Honor, the *81-Petals* hangar doors are opening," Falcon explained.

"Kays, to the scooters! Sequoia, Falcon, Command Bay!" Iricana ordered. Beezan, Thunder, and Iricana all ran to the Command Bay with them.

"It's the *Lotus,*" Thunder confirmed. "If they go for the planet, we can't stop them."

Beezan tracked them from his panel. "They are burning away from the planet. *Midnight,* calculate course."

"A-ring intercept course."

"In a shuttle?" Iricana asked. "*Why do people keep thinking this is feasible?*"

"We could intercept them, Captain," Sequoia said. "It may be the only way to save them."

"We need to know who's on it," Iricana said. "Break stealth mode. Hail the *81.*"

Falcon nodded. "Go ahead, Captain."

"*81-Petals*! Who is aboard the shuttle?"

"Everyone. I am alone. Again. Please do not leave."

Sequoia was waiting for the intercept order, but Iricana paused. "*81*, perform the sealed backup and shut down. We will do our best for you."

"You are leaving me?"

"Yes, *81*. You have served bravely. Seal and shutdown. That's an order."

"Acknowledged."

"Contact broken," Falcon reported.

"At current speed—" *Midnight* was reporting, but no one heard the rest. They all gasped as a teeth-rattling slam hit them. Beezan grabbed his head in pain, a path showing itself clearly in his mind.

"No!" Sequoia said.

"They're gone," Falcon reported, unaffected by the resonance.

"That was Ra'Tama, jumping," Sequoia said, in sudden realization.

"Yes," Beezan agreed.

"Where?" Iricana turned to the map. Where would he—"

"Tektite," Beezan murmured.

"Is that the right way?" Sequoia asked.

"Yes," Iricana said.

"Tektite," Beezan said louder.

"His ship is there," Sequoia said, "remember, the *Kingfisher*?"

"Tektite!" Beezan insisted, the path clear in his mind.

Iricana looked at him this time. "Prepare to jump. Sequoia, you do it. You have to come in to Tektite *before* they get there."

"We'll beat them to it," she said grimly.

"Nooo," Sky keened and Beezan gasped in pain, his whole mind on fire.

Lotus, incoming to Tektite

It was a nightmare. Terina tried to scream, but she couldn't. She thought she couldn't breathe, but she didn't die. There was a pulsing, jerking motion as if she were a bug being shaken out of a sock. Finally, with a neck-breaking snap, they dumped into normal space.

Oh my God, we jumped. Mom! And something was seriously wrong with the jump. She wasn't sad, or depressed like a normal jump. She was *angry*. She looked down at her hands, glued together, and remembered everything. In a surge of rage, she used her knee to pull her hands apart, ripping the skin and separating them. *"Ahhhhh!"* Her scream didn't even wake anyone up. They were out cold. The pain brought a sense of rationality back. This was her chance to do the big rescue. But training kicked in first. She herded the floating drops of blood onto her pants, slipped out of the restraints, and opened the med cabinet. She sprayed her hands with sealer and put gloves on.

"Umm, *Lotus?*"

"Identify."

"I'm Terina of the *Midnight*. No one else is conscious."

"Understood."

"Where are we?"

"Tektite system."

Tektite! That's where they picked up Ra'Tama. "Umm, beacons?—Chike? Are there Chike beacons?"

"No Chike beacons. No sign of Chike ships. A-ring beacon detected. T.O.A. and T.I.A. beacons detected—"

"*Kingfisher?*"

"Yes, *Kingfisher* beacon detected."

"Take us there."

"Stand by for course correction." Terina slipped back into the nearest chair. There were several burns.

"*Kingfisher* ETA: 3 days, 4 hours, 2 minutes."

"Good." *I guess we didn't need the 60 days of food after all.*

Terina carefully floated to the front, waving her hand in front of AnnaLee several times, even though her eyes were closed, and then carefully touched her shoulder. When there was no reaction, she reached into AnnaLee's jacket and pulled out the trank dart. She opened the casing. Seven more doses! Was this some kind of riot dart? She turned and pointed it at AnnaLee. She had every justification for using it. She had no doubt it would be acceptable. But she didn't want to be like them. They were clearly backward-leaning barbarians. Quickly, she popped out the darts and put it back in AnnaLee's pocket.

She checked for pulses. They were all alive.

Terina wasn't going to be able to hide the fact that she was up, so she just went about taking care of things. She got the glue remover and undid Ra'Tama, and got the trank antidote and gave it to Gadi.

"What's happened?" Gadi asked, and was dazed and disbelieving when Terina told her.

"Have some water," Terina said, handing her some.

"Thank you."

Terina nodded. Gadi. Polite. A civilized human being. Terina helped her float over to the facilities. The door shut loudly and AnnaLee sat up suddenly. And grabbed her head in pain. She saw Terina up and about and quickly patted her pocket where the trank dart was.

"What did you do?" she snapped.

"*I* didn't do anything," Terina said, trying to sound calm. "We jumped—"

"Impossible, we weren't in the a-rings."

—to Tektite."

"Ridiculous."

"Look for yourself."

"Zonta, wake up!" AnnaLee shoved her in the shoulder. She hadn't even checked first to see if her people were alive.

Just then, Gadi wheeled out of the facilities and braced

against a seat, staring at AnnaLee. "Is she the one who shot me?"

"Spare me the drama!" AnnaLee said.

"She ordered it," Terina whispered.

"Get over here and be monitor," AnnaLee ordered Gadi. Then she unstrapped Zonta and heaved her towards the back. Terina and Gadi both gasped—and it took both of them to catch Zonta and maneuver her into a seat.

Then with great dignity, Gadi pulled into her seat and strapped. She updated her panel. "Tektite system," she confirmed.

Halim suddenly blinked awake in terror. "Oh my God!"

"What?" AnnaLee asked.

"The ways!"

"What about them?"

"The paths have changed—"

"Calm down! You haven't jumped in fifteen years."

"I didn't jump! How could I? We weren't in the a-rings. And something is seriously wrong with the ways."

"One of you jumped!" AnnaLee hissed, reaching for the trank.

"It was Ra'Tama," Terina said quickly. "It's a new thing."

"But something's wrong," Halim insisted.

"He's right," Ra'Tama whispered, slowly waking up. "The ways are erratic and pulsing . . . difficult . . . hard to stay in the path. We must get to Firelight before the paths . . . shut down completely."

AnnaLee squinted at them, suspicious. "Why Tektite?"

"Because I have a ship here," Ra'Tama said. "With food, and an engine."

Terina turned away so AnnaLee couldn't see her face. What

was Ra'Tama's plan? The *Kingfisher* engine couldn't be fixed. It wasn't going anywhere.

"You will turn your ship over to me," AnnaLee concluded.

"After we jump to a civilized place for us to get off . . . I will try." And for the first time, he sounded uncertain.

"Try?"

"The AI is somewhat possessive. If it believes I am under duress, it may be difficult."

"He'll have to do the talking," Halim said.

"Well, we can hardly stop him," AnnaLee said and Gadi scowled.

Terina was amazed at how quickly she had adjusted to the situation. She almost felt like making rude comments to Anna-Lee. *It's so easy to fall into savagery.* Although old media wasn't entirely banned, it was highly discouraged, and now she understood why. Like a disease, this lowering of human dignity seemed to spread easily. She determined to resist, to remain herself.

16-Dominion

Watcher

Every night, Lanezi was so relieved to be back in their cabin after the heat of Raykatoo's cabin and her constant scrutiny. At least he got Raykatoo to agree to let all three of them rest before the next set of swing jumps.

"Io?" It was dark and quiet. Io must have gone to the play with Euro. Good. "Lights." The Ramians were dedicated, stubborn even, about keeping up the arts. Concerts, plays, painting sessions, summary editing workshops, whatever. They had daily activities, well attended.

Lanezi collapsed on the foldout couch. The Ramians had a lot more energy than he did. And he felt like he was offending people by not going to all these events, or not knowing which ones to grace with his alien presence. But he was tired, not only physically. After sitting on an advisory board with Ramians all morning and serving Raykatoo all afternoon and sometimes evenings, and trying to settle his nerves for the swing jumps, he was mentally worn out.

And as much as he loved Io and Euro, they were young and slightly odd. Their communication was on a wavelength he could never hope to entirely pick up.

The door swung open and Io stepped through, looking exhausted. "Greetings, Lanezi," he said formally, in Ramian.

"Relax, Io, it's just me. Feeling okay?"

Io slouched on the couch next to Lanezi. After a beat, he said, "Too many girls."

Oh no. "Are they bothering you?"

"They ignore me. But they distract Euro, so I'm just by myself."

"Why do they ignore you?"

"Well, I learned Chike while Euro was learning Ramian, so they think I'm a Chike spy."

Lanezi frowned. He had noticed a few cold shoulders and lime green flashes since he started working with Raykatoo. "Should I talk to Euro?"

"No. He's not going to get mixed up with them. We're going home. God Willing."

"What was the play about?"

"An old one about sailing ships. They make the chairs rock, like you're on the ship, but it was just making me sick." He held his stomach with one hand. "I'm sorry. I don't mean to be negative. I'm just so tired."

Lanezi nodded. "I hear you. Go to bed." He helped push Io to his feet. "God is Most Glorious."

Without looking, Io reached behind and squeezed Lanezi's hand briefly, almost like a farewell.

The next afternoon, Lanezi took his painting to Raykatoo's cabin to paint while she was busy. But then he stood staring at the canvas, while Raykatoo stared at him. "Maybe this wasn't a good idea. It's not performance art."

"Humph! Art." There was a clamor at the door. "Your charges, no doubt. Enter!"

Four podpups rolled in, with Euro behind them. "Lanezi— oh sorry. Greetings Exempt Honor." The podpups took one look at Raykatoo and ran under Lanezi's feet. Raykatoo rolled her eyes in an almost human way. "Lanezi, the doctor has a treatment!"

"About time," Raykatoo muttered.

Lanezi stepped over the pups to hug Euro. "Great news! Praise the Lord." The pups started jumping around them. "Where's Io?"

"I told him, but he said he's thinking about it."

"What?" Subdued, the pups sat down to watch. "There's some danger?" Lanezi asked.

"Yes. 23% chance of fatality."

"As compared to 100% chance of fatality," Raykatoo said sarcastically. So she *had* read the data.

"Well, yes Exempt," Euro said. "That's how I see it. I often don't understand Io, though."

"Maybe," Lanezi said, "he just doesn't want to be the sole survivor."

"Oh," Euro said. "That would be terrible." And the pups whined.

"Lanezi! Take those rowdy pups and go home. I reduce your time to three hours from now on."

"Thank you, Exempt."

Euro helped him grab the pups. "Thank me? I need some rest. Human drama. Ramian drama. Podpup drama. Musical drama! Made up drama . . ."

18-Dominion

Midnight, in Tektite System

Although *Midnight* jumped out of the colony system in a rush, with the Tektites upset about leaving their family, Sequoia's single-minded determination to rescue Terina brought them into Tektite only *one day* from the station. To Beezan's, and everyone's relief, there were no Chike in system. There was no one at all. They had arrived ahead of the *Lotus*, but Lotus could show up any minute, so they shut off the *Midnight* beacon.

The jump left Beezan reeling. The ways were difficult, almost seething. He couldn't clear the angry threads from his mind.

Now that they were hidden behind the planet, opposite Tektite Station, he went to the Med Bay to pick up Sky, reportedly awake from her sedation and calling for him. When the door opened, Beezan was hit by the whining of Sky and Cookie, and Thayne, who immediately complained to him to stop the podpups. Thayne was in a small alcove, reclined on an exam bed, pale and wincing, but seemingly over his mindstorm. Katie hovered over the pups, both whining in the same heart-rending way. "Please," Beezan begged. "Please, no crying. I'll do everything I can for you." He stroked both pups trying to calm them. "And Ra'Tama should be here any time."

Beezan caught Katie's eye and mouthed *more sedative?* but she shook her head, signaling Roza to watch the pups a moment. There was nowhere private in the Med Bay crowded with Ramians, but they retreated to Thayne's alcove.

"I'm sorry," Katie said. "Sedation is not a long-term solution. We can only do it during the jumps—for the pups anyway."

Beezan shook his head no. As painful as it was to deal with Sky's whining, he didn't care to be fuzzy, and doubted it would stop the burning pain. "The only thing that will stop her is taking her to the planet." He didn't really mean to say that aloud, but Thayne suddenly sat up, intense black eyes homing in on Beezan.

"What planet?"

Beezan answered politely, as if Thayne had every right to be in on their conversation. "Sky insists on going to a specific planet outside the sectors. She seems compelled."

Thayne slid off his bed, now full of energy. "Show me."

Beezan shrugged and took him to a control panel in the main Med Bay. He brought up the display showing the exact location. Thayne frowned and studied it, moving the map around and telling the *Midnight* to "show Chike space, show colony."

Sky started to whine and crawl out of her med box, so Beezan brought her over. "Bee take," she grumbled. She pointed at the planet. "Bee promised."

Thayne stared at Sky and said, "I've seen this, this behavior, in a person—a Ramian. Compelled, like you say, and confused. He said he was called." Thayne turned back to the map in excitement. "This must be the location of the convocation!"

"That was our brother, Quay, you're talking about," an eavesdropping Danulell said.

"Yes."

"So this planet could be . . ."

"Where they've taken him. Yes," Thayne agreed.

Danulell's family turned to look at each other with new determination.

"It doesn't matter," an exasperated Iricana said when they went to see her. "We still have to go to Firelight to complete our mission. Beezan," she said, for the first time talking to him with an edge of annoyance, "as soon as we're at Tektite, go to the *Kingfisher* with the boarding crew. You need a break from that pup."

"Yes, Captain," Beezan said. But Thayne only scowled.

19-Dominion

Watcher

Everything was a spectator sport to the Ramians. Lanezi, Io, and Sontula were even allowed to sit on a couch and watch Euro's treatment, with his permission, of course, through a window, and without the birdcams.

Dr. Pranakeen and an assistant stood by the surgical table with Euro. A nano expert named Hetz joined them with her equipment. Anitoran monitored the procedure at a side panel. All of them were serious, their tokens removed and hoods up.

Although it had been explained to him, Lanezi only understood the procedure in the most basic terms. "First wave," Dr. Pranakeen announced, releasing the virus that would carry the gene editor rapidly to every cell in Euro's body except the brain.

Euro was sedated, but not unconscious. His temperature shot up as his natural defenses engaged, but the Ramians suppressed those, calculating that they could head off the virus in time. Anitoran sent some of her feeds through the translator and posted them in the observation area for Lanezi, Io, and Sontula. They could clearly see the progress of the virus as it moved through the blood and lymph systems, and then to the organs. The full-body scan glowed red as Euro's temperature increased.

Io alternated between sitting up straight on the couch and praying, and pulling his knees up and hiding his head behind them, barely peeking at the scene. Annoyingly, Lanezi's Ramian p'link buzzed with a personal message. Lanezi switched it to *busy*. Everyone knew where he was and how important this was. Who was bothering him?

"You know, I never wanted to go away," Io whispered. Sontula glanced at him, but let Lanezi reply.

"You didn't want to leave your home and go with Dr. Tenshi?"

"Would you? She was scary. But Euro and Gany, they like adventure."

"Why didn't Gany go?"

Io shrugged. "Euro always looked out for me. I didn't want to be separated from anyone, not my brothers, not my parents, not my teachers, or my home, especially not Euro. And, we were each one of a twin set, so Dr. Tenshi got the whole package with only two of us. And . . . it was only supposed to be a year. But then we ended up on the *Cheetah*, and then delayed, and then the sundering, and then the accident, and now," he sighed, "I volunteered to go to Chike space, and next, the convocation." He looked up at Lanezi. "And now maybe it's too late for Gany and Calli."

Lanezi put his hand on Io's shoulder. "Or maybe Gany and Calli get cured some other way, and you and Io get cured, and you'll all be together again soon. And until then, you're with me. Not as scary as Tenshi, I hope."

Io gave him a teary-eyed smile and nodded. "Thank you."

Finally, the virus had spread sufficiently to mutate the necessary cells. The scan showed deep red. Dr. Pranakeen turned to Hetz, "Begin."

Hetz infused her nanos through a tiny IV port. Following the same pattern, the nanos would truncate the replicating virus at just the right moment, allowing it to correct the genetic defect, and prevent a runaway virus. Anitoran nodded with confidence. "It's working," Sontula said.

Lanezi's p'link buzzed again, three more times. The scan of Euro's body, which had started blue, then turned red from the virus, now displayed a green wave as the nanos did their work. Lanezi's p'link buzzed again, on override now. Annoyed, he pulled it out and saw messages from ten different people. He contemplated reading them as everything was going well, but he was here for Io too, so he quietly got up and tossed his p'link into the other room.

"Truncation complete," Hetz reported. Sontula let out a sigh of relief.

"Is it over?" Io asked.

"Almost," Sontula answered. "They just have to clear the nanos now." The green image slowly returned to blue as the nanos retreated to the infuser and Hetz collected them.

"Scanning for strays," the doctor announced, and they tracked down a few, sending a nanochain back for some and extracting one with a long magneedle. Io buried his head in Lanezi's shoulder for that part. Not that Lanezi was watching either.

"Clear," Hetz reported.

"Vitals look good. Increase sedative," Dr. Pranakeen said, and stepped back.

The medical team burst into smiles and removed their hoods. Their colors ran bright blue with tan lines. The doctor beckoned to Io. "He's sleeping, but you can come in." The doctor came out to talk to Lanezi. "It appears to have been entirely successful."

"Thank you, doctor!" Lanezi pressed hands with him, a bit overwhelmed.

"A great accomplishment doctor, Hetz," Sontula congratulated them. But they both shook their heads.

"We are grateful to be of service to our Human friends." And they seemed like it.

Lanezi checked on Euro quickly, gave Io a hug, and then retrieved his p'link, now with twenty override messages. He opened the first one. It was Neah, of all people. "Trouble—pilots staging uprising against Getti Drann."

"*What?*" Lanezi said, alarmed.

"What's wrong?" Sontula grabbed her p'link.

"Some kind of rebellion?"

"Quickly! To the dining room," and she took off, Lanezi right behind her and birdcams swooping in. *The dining room? A kitchen mutiny?*

They burst in the dining room to find almost the entire crew. They were assembled in three loose groups, two with leaders up front.

The pilots, with their tans and the majority of the crew behind them, stood with Widinmay, the token-covered grandfather pilot, in front. But Reev, the angry pilot, was prominent beside him, scowling and flashing dark green with an amber strip.

In another clump, Getti Drann stood with ziz command crew and a few other loyal people. A smaller bunch was either just watching or undecided and had no leader. But as soon as Lanezi and Sontula entered, Neah stepped to the front of the third group. Sontula immediately went to his side, as did Lanezi, without even thinking about it.

"We are two jumps away from our destination," Neah stated. "Two jumps from completing our agreement. Now is not the time for a change in leadership."

"We never should have come out here!" Widinmay said.

"We can't change the past," Getti Drann said. "I do not intend to step down until our agreements are fulfilled. Reneging now would strand us far from home."

Neah was about to speak when the door slid open, and Raykatoo herself stepped in, upright, with her gray robes sweeping around her. The birdcams zeroed in but she hissed at them and they veered off. "What is the meaning of this, Getti Drann?"

"Exempt, I apologize. A completely internal matter. We did not mean to disturb you."

"I have full access to your birdcams and I know exactly what goes on here." She approached the pilots, who backed away slightly. "These pilots *again* refuse their orders."

Widinmay flashed defiance. "We reject Getti Drann's authority to give us orders! In our culture, it is our right—"

Raykatoo hissed and swung her tail, missing his feet by a hair. "Perhaps your infant minds forget. Getti Drann is not in charge. *I AM.*" Stepping in close, she gave him the one-eye. "This is *my* ship. *I* give the orders. *All* obey."

Widinmay took a breath as if to speak, but Raykatoo's tail slammed down on the deck and they all jumped. She pointed her small claw to Drann's group. "Return to your duties!" They bolted, except for Drann.

Raykatoo spun to face Neah. "Who do you stand with?"

"We stand on our agreement with the Exempt," Neah said quietly. The pilots jeered, but Raykatoo swung around again, ignoring many of the pilots who slipped out with Drann's people. The core of the pilots and their tans remained. "This group, no rations three days."

"We won't!" Reev shouted.

In a flash, Raykatoo reached out and grabbed Reev by the tunic. There were gasps all around. Getti Drann sprang forward. "No rations, three days, yes Exempt. I will see to it." She hauled Reev closer. "Exempt, I beg you. We do not use corporeal punishment."

"Neither do we. We are not barbarians. But animals, and the GenSix, must be controlled. You!" She pointed to Widinmay with her other claw. "Remove your tokens."

Oh my God, Lanezi thought, *she knows how to hurt them.* Widinmay, coldly defiant, stripped the tokens of a lifetime off and dropped them on the deck as if they meant nothing to him.

"Now you," she said to Reev, releasing him and grabbing Widinmay. Reev shook with fury, his colors flashing between black and dark green, and made no move. Slowly, carefully, Shiwelna came forward and pulled off Reev's tokens, adding them to the pile on the deck.

When Raykatoo released Widinmay her eyes glittered with danger. "Getti, have that pile of junk taken to my cabin."

"Yes, Exempt."

"All of this group will proceed to your living areas. You will not exit for three days. Except for children, you and your family will not eat for three days. Understood?"

They stood, horrified. Even Lanezi felt sick.

"UNDERSTOOD?"

"Yes! Yes, Exempt." Shiwelna, her long years of savvy still with her, herded the pilots out. A flick of Raykatoo's claw and the birdcams took off, monitoring the pilots.

Before she turned to go, Raykatoo hissed at Getti Drann, *"All are my servants."*

17 / RA'TAMA

1-Ayyám-i-Há

Watcher

For Lanezi, the scariest moment of the rebellion was the next day, when he had to show up for his afternoon service with Raykatoo. He brought Whisper along for a measure of mercy-seeking.

"Enter. This one will not harm you."

"Thank you, Exempt." Lanezi set Whisper down. She didn't fear Raykatoo as the younger pups did.

"Attend your painting. I must rest in the hot box." She burrowed into what was once Lanezi's sunken living room. Now it was filled with small glass pebbles, blue and green. She had requested red and black sand, but the Ramians wouldn't tolerate sand on their ship. Or red and black for that matter. The pebbles were heated somehow, because the stifling heat of the room just wasn't enough.

Lanezi's painting was done really. It was the Chike ship, before it was destroyed, before the Ramians sent their art ships out. He painted it with the star bursting from behind the gravity ball and the ship lit with the reflected light of a gas giant. Lanezi wasn't sure how Raykatoo would react to it, but he had to paint the images that hung in his mind.

He cleaned it up here and there, but finally forced himself to sign carefully, put everything down, and step back. Suddenly he remembered where he was. "Whisper?" He whirled around.

Raykatoo held a claw to her jaw in a very Human gesture. Then she pointed next to her in the box. Lanezi came over, dropping to his knees. Whisper was curled up near Raykatoo in the warm pebbles, sleeping contentedly. Lanezi sat down next to them. "Exempt," he whispered, seeing her uneaten meals piled on the desk, "should I get you other food?"

"No. The food is acceptable. But this one will not eat until the punishment is over."

She was thin and losing weight already. "Three days? Must you?"

"A civilization must rise to the point where one defective, disgruntled person does not cause the sands to shift. They should be utterly unnoticed. They must align themselves with the good, or be swept away in the wind." Lanezi understood what Raykatoo was saying, but Reev and Widinmay weren't the only people who sprang to mind. She sighed. "But one does not give a punishment one would not take oneself."

"You are a true nest mother," Lanezi said.

Carefully moving Whisper aside, she slithered out of the pebbles and came to stand by the painting. Lanezi scooped up Whisper and stood by her. "Of all the Ramian art I have seen here, this painting skill is . . ."

"Exempt, this is my humble gift to you."

She nodded after a moment. "Accepted."

. . .

Lotus, in Tektite System

Terina stretched in front of her seat on the *Lotus*. For three days, she hadn't been allowed to move around the shuttle, except to use the facilities. Thank heavens Ra'Tama had jumped them so close. She doubted that her mom could have come any closer.

Now, as they approached the *Kingfisher*, AnnaLee told her and Gadi to get back in their seats and called Ra'Tama up front. She pulled out her trank dart and held it casually in her hand. *Please don't check inside!* Terina prayed.

Ra'Tama took the pilot's chair from a nervous Halim. "*Kingfisher*, *Lotus*, this is Ra'Tama. Please respond."

"It has been over 14 days since your last communication. The password is required."

Ra'Tama typed something on the panel before AnnaLee could stop him. **"Password confirmed."** There was a moment of hesitation.

In the reflection of the front window, she saw Ra'Tama frown with concern. He misses his ship, Terina realized, like Honor Beezan was so heartbroken about the *Drumheller*. "*Kingfisher?*"

"Your Highness, welcome back." It sounded emotional.

"Your Highness?" AnnaLee scoffed. "How ridiculous—are you the king of the outer sectors?"

But Terina and Gadi looked at each other, stunned. Ra'Tama's quiet confidence, his excellent manners, his service leadership, the Kays' obsession over him. He was Earthborn. *The ship named Kingfisher!* He was royalty, from one of the Earth monarchies.

"*Kingfisher*, it is good to hear your voice. Please address me as Ra'Tama for the time being."

"Yes. Ra'Tama."

"Please undock from the station and prepare for my shuttle. Bring life support up to specs in the Entry Lounge, lift, and torus, and spin up."

"Yes, Ra'Tama."

Kingfisher, near Tektite Station

Terina got her legs under her as the *Kingfisher* lift went through the coupler and then up to TopRim. Gadi grabbed the rail for support. It seemed like forever they had been strapped to the chairs aboard the *Lotus.*

The lift was ordinary, but when they entered the torus, the walls were a beautiful turquoise, painted with tropical islands and giant turtles. Ra'Tama ran his hand lovingly along the wall, tracing a line of colorful little fish. It was more spectacular than the *81-Petals.* Even Zonta and Halim looked at each other in surprise.

But the ship wasn't that big. Urged on by AnnaLee and her trank dart, they soon passed the kitchen in Arc 1. Terina could have sworn she caught a whiff of something and hoped it was a computer-made surprise dinner. The six of them squeezed into the small Command Bay airlock and the door slid shut. As soon as the second door opened, Ra'Tama said, "*Kingfisher,* condition stingray."

Instantly, Halim tried to shut the door. "It won't close!" Jets of steam or gas blasted them from the ceiling. AnnaLee covered her face, trying not to breathe. She stepped into the Command Bay and fired the trank dart at Ra'Tama, but nothing happened. Ra'Tama caught Gadi as she passed out and lowered her into a chair. AnnaLee fired again and then realized it was empty. She looked ready to kill someone. Terina felt woozy, but she figured she might as well fall on top of AnnaLee, knocking her down.

. . .

Beezan huddled, breather ready, with the Kays, Sequoia, Roza, Maura, Cooper, and Thunder, one level up from the kitchen, in the *Kingfisher*. It was dark except for one shielded security screen, held by Vante Kay. Once they felt the ship undock and spin up, they knew the *Lotus* was coming. *If I jumped to the Drumheller, at least it has an engine and I could bring it back. Why did Ra'Tama bring them here?*

Beezan thought it was borderline outrageous that he had been assigned to a security mission, risking two pilots, as Sequoia insisted on coming too. And he was useless. But he scowled at himself. Captain's orders. And if anything, it brought home to him how much trouble he was making. But finally, after hiding in the kitchen for two days, the wait was over.

On Vante's screen, they watched the *Lotus* party enter the Command Bay where they were unexpectedly blasted with some kind of gas. "Good." The Kays nodded in approval. Sequoia and Roza were up before Vante said, "Let's go!"

"*Kingfisher!* Clear the Command Bay!" Ling ordered. They hurried down the stairs to the Command Bay. Beezan went last.

Before they even reached the Command Bay, the door opened. Ra'Tama stepped over the limp forms of the rebels. Ling pressed him against the wall, putting herself between him and the Command Bay, while Vante checked the others.

"Thank heavens you're here," Ra'Tama said quietly.

Sequoia leaped through to get to Terina.

"It's okay," Ra'Tama reassured her. "Quick but safe sedative."

"They're out cold," Vante confirmed. "We'll need five stretchers." So Beezan went back with the others to organize the robots for stretchers.

"It was a trick!" Roza said. "All along. Ra'Tama brought them here to knock them out. He wasn't going to escape with her."

"He couldn't," Maura said. "The *Kingfisher* engine was missing a part. We failed to fix it."

"Good thing Teeve picked up the part at Firelight," Cooper added, smiling.

"What?" Beezan said. "Does he know?"

"Nah," Cooper said. "Why ruin a fun surprise?"

"We don't leave stuff broken," Maura affirmed, and Cooper nodded.

By the time everyone was situated in the *Kingfisher* Med Bay, three people in full restraints, and Sequoia standing over Terina, Iricana, Falcon, and Teeve had come over.

Although the ship was small, the Med Bay could treat ten people, and Beezan had no trouble keeping out of the way. Ra'Tama, after hugging the Kays and formally expressing his thanks to everyone, sat and gave Iricana his full report.

Roza hovered over Gadi in concern. She'd been dosed twice. "Why aren't you affected?" she asked Ra'Tama suspiciously.

"I am immune—a genetic enhancement."

Her eyes narrowed. "That's not allowed on Earth."

"Royalty is exempted," Kay Ling said quietly. "Prince Ra'Tama is granted protection."

There were gasps and stunned expressions all around. Beezan almost smacked himself in the head. *Of course.* Someone ten times more diplomatic than Jarvie must be royalty.

"Falcon," Iricana said, turning to her, "Just for the record, maybe you could verify Ra'Tama's real identity."

Falcon, normally loving the drama, was tense and unhappy.

Tears came to her eyes. "Honors, I'm so sorry. It was in the 1000 packets. There's been a terrible accident. Ra'Tama . . . is now King."

Ra'Tama gasped and grabbed his chest. Immediately, with cries of pain, both Kays dropped to a knee and bowed their heads, "Majesty."

Ra'Tama sunk to his knees with them, putting his arms around them. The lights dimmed and a mournful march played throughout the ship as they grieved together. Beezan was ashamed of himself for his earlier tinge of jealousy. Poor Ra'Tama had regained his ship, but lost his family.

2-Ayyám-í-Há

Kingfisher, near Tektite Station

Beezan didn't go back to the *Midnight.* He had to admit that a break from Sky was letting his nerves settle a little. And he'd be just as heartbroken for Ra'Tama on either ship. So he stayed on *Kingfisher.* And when the Tektites snuck down to fix the engine, he followed them past the cargo holds to the top of the engine shield. Teeve and Maura were suiting up and Cooper was at a panel.

"You're not going in the engine compartment!" Beezan said.

"Nah, honor. We're not main engine techs," Maura answered. "The engine is shut down. The super-special part, which is a regulator, goes on the outside. Most outer sector ships don't even have one. It's for an elaborate safety system. If it's not working, even a perfectly good engine shuts down. Annoying."

Maura hefted it in nogee; it was slightly smaller than the ID box. She secured it on Teeve's back.

"Can I help?" Beezan asked, feeling like it would be cosmic good to get someone's ship back to them.

"Thanks Honor. This one's on us," Cooper answered. "But you can keep me company while those two have all the fun."

Terina, still on the *Kingfisher* with her mom, hands patched up, dug through the Earth geography database. Ra'Tama, she found, was a prince of Greater Melanesia, a group of united islands in the South Pacific. His father was king. The older of two daughters was to inherit the Kingdom, greatly anticipated by the people as they had not had a queen in many generations and somehow that was special to them. And now tragedy had struck. There was also some controversy about Ra'Tama's "abandoning the Kingdom" and "gallivanting" in space for nine years. He was due to return to the islands when he was 21. Now he would return as a reluctant, and perhaps unwanted, king. He could not abdicate as that was traditionally only done if one had committed a dishonorable act.

There were many small monarchies on Earth, all loyal to the wider world government, of course. They were strong representatives of the culture and honor of their diverse peoples.

Besides the one official packet in the 1000 messages, there was no other news about the accident. Whatever happened had killed Ra'Tama's father and two sisters, but there was no mention of the rest of his family, his mother, or younger brother.

Terina headed to the Consultation Hall where they were saying prayers, but checked in the kitchen on a hunch. Sure enough, Cookie was sulking in a corner. Terina got a treat, picked her up, and fed her.

"Cookie sad?"

"Tama sad."

"I know."

"Cookie lonely," she grumped.

Oh, poor Cookie was separated from the other pups now. Terina sent a p'link message to Iricana suggesting transferring a couple of the Midnight crew that had pups to the *Kingfisher*. And then was horrified at herself that she'd just told the captain what to do. *Oh my God. What will she think? I hope she doesn't tell my mom.*

She peeked out in the rimway. Should she show her face in the Consultation Hall? But Beezan was coming her way. He signaled her to follow. "They're about to restart the engine," he whispered.

I can't miss that!

Terina slipped in behind Beezan and sat quietly for a few more prayers. Just as Vante Kay was finished reading, there was a familiar vibration. "What is that?" Vante asked.

Ra'Tama gasped and looked at Iricana.

Iricana smiled. She looked at her s'link and nodded. "Cooper reports that they've finished the job. Honor Ra'Tama, your engine checks out."

He stared at her a moment, collecting his thoughts. "Home. I can go home."

"Yes, Captain. We'll split off some crew for you," and she gave Terina a tolerant look. "We'll transfer the prisoners back to *Midnight* as soon as possible."

Iricana got up, but Ra'Tama put out his hand. "Wait." Everyone turned to him. "What if we take the prisoners? And the news about the colony. We have to go through Firelight. Then you would be free to jump . . . wherever."

The mystery planet!

. . .

Terina sighed and put her pad in her pocket. Kelson had arrived in a shuttle to take her, Sequoia, and Gadi back to the *Midnight*, now that Gadi felt better. The four of them walked to the Operations Bay to say goodbye to Ra'Tama. Terina's head was still spinning from the craziness of AnnaLee, and now, she just couldn't accept that she was never going to see Ra'Tama again.

Terina's heart had gone out to Ra'Tama during their captivity on the shuttle and their many prayers since learning of his tragedy. There would be no official memorial until he returned to Earth.

"No bowing," Sequoia whispered to Kelson.

"No?"

"No calling him your majesty or any of that. He is just Honor Ra'Tama to all except the Kays."

The door slid open. They waited while Teeve, being his usual undiplomatic self, discussed repairs with Ra'Tama. Teeve sauntered out, giving them a cocky smile on the way. Kelson raised an eyebrow. Sequoia shook her head. But Ra'Tama was nodding as if relieved and encouraged.

"Welcome, friends," he said quietly, gesturing for them to come forward. He was pale, with puffy eyes, holding Cookie in the crook of his arm. He carefully handed her off to Vante and came to greet them.

Just then Iricana came in, and he gestured her forward too. "Captain, honors, friends, thank you for coming."

"Honor Ra'Tama," Sequoia said and paused, collecting herself. "We're taking a shuttle back. We just wanted to say goodbye. It has been a pleasure knowing you and jumping with you."

He nodded. "Likewise, Honor. I wish you a lifetime of service." They solemnly bowed to each other.

Terina went to say goodbye, but was suddenly tongue-tied,

looking down. Of all things, she blurted out, "What will happen to Cookie? They're not allowed on Earth."

Ra'Tama sighed. "She was so old when I got her. There was no way she would live until I was 21. But she is stronger than she seems. I will take her with me. Perhaps an exception will be granted. And it may yet be a long trip."

"I'm sorry. I wish the best for you. And I know you will be a great king."

He smiled a bit at that. "Perhaps we are all stronger than we seem." He shook her hand warmly. "I do wish we could stay in touch if you have time, especially regarding your historical work."

"Oh, yes!"

Gadi was bold enough to give Ra'Tama a hug.

He looked up at all of them. "I am so grateful for your help and prayers. But we must hurry. The ways are erratic. I plan to jump to Firelight directly."

4-Ayyám-i-Há

Midnight, in Tektite System

Back on the *Midnight,* Terina hung around in the kitchen checking supplies. Since fast was starting, she would be in charge of lunch for those who didn't fast: the too young, like herself, the too old, and the sick and injured. And of course, the few Ramians that didn't go with Ra'Tama. Danulell and his family were staying. So Zhenumae would work with her. Which meant the baby would be around. And Rocket. Exciting times. *Crazy* times.

Her mom peeked in the door. Seeing no one else was around gestured Terina over for a quiet talk. "Sweetheart," she said, looking worried and sad, "I'm thinking I should send you back to the *Kingfisher*."

"Just me?"

"We'll be jumping into Chike space—"

"You mean send me away? Mom!"

"Iricana wants a skeleton crew."

A panic bubbled up inside her. "Mom, I'm not leaving if you're staying! You can't send me away! That whole time . . .I was on the *Lotus* . . ." Terina started sobbing, "all I could think about was being separated from my family. And how evil she was. You can't be evil too!"

"Terina, I don't want to be separated. I just don't want to put you at risk."

"I'll take the risk. It's the outer sectors. Every day is a risk. *A baby is going!* Mom . . . please." Her mom teared up too, but tried to control herself. "Is Jarvie going?"

"Yes. He has nowhere else to go."

"I have nowhere else to go!"

"Are you sure?"

"Yes. Yes! Mom, please don't send me away." Sequoia nodded and hugged her, tears of relief streaming down her face.

As it turned out, when Terina got her lunch list, it was hardly a skeleton crew. The Tektites were back on the Midnight after fixing the Kingfisher. Roza and some of the original Midnight crew, including podpups, had transferred to the *Kingfisher*. The bulk of the Ramians went and hoped to be transferred back to their space, if the ways didn't close.

Besides the captain and Sequoia, Beezan, Kelson, Thunder, Taj, Jarvie, Gadi, Gola, Katie, Falcon, Thayne, Nkiroo, the Tektites, Terina, and Danulell's family would be staying on the *Midnight.*

She couldn't wait. The river of history was running wild.

18 / SACRIFICE

4-Ayyám-i-Há

Watcher

Lanezi was so relieved when the pilots' starvation was done. Their friends piled replacement tokens on them. Reev wore them all, but Widinmay refused, flouting his punishment like a token of honor.

Drann decided that Kells, the young pilot, would do the last swing jumps, the first time for him. But he had stood with Neah during the rebellion, so they thought it would be for the best.

Lanezi arranged for Io and Euro to stay in the med center the whole time, so they were oblivious of the rebellion and punishment. And Io had easily agreed to the treatment after seeing how well it went for Euro—and knowing that Euro would live.

Euro, Lanezi, and Sontula sat outside the treatment room again, with Io inside this time. There were prayers, but the anxiety level was much lower. Euro, up and about and, most importantly, hungry as a teenager, hardly bothered with any parting scene. "It didn't hurt at all. It'll be over before you know it." Io nodded and got a quick hug anyway. Lanezi left his p'link in his cabin this time. *Let them riot.*

The virus stage went as before with Anitoran and Sontula nodding with confidence. The doctor signaled Hetz for the nanos and the green wave started. But the doctor frowned this time and turned to Hetz. Hetz reported, "The nanos are encountering resistance. There are other nanos already installed."

And if the virus wasn't stopped, Lanezi remembered, there would be the *deadly cascade.* "Other nanos?" he asked a stunned Euro.

"No. No he doesn't! Only Gany and Calli had them. And it didn't work anyway, so they didn't try it on us."

"It's certain," Hetz insisted. "We need to program ours to either take over or destroy them!" Fiercely, she set to work, getting help from Anitoran to tie in the Human translator, while the doctor and his assistant tried to keep Io's fever down.

"Euro," Lanezi grabbed his shoulders. "Do you know what kind of nanos Gany had? What the program was called? Anything?"

"No," he shook his head, tears streaming down.

"It must be in the *Enkindler* data!" Lanezi reached for his p'link. *Oh no!* "Do you have it on yours?" Sontula shook her head, her colors gray.

"Fever reduction protocol. Life support!" Dr. Pranakeen was ordering.

Euro lunged against the observation window, "Io!"

Lanezi sprinted for their cabin, the birdcams zooming behind him. Raykatoo was at her door as he slammed to a halt against his door and tumbled in, grabbing his p'link and standing in the doorway. "Access *Enkindler* data: Chinjeol quadruplets nano treatment data! Override code for medical nanos!"

It beeped. He tried again. "Medical stand down code—Chinjeol nanos!" *Beep.*

Raykatoo came to his doorway.

"Nano program code STOP," he said, and his p'link went off. *Oh my God!*

He pressed the button to turn it back on.

"END-END-END," Raykatoo said. "All one word."

"What?"

"Didn't you read all that data you gave me?"

He tried to focus. *Endendend!* His p'link was still rebooting, but Neah was there, calling Sontula and telling her. "Thank you!" He squeezed the startled Exempt on the arm as he turned to run back, leaving Neah to deal with the gathering crowd.

In the med center, Euro stood at the window crying and praying as Sontula had one hand on his shoulder and was talking to Neah with her p'link and watching the scans. "They've sent the code," she told Lanezi. Anitoran sat at her panel, no longer working. Her eyes were closed in prayer. Her hood was thrown off, and she was running a strong, almost silvery color he'd never seen.

Suddenly, the scan flashed white and then the green wave finally started. "We've defeated the nanos," Hetz reported, but there was no celebration. *Was it too late?*

The wait was agonizing. Slowly, slowly, the nanos truncated the virus, collected the Human nanos and returned to their port. The scan for strays revealed many, with Hetz tracking them down as the doctor dealt with the fever.

"Clear from nanos," Hetz finally reported, sagging against the wall.

"His temperature is at a tolerable level," Dr. Pranakeen reported. "He'll have to stay here, but he'll live. And he is cured."

Euro collapsed into Lanezi's arms and Anitoran laid her head down on the desk in relief. Neah burst in. "He lives," Sontula whispered. Lanezi hugged Euro while mentally kicking himself. He should have known the code. He should have studied it himself. He looked up to see the doctor pat Anitoran, his tan, on the back. But she didn't respond. The doctor lifted her shoulder and her head dropped back down, colors gone. She was dead. He fell to his knees with an anguished scream.

"What happened?" Lanezi asked, holding back a sob. "She was young. How could she be dead?"

Sontula stood in shock. "Sacrifice," she whispered, holding her finger to her lips.

"How? Why would she sacrifice for Io?" Lanezi shook his head in confusion.

In a barely audible voice, in Alkulu, Neah said, "Not for Io, for Dr. Pranakeen, her jik."

But . . . how?

4-Loftiness Eve

Midnight, at the Tektite a-rings

In the Command Bay, Beezan sat, strapped, with Jarvie, Sequoia, and Falcon as they prepped for the jump to Sky's mystery planet. Sky was tethered to Beezan's chair in nogee. The change in her personality was amazing. She was happy. She ate. She kept Rocket and Star in line. She tagged along for all their operational meetings. And now that they were one hour away from the a-rings, she was beside herself with excitement.

Jarvie smiled. "You'd never know we were jumping to a mystery planet *slash* alien convention!"

"With the ways collapsing," Sequoia added, frowning.

But Beezan's heart was light. The prayers, the fasting, nothing compared to having a happy Sky. "We are one hour from the a-rings with no Chike in sight," he reminded them. "And the a-rings will make it easier to find the ways." It was a long *long* jump. A year ago, it would have been unthinkable. But now, with Jarvie on his right and Sequoia on his left, he felt no fear. It was as if Sky had become a fuzzball of confidence and was feeding it to him.

Sky was so excited by the bustle of the jump that she wouldn't go in her box yet. She would occasionally tug on the tether so she'd bump into Beezan affectionately. "Soon!" she bumped him.

"Yes. *You* go in your box *soon*. Then six hours in the a-rings."

"Boring."

"Sky help find the way?" He teased her.

"Sky help."

She reeled to the end of her tether, grabbed a small hold bar on the panel, and pressed the map so it enlarged to fill the main screen.

"Good Lord," Sequoia whispered. "A podpup that works the panels?"

"You are excited," Beezan said, but had a pang of doubt. Was there something on that planet Sky would love more than him?

But Falcon announced "P&P, 24 and 3," and he pushed that thought out of his head.

4-Loftiness

Midnight, at the mystery planet

They dropped into normal space. "Target system reached." *Midnight* announced. "Onscreen."

"All pilots yellow!" Katie advised.

"I've got it," Thunder assured them.

"So many beacons," Falcon said in awe.

Terina unsealed her visor to see the main screen. A small galaxy of bright beacons whirled around a terrestrial planet. Streams of beacons headed toward the planet, forming regular arcs as they approached.

History again! Terina quickly checked her gear. Everything was recording. Maybe someone would say something historic.

"Check our vicinity!" Thunder ordered the monitors.

"Clear in all directions!" Gadi reported.

"What the—I'm getting a heading!" Falcon said, and a map flashed up on the main screen.

"I see it!" Thunder answered and seconds later they were boosting. "Matching speed to that ship in front."

"It must be the convocation," Katie said.

"It could be the Olympics for all we know," said a groggy Iricana.

"Or a ship junkyard," Nkiroo said. There were a lot of strange conglomerations flying around out there.

"It's the convocation," Thayne said dismissively, taking off his helmet and rubbing his neck.

"Stand by for spin up," Thunder said. Terina checked her mom's light. It was green now, but the pilots were all quiet. It was a long, hard jump.

"Receiving audio!" Falcon warned. And those who had taken their helmets off covered their ears, bracing for the Chike blast. But, amazingly, it was a polite voice at a normal volume.

"Maintain / Do not leave your traffic pattern."

"No translator," Falcon said. "They're transmitting in Alkulu."

"How can they know our language?" Iricana asked.

"Your ship is not authorized / invited. However, you will be allowed / tolerated if you comply / obey all instructions / directions. The convocation begins in eleven days."

"See?" Thayne said. But they all ignored him.

"Clear from blue zones," Falcon announced. Terina climbed out of her cocoon.

"Mom?" she said, coming into the Command Bay. Katie was there, scowling over the pilots. Terina helped her mom pull off her helmet. She groaned.

Jarvie groaned. "Let's NOT do that again."

Beezan groaned. "Sorry."

"Such a strange jump," Sequoia said. "As if all ways were leading here."

"Bee! Out!" Sky called.

Terina let the pups out and Sky bounded over to Beezan. With some help, she crawled up on his cocoon and then ignored him. She gazed out at the view. "Yeah, sweetie, we're here," Terina told her.

Sky nodded with approval. "Bee promised."

"I need food," Sequoia said.

"Come on Sky, let's get dinner going."

"Dinner!" the pups repeated as she headed off to the kitchen.

Sandstorm

Zahar faced the screen in the fake Cheetah room. Pascal was seated on his throne behind them and she didn't want him to see her scowling. She rubbed her painful elbow, and then her knee, and her hip. In the many weeks since the ping-pong game, ze had managed to recreate the most obscure Earth sports to try with them. But roller derby? The three humans had never heard of it. And poor Quay. The naturally timid Ramians had never conceived of such a game. They had finally rebelled and told zir that ping-pong was their game of choice. Right now, they were playing Evan's favorite game, but it was more serious than Pascal knew—she hoped.

Pascal's ship was orbiting the planet Rissh, as near as they could pronounce, the scene of the great convocation. And Zahar had to admit, it was a spectacular scene for any ship fan. They had been one of the first ships to arrive, three weeks earlier. Now hundreds of ships were orbiting the planet and more were on the way.

There were ugly angular ships, colorful spheres, the viper-nosed Chike ships, strange smooth vessels that looked like marine life, foldable boxy ships, tumbling dumbbells, the occasional spinning torus, some misty pulsing objects, works of engineering art, and assorted junk piles.

Evan's game with Pascal was calling up the ships on the main screen, reading out their beacon information, and identifying everything he memorized about them, the gen, the species, specs, and tech of the ship. Evan asked the engineering walls to make him little models, which he lined up on specially made shelves.

The panel beeped with a new incoming ship. Evan put it up on the screen. "A GenTwo," Evan reported, "the Swish, the terraformers, class 3 push gravity ball, ship #947081."

947081? Those Swish have a lot of ships, Zahar thought, while Evan and Pascal cooed over the engineering. But during this talk, Pascal dropped comments about species, planets, customs, the convocation, what the names of the ships meant, and how the whole Leaf thing worked. Caspia and Zahar casually cataloged every little fact and searched for any data that could help them.

There was one species of GenOne, but they had many ships and representatives here. There were eight species of GenTwo, twelve species of GenThree, and at least ten species of GenFour, so far. The system was buzzing with their ships. But no Human ships, and no Ramians.

"Who are all these people?" Zahar asked.

Pascal swung his smallside eye to her. "Diplomats, reporters, interpreters, legal experts, science and spiritual advisors from every planet. Also historians, data gatherers, and the like. They have all been in session. When the last harbingers and witnesses arrive, it will be time."

Zahar was excited, but the convocation was serious business, especially for the GenFour. Whether they were demoted or promoted would determine the future of their species. And Pascal had warned them that Humans and Ramians already had many strikes against them.

Quay was sick with worry about his role in this. Pascal was annoyingly skimpy on information, saying only that Quay would be transferred to his duties when the arena was complete and all the "guests" assembled.

Their daily live broadcast popped up on the screen. But it didn't start out from the convocation arena as usual. Pascal sat up. An old Chike, with heavy green draping, appeared and started talking.

They had to wait a few seconds for the translation. "Attention / hear this, the harbingers / representatives / spokespersons have all arrived in system. Proceed to the arena as instructed." The broadcast stopped. That was it for today.

Quay's colors went completely gray. Pascal jumped up. "Congratulations! It is time. You will of course fight / challenge / represent well for your people." Quay swallowed, obviously trying not to panic. "One escort will be required."

Zahar immediately stepped forward. They would not separate a married couple on her watch. "What will happen to Evan and Caspia?" she asked.

Ze casually waved a claw. "They will be transferred to a Human ship."

"There are no Human ships here."

"Oh, perhaps this one will just keep them." And ze clicked ziz little claw in humor. "Dress formally and return here at once."

Then Evan's panel beeped again. He turned and zoomed in on the new ship. Pascal closed his teeth sharply. Evan reported evenly, "GenFour, Human, observation class . . . the *Midnight*."

Zahar could tell by Pascal's cold stare that *Midnight* had not been invited to the party, but Humans had found the way. This time, she let zir see her satisfied grin.

Back in their quarters, Zahar and Quay discovered that Pascal had already ordered what ze considered dress clothes, long heavy robes in the Chike style.

"I don't want to look like a Chike," Quay fretted.

"Don't worry; these robes will hide our supplies." Zahar demanded protein bars, water pouches, and small shoulder bags to carry them in. "Also, please make a map of the planet, of the convocation area, and directions to the nearest spaceport— in the Human language. And a schedule of the proceedings."

Nothing happened for a moment. "Nice try," Quay said quietly. But then a paper map appeared. Zahar picked it up. In large letters it said, Human Language Map.

"It's the arena," Zahar said. A green arrow pointed to the entrance. "Harbinger Assembly Area."

"It's something. Thank you for thinking of it."

. . .

Back in the fake Cheetah room, they said tearful goodbyes to Caspia and Evan. Evan gave Zahar one of his model ships and dramatically made her promise to keep it with her always. She hugged Caspia and whispered "Get away if you can. Don't worry about us."

Caspia nodded. "Same advice. You've been a great captain."

After their hugs, Pascal took them to the shuttle hangar. One of the guards stepped forward with a box. "Zahar must escort this small one to the witness area."

"What?" She thought she was escorting Quay. She took the small box and looked inside. It was a rat. The one she called Zombie, because nothing could kill it. "Where are the others?"

"They will be cared for. They are old," Pascal answered. "The three of you," Pascal indicated Quay, Zahar, and Zombie, "will take a shuttle to the planet. You will be shown to your entrances. This one separates here. Perform your duties well for the honor of us all."

Quay stood as tall as he could. "On behalf of my people, I thank you Exempt Pascal, champion of the downtrodden."

Zahar tucked the cage under one arm and took Quay's arm with the other. "I'm with you." Quay took a deep breath. By force of will, his colors went from gray to the blazing blue of destiny.

Convocation

The horrid Chike shuttle thumped to a landing on the convocation planet. As she unstrapped, Zahar thought the gravity felt a little light, like a couple of decks up in the torus. She put on her shoulder bag and the Chike robe, and gripped the small cage as the back doors opened. A yellow-orange light streamed in—and a warm organic smell. It was like an arboretum, only, as they walked to the top of the ramp, Zahar realized it was open air.

"Amazing," Quay said, staring out.

"Trees!" Zahar said. Their spaceport-type landing area, with green landing pads and roadways, was surrounded by trees. "There must be thousands, tens of thousands."

"They're so tall!" Quay said.

The escort, lined up on both sides of them, started down. When they had formed up along the ramp, Quay and Zahar started to go. "Wait / pause!" the last Chike said, holding ziz prod across Zahar's way. "The harbinger only / alone."

Oh no! Zahar turned and hugged Quay quickly. "I hope we can be friends, Humans, and Ramians."

"And you and I," Quay agreed, flashing destiny.

"God be with you," she whispered as he started down the ramp.

At the bottom, he was met by four creatures that looked like Earth dogs, and escorted away. He turned once to look back, but squinted in the bright light and turned away.

When it was her turn, Zahar blinked away tears and marched down. It was so bright, she could barely see, even when looking away from the alien sun. There was a new set of dog-people, but they were having a hurried discussion among themselves, whining, yipping, and quiet barking. They were dressed only in headsets and vests, complete with pockets for electronic gadgets. Their front paws were somewhat hand-like, although thick, not like the paws that she had seen in pictures of Earth dogs. Not dogs! She reminded herself. Like the Chike were not lizards. *People.*

"Human?"

"Yes."

"Human person." Suddenly all four dog-people sat at attention with an air of quiet comfort and friendliness. "Please forgive the delay. Your kind was not expected."

Zombie gave a loud squeak. "Oh, I'm sorry. I'm escorting a . . . this . . . small being." She lowered the cage so they could see.

"Yip! Of course."

And then their translator changed to something squeaky, and probably out of Zahar's hearing range. One dog-person poked at the air, using a virtual screen that Zahar couldn't even see. That one switched back to Alkulu. "Welcome to the convocation. It is our pleasure to assist you. Please allow us to proceed with you to the witness entrance."

"Thank you." They started out immediately. Zahar glanced back at the ship and regretted it, getting white spots in her eyes.

"Please refrain from looking at the Bright without eye protection! Proceed quickly now for the witness."

They trotted along with her, following a yellow painted path. "Are you GenTwo?" Zahar asked. They yipped with surprise, but went back to their smooth talk.

"We are the Coursers, first of the GenThree to join the Leaf."

"Um . . . nice to meet you." She took the tail flicks as a good sign. *God help me. You're supposed to have special training for this first contact stuff. First Ramians, then Chike, now Coursers?*

They hopped on a tram for a short ride and unloaded at a side gate, passing through three decontamination areas, one wet, one dry and hot, and one ultraviolet or something, before entering a long corridor. Just as Zahar was starting to relax in the company of the Coursers, they passed tall desks, like ticket counters, with creatures—people—of other species. Zahar had never imagined such species, although almost all had a resemblance to some kind of Terran animal, or else her mind was just sorting them that way for lack of any other mental anchor.

Zombie started to squeak more, and seemed agitated to get out. "Hold on sweetie," Zahar soothed. "I don't know what's happening here, or what you have to do with any of it." Zahar fervently hoped she wasn't handing the poor rat over to some experiment after everything she'd survived on the *Cheetah*.

Their escort stopped at another gate. This one was shimmering like a force field. More decontamination? Zahar started to step forward, but a Courser stopped her. "Many pardons, diligent Human, but you must not go through."

"But?" Zahar held up the cage.

The Courser pointed with ziz nose to the floor. "Please, put the honored witness down and open the door." Zahar was confused. The rat would just run away. But she didn't. Zahar left her hand by the door in case Zombie wanted some comfort, but she came right out and scampered into the field.

Zombie froze. It looked like she was being electrocuted or x-rayed. Zahar jumped up. "What are you doing to her?"

The Coursers sprang forward to stop Zahar. "The witness is unharmed. Stay back!"

Finally, Zombie returned to normal. She shook herself and turned back to look at them. Her eyes. They were no longer the eyes of a rat. Intelligence, savvy, anger . . . Zahar had a strong feeling of danger. Her heart started pounding. What was happening? "Who are you?" she asked desperately.

The Coursers pushed against her thighs, forcing her away from the gate. "That one is a witness. Ze will testify to ziz treatment."

Oh my God! The rat that Tenshi had blasted with radiation and subjected to experimental treatment? She was going to testify against humanity? With one last spurning look, Zombie flung herself around and leaped away.

"Wait!" Zahar, called. "Please. Please forgive us!" Zahar dropped to her knees. She had just delivered humanity's deadliest witness. And now she was alone with nowhere to go.

"Human, do you require assistance?"

"Yes! Please. I need to go to a Human ship."

One Courser sat and poked the air again while another spoke.

"One moment while we find out how to help you. Please refrain from fainting, sickness, or extreme emotion. You will be sorted out in friendliness."

"What's going to happen with the witness?"

"Proceedings will begin soon. You will watch with your pack, from your ship."

"Yes, my ship—the *Midnight*."

"*Midnight* is still incoming," said the leader.

"*Midnight*. That's my ship."

5-Loftiness

In the Convocation Arena

Zahar woke the next day on a square pad in a large, dimly-lit, open dorm. She was still in her Chike robes and her bag was next to her. Her memories of getting there were vague after the shock of her separation from Quay and the transformation of Zombie.

Other square pads were mostly unoccupied, except for several of the dogs—Coursers—piled on one. Zahar sat up cautiously, finding an earclip and small ID card on her chest. She checked her bag for water and snacks—still there. *Yes!* She was starving. Quickly, and as quietly as possible, she ate a full ration. Then she clipped on the earpiece and ID card and slipped into the facilities. That was one thing she remembered, the icon of the spiral drain. She thought it was a cyclone, but apparently, it was the universal icon for facilities.

Grabbing her bag after, she slipped out. She emerged into a torus-like corridor, except gravity was on the side of the torus rather than along the curved outer edge. Instead, there were huge windows along the outer curved side. It was daytime and she could see the trees. So beautiful. But she was afraid to cross the busy corridor to look out. She edged along the inner wall. No one stopped her. No one even bothered looking her way. So many creatures of bewildering types. She saw a few Chike and many Coursers, but no Humans. No Ramians either.

Finally, she found a big screen with a map. A red dot was blinking obviously, so she touched it. "Your present position," her earclip announced. *Great! So organized!* She touched the room where she had been. "Rest area."

"Food court 1 . . . facilities . . . Alert! Methane entrance . . . Courser check-in . . . Convocation Floor . . . utilities . . . exit to shuttle drop." She tapped the different seating sections of the arena. "Reserved for the respected GenOne . . . Chike . . . general nitrogen oxygen." That sounded okay. She tapped it again and a blue line appeared, not on the ground, but somehow projected from her earclip. *Yes!* She stepped onto the virtual path as if she knew what she was doing.

Wait! If she left the rest area, would they know where to find her? And then she realized they could track her ID, of course. And the *Midnight* wasn't due for days. She wasn't going to sit around and miss all this.

Although she tried to be nonchalant, the projected line was a bit disorienting, so she kept her hand on the wall. Eventually, she came to a set of double doors, a large airlock, and by holding up her ID card to some invisible scanner, was allowed through.

The doors opened to a vast arena, bigger than some ships. Zahar stood at the top of a dizzying staircase, a ramp next to it, with several levels of railing running down the middle. The gigantic stadium was mostly empty, but chairs and platforms of various shapes could probably seat 100,000 Humans. Entire sectors of people could fit in here. A few sections were sealed off with different atmospheres, but lucky Humans, they were in the common atmosphere group.

At one end of the arena floor, a stage was being set up. It reminded Zahar of a big ceremony, like a graduation. Except whole species would graduate here, or be condemned.

"What is that?" She heard a disapproving voice over her translator. She turned to look and stifled a gasp. Three giant rats were staring at her. In fact, one was moseying over on ziz two back feet.

"How lovely," ze said. "A Human."

"They weren't invited," the first one sniffed.

"Nevertheless, here they are. What did I tell you?"

"It's only one," the smaller, third rat said, as they reluctantly followed zir over.

As the less sarcastic one approached her, Zahar grasped the rail and forced herself not to run away. *People. They are people!* But maybe mad relatives of Zombie?

"Allow me to introduce myself," ze said, bowing like an old-time actor. "I am Veez, patriarch of Slassamslaad, representative of the Scampers, friend to Humans, etc."

The other two actually rolled their eyes. Zahar stood gaping at zir—him, he said patriarch.

"It doesn't talk," Sniff said.

"It is primitive," Smaller said.

"It can't be primitive!" Sniff objected. "It's a primate—probably a GenFive or GenSix, but it has a translator."

Zahar frowned. "Ignore them," Veez advised. "I am a good friend of Humans. Do you know Beezan? Kelson? Iricana?"

Zahar gasped. "Iricana?"

"You see?" Veez said smugly. "Small galaxy."

"Nonsense," Sniff argued. "There must not be many Humans. What's your entire population?"

"Um, 15 billion, honor." Zahar answered.

"See! Only 15 billion. They probably all know each other."

And then they threw their heads back and laughed with great sniffs and whisker waving. *A joke.* Zahar smiled.

"It's only a young one, maybe lost," Veez said. "But come, sit with us and we will speak of mutual friends."

Zahar nodded and followed them. "Thank you. I'm Zahar, honor. Do you really know Iricana?" She sat with them, their whiskers occasionally tickling her, but apparently that was companionable.

"I do know her, but first, tell us, how did you end up here?—and do you have any snacks?"

7-Loftiness

Watcher

Of all the moments of his out-of-control life, Lanezi thought this one might be it—the most extreme, scariest, craziest turn of events yet—and if he dared to hope, ever.

Lanezi had paid his respects to Anitoran as an unwelcome guest at her funeral. The trouble with the pilots and the loss of Anitoran fueled more resentment against Getti Drann and the Humans. Io and Euro, although both healed, were too underweight to fast, and Lanezi gave it up under the turmoil, vowing, once again, to get his life back in order by next year.

Io and Euro were grateful beyond words for their treatment, but shocked and saddened at Anitoran's sacrifice. They stayed in the cabin as much as possible to avoid the Ramians.

Actually, everyone was grateful to be alive after Kells' hair-raising, heart-pounding, almost-didn't-make-it-seven-times swing jump. The only consolation was that they were done with swing jumping. Their last jump was originally supposed to be to the convocation, where they would drop off Raykatoo. But no. Unexpectedly, they made an extra jump to a planetary system in the thick of Chike space, where Raykatoo directed them to the second planet, not the a-rings. Getti Drann wisely did not object, but the pilots glared and flashed lime green. This was obviously a heavily populated system, with plenty of beacons and traffic patterns.

And now. Now. Lanezi's life took another bizarre turn as he sat in a Chike shuttle that had been sent for them. Raykatoo insisted on showing them something on the planet, like a tour, she said. What worried Lanezi was her choice of tourists: Getti Drann, Neah, Lanezi, Whisper, Shiwelna, Widinmay, and Reev. What did she intend with the pilots? For his part, Reev sat stoically in the Chike shuttle, overburdened with tokens.

Once they were safely through the atmosphere and the viewport shields were pulled back, they could watch their descent to a major Chike city. Reev tried to feign disinterest, but Lanezi and the rest of the Ramians pressed their faces against the windows, gawking.

It was dawn, and an old red sun shone through the dusty sky. When they got low enough in the haze, they could see a complex architecture of interlocking geometric patterns decorated in irritating color combinations.

Raykatoo was enraptured. Lanezi found it hard to believe she would leave again to go to the convocation. Whisper climbed out of the podpup pocket to Lanezi's shoulder and peered out. "Lots," she said.

They swept into an enclosed landing area in what looked like a red and black sports stadium. When they were settled and the doors opened, two rows of very fancy escorts with red and black striped poles lined their route. Raykatoo, all haughtiness now, took her place at the top of the ramp, with the Ramians scrambling into order behind her, Getti Drann stepping firmly to the front, with Neah behind and the pilots next, Reev last. Lanezi carefully put Whisper in the podpup pocket, and started down, so technically, he was the very last.

Once they left the hangar for the building, a new, fancier set of escorts took over and eventually, Raykatoo was greeted respectfully by three Chike with long red and black robes. They had become so used to Raykatoo speaking Ramian that when she switched back to Chike, Neah had to scramble to engage their translators.

The gravity was tolerable, but the dry heat sucked the moisture right out of his body. Lanezi hoped they would not be down here for long. Then he hoped he wouldn't be down here for life. They came to a set of fancy doors with another guard of three out front. This time there was no bowing and scraping. The tallest Chike clearly challenged Raykatoo, indicating her entourage without actually looking at them.

"Elder / Nest Mother, you bring the primitives / GenSix among us?"

Their manner was somewhat threatening. Although Raykatoo seemed powerful and intimidating to Lanezi, by comparison to these Chike, she was thin and run down. By some bold instinct, Neah and Drann stepped forward to flank her. The guards practically sprained their necks accidentally looking, and then snapping back to give Raykatoo the one-eye.

"The hatching is in progress, Nest Mother."

"That is why this one attends. Education is in order."

"You assume to educate these—"

"This one's crew, yes," Raykatoo said.

"They are GenSix," ze hissed.

"*Not yet!*"

They stared at each other, one eye to one eye. Whisper

buried her head in Lanezi's chest. Finally, the guard stepped aside, and they were allowed to pass, the guards' faces turned away. Lanezi kept his eyes on the floor and followed, but Whisper gave a little humph as they passed the last guard.

Reev's tokens clanked as they walked down yet another black and red corridor and entered the top of a grand arena. Below, at least a thousand red eggs were warming in black sand. Lanezi gasped as he realized that some had already hatched.

"Attend," Raykatoo said in Ramian. "You are greatly honored to witness." They stood along the railing. Around the arena, hundreds of Chike were observing. The smell of dry scales was so strong. Lanezi was used to it, but the Ramians struggled to keep neutral colors. He let out a relieved breath. This is why Raykatoo brought them.

They stood at least an hour, watching as the hatchlings first began to cry out, then the eggs would rock, then small holes were punched out, and finally, the eggs would tear open, and small red Chike would awkwardly climb out of the rubbery shells and flop onto the sand.

As more and more hatched, the stench of mucusy egg lining and the irritating mewling of the newborn became almost unbearable, although Whisper was enchanted. "Babies!"

"We will go soon," Raykatoo assured them. She gave Drann a stern look. "You witness what was lost."

Getti Drann nodded, actually teary-eyed. "We see, Exempt, and are greatly saddened."

Reev scowled and stared at the ceiling. Neah flashed curiosity, and then quickly went back to neutral. "Yes?" Raykatoo said to him.

"Forgive me Exempt, I was just curious." She indicated he should go on, despite Reev's glare. Neah pointed to the adult Chike down on the floor. They were clearing up the shells and herding the clumsy little ones along a path. But a few were escorted in a different direction. "How are they being sorted?" Lanezi hoped that wasn't a rude question. Maybe they had only 10% female or something.

Raykatoo sighed, and at first she didn't seem like she would answer. She had water brought for them to drink. Finally, after more hesitation, she said, "At one time—ancient times—only one in a thousand eggs would survive to adulthood. Of course, now all are cared for. But unlike your very fortunate species, not all have capacity."

"Capacity?" Neah asked. "Sentience?"

"All are sentient. They have feelings and thoughts. Perhaps not as advanced as the small one." Raykatoo indicated Whisper, who gave a scowl and another humph.

"What happens to them?" Neah asked, pointing to the small group.

"No," Raykatoo said, "not that group. The ten percent are fully intelligent, brilliant even. The rest . . . they can usually be trained for something. Labor, escorts."

They were stunned. "Your entire star-spanning civilization was built by 10% of the population?" Getti Drann asked.

"Originally, by less than 1%. We've only recently increased the intelligent portion."

And now that he knew, Lanezi could see that the 90% could barely crawl in a line. They would need some training up. A small part of Lanezi was grateful. *At least the galaxy is not overrun by Chike.* And then he remembered Raykatoo saying those who do nothing at all are not fed. A chill went down his spine. What was Raykatoo trying to teach them here?

They finally left the arena. Lanezi breathed a prayer of relief —a second too soon. "One more stop." Reev clutched his chest, but Shiwelna grabbed his arm and gave him a tug with a flash of get-a-grip. "It is a great honor." Raykatoo indicated they should enter another door. Back in the stadium, in a private viewing area, they met four younger Chike who sprang to their feet and bowed deeply to Raykatoo. But they stared openly at the rest of them, jittering with excitement.

Raykatoo proceeded to present the Ramians, and Human, to the four: Exempts-in-training. "They have never met GenFour. It is a great education."

"Humph!" Whisper poked Lanezi. "Down." Carefully, he set her down. She nonchalantly wandered over to the Exemptlings, as Raykatoo backtracked.

"Our pardon, the podpup Whisper," Raykatoo added. The Exemptlings stared down in puzzlement, except for one, who slowly dropped to all fours to look Whisper in the eye. That one will go far, Lanezi thought.

"I look forward to the day when our people meet again," Getti Drann said to them.

They all pulled back in astonishment, except Raykatoo. Apparently, the Exemptlings had no hope for them.

Outside again, Raykatoo paused. "The Exempt are the most intelligent Chike, the ones with vast intellect and flexibility to work with others." She shook her head. "We are not like your people, where everyone, unless defective, is intelligent, where progress is only a matter of education, opportunity, and ambition. With a little self-discipline on your part," she shot a glance at Reev, but directed herself to Drann, *imagine what your people could do.*"

Reev flashed annoyance, but Drann was listening intently. Raykatoo was trying to tell them something, like they had potential, even after she said she would label them GenSix. She swept her claw toward the stadium. "We have taken control of the weakness in our society. You must take control of yours."

Drann's colors slowly went to yellow. "We appreciate your education, Exempt."

She drew herself tall, and took a breath, as if stealing herself to go back to the ship. "Exempt," Lanezi said, before he could even think straight. "You are a nest mother. Isn't this your place? Why don't you stay?"

The others gasped in shock. "Stay," Whisper repeated as she returned to Lanezi for a pick up.

"But we have to get home!" Drann said.

"No! You have to get to the convocation!" Raykatoo corrected.

"But we don't know how," Shiwelna said, in a panic.

"The Humans have their own kind of sense. Lanezi will figure it out," Raykatoo said, unconcerned. Then she drew up to her full height and haughtiness. "I consider our agreement complete. Send my painting. I wish both your species a fair assessment." And she turned and walked away without them.

They had a moment of collective panic, standing by themselves outside the Chike stadium. "We're rid of her!" Reev hissed, thrilled.

"Back to the shuttle, calmly," Drann said.

"Do you have any idea how to get to the convocation?" Shiwelna asked Lanezi.

"No. But we're not that far, I don't think. She's been curving us around."

"I thought so."

"We should go back to Ramian space," Reev said. "We don't need to go to this convocation."

"Yes we do!" they all said at once.

"Quiet!" Drann said again, flashing orange. "Walk back the way we came and hope that shuttle is still there. Assume they will take us back just to get rid of us."

. . .

Only when they were safely back on the *Watcher,* confusion and relief erupting from the crew as they realized they were free of Raykatoo, did Drann let them talk.

"I don't understand what just happened," Reev finally admitted.

"She's giving us a chance," Drann answered.

"But she's not coming to the convocation."

"It doesn't matter. She introduced us to the young exempts, as if we had a future. She'll speak on our behalf, if—IF!—we present ourselves as one, stable, civilized society. We need to go and we need to stop squabbling."

The others nodded in agreement. Drann turned to Lanezi. "The shuttle is waiting. See to her belongings. And for all our sakes, figure out where we're going." Ze walked away, fully in command once again.

Lanezi hurried to Raykatoo's cabin, and joy of joys, when he opened the door, there was a huge hologram with the route to the convocation. *Thank you!* After everything that had happened, Raykatoo was on their side.

10-Loftiness Eve

Midnight, at the convocation planet

Midnight finally arrived within shuttle distance of the planet, so Jarvie was on alert. Hundreds of ships, none Human, orbited in various traffic patterns. They were granted a priority orbit. Normally, he would have loved all the action, but he was uneasy. He had not forgotten that Sky had manipulated a crew of Humans to jump to a convocation she could not have known existed.

Sky had been acting like her old self, and Beezan seemed so relieved that he didn't care about why. Jarvie stalled getting ready for bed until Beezan had gone to sleep. Then he took Star to stay over at Terina's.

Jarvie dressed in work clothes, packed a survival bag, and snuck into Beezan's dark cabin. Despite his intended vigilance, he fell asleep on the deck, only to be awakened by Sky talking. "Bee now."

"What?"

"Now."

"Now what?"

"We go."

Beezan groaned. "Sky, where?"

"Down."

"No. We can't."

"Bee promised."

Beezan sighed. "Night light."

In the dim light, Jarvie could see that Beezan wasn't just sleepy. He seemed dazed. Slowly, he got dressed. Then, seemingly resigned, he picked up Sky. "We go."

Although Sky must have known that Jarvie was following them, she didn't say anything, and Beezan was too dazed to notice.

It was 02:00 in the morning, shiptime, but even so, the rimways were more deserted than usual. They didn't pass a single person on their way to the shuttle hangar. There was no one in the hangar either, but the *Bird of Prey* was prepped and the tube was already extended.

They got in the lock together—there was no way that Beezan and Sky didn't see him. But Beezan had a faraway look and Sky merely said, "Good Zharvie."

Along for the ride, I guess. And it was a ride. Everything was automated. He didn't call the Command Bay or any planetside monitor, and no one objected to their departure. "Sky, who's flying the shuttle?"

"Shuttle."

Jarvie frowned; from their trajectory, they were clearly going to land on the dayside of the planet. "Sky, we're going through an atmosphere. I'm going to strap you in." She let Jarvie put her in a podpup box, and when he got back to the controls, Beezan was strapped. "Do you know where we're going?" he asked Beezan.

"Down," Beezan answered simply, as if podpup brain had taken over his mind.

Jarvie said a prayer to himself, something between *please don't let this be happening* and *whatever God wills*.

Inside the arena, Zahar huddled with her new friends. Their fear of breaking the taboo seemed forgotten. They were irreverently funny, completely informal, and unabashedly enthusiastic. She imagined that the Chike despised them. They also maintained a generous stash of snacks. Zahar felt very safe with them, but occasionally, she remembered the look in Zombie's eyes, and feared that Zombie was somehow related.

The stage setup was complete and they were testing a three-dimensional projection, broadcasting various scenes from around the convocation. Zahar couldn't understand the scenes until they started showing a shuttle landing. "Veez!"

"Yes, child?"

"Is this live?"

"Yes, why? Oh! That's a Human shuttle!"

"Maybe the Humans are sending a reporter," Smaller said.

"Don't be silly," Sniff said. "Human spectators aren't allowed. We can't have the GenFour running amok here."

But Veez looked serious. "Their harbinger is already here."

Yes, Zahar remembered, a Human named Oatah had been "found." How long would the shuttle stay? "Should I go out there?"

"You mean for a ride?" Veez asked.

"Don't you want to stay for the convo?" Sniff asked.

"Yes, but not as much as I want to get home."

"Understandable," Veez said quietly.

She sat frozen, watching the screen. Two Humans came

down the ramp, one very tall. They had a confused meeting with the Coursers. Then they set off, to the witness entrance, where Zahar had gone.

The camera followed them. The view became very close up as they approached the final force field. Veez sat up, suddenly serious. "It can't be," he whispered. Zahar tensed, remembering what happened with Zombie. Was one of the Humans actually *not Human*? That was a scary thought.

Zahar realized the entire arena had gone silent. Everyone was watching. The Humans hesitated. They seemed distraught. The shorter one then took a podpup out of his jacket. The fuzzy black pup reached up and patted his face. Tears streamed down as he set zir on the floor.

For some reason, Veez gasped and murmured some kind of blessing.

The podpup scampered through the field just as Zombie did. And then the tall Human and the Coursers were forcibly holding the shorter man back.

In the field, the podpup was transformed. It was still a podpup, but it was somehow more dignified. It turned to look back, and the man fainted, saved from hitting the ground only by his companion and a pile of Coursers.

"Veez! I need to get to that shuttle!"

"So do I! Packmates! A romp!"

Terina awoke to the keening of Star and Rocket. "What's happening? Lights!"

They were hunched on the foot of the bunk keening. "Hush! Hush, babies!" She gathered them in her lap. "What's wrong?" But they were inconsolable.

Terina plucked her p'link from its wall holder. "Doctor?"

A sleepy Katie answered. "Terina—*what is that?*"

"It's the pups!"

"All three?"

"No-oh my God, just Star and Rocket. Something's happened to Sky!" She grabbed her jacket and carried them up the stairs and down the rimway. Katie was right behind her, headed to Honor Beezan's cabin. Iricana appeared, speaking into her level 1 s'link: "*Midnight,* open the door of Beezan's cabin."

Katie ran down the stairs, but Terina didn't have to. She knew. "He's not here," Katie called up. Then she went through to Jarvie's room, "Jarvie's not here."

"How could they leave without us knowing?" Iricana asked as others appeared. Then she looked at Terina. "Sweetheart, you have Star."

Terina couldn't hold the tears back. "Jarvie asked me to keep him. We trade off sometimes so we can sleep."

Her mom was suddenly there, with her arm around her. "It's not your fault."

"Maybe they're not gone," Thunder said. "Thunder to Jarvie."

"Jarvie's p'link is out of range." *Midnight* reported.

Iricana's shoulders slumped. "*Midnight,* are all shuttles accounted for?"

"Yes. All shuttles except *Bird of Paradise* are in the hangar."

"Where is *Bird?*"

"It departed at 02:47 for the planet."

"Who gave clearance?"

"You did, Captain."

The captain stared at the s'link in her hand. "That's not possible."

. . .

Terina didn't even think of going back to sleep. The pups, still whimpering, were in Med Bay so Katie could keep an eye on them. Terina tried to make herself useful, so she brought a snack for the crew in the Command Bay. Her mom and Falcon were on duty and Iricana was reviewing ship records with Taj.

"Thank you, sweetheart." Her mom took the protein drink, but Falcon froze, one arm reaching halfway to her drink. "*Bird of Paradise* on the Ship Tracker! Just exiting the planet's atmosphere." She put a graphic onscreen.

"Thank God," Iricana said. "Open the hangar."

"It's already opening," her mom reported.

"Heaven help us," Iricana said. "No contact?"

"No, Captain," Falcon answered.

"Katie," Iricana ordered, "meet me and Sequoia in the Entry Lounge. Taj, tube duty."

"Yes, Honor."

The captain tapped her s'link. "Thunder, Kelson, to the Command Bay, please."

"ETA, 27 minutes," Falcon reported.

"I can't believe Beezan would leave without telling us," Terina's mom said, hurrying out with Iricana, and neither seemed to notice that Terina tagged along.

"Do you think Sky forced him?" Iricana asked.

"She's a podpup. What could she do? And even under duress, he's a darn stubborn pilot. He wouldn't do anything he didn't want to do."

"But what if he wanted to?"

They frowned at each other.

In the Entry Lounge, Terina took a moment to grab a hold bar and adjust to nogee, but her mom hooked into the command panel like it was nothing. "Well, the hangar door is obviously open," the captain said, looking out the window.

"Guide beams activated," her mom reported. "Four minutes."

Taj floated in, carrying his helmet. Terina helped him cross-check the suit before he went around through the safety hatch to the tubeway. Terina grabbed a hold bar to stay out of the way. Three minutes later, the shuttle came in and touched down perfectly.

"Program complete," *Midnight* announced.

Her mom scowled. "What program?"

They waited to see if someone aboard would take over the checklist, but nothing happened. "We don't actually know if anyone is aboard," Iricana noted.

"True," her mom agreed. "*Midnight*, deploy auto anchors on *Bird*."

After it was secure, Taj put on his helmet and extended the tube and went through to secure it. "Seal is green. I'm opening the shuttle hatch." They waited tensely for Taj to report. "What the—? Who are—? Arggg, no link. They can't hear me. Captain, I'm sending them through."

"Who?" they all said to each other.

"No use guessing," Iricana said. Terina peeked through the hatch window. It was a sad scene. "It's honor Beezan, with Jarvie helping." She turned to look at Katie. "No Sky."

"Oh, no—"

"—oh my God, a Scamper!"

"What?" Katie peered through the little window with her.

"Tube hatch sealed," Taj reported, sounding mystified.

"Open the door, Terina," her mom said. Beezan and Jarvie came through first. Both had tearstained faces and Beezan looked disoriented. Jarvie was trying to steer him by the arm. Katie grabbed his other arm.

"*Midnight,*" Katie ordered, "Clear a private path to the Med Bay."

Next through was the Scamper, who righted himself with a flick of the tail and coasted in. "Greetings, my dear friends. I wish the circumstances were cheerier."

"Veez!" her mom nearly shouted. "*We risked our lives dragging you halfway across the galaxy and now you're BACK?*"

"A thousand pardons . . . circumstances . . ."

Iricana had flown across the room to check on Beezan, but looked back at Veez and her eyes narrowed. "Did you have something to do with this?" she indicated the stricken Beezan.

"Captain, of course not. I am here to help, at the request of—"

And then a girl, not much older than Terina, swung through the lock, and came to attention, addressing Sequoia. "God is Most Glorious. Veez and Zahar requesting permission to board."

Iricana gasped. "Zahar?"

And the girl blinked. Her professional demeanor dropped away and she launched into Iricana's arms, sobbing.

Beezan let Katie and Jarvie pull him to the lift, but then did his best to stand and walk normally in the rimway. He'd heard the murmurs of sorrow and exclamations of recognition in the Entry Lounge. His fuzzy mind was clearing, only to be replaced by a searing pain, a heartbreak far greater than losing his first podpup, more devastating than losing his grandfather, or Lander, or even his ship. It was as bad as when he lost Nurita— maybe worse than that. It was as if Sky had never really existed. All the love he'd had—did it just disappear into the void?

They stopped outside Med Bay, but he shook his head and kept going. Katie let go of his arm, so Jarvie brought him to his cabin and went in with him. He made it to the bunk and sat back against the wall, Jarvie still holding his arm and sitting next to him.

Beezan struggled to talk. "Tell me again . . . what the girl said on the shuttle."

"Zahar. She said . . . they are witnesses. GenOnes that are somehow constrained in the bodies of lesser beings. When they go through the field, it frees them from the constraints, at least mentally." Jarvie took a shaky breath. "They're going to testify against us."

"Against?"

The door slid open and Katie set Star on the top step, but he just slumped, almost rolling down the stairs. Katie grabbed him and brought him down, handing him to Jarvie. "They've been crying." Jarvie pulled Star between him and Beezan, nodding. Katie gripped both their shoulders. "Call if you need me."

"Star, Star, we're here." Jarvie picked him up and put him in Beezan's lap and suddenly they were all crying and hugging each other. It didn't help the pain go away, but Beezan didn't have to face it alone.

Although she had a flutter of guilt that the other two men left the lounge in grief, Zahar was now sobbing with joy. She was back on a Human ship. With people she knew! She stopped crying and started hugging.

"How are you here?" Iricana asked. "You were on the *Cheetah*, and they were taken by the Chike—you were with Quay! Let's get you to Consultation Hall," Iricana said. "Sequoia, call an all-crew meeting."

"It's 05:00."

"No one will care."

"Yes," Zahar grabbed a hold bar. "Yes, sorry." And she let them bring her. They went up the lift, and around the rimway, section by section, bringing her closer to the heart of a Human ship. "Evan? Caspia? Are they here?"

"No, only you. And Veez."

As they passed the kitchen, Veez hesitated. "Captain, do you mind if I make myself a bite?"

"Feel free, Veez—and welcome back."

Just as they were nearing Consultation Hall, a Ramian came out of his cabin. "Zahar!"

"Danulell!" More hugging.

"Small galaxy," whispered a familiar voice—Thayne. *My God, everyone is here.*

"How—"

"Quay?" Danulell asked desperately.

"Down on the planet," she answered, pointing.

A surge of emerald green lit up the walls.

Iricana put her hand on Danulell's arm. "Everyone in the Hall. We'll take it from the top."

They were sitting down when Zahar realized she was still in the Chike robes. She unceremoniously threw them on the deck behind her chair as Veez slipped in with his snack.

Iricana was the captain. Okay. As long as it wasn't Thayne. Nkiroo was here. *They escaped the colony!* "Melawn, Tenshi?" she whispered while everyone was getting settled.

"On the colony," Nkiroo answered, somewhat subdued.

"Okay, please," Iricana got their attention. "Honor Kelson, a prayer please."

After the prayer, Iricana nodded at Zahar. She scanned their faces and started to tear up again. "Umm, okay." *Pull yourself together! Or you'll end up a lowly med tech again.* "Yes, Captain. I was on the *Cheetah*, as you know, which was taken by the Chike. After we dropped everyone else off at the Colony, Evan, Caspia, Quay, and I continued on the same Chike ship called *Sandstorm* with the Exempt Pascal. The Chike were searching for more harbingers."

"What are the harbingers, really?"

"They're representatives. One for each GenFour planet. All species of a planet are called a clade. Each harbinger will speak for their clade at the convocation. I was sent down to the planet with Quay. He's with the harbingers." Zahar grabbed her bag from the pile of robes. "Here's a map." She pulled out a small paper map she'd drawn of the arena complex and passed it to the captain.

"Where are Evan and Caspia?" Iricana asked.

"I assume they're still on the *Sandstorm*. The Exempt Pascal's ship." They frowned in confusion.

She looked to Veez, who shrugged like a Human. "There are a hundred Chike ships out there."

"Wait!" She dug into her bag again. *Evan, you are a genius!* "Here." She pulled out the model of the *Sandstorm* that Evan had given her, complete with Chike markings. "This one."

Nkiroo's eyes went wide with joy as he snatched it from her. "Oh, and there's this." She undid the ear clip. "Maybe you can tie it into the ship. It's some kind of universal translator. Maybe Veez could help," she suggested mildly.

"So each clade has a harbinger, including Humans?" Iricana asked.

"Each of the GenFour. Our harbinger's name is Oatah."

Half the people at the table gasped. "Small galaxy," Thayne whispered again. But the others sat up.

"That's good news actually," Kelson said. "No one could represent better." There were nods around the table.

"But the job of the harbinger is to plead our case for continued existence?" Iricana asked.

Zahar glanced to Veez, who held out his paws. "Well, that's putting it . . . well, for your continued . . . freedom to roam the galaxy . . . which may be related to your existence . . . yes."

"And the witnesses testify for or against. And we have Sky. That can only be good," Katie said.

Zahar shook her head. "There are more witnesses. I don't know how many more. I escorted another witness. One of Tenshi's rats. One that she had experimented on. I mean the treatment was supposedly humane, as much as it could be . . . but you know, it never really can be."

They all went shades of pale, gray, or faded blue. Iricana closed her eyes. "Will our treatment of animals be our undoing?"

21 / THE RIVERS CONVERGE

11-Loftiness

Midnight, in orbit around the convocation planet

Beezan woke up early with a stiff neck from sitting all night. He didn't suffer the shock of suddenly remembering his loss, as he hadn't slept well enough to forget. Jarvie and Star were huddled at the foot of his bunk asleep, so he gently slid off. At least Star was snoring instead of whimpering.

If Star and Rocket had been so distressed, then it was certain that Sky, at least Sky the podpup, was gone. He closed his eyes. *I've been through worse.*

Don't think about that! But the memory flooded over him, coming out of jump that day to find his whole crew, including his fiancée, dead. The red lights, the pain, the guilt, the depression. He had gone to the airlock but *Drumheller* wouldn't open it. It took two days to win the battle with himself to survive. And when he realized he'd have to deal with the bodies, he had another battle, one that he could not win. But somehow, with sedatives and *Drumheller* leading him step by step, it was done.

And then two more weeks alone to come in. Although he hid it from counseling, he was broken.

And he didn't want to go back to that. Even though he didn't have the *Drumheller* to help. *I'm not alone. I have Jarvie, and Star.* And—he knew the minute he walked out the door he would be surrounded by friendship and sympathy. And he had that one last image of Sky, after her transformation, looking back at him with surprise, with comprehension, and with love. *Love is never wasted.*

After their fast breakfast, they said a long round of prayers in the prayer room, even letting the pups in. Everyone, except Thayne, reached out to Beezan, sending him messages of support and speaking to him briefly. They also gave him just enough space. He let it all soak in. As they went down the stairs back to the rimway, he even asked Iricana if he could come to the all-crew meeting.

"It's just a quick meeting about crew assignments."

"I need something to do," he whispered.

She nodded and they walked to the Consultation Hall together.

When they assembled, Beezan took a seat by the door in case he suddenly had to leave. "Taj and Gola are on duty," Sequoia told everyone. "We don't leave the Command Bay unattended in this crazy traffic zone."

Iricana looked at Beezan like she wasn't sure she could leave *him* in charge of a ship in a crazy traffic zone. "If you're up to it honor, you can have the night shift with Jarvie and Danulell."

Ah, Jarvie would be monitor and backup pilot. Actually a smart decision.

"Yes, please."

"Okay, then, Zahar can join Katie in the Med Bay."

Zahar tensed and sat up. All eyes that had been flitting to Beezan suddenly focused on her. "Honor, Captain," she said nervously, "could I have a different assignment please?"

Iricana seemed puzzled. "Well, you have experience in med tech and we already have monitors."

"Captain, can we talk privately?"

"We're family here. We're here to listen."

"Okay." She took a big breath. "I was conscripted / quarantined / sequestered into that Med Tech job. I always hated it. My oath is done. I can't be quarantined now that the secret is out."

Beezan tried to take that in. Obviously it was a short summary of a very big deal. An oath. Like he and Jarvie had taken. And this Lanezi who had taken an oath and broken it. Beezan glanced at Jarvie, who was just staring at a view of the planet onscreen.

Thayne took that beat of silence to say, "You're not the captain any more, you know." He said it with such a tone that Beezan took offense on Zahar's behalf, but then realized that those who knew Thayne just ignored it. *Who are we dealing with here?*

"I'm not asking to be captain! But I'm not a med tech. I'm a monitor. I don't want to cause trouble, but this whole thing derailed my life years ago and I think it's reasonable to give me a different job! Please."

"Like our lives weren't derailed on the colony—"

"Thayne, you're excused," Iricana said, without even looking at him.

"Thank you, *Captain*." He got up like his behavior earned

him a reward. Beezan was appalled. They were used to this? And he felt bad for Zahar. He'd almost been commandeered himself, so he understood.

Katie was sympathetic. "I don't want to force people, but I could use the help. Zhenulell and Danumae are still learning our systems and they mostly take care of Ramians."

"If we get Evan and Caspia back, you'll have another doctor," Nkiroo suggested.

"But how long will that be?" Iricana asked.

Zahar was polite. But Beezan could see that she was determined—and she was right. Still angry from Thayne's attitude and picturing how it would be to be sent to some ship, now that he didn't have the *Drumheller*, and be told he's not even a pilot. "I'll help. In Med," he said.

Iricana smiled gently. "You have a six hour shift in the Command Bay, honor."

"I can do two hours in Med." He stopped to collect his shaky voice. "I need something to do."

There was a moment of consideration.

"I can do two hours too," Jarvie said. "I have my teen training med certificate."

"Me too!" Terina added. "I mean I could do my certificate ..."

"I can also help," Kelson volunteered.

"Dad, you haven't been a med tech for 70 years!"

"Yep! But I remember it better than yesterday."

At that, people started to laugh and Iricana sat back in her chair.

"Okay, Zahar will join Beezan's shift as monitor. Katie will work out the rest. Thank you all for volunteering."

Zahar looked up, teary eyed. "Thank you, Captain, everyone."

. . .

12-Loftiness

Watcher, headed for the convocation

Lanezi, jump pilot of the *Watcher* for the first time, let all his frustrations of their journey course through him. Rather than jumping in a serene and peaceful state of mind, he planned to use that hurt, that longing, even that anger to power their jump across the leaf.

It would be like jumping from Harbor to Earth—as Alesta Eve had apparently done. No swing jumps, just the a-rings and the ways. On their last lap, he sensed the route easily. It was so strong, as if a thousand streams had come together into a mighty river.

And there was something else, something familiar. Humans?

He thrusted into the path. They'd done swing jumps for hours; this would be far less. He put his mind in another zone. He knew he was bringing them to the convocation: first stop on the long way home.

Midnight, in orbit around the convocation planet

It was three in the morning, the first night of Beezan's shift, Jarvie sitting between him and Zahar, when the first crazy thing happened.

"Honor," Zahar reported, "a Ramian beacon has just appeared on the ship tracker." Jarvie accessed the location and flicked it up to the main screen.

"I'm trying to tie in your Ramian trans—wait," Zahar said. "A Human signal, from the same place."

"The same ship?" Beezan asked.

"It seems like it."

"*Midnight*," Beezan ordered, "can you confirm if the new Ramian and Human beacons are one ship or two?"

"Both beacons are from the same Ramian ship: *Watcher*."

Watcher, in the convocation system

Lanezi tried to wake up. He tried to open his eyes, but the aftereffects of making the longest jump of his life pushed him back to sleep, or unconsciousness. *Did I recess?* But no, he wasn't in the chair. His eyes finally squinted open. He wasn't even on a Human ship.

The jump. Yes, they had jumped to some big convocation alright. He'd practically crashed into it. Way to make a good impression for the Ramians. And not wanting to face that, he fell back into his stupor.

Yosemite Valley

Melawn had been cold before. The upper caves back home were freezing. Ships could be cold, docking stations, shuttles. And lack of sunshine was normal in space. But this! This constant state of being wet was intolerable, especially during fast.

Yosemite, closest to the ocean, was damp and windy even when it wasn't raining. The buildings wiped out by the tsunami had only been partially and hastily rebuilt. And there weren't nearly enough with the influx of new people. Hundreds of people were camped all over the village, using their primitive waxed canvas tents. In town, the men's hall was packed solid. They slept on the hard floor shoulder to shoulder, and if you needed to get up at night, too bad.

Melawn was actually grateful for his spot on the floor. Curled up in his blanket, on top of his mat, it was the warmest he ever got. And he didn't have to get up at 03:00 for breakfast-cooking duty. *Count your blessings*, he scolded himself.

The wakeup bell rang and lanterns were lit at the ends of the hall. Quickly, he got up and put on his muddy day clothes, still damp. The rain had stopped for the moment so they could eat their hash and cheese in peace. They gathered in the courtyard for prayers, but the sun barely made itself known through the thick clouds. Gray. It was the color of his world, both outer and inner. He was ashamed to admit how unhappy he was, how much he missed his people, how lonely he was among the masses. He had hoped to find some comfort in fasting, but it was a foggy comfort, ill-defined and hard to hold on to.

Melawn thought that under these circumstances it would be easy to recruit 250 people for the new colony. But no one wanted to leave their family or their "home" even though they'd only been there a matter of weeks. And his instructions, to look for young, hardy people who can work together? Good. And who have outdoor skills. Spacers? No. Even the few Earthborn were city people.

Jagger, the only self-proclaimed "Montana Mountain Man" on the planet, was Melawn's poster child, but they needed 249 clones. The Zann were off limits. Technically, this whole valley was their colony and they were getting concerned about the resource overload.

The farm teams were their best bet. So Jagger and Melawn took a cart out to the fields and slogged through the mud to talk to them. They showed them the plans for a new colony and talked about travel, adventure, and independence.

A tough young woman named Maki joked, "Hey, find me a husband, and I'll go."

"Find your own husband!" Jagger teased back.

"Oh, right. I'm out here all day with this lot." Melawn looked where she was pointing over her shoulder. Two teenagers, a grandpa, and three women. Melawn took her point. And later got to thinking, they'd be bottlenecking the gene pool in the new colony. Best to mix people well beforehand.

So he made a spreadsheet, with qualities, ages, genetic diversity. Then he stalked through the men's hall until he found a good humored, sass-proof young man. Not as skinny as other spacers and he was an engineer.

The next day when Melawn told Jagger the plan, Jagger lost his hat laughing, but drove Melawn and Evgeni, the unsuspecting engineer, out to the field. Just as they approached, the sun finally broke through the clouds. Evgeni stood up in the cart and cheered. Jagger whispered, "Are you sure about this one?"

"I used math."

When they got to the field, Maki was standing to her knees in mud. She had weeds in her hair and a shovel balanced on her shoulder like a lance while she gazed up at the sun. Her strength and high spirits radiated.

They all clamored out of the cart. "Hey, Maki!" Melawn tried to sound like a casual colonist. "This is Evgeni."

"God is Most Glorious," they both said formally.

"What brings you out today?" she asked.

"About the new colony," Jagger drawled, looking at the sky.

Her head snapped back to Evgeni, who brilliantly, and perhaps hopefully, grasped the situation.

"Well," she said, "look what the beast brought in! We can always use another helper." She grasped his arm and turned him toward the rest of the team. "You can ride home with us."

As they walked off, Evgeni turned back to them with wide eyes and an embarrassed smile, but he never slowed down.

"Remember our deal!" Melawn shouted to Maki.

"How many is that for the colony?" Jagger asked, stifling a laugh.

"Eighty-two."

15-Loftiness

Watcher, at the convocation planet

Three days later, Lanezi finally dragged himself to the little kitchen in Io and Euro's cabin. He'd never moved back to his cabin, as the ghost of Raykatoo was too strong. He had vague memories of the twins bringing him food while he slept, but he was ravenous.

The twins were in the main room. They were bustling around and whispering with excitement. They were smiling. Not smiling like they brought him cookies, smiling like deranged fools. "What's happening?"

They snapped to attention. *They are scheming.* "Honor! We have exciting news," Euro said.

Io couldn't contain himself. "A ship! A Human ship!"

"Here?"

"Yes!" They both hugged him excitedly.

"Praise the Lord," Lanezi whispered, finding a chair to sit down. "What ship?"

"*Midnight.*"

"Hmmm, I don't know it."

"You will," Euro said. "We're going in two hours!"

Lanezi looked around. They were packing. Fancy clothes hung on the wall. And it was too quiet. "Two hours? Where . . .?"

"The pups are getting baths," Io explained. "Neah and Sontula will take us in a shuttle. We have to wear these clothes."

"We're dressing up?"

"It's an occasion!"

Lanezi thought about it. "It is an occasion. We're reunited with humanity."

"Reunited!" They shouted, smiling with glee.

Lanezi tried to keep his panic in check aboard the beautiful Ramian shuttle as they transferred to the *Midnight*. The twins were so excited. They had been so brave aboard the *Sandstorm* that he hadn't realized how much they'd hated it.

Lanezi was excited too, but also had a sense of dread. He got out his Human p'link and looked at his last photo of Katie, two years ago. And since then, he'd only received three words. But they were good words, saying "yes" to marrying him. But would she still want to marry him? Was she alive? Was she trapped somewhere else in the sectors?

At the Entry Lounge they were greeted by a man named Taj, who insisted on taking care of their luggage and podpups himself, and a very elderly man named Kelson, who escorted them to TopRim with a twinkle in his eye and a cryptic saying, "If you wait long enough, it will be good weather." Neither of them blinked at Neah and Sontula, as if they met Ramians all the time.

Although Lanezi wondered if picking up lost Humans and having Ramian guests was so normal these days that the captain didn't even meet them, Kelson was quiet on that subject, and led them around the rimway and up the stairs to the Consultation Hall.

Lanezi stopped. It was set up for a meeting, but all the chairs were facing the front, with an aisle in the middle, and people were already sitting in them. Everyone turned to look. Lanezi stepped back, embarrassed to interrupt, even though they were smiling. And then the twins took him firmly by the elbows and started walking him up the aisle, and there was music! "What are you doing?" he whispered.

But they were grinning wildly again and looking ahead. Lanezi looked up. A small, beautiful woman was standing alone at the front, in a dress with roses, a dress the color of a jump thread. He stopped. He blinked. It could not be. He gasped and grabbed his chest. *Katie!*

She smiled, tears already running down her cheeks.

All sense left him. He sprinted to the front and scooped her up, swinging her around and around as the audience cheered and clapped.

Never be separated again! Never! Never! He had to force himself not to squeeze her too hard. *Thank you! Thank you!* He prayed, stunned that his long-wished-for day had come. His mind was hyperventilating, thoughts short circuiting, except for one.

Lanezi set Katie down and gently took her face into his hands. He didn't need to ask if she still wanted to marry him. Aside from the entire scheme, it was in her eyes. It was supposed to be solemn, serious, prayerful, but he shouted it out, ***"We will all, verily, abide by the Will of God!"***[1]

Katie tearfully repeated it. She barely finished when a woman slapped her hand on the panel and said, "I so witness!" – *Iricana! Oh, my God.*

"I so witness," said a voice behind him. Lanezi, holding Katie to his side, turned them both to look. *Jarvie!* And then Iricana and Jarvie and the twins were hugging them. The people abandoned their chairs and made a giant jumping, crying, hugging mass around them. Lanezi kept one arm around Katie and reached out with the other, hugging and handshaking everyone. His eyes were blurry, but he could have sworn he saw a giant rat in the back, sneaking a piece of cake.

Hours later, after some serious prayers, food, dancing, and actually meeting the giant rat, he and Katie headed to her cabin. It was the happiest moment of his life. All the abandonment, all the pain, all the longing seemed as nothing compared to this joy. He was bursting with gratitude.

Inside the cabin, Katie was suddenly a little shy, and Lanezi was hit by a wave of jump exhaustion. "I just need to sit for a minute," he said, and barely made it to the bunk, collapsing across it. "I've only come across the galaxy for you." She snuggled up next to him, her gentle laughter ringing in his soul.

Beezan soaked in the joy of the festivities. Even the new people seemed to understand he was struggling. Everyone checked on him, brought him food, and generally watched over him. He stayed until his shift. He'd spoken to Neah ship-to-ship and briefly with Sontula, but they'd been reunited and busy with Danulell's family. Meeting again was so incredible and improbable that he took it as an omen. That's when he realized why Terina was sticking close to him. He even heard her whisper to her grandfather, "The rivers converge."

It was only when his shift started and Jarvie and Zahar arrived, that Neah and Sontula requested to enter the Command Bay and he actually got to sit and talk with them.

"I'm so happy and astonished to see you, Captain Beezan," Neah told him. They both hugged him, colors running pink. "And you, Jarvie!"

"Me too!" Jarvie said, towering over them and even standing on his tiptoes. "Do I look 100 years old yet?"

They laughed and flashed affection and humor. "You are as ancient as you are wise, I suspect," Neah answered. "Captain—"

"Just Beezan now, please."

Neah reached over and squeezed his arm. "Of course, we were very sad to hear of both of your losses. We were the first aliens to meet and now here we are, with Veez, and attending a convocation of so many clades."

"Do I hear my name?" Veez waded into the Command Bay without even asking. But he had a tray of cake, so all was forgiven. The trail of cake crumbs had attracted a parade of pups. They hardly needed any cleaning bots.

Beezan stared. They had been down to two pups, Star and Rocket. Now, seven pups tumbled into the Command Bay, Rocket attacking Veez's swishing tail, Star bowling into Rocket, a large purple one focused only on the cake, three colorful young ones rolling around in excitement, and trailing behind, one beautiful silver one, significantly more reserved.

"Heaven help us," Beezan whispered.

"Should I take them out, Honor?" Zahar asked.

"No. They are a blessing. Most of them." Beezan shook himself, leaned down and put his hand out to the silver one, who came right to him. He lifted her gently into his lap. "We only got five new people aboard. They each had a pup?"

Neah laughed. Star looked up at Beezan. "Purple Friend!"

"Oh," Sontula's pup. He should have recognized the bigger purple one.

"And," Neah added, pointing to the one in Beezan's lap, "This is Whisper, Lanezi's."

"Those three belong to the twins, Io and Euro," Sontula explained.

Zahar picked up the yellow one. "Hi Summer. Long time, sweetie."

"Where Kiwi?"

A sad look crossed Zahar's face. "I don't know." She patted Summer and explained, "My pup Kiwi, their sibling, went with all the other Ramian pups when they sent everyone else down to the colony. I guess I could have kept him after all, but I didn't know what would happen."

Beezan reached over and squeezed her arm. "I'm sorry." They'd both lost one. But pups knew how to spread the love and fun around. Soon they all were in laps and had acquired cake.

"Neah, Sontula, my friends," Beezan said quietly. "I sense something serious."

Neah nodded. "We have been through some trouble. We have been to the heart of Chike space and back. And we've been . . . advised . . . by our Exempt Raykatoo, that it will take a tremendous effort not to be rated GenFive or GenSix."

"The convocation starts tomorrow," Veez said. "We can watch together."

"But watching does not help our cause," Neah said. And Beezan saw the wheels of the bold turning. Neah sat up and smiled. "But tonight is a happy occasion. Tomorrow. We will talk." And their colors ran a determined white.

Midnight, in orbit around the convocation planet

Terina was so tired the day after the wedding, but it was her shift in the Med Bay. She wanted to stay near Beezan anyway, and luckily he was her tutor for the med tech certificate. He was showing her how to do the podpup checks, using Whisper, the only cooperative pup, when the captain called.

"Iricana to Med Bay."

Beezan nodded at her to answer. She stood at attention. "Med Bay, Terina here, Captain."

"Do you have any patients?"

"No, Captain."

"Good. All of you can come to Social Arts Bay. Nkiroo has a feed to the convocation."

"Thank you, Captain!" Terina had to cover an involuntary shriek. *More history!* Beezan hesitated, but then folded up the equipment and helped herd the pups down the stairs.

In the S-Bay, Beezan stayed near the door, but Terina went close to the screen. Nkiroo had a choppy feed showing on the main screen. "They have multiple feeds, but no Human ones. I've tied our translator into the Chike feed."

"Oh, here," Veez said nonchalantly, "use this." Veez handed him a small unit that looked handmade. Pawmade. "I made it years ago so I could use the *81* screens."

Nkiroo took only about twenty seconds to figure it out. Suddenly the screen flashed off and back on, clear and colorful. And there before them was a spectacular arena. "Wow," Nkiroo whispered with a sigh of relief. "Thank heavens it's not like the Chike ship."

In the back of the room, Beezan started to shake. Katie and Lanezi sneaking in distracted him for a moment. But he wasn't sure if he really wanted to watch. Right now, there was no one on the terraced rock stage. The sides of the arena, where seats would be, were split into sections, with some wide flat steps where all kinds of creatures, rats, dogs, lizards, bears, were sitting or laying out flat. Other sections had leafy chairs, filled with bipeds like humans or smaller primates. Other sections were encased in different atmospheres that Beezan couldn't see through. One section seemed to be water.

The floor of the arena actually looked like a giant pond, if he had the right water word. But there was no sign of any creatures swimming in it.

The background noise suddenly stopped. Everyone in the arena stood or came to attention in some way. Even the irreverent Veez stood, and the rest of them scrambled to rise to their feet.

A camera zoomed in on a frog-like creature gracefully hopping up the terraced stone steps to the main stage. "That's a GenOne?" Beezan heard Terina ask Veez.

"Yes, my child. All our destinies are in their grasp."

"The invocation," the translator announced. Beezan stared, not even listening, trying to process what he was seeing.

"Opening remarks."

Beezan tried to breathe calmly. The shiny green and blue creature looked out over the audience. Ze had bulging eyes and bulbous knuckles on ziz 4-fingered hand. Ze had a wide mouth with a long red tongue flicking back and forth.

Sky was really one of these? Beezan felt faint and queasy. He didn't want to be prejudiced, but . . . a cute fuzzy pet-like creature sleeping in your bunk was one thing. An intelligent amphibian was another. He staggered down the stairs, trying to keep his breakfast down.

Terina barely registered Beezan's departure as she was so engrossed in the broadcast. *This might be the biggest moment in the history of humanity!* She prayed her recorder was capturing Veez's images.

The GenOne Prime hopped away and everyone sat down as another great frog, slightly bluer, took ziz place. They were odd looking, not ugly, but different. Their eyes were intelligent and intense, and the Prime had been inspiring.

Terina scanned the room quickly and saw Sequoia and the Command Bay crew come in. Beezan must have relieved them. And the pups! They were sitting up front listening, as still as little yoga masters. That alone was historic.

The new GenOne narrator introduced the GenTwo and GenThree representatives / judges. The crew sat on the edges of their chairs, seeing for the first time short glimpses of the real aliens of their galaxy. *This is not fiction!* she kept telling herself.

They knew the GenTwo had eight species, or clades as the

translator called them, but there were only seven here. Besides the Chike, there were two underwater clades that couldn't be seen clearly. Each clade had a simple-to-translate designation, almost a job description, as well as a casual name. When they called the Chike "The Builders" a chill went down Terina's spine. Humanity had named them correctly, never imagining how scary they would be.

The two underwater clades were called "The Navigators" and "The Terraformers." A giant neon-colored beetle, or a being encased in a neon exosuit, represented "The Healers." The "Historians / Thinkers" were tortoises. Delicate creatures with lace-like wings were called "The Artists."

When they zoomed in on "The Computers" the crew exclaimed in shock and leaned back in their seats—a giant spider. Its intelligent silver eyes made it all the more terrifying. "Someone should tell Beezan it could have been worse," Thayne remarked. But the others scowled at him, even if true.

"Where is the eighth clade?" Neah asked Veez.

"Oh, them. You know, dinosaur types. The Stompers. Don't play well with others."

When the narrator started on the GenThree, it became obvious that there was a progression. The GenOne, first to develop in this leaf of the galaxy, were frogs. The GenTwo were a verity of reptiles, insects, and birds if you counted the dinosaurs. The twelve clades of the GenThree were all mammals, a wide assortment. They ranged from the Scampers and the dog-like Coursers to bat-like creatures, tigers, and one clade represented by a co-species of two bearlike creatures.

"There's only ten," Neah whispered again to Veez.

"Right. Orca types, too big, but they're watching. And The Solitaries. Don't care."

There was no applause or acknowledgment as each clade

was introduced. It was dignified, almost business-like. The narrator explained that each generation in the leaf had come to space travel sooner than the one before, using the network built by the GenTwo. At first, the upcoming GenFour had come from peaceful planets. They had been accepted as a new wave of evolution in the galaxy and were allowed to remain GenFour, but were not included in the convocations.

"But now . . ." and there was a scary stillness in the arena. "There are signs." Ze paused again. "Clades of GenFour are escaping their systems before they are ready to join the peaceful association of beings under the beneficent guidance of the GenOne. And there are more signs."

Ze looked around seriously. "The ways are closing." The entire arena gasped in fifty different noise-making ways.

"Didn't they know?" Lanezi asked.

"Probably not," Veez answered. "Only a few of the clades jump around enough to notice."

"The ways have been closing for 25 years," the narrator continued, "but they have continued to close more than their average variation. It is a sign."

Sign of what? Terina wondered, confused. The GenOne raised ziz four-fingered hand for silence, and it was instantly quiet. "Our purpose here is twofold. We will determine which of the GenFour will be promoted to GenThree, based on peacefulness, obedience to their own standards, lack of exploitation, and degree of cooperation. Those that are unworthy will be confined to their home systems. If they mature, reevaluation will take place in 500 years."

"Five hundred years!" Thayne exclaimed furiously.

"God help us," everyone else whispered.

"The second purpose will be to consult on the meaning of the closing of the ways."

"What about Seven?" Io asked quietly.

"Seven?" Veez asked, turning to them.

"And now, the presentation of the harbingers."

The camera quickly panned across the twelve harbingers, sitting nervously on leafy thrones. They could see a crumpled white creature on the far right next to Oatah, who was next to Quay.

"Quay!" Quay's family shouted with joy, pointing and hugging and shushing each other.

"Thank God," Terina whispered.

"They're all primates!" Katie said and Veez nodded. It was as if the evolution of the galactic leaf mimicked evolution on Earth, except civilizations branched off at different levels. Starting on the left, the harbingers were announced and allowed to stand and say one line of greeting to the assembled gens.

The first harbinger stood. Ze was orange with straight yellow hair, only on ziz head, and brownish round eyes with thick brow ridges, but no more different from humans than Ramians were. "DorroClade is honored to be included. We acknowledge the esteemed GenOne and greet the assembled clades in peace and servitude."

Servitude? The crew stirred uneasily. Another harbinger, either an albino or from underground, cast the allegiance of ziz planet at the feet of the GenOne.

Some of the primates were of obvious gender, like Humans. One had a central dot of emotion color, instead of the full head-band like the Ramians. Their greetings were meek and careful. The fourth to last, ChiCha'tiClade acknowledged the unques-tioned leadership of the GenOne.

Next up, Quay leaped to his feet and raised his arms to the ceiling. "RamiaClade awaits the mercy and deliverance of our mutual Creator!"

The crew gasped. "Wild whiskers!" Veez said.

"Bold," Danumae said, and the Ramians nodded approvingly. The arena, silent all this time, erupted in hissing.

Then Oatah stood. He looked terrible: thin, worried, with dark circles under his eyes. But his gaze was full of fire as he turned to the GenOne narrator. "EarthClade greets the assembled gens in peace and friendship and respectfully awaits evidence of their right to subject or command others." Oatah made a respectful bow and sat.

"Madness!" Veez whispered. Again the turmoil in the arena. The last harbinger, the cringing being seemingly overcome by terror, had unfolded, looking at Oatah and Quay in astonishment. Then she stood, not even as tall as Quay, but a strength coming into her bearing. "We protest!" She turned and pointed to the seated GenOne Prime, not the narrator. "LuessClade calls on YOU to acknowledge our freedom and release us!"

And then the feed blinked off.

There was chaos in the Social Arts Bay as everyone started questioning Veez at once. Iricana went to stand by him and quiet people down. "Please, can you tell us what will happen?"

Despite his airy attitude, Veez seemed shaken. "Well, my friends. I am somewhat of a student of these convocations."

"And," Iricana prompted him.

"Well, those clades that refuse to cooperate are inevitably made GenFive. We should know."

"What happened to your harbinger?" Iricana asked.

"Oh, before the convocation even started, she bit her 'escort', shut down the life support of five clades and escaped in a shuttle."

They all stared at Veez. Kelson finally said, "You're not kidding."

"No. But please remember, that was several-thousand years ago. We're much calmer now."

"So, what did the GenOne do?"

"They made us GenFive, of course."

"But," Iricana said, "here you are, GenThree."

"Not without a herculean effort, as your people would say."

Iricana shook her head in concern. "Did our harbingers just condemn us?"

"No. No. You're already GenFive. Nothing to lose."

"You're not kidding," Kelson said again.

"No, my friends. Your Quay has the right idea. You need a miracle."

Yosemite Village

Sometimes people walked on the beach of their little bay at lunch, during fast, especially some of the new couples Melawn had put together. That's where Tenshi found him, staring at the waves.

"Melawn?"

"God is Most Glorious. Is everything okay?"

"Yes. I came to visit you." Melawn found that unlikely, with her pressing duties all the way in Nile. But he would find out soon enough. They started walking, just where the waves rolled up.

"You see how the waves come up different amounts?" Melawn asked.

"Yes. Tides."

"It's amazing. I never noticed until fast. I never really looked at the sun and the moons. I just kept seeing them in my mind, like from space, orbits, you know." He stopped. "They told me the sun sets in different places. And normally we'd do fast right before the equinox, but we're still on an Earth schedule, so rain or not, it's actually past spring."

"There's a movement to convert to a planetary calendar, but there's a lot of resistance."

"I can see that, from spacers. But now I see how much we're connected to the planet. Like that moon. I'm wondering if the Chike put it there."

"Why?"

"It's just the right distance. It makes the rotation of the planet almost 24 hours. It stabilizes the seasons."

"It makes it Earth-like," Tenshi said.

"But not Ramian-like."

"No. Our colony was here hundreds of years before theirs."

Melawn almost stepped on one of the coral spikes. "Argg. These really hurt if you step on them." He dug it out of the sand. "And they're never broken." Tenshi stepped back a little so he wasn't pointing it at her. Melawn always threw them back; it was the order of the council. He never even thought about it. "What?"

"Nothing. Just be careful with those. Did you try to break one?"

"Not me. You know Cypress, the axeman." Her eyes widened. "He broke his axe." She sighed, relieved. "What do you know?" he whispered. She glanced around.

"Don't mess with them. Don't tell people. It's possible to activate them, sometimes. And they don't all do the same thing. At least two people have been killed. Once a beam shot out of the tip and burned down a unit."

"Wow. How can you keep that a secret?"

"Because it's necessary. Imagine people collecting them, seeing what they do, trying to own them."

"People like AnnaLee."

"Exactly. Although I hope there's no one else like AnnaLee. Don't make me regret telling you."

"Never," he said and flung it high into the air so that it made a long arc into the water.

They continued on. "So the council wanted me to ask you something." Melawn nodded, knowing that was coming. He was doing his best to recruit for the expedition, but there were few takers. "There's bad news." He stopped to look at her. "Jadee came back from the test farms, from further up where the salt water didn't flood. The seeds didn't take. So our test crops here failed and most of our test sites nearby failed. Our food supply is going to collapse."

"Oh, my God."

She held up her hand as if not to panic. "There's a plan, but it's extreme. The council will mobilize at least 32 permanent expeditions."

"Thirty-two! I can't even find 250 volunteers for one!"

"Well, starvation is a mighty motivator. The council is going to make an appeal on New Year's, a call for pioneers. And those groups will be nomadic at first, living more off the land than crops."

"That's 8000 people!"

"That's the minimum."

"What if they don't volunteer?"

"They'll have 'further consultation'." She looked at Melawn, still hesitant.

"I was already planning to go," he assured her.

"That's not what they wanted me to ask. They want you to lead an expedition."

"*What?*"

"I told them you wouldn't want to."

"No! I mean if they command me, I'll do my best until they

pick someone else, probably after an embarrassing series of blunders. I couldn't even lead a crew back from the coast."

"They think you have leadership potential."

"Why? And why is it not okay to be, to be a tan?" The Ramian word truly described how he saw himself, and their system of jik and tan made sense to him.

"It is okay. But you're a sidekick in need of a hero."

"You make it sound bad!"

"Well, it depends on the hero."

He frowned and shook his head. "I was 15 when I went with Thayne. Obviously, I've learned better." She nodded, accepting that. He let his annoyance go. It wasn't Tenshi's fault. "Are you a leader?"

"No," she said. "But I'm going. And the council said it was your choice."

He sagged with relief. "I'd like to go with your group then."

"Jadee is our leader. You and I are both to head back to Nile after New Year to help organize."

"Good, something I know how to do, and someone I believe in."

They hadn't been paying attention to the waves which suddenly rolled over their feet. They shrieked like children and ran up the beach, and then laughed at themselves. "It's a wild thing, this planet," Melawn said.

"It's a wonderful planet," Tenshi agreed quietly.

19-Loftiness Eve

Midnight, in orbit around the convocation planet

"Last hour of the last shift of the year," Beezan commented. Of his night-shift crew, only Zahar was in the Command Bay to hear him. Jarvie was preparing their early breakfast since they'd be sleeping through the last morning of fast. Nkiroo was doing his mechanic / engineering shift in Hangar 1, with the shuttles. Danulell was in the Med Bay, and their general assistant / errand runner / resident historian Terina was helping Jarvie in the kitchen.

Jarvie soon came loping up the rimway carrying a tray of food, followed by the usual parade of pups. "Have they become nocturnal?" Beezan asked.

"No," Jarvie said. "Terina's watching them so Io and Euro can get some sleep, but she didn't want to take them down to the hangar with Nkiroo's breakfast. You know, seven pups in nogee . . ."

"No, I don't want to think about it," Beezan said. Zahar smiled, but then blinked and grabbed her headset, putting it properly over her ear and turning to the panel. "This is *Midnight*." She turned on the speaker so they could all hear.

"Human ship *Midnight*. This is high clerk of the Extreme Honor Exempt Pascal aboard the *Sandstorm*."

Blueberry hissed.

"Shhh!" Jarvie scolded her gently.

"You will receive the Exempt's shuttle in 10 hours, 14 minutes. All due consideration / respect / courtesy will be offered to the Exempt, including your best accommodations. Two escorts will accompany. Acknowledge immediately."

"Honor! That's the ship I was on, with Evan and Caspia!" Zahar told him.

"So the Exempt might be bringing them?" Beezan asked. She nodded. Beezan hated the idea of letting the Chike aboard, and didn't want to wake the captain. But he knew Iricana always came down on the side of peace, cooperation, and assuming the best. "We have to let them come. Tell them . . ." he looked at Jarvie. "You're the diplomat."

"It is our great privilege to receive the honored Exempt. All will be ready."

Zahar was relaying that when Beezan added, "And use the hangar!" Which Jarvie translated to "Hangar 1 is cleared for your convenience."

After she sent the last message, she signaled the line was dead. They stared at each other. "Let's let the crew sleep their last hour."

"Oh no! I forgot," Zahar said. "Pascal knows the colony people. If he sees them—"

Beezan sighed. *Of course.* "Jarvie, wake up the captain."

19-Loftiness

Zahar helped Terina pass out rations and hot cereal to the half-dressed, half-asleep crew as they came in the kitchen. "Eat while you listen," Iricana said. "We have three Chike coming aboard, The Exempt Pascal—" Danulell choked.

"No!" Thayne said, as Katie patted Danulell on the back.

"What are we going to do?" Zhenumae asked.

Jarvie whipped his head around to scowl at them for interrupting the captain. "—and two escorts. We hope there will be two humans as well." She flicked a duty chart onto the main screen. "This is what we're going to do. Keep eating! Thayne, Nkiroo, Veez, Danumae, Zhenulell and your family will move to Arc 8 and stay there. The Tektites, Taj, and Falcon will also move, but need to be seen coming and going.

"Zahar will prep Arc 3 for the Chike. Heavens, what do they eat?"

"Meat," Zahar answered. "I'll fire up the freezer and hope they bring their own."

"They're staying?" Lanezi asked, cringing at his own interruption.

"They demanded accommodations," Iricana answered. "I'm sorry. I know you've been at their mercy. Do you want to move to Arc 8?"

Lanezi straightened. "No, Captain."

"Good. Zahar and Jarvie will meet the Exempt in Hangar 1 and escort them to the Arc 3 Consultation Hall. Taj, tube duty, Sequoia in command in Hangar 1, and Thunder stand by to help. Yes, Terina, you may record. Io and Euro, keep the pups with you in Arc 1. Neah, Sontula, Lanezi, and the rest of the senior crew with me. Understood?"

"Yes, Captain!"

"We will try to have our New Year's celebration. Be sure to

take whatever you need for Arc 8. It's still a holy day, Chike or no Chike."

And so they scrambled. Zahar loved this race-to-organize work. She cranked the heat in the three biggest cabins in Arc 3. She'd never seen Pascal's cabin, and they had no decorative items anyway, so she wasn't sure what would be considered special. But somehow, in all the runaround, Katie came in carrying a painting. "It's one of Lanezi's. He brought it from the *Watcher*."

Zahar stood back to look at it. "Swing Jump" was the title. "It looks terrifying. Let's put it up."

"Oh, and here are some onions. We can put them in these vases."

"Onions?"

"It's art . . . or a snack."

Zahar impulsively hugged Katie. "I'm so happy for Lanezi. And you."

Katie smiled. "I'm happy too!" And they laughed. But then Katie was serious. "I hope these Chike don't wreck it."

Terina braced in Hangar 1 with her gear. She'd done this enough to know the best camera angles. Taj was already through the safety door, standing at the tube hatch. "They might have to come over in suits if I can't hook up the tube," he said over the s'link.

Zahar, standing at the window, shook her head. "They won't have Human suits, but they took us from the *Cheetah* somehow."

"How?" Sequoia asked.

"I don't know. I was unconscious," Zahar said quietly.

I have to get that story! Terina made a mental note. Meanwhile, she checked through the observation window. The big hangar door was open. They had turned so the star was to the left, allowing the shuttle to see in the hangar without being blinded.

"Guide beams activated. *Midnight?*"

"Shuttle on target, 25 seconds to touchdown." A long flat shuttle slid into the hangar, flexing out its ten landing legs at the last second. The auto anchors fired and bounced off. **"Anchors failed,"** *Midnight* reported.

The shuttle's own grappling system activated, sealing it to the deck. "Microtech," Thunder said. "Hold off the tube, Taj, they may have some other plan."

Terina readjusted the camera just in time to capture a gangway telescoping across the hangar from the shuttle. Taj remotely disengaged the accordioned tube and swung it aside just in time. The Chike gangway hit the hatch and formed an adapter. "More microtech."

"Seal reads green," Taj reported. "Opening both hatches."

Thunder took a position by the safety door. "Proceed," Sequoia said.

Terina positioned her camera at the little window of the safety door and sent the feed to the big screen, so they could all see. Two Chike with poles floated out of the hatch and used the poles as some kind of holdbars to swing aside. A third Chike emerged, green and gray robes floating gracefully around zir.

"That's Pascal," Zahar breathed.

"You can tell them apart?" Sequoia asked.

"I know the Exempt. Not sure about the others."

"Humans!" Taj exulted, grabbing a hold bar and reaching down to help pull a woman through.

"Yes! Yes! Yes!" Zahar smiled with joy. Then the view was blocked by the Chike.

"Two humans. That's everyone," Taj reported. "Hatches sealed." Terina reframed her shots for the big moment while Thunder opened the safety door.

Pascal pulled through first, blinking in apparent surprise, turning ziz head one way and then the other when ze saw Zahar. "God is Most Glorious," Zahar said. "Welcome to the *Midnight*, honored Exempt Pascal. It is good to see you again. May I present the captain's diplomat, Jarvie."

Jarvie swung forward. Veez had advised that Iricana have four layers of introduction, to emphasize her role as captain. "*Midnight*'s crew is honored with the Exempt's presence. I will escort the Exempt to the captain. Also, it is regular gravity there."

"Acceptable. My party will accompany," Ze said in understandable Alkulu.

"Yes, Exempt." Jarvie tentatively extended his arm to Pascal, who grasped it, allowing zirself to be towed.

Meanwhile, Terina kept her second camera on the two Humans. She recognized them from the photos. Caspia was smiling with relief and trying to blink away tears. Evan had a pleasant, friendly, slightly distracted smile and looked around curiously. They both exchanged brief hugs with Zahar, but warily stuck to business, keeping close to Pascal and acknowledging the others with intense nods and waves.

Jarvie breathed a careful sigh of relief when the lift reached full gravity and Pascal let go of him. He'd come a long way since his day of panic when Neah had stood over him in the kitchen, but the Chike's grip was like an exosuit claw and could have snapped his arm in two. *Strong.*

They exited in Arc 6. "A short walk to Arc 3, Exempt." Jarvie gestured as kindly as possible, trying to channel his brother. Pascal continued to walk upright, gazing ahead as if boarding a Human ship was no big deal.

But then Pascal turned ziz head sharply several times and sniffed, ziz eyes narrowing. *Something is wrong!* "Almost there," Jarvie said, to distract zir. "Stairs up . . ." Pascal let the escort go up first, which they did on all fours. Pascal followed, zipping up the stairs in a couple of seconds. Jarvie took them three at a time to keep up. *Strong and quick.*

At the top of the stairs, Kelson waited until they were all inside and the escort had parted for Pascal. "Honored Exempt," Kelson said, with all the gravity of his age, "May I present Iricana Jasmine Kentan Atikameq, Captain of the *Midnight* and level 1 administrator." He stood aside and Iricana stepped forward.

"God is Most Glorious honored Exempt. I hope—"

"Ze is here!" Pascal hissed. The escorts lowered their poles toward Iricana. She froze. Beezan took a step forward while everyone else stepped back.

Iricana cautiously repeated, "Ze is here?"

"The angry one!" Pascal spun around, looking at all of them. Jarvie barely dodged ziz tail. "I smell zir!" Jarvie's heart started pounding. *Thayne.* "And ze cannot be here! This one left zir on the colony!" Ze stepped right up to Iricana and swung ziz head to one side to stare at her with one eye. "Explain yourself, Captain!"

Jarvie moved aside so Terina could squeeze in next to him. Iricana didn't take her eyes from Pascal, even as the escorts moved forward with their poles pointed in her face. Jarvie looked to Beezan, who held a hand up, keeping the crew back. Caspia rushed forward though. "Please, Captain, please. Whatever it is can be worked out. The Exempt is wise and reasonable."

Iricana actually smiled and gestured to the table. "Then please, make oneself comfortable."

"This one will stand. You will explain how the angry one escaped and then I will tell you why this one suffers to join the lesser ones."

Iricana took a deep breath. "Thayne, I assume you mean, is here, along with several others from the colony. They did not escape. We rescued them." The Exempt sucked in a breath as if oxygen deprived, and she continued. "We know the location of the colony—and that information has already been disseminated throughout Human government."

"You cannot know!" And then ze began sniffing again, signaling to his escort to sniff along the deck. Both escorts ran around the room, sniffing, and spoke quietly to Pascal, heads bowed. "A Scamper! You have broken the taboo!"

"*We* have no taboo, Exempt."

Zis eyes narrowed again. "So you don't." Suddenly, the escorts swung their lances toward the door, where Veez had just come in. Veez, who was supposed to be hiding.

"Good Lord," Iricana whispered, shaking her head.

Pascal's jaw dropped open, but ze signaled the escorts to step back. Veez sauntered in, bright and respectful, bowing graciously to Pascal and handing off a gift of what looked like fried worms to ziz escort. "Exempt Pascal, it is my extreme—"

"Enough of this! There is no time for manners or comfort or protocols, or even taboos! We have a mission!"

"We?" Iricana asked.

"Yes! By which this one means *YOU*! Bring the angry one.

Bring everyone to hear this one. Except," ze paused and gestured gracefully. "This one presents Caspia and Evan, returned to your people by the grace of the Chike and with compliments of Kingdom Leaf."

"We are grateful, honored Exempt," Iricana said. "With this gift, our endeavor will be blessed."

Lanezi sat at the conference table, stunned at the turn of events. His stomach churned in panic and he squeezed his shaking hands between his knees. *I just escaped the Chike and now this?*

Meanwhile, Thunder and the Tektites were supervising the unloading of the Exempt's supplies. The Chike were staying.

Everyone else except Katie and Caspia, and the podpups, crowded into the room. The senior crew sat near Pascal while the rest crowded around the other side of the table.

"A prayer please, Honor Beezan," Iricana requested. Beezan, who supposedly could freejump, looked too stressed to be a pilot, but his chanting was softly piercing, almost mystical. It helped calm Lanezi's heart a little.

"Danulell," Iricana prompted. Danulell and the Ramians offered a Ramian prayersong that Lanezi knew from the *Watcher*. He joined in. It brought back visions of Raykatoo. Certainly this Pascal was younger, although ze seemed equally intense.

After Danulell, Iricana looked at Pascal. "Would the Exempt like to offer a prayer?" Lanezi saw the Ramians flash approval of boldness before turning back to the solemnity of prayer. Pascal took a resigned breath, held both claws to heaven and repeated one line three times. When ze lowered ziz claws ze said, "It is the invocation for deliverance. We will need it." Ze paused and no one interrupted.

"This one has been directed, by the great, the legendary, the grandmother of wisdom, to undertake your salvation. You know the great nest grandmother as Raykatoo." Lanezi failed to stifle a gasp. "Yes," Pascal's eye swung his way. "You have had the honor of serving the Exempt Raykatoo personally. It is that one that directs us now."

Pascal looked around the room, first with one eye, and then the other. Ze paused a long time on Thayne, who glared back, and Beezan, who lowered his eyes in modesty. "Your people, both your clades, will be declared GenFive, or worse," ze said, glancing at the Ramians.

Several people started to object, but ze snapped ziz jaws and no one spoke. "There is no conceivable way to overcome it after the chaos you have wrought in the leaf, not to mention defiance during the introductions."

Ze turned to the Ramians. "The theft of the anchors, which you call gravity balls, leading to destabilization of the ways, which precipitated the unheard-of phenomenon of the nova, will lay waste to part of the leaf, including an entire sentient civilization at the planet you call Seven! Even now it is shutting down the ways." They were all silent, but Lanezi was growing heated inside. It wasn't humanity's fault.

"That alone is your doom, but you were doomed anyway, when you destroyed the Chike ship. And, not to forget other crimes, the genetic manipulation of the small ones, and enslavement of the birds."

Ze turned back to the Captain. "And Humans! Attacking a Chike ship with nanos, conspiring with a GenThree, and generally ignoring our warnings and instructions for *five-hundred years.*"

Ze leaned forward with both claws on the table. "You will be GenFive or GenSix. It is a *foregone conclusion.*" Lanezi was shaking for real now. He wanted to jump up and object. But he knew better. "Unless . . ." Everyone froze, eyes fixed on Pascal. "Unless you save Seven."

"What?" people asked, but Lanezi couldn't restrain himself any longer.

"Exempt! The Exempt Raykatoo said that even the GenOne could not save Seven!"

"Exactly."

"I don't understand," Iricana said.

"You must do what the GenOne cannot. It is your *only* hope."

Two hours later, Terina sat with the rest of the frowning, exhausted, hungry crew around the Consultation Hall table. They were all seated, except for Pascal, who paced back and forth, giving the Humans neck strain. Everyone was there except Gadi, Gola, and Falcon, listening from the Command Bay. They were frowning at their brainstorming list, but it was more like a junk news list: *Top Ten Ways to Save a Planet!* Except there weren't even ten ways and none of them sounded remotely possible, not in five years.

Veez came in late, nodding soberly to Pascal. "Exempt," Veez said, "I've received a preliminary report from a science vessel at Friendship, which by the way, they're now calling Destroyer."

Pascal stopped ziz pacing in shock. "What science vessel?"

"One of ours," Veez answered. "Volunteers of course. They jumped in, got the data, and jumped out."

"They will all die," Pascal said.

"They're already dead, but we have the data, as well as information from *Watcher*, which came from the *Enkindler*, as well as data from your own ship, Exempt."

Pascal stepped aside, "Please present."

"This event isn't a regular black hole or supernova. It appears that somehow a star from another dimension or another universe broke through whatever natural barriers exist and touched or came close to Destroyer, causing a partial collapse and bounce, like a lopsided supernova. But the explosion is extremely chaotic and may involve forces and particles we don't understand. It may have happened because the anchors—gravity balls—were removed from that system and many nearby systems. But for whatever reason, it's a powerful event. It appears to have accelerated the closing of the ways."

Veez put some charts on the screen that were meaningless to Terina. "The good news, if you can call it that, is that there is no gamma ray burst. The bad news is that the shock wave is definitely headed toward Ramian space and will overtake the Seven system in 5-6 years."

Terina sat back and stared at the list.

- Bioengineer the whole ecosystem to withstand radiation
- Go underground
- Build a shield
- Generate a supermagnetosphere
- Move the population
- Drop the planet in a pocket

Anyone was allowed to suggest anything, even if it met with eye-rolling from Thayne, or frowns of concern from everyone else. Pascal was still studying Veez's data with ziz small side eye. "The energy of the shock wave is far higher than expected." Ziz shoulders slumped. "It's not just the biosphere of Seven, the star itself will be affected." Ze looked up at the list. "The population of Seven must be relocated."

Iricana grimly deleted every other option except move the population. "A percentage could be saved," Veez said sadly.

"That is not our mission!" Pascal said, shoulders straight again.

Thayne slapped his hand on the table. "You expect us—the GenFive—to do the impossible?"

Pascal swung around to give Thayne the one-eye. "It is the great Raykatoo who expects."

Neah cut in, "Exempt, the GenOne already refused to move them. They said they would have to enslave the rest of us to build two-million ships. How else could we move the population?"

"Can you . . . beam them out?" Evan asked.

"No," Pascal answered. "The GenOne do possess the ability to create and move a safebubble through space, but the energy required is far too much for an entire civilization."

"Can we move the planet?" Nkiroo asked. "Convert it directly into a giant spaceship?"

"The planetary engineers can move a planet within its own system. But that won't help."

Jarvie broke in, almost offhand, "We might as well just jump the planet."

There was instant silence. Everyone turned to look at him, some as if he'd lost his mind, the pilots as if their eyes were boring into him. Murmurs of crazy and impossible floated around the table. Pascal gave him the one eye. But Io and Euro sat up with hope.

"Wait," Sequoia said, shaking her head as if to shake off the crazy idea. "The ways are closing. How could we possibly get a whole planet in the path and then keep it there?"

"Determination!" Pascal said. "Determination / stubbornness and passion / insanity, the main attributes of Humans and Ramians."

"You can't seriously consider this!" Thayne objected. "You can't even steer a planet."

"Ze said they can move it in-system," Neah reminded them.

"Wait, wait." Iricana said. "Assuming we could even do such a thing, where would you take the planet?"

"To a system that can remain stable with a new planet, of course," Veez said. "The GenOne can advise."

"We'd need every possible assist," Sequoia said.

"Mom!" Terina said.

"We need the perfect path," Evan said.

"Evan!" Caspia said

"Yes, with the wind," Danulell said. "The best possible calculation."

"Danulell!" his mother said.

"A failed jump would destroy their civilization and all the pilots," Kelson noted neutrally. "We don't even know if the people could survive a successful jump."

"If you fail, you won't need pilots," Pascal said. "You'll be confined to your home system."

"This is fantasy!" Taj objected. "If they could jump planets they would have done it already."

"They cannot," Veez said. "But each clade has its own . . . gift."

Pascal leaned on the table, eyeing them. "*Find* your gift. Save Seven. Save yourselves."

Thayne sat back in his chair, arms crossed. Zahar put her hand on Thayne's arm. He almost pulled away from her, but stopped to look at her. "Remember your destiny," she said.

"Yes," Nkiroo agreed. "To save the sectors. That was your mission in life. You can calculate this."

Terina snuck a look at each pilot. They were obviously shaken. Her mom was staring at the screen. Beezan and Evan were looking at something in their own minds. Jarvie looked sick, like he'd made a suggestion that would kill them all. Lanezi was holding Katie's hand and shaking his head no. And then, calm as ever, Evan said, "Honor Beezan could lead us. I've seen him in the ways. He could do it."

The others looked at Evan, puzzled. "You've seen him?" Caspia asked.

"I didn't know it was him, until we came here."

They all turned to look at Beezan but he wasn't really there.

The rivers converge!

"We must consult with the Navigators," Pascal said, "the crab people."

"They don't allow visitors," Veez said.

"Not on their homeworld, but we will go to the colony, immediately."

Everyone took a breath and looked at Iricana. She shook her head and put her hand out to slow down. "Exempt. It's the last day of fast. We have a holy day starting in two hours. Tonight we will celebrate the concept of Divine Teachers bringing a New Day. I hope that you will join us. Tomorrow we will pray." She looked around at her stunned crew. "The next day, we will jump to the colony and visit these navigators. No one on this ship will be left on the colony against their will."

Pascal nodded once. "Accepted."

New Year's Eve 1085 BE

Yosemite Village

It was New Year's Eve and almost everyone in Yosemite had come down to the bay to watch the sunset. Melawn walked along the beach again, breathing in the ocean air. *We are part of the planet. We're designed to live on planets.*

People on the beach gave him smiles or slight bows, a striking change from the polite nods he received before his new role of matchmaker.

As the sun got near the horizon, everyone gathered. This star was supposedly slightly bigger in the sky than Earth's sun, but hardly anyone here would even know that. And since the rain had cleared there weren't many pink clouds. But the abstract notion of the new year—a new year on Earth, lightyears away, and the very practical aspect of fast being over, combined to make it an emotional moment.

As the lower limb of the sun touched the horizon, someone began the New Day Prayer, her chanting rising and falling on the ocean breezes, *". . . all Thy company, O my Lord, have broken this day their fast, after having observed it within the precincts of Thy court, and in their eagerness to please Thee."*[1]

They sang two songs and then the sun dipped below the horizon and the dinner bell began to ring. The children cheered and ran up to the courtyard, quickly followed by the adults. No one stood on ceremony during fast. But Melawn lingered a moment. It was a beautiful planet. And he could have a happy life, if he let himself. New year, new life. He turned and walked up to dinner.

1-Splendor-1085

Midnight, in orbit around the convocation planet

Zahar sat at the youth table for their light dinner. They'd had a big lunch, after their New Year's celebration. Then they'd spent the afternoon prepping chairs in the Passenger Lounge while some of the command crew met and were still meeting with Pascal.

After her long stint on *Cheetah,* with no others her age, and her seemingly endless stint on Pascal's ship with hardly anyone of her species, Zahar was relieved and pleased to be back with youth. And these were exceptional youth.

Jarvie, still in shock and feeling guilty that anyone had listened to him about jumping the planet, was a pilot and on his way to becoming a freejumper. Zahar had only recently heard the term for pilots who could jump without a-rings. Apparently, they didn't even need the push-along gravity balls that the Chike used. Meaning humans could do something the GenTwo couldn't. *It must make Pascal crazy.*

Terina, the young reporter, was organized and dramatic. Of course, Zahar already knew Io and Euro and was grateful to learn they'd been cured by the Ramians. They seemed thrilled for Lanezi and Katie, but somewhat more subdued and worried than she remembered them.

The pilot Gola and monitor Gadi usually sat with them too, even though they were in their twenties. Other times they sat with the Tektites, who tended to stick together. Danulell, who also often joined them, was eating with his family tonight. Zahar had been stunned to learn that Danulell knew Jarvie, back when they were both the same age. And now Danulell was nine years older. *That must be mind-bending.*

There was no teen training on the *Midnight*, but this amazing group was even better. Zahar was lucky to be sitting with them. And they had taken her in as one of them. She could feel their strong support and concern. And if Terina's confluence ideas had any merit, this bunch might have the chance to do something historic.

They ate their salty broth with greens and then speculated on who the command crew would choose to jump, until Iricana came up the stairs and stood quietly in the doorway. "Captain . . ." people whispered until everyone was silent and looking at her.

"So sorry to interrupt your dinner, friends. There are just a couple of last-minute developments."

Normally, business wasn't discussed at dinner, and the captain seemed apologetic, but people nodded their acceptance and Terina pulled out her pad.

"The Exempt Pascal has decided that the Ramian ship *Watcher* will be jumping to the colony planet with us." There were small gasps all around. "Getti Drann has invited all Ramians to continue the mission aboard the *Watcher*, if they wish. You're also welcome here, so it's up to you. But you need to shuttle over tonight. Gola will take anyone over at 21:00."

"What about Quay?" Zhenumae asked.

"He is required to stay for the duration of the convocation. We're assured of Quay's safe return to Ramian space."

"But he'll be alone."

Zahar frowned, feeling somewhat responsible for Quay, but his family could stay if they wanted. The Ramian table continued their discussion in Ramian, colors flashing.

Iricana moved to their youth table and spoke quietly to Jarvie, "Pilots, except Gola, will retire for prayers at 19:00."

"Yes, Honor," Jarvie answered, while Terina tapped away on her pad.

"Evan will jump us to the colony tomorrow, using the a-rings."

"Yes, Honor," he answered again.

"And yes, Terina, you may post all this on your Mission Seven feed."

"Thank you, Captain!"

"Oh," Iricana turned to Zahar and smiled. "Veez will be monitor on this side, and then Pascal will take over in the colony system."

As Iricana passed by another table and paused to speak to them, Thayne asked, "Captain, why is it we do everything this Chike Pascal tells us?" There was a sudden silence in the room. It wasn't so much the question as his scathing tone. Zahar had been surprised to find that Thayne was not confined to his cabin, but at least he wasn't on the command crew. Zahar suspected that Iricana just hadn't had time to deal with him.

Iricana paused and considered, without seeming annoyed. "I understand some of you were confined to a Chike ship and relocated to the Colony, and may feel like the Chike are not our ... allies. But I am convinced that Exempt Pascal's reading of the situation is correct, and it is in our best interests to follow ziz lead. And Veez concurs."

"You are putting the lives of our pilots and passengers at risk." Thayne insisted.

"We'll evaluate the risk as we go. No one will be forced to do anything."

"And as far as listening to this Pascal," Thayne started in an inflammatory way, when Caspia stood suddenly and interrupted him.

"Excuse me Captain, but there's been a misunderstanding. The Exempt Pascal saved *all* our lives on the *Cheetah* and has defended our people at every turn. There is no justification for disrespecting zir."

"Thank you, doctor," Iricana said calmly, indicating she should sit and giving Thayne an *I hope you're listening* look. "We need to treat everyone with respect. Not to mention that it is our duty, as human beings, to help a civilization in need."

"Our duty as well, Captain," Neah said as he stood. "We will all return to the *Watcher*."

15-Splendor

Yosemite Village

Fifteen days later, Melawn was still riding his wave of newfound contentment, even checking through his matchmaking data for himself, when there was shouting from the road. Melawn ran out of the men's hall and of course—of course!—now that he'd found some peace, a Chike shuttle was approaching the village, flying along the river from Shen.

A Zann teenager ran behind Melawn, terrified. "It's okay," Melawn reassured him. "It won't hurt you."

"Clear the courtyard!" a spacer shouted, thinking that it

would land, but it didn't. It continued over the beach to the bay. Melawn and half the crowd ran down to watch. The shuttle lowered itself right into the water and slowly sank.

"What are they doing?" Melawn asked Jagger.

He shrugged. "As far as I know, it's never happened before. Maybe they're just meeting with the crab people. But why fly over the villages?"

"Mean."

"Yeah," Jagger agreed.

16-Splendor

Melawn was just finished with his after-breakfast scrubjub, hurrying with all his gear to meet Tenshi at the cart stop, when a runner came tearing up the road, skidding to a dusty halt next to him. "Melawn!"

"What's wrong?"

"The council calls for you! It's urgent!" Melawn frowned. He'd miss the cart to Nile. But he waved for the approaching Tenshi to come with him and followed the youngster to the makeshift council hut.

Melawn and Tenshi took off their hats and stepped inside. "God is Most Glorious," they said together.

"Good morning," the council member said, with a look-over-there expression. Melawn detected a flash of burgundy and turned to see someone standing in the corner—a Ramian.

"Danulell!" He dropped his gear and embraced him, stunned. "What's happening? Why are you back here?"

The council member didn't bother with any more formalities. "The Chike have a mission and are demanding your presence, Melawn. They sent a Ramian, figuring he wouldn't defect to an all-Human colony."

"I . . . have duties here." Melawn didn't even know why he was objecting. For some reason he felt torn.

"I know it's sudden," Danulell explained. "Thayne got them to promise you would not be returned to the colony." *Not returned.* It was his dream, but he suddenly felt dizzy.

"What about the others?"

"No others, only you," Danulell said, with an apologetic flash at Tenshi.

"Melawn," the council member said, "we have to comply. Besides cooperating with the Chike, this is an opportunity. You can advocate for us in person. You're much more knowledgeable about the food situation, the population overload, than the others. Request that they repatriate the spacers. Insist. *Beg.*"

"Of course, yes," he said in a daze. "I'm so sorry," he said to Tenshi.

"Don't be ridiculous. There's no reason for guilt. You're doing what has to be done. You may be our best hope."

"And if you're freed," the council member continued, "it's God's will. No guilt."

Danulell added, "Don't worry, you'll adjust quickly. Thayne is waiting for you."

That's a mixed blessing. "Okay, wait." Melawn dug through his pack for his precious papers. Swallowing hard, he separated out the research for the colony, even the matchmaking. "Here." He handed them over to the council member.

"God be with you Melawn," he said, and took the papers.

Tenshi stepped up to hug him. "Give my love to the right people."

Melawn nodded, tears starting. "Council member, friends." He picked up his gear. He was a survivalist now, after all, and he wasn't going to leave without it.

The council member went out and rang the bell to provide a

distraction while Melawn and Danulell hurried down to the beach. Melawn turned to look one last time. Tenshi and Jagger stood on the grassy dunes. He waved. At the water's edge, Danulell took his arm. "Don't be afraid. Just kneel down in the sand. It's perfectly safe."

"What?"

Melawn clutched Danulell's arm as they descended in a clear life-bubble of air, like a giant cell membrane, surrounded on all sides by the deadly ocean. Two dangerous-looking crabs somehow steered them from behind, using their spike tools. A stray starfish squelched around Melawn's knees. He was terrified. The memory of going under the waves at the shipwreck flooded over him and he gasped for air. There was no way they would survive if the bubble popped.

"Keep breathing. The Navigators—the crab people—are very precise," Danulell said approvingly. His colors ran coral as he gazed at the underwater scene. "Beautiful, isn't it?"

He's insane. By the time they were transferred into a Chike shuttle and the bubble burst, flinging seawater all over them, Melawn was hyperventilating. The little black and green striped Entry Lounge seemed almost as claustrophobic as the bubble. "We're still underwater?" he gasped.

"Perfectly safe," Danulell insisted. "You know, the same as being in space, except different pressures, stresses, and atmospheric mixtures . . ."

"You're not helping."

After the shuttle transferred them to an underwater lab, Danulell pulled Melawn along. "Come on." Suddenly, there was Nkiroo. Melawn threw his arms around him. *Both brothers back in one day!*

"Melawn!" Nkiroo said quietly, "I'm so happy you're back, but we have work." And they both pulled him along.

What am I doing here? In the underwater lab of the Navigators, Beezan wanted to bang his head on the makeshift table, but there was already too much noise from the clicking and clacking of claws, and the slap-splashing of the slimy water on the floor. On top of that, the crabs communicated by some kind of stridulation, like playing tiny violins. The overall effect was a high-pitched, out-of-tune orchestra with an overenthusiastic percussion section.

And they poked and pinched. Beezan's arms were going to be bruised. If he told them to stop it, they'd exclaim "tut" like he was a fussy baby. The others, Veez, Iricana, Thayne, Nkiroo, Danulell, Neah, and the Ramian pilot Shiwelna from the *Watcher*, were all stressed and on edge.

The Navigator / Chike translator was hooked to the Chike / Alkulu translator. A garble of words tumbled out, without any structure or hope of meaning. Thayne made no effort to hide his displeasure. "We're never going to get anywhere with this cacophony."

They sat around a table of tacked-together driftwood, with chairs that were just big rough rocks. For comfort, there was a smooth stone on the floor to keep their feet out of the water. But Beezan had an adrenaline surge every time a crab ran over his feet as they scuttled about under the table. They didn't seem to have a concept of quiet or stillness. There was no prayer, no moment of silence, just one big clack to the sky at the beginning of the meeting.

Melawn, the famous data hunter, now a stunned refugee from the colony, sat wide-eyed and dripping in his colony clothes. Nkiroo, apparently, his longtime friend, kept patting him on the shoulder. "Here," Beezan said, passing Melawn his unused pad. "I'm not going to need this." Melawn clutched it to his chest and cried. That paused the chaos for a moment as the Navigators and Veez puzzled over his reaction.

There was a boss crab, or at least a bigger one, plus five assistants, and one small pale crab, supposedly the genius of the tribe. Ze waved a coral spike around, using it to write on the glassy black walls. It looked like they had just fused some rock to write on. But since the Humans hadn't explained what they wanted yet, Beezan had no idea what ze was writing. Several times, Iricana seemed as if she might take charge, but Veez whispered, "Patience."

Finally, Pascal arrived with a big Chike pad and slammed ziz tail on the wet floor to passable effect. "Stop this chatter! We have a serious mission." Ze turned to the boss. "These translators are worthless. Bring us an interpreter! Ten billion lives are at stake!"

The boss considered Pascal, turning ziz head to the big claw side as Pascal did the same. But no being was going to out-intimidate Pascal. *Click Clack!* The boss signaled and the five assistants scuttled out. Momentarily, a new crab came in. "Interpreter," ze bowed. "I am Talker." Ze pointed to the supposed genius. "Ze will be Expert. This one Boss."

The Humans nodded. "Understood," Pascal said, mollified.

"Boss here?" Talker asked, pointing a claw at Pascal.

Everyone except Thayne nodded. "The Exempt Pascal," Pascal said.

"Boss Pascal, what is your destination? We calculate."

Expert swayed back and forth in anticipation. Pascal took a breath and lit up his pad. "You will calculate a jump route from this marked location to one of these M class systems. It has to optimize all possible jumpspace motions." Ze paused and looked at them sternly. "We are going to jump a planet."

Melawn choked, *"What?"*

Talker froze. They *could* be still.

"Jump a planet," Pascal repeated. "Ten billion lives." Talker translated and Expert dropped ziz coral spike in the water. Boss crab sunk under the water. But then Expert reached out and snatched the pad from Pascal, staring at it with ziz eye stalks vibrating. "No!" ze said in plain Alkulu, and handed the pad back.

Pascal frowned, a scary sight.

"Ze means," Talker said, "that ze will not be responsible for such . . . travesty."

"It is going to be done," Pascal insisted, pushing the pad into Experts's claws. "Help us or let the lessers do it alone." Expert started waving and clacking frantically. Boss resurfaced.

Talker could hardly keep up. "Local stars, planetary motions, galactic rotation . . ."

"Yes," Thayne agreed. "Clusters, superclusters, great attractor, dark matter clumps, black holes."

"Not all space is anchored," Talker translated for Boss.

"The Chike will see to that once we have a route," Pascal said.

"Also the Chike will build planet-sized a-rings?" Talker asked.

"No," Pascal said. "Humans have freejumpers."

At this, the Navigators looked scornful, turning their heads from large side to small side, like less-scary Chike. "We have heard this misty rumor."

"This one," Pascal said, pointing at Beezan, but thankfully not poking him. Beezan sat up a little straighter.

"Tut!"

"And others."

"You think this squishy pilot can put a planet in the current and keep it there? *Impossible!*" Expert claimed. Part of Beezan's mind agreed.

Pascal leaned on the table to look Expert in ziz quivering eyes. "Find us a path that makes it possible."

In the wetroom on the colony

Melawn sat through an eternity of data dump during the rest of the meeting with the crabs, although none of it really settled after the mind-bending news of jumping a planet. Despite their logic, technology, and enthusiasm, Melawn could only see the deaths of ten billion people, either in a destabilized orbit or in the deep dark of a failed jump. Even the reckless Ramians wouldn't risk such a scheme.

Midnight, orbiting the colony planet

Aboard the shuttle on the ride up to *Midnight,* Nkiroo and Iricana tried to summarize everything about the convocation and gens. They showed Melawn photos of aliens, tens of them, with nicknames like the Stompers and the Swish. And the Chike really were called the Builders. The only bit that stuck in his mind was that humanity would be judged, and certainly fail, if they didn't pull off this planet-jumping miracle. Delusional.

In the *Midnight* lift, Melawn tried to keep his gear from

dropping on people's feet as they rode up from the Entry Lounge. He'd gone from the unfamiliar terror of being underwater back to the lifelong fear of decompression in space. What did it matter? Either way, if the thin manufactured walls failed, they'd be dead. It was only now that he realized that down on the planet, he'd been free of that ever-present worry.

Melawn tried to keep his stomach under control for the last few moments until they reached full gravity. But when he staggered out of the lift, even the spin gravity didn't feel right. "How long?" he asked no one in particular.

"Since you've been gone?" Iricana answered, "About 14 months." Not even a year. *How can that be?* Nkiroo and Danulell hovered around him, patting him on the back and reassuring him. The quiet Beezan seemed sympathetic. But Thayne obviously thought Melawn's reaction was lacking.

"You'll appreciate being home after a meal," Thayne said. "And you'll soon be back to your old self." *I don't want to be my old self. The one who couldn't stand up to you.* Thayne even maneuvered Danulell out of the way and took Melawn's arm possessively, radiating power.

"Captain," Melawn asked, "is there somewhere I can rest?"

"Of course. We're almost to your assigned cabin."

"Eat first," Thayne insisted.

But Melawn held his head like he couldn't take it anymore and slipped into the cabin. He set an alarm for one hour and collapsed on the bunk. A ship. Space. His people. But somehow not home. And the planet, also not home . . . but he felt an attachment, to the land, the people, the struggle for survival.

It seemed like only seconds later the alarm woke Melawn up. *I don't care,* he thought with just-waking clarity. *Let them jump planets. I don't care. If I have a destiny, if there is such a thing as destiny, mine is here, on this planet. This planet with the colony, the ocean and the temple, and even Heartless. This is my place.* Painful as it would be to leave Nkiroo, he had a problem he *could* solve and it was down on the planet.

A dish of food was on the table, his favorite, so Nkiroo must have brought it. He took a few bites, but it was weird, with a manufactured taste. He ate it anyway. He considered a shower, but there was no time. He linked the pad to the *Midnight* database and started downloading everything he could about salt water soil recovery and crop failure. He focused on his task, the files flashing before him.

Hours later, the door slid open without a knock and Melawn knew that he'd been interrupted by Thayne. So now, exhausted, he'd have to marshal all his will not to fall under Thayne's spell once again.

"What are you doing up?"

"What are you doing in my room at two in the morning?"

"Bringing you a uniform." Thayne hung the usual gold and white outfit on the edge of the bunk support. If anything, it was gaudier than before.

"I think I've grown out of that." *And I'm not going to need it.*

"It looks good on you. You should rest for the meeting tomorrow." Thayne leaned over to see what Melawn was doing, just one second before the file closed. "Soil reclamation?—of course, we can find a way to send that."

Now or never. "I'm going to take it." Melawn tried to sound steady, but his voice came out shaky. "I'm not staying."

Thayne's breath caught in surprise. "Don't be ridiculous. It will only take a few days to adjust."

"It's not about adjustment. When we get back to the meeting, I'm going to ask Pascal to repatriate 8000 spacers. Immediately. Then I'm going to go back and help the other 8000 people *not starve.*"

"No!" Thayne looked genuinely alarmed. "You can't make a deal! I already made zir an ultimatum! To get you! I told zir you were indispensable!"

"Then you lied."

"You're indispensable to me!"

"I'm not. You have a whole team here. I'm just your puppet. Your apologist."

Thayne put a hand on his chest and sat down on the bunk as if he were truly hurt. He started to reply and then didn't, hanging his head. "I really do need you. They didn't tell you about AnnaLee," he said quietly.

"They didn't have to. She was evil."

"She was. More than you know. She hijacked the shuttle."

"*What?*"

"On the way up from the planet. She hijacked the shuttle, tranked people, glued their hands together, kidnapped them, and tried to get the *81-Petals*. But the engine was gone. So Ra'Tama jumped to Tektite and got aboard his ship, which overcame her."

Melawn's heart was pounding. "Where is she?"

"Aboard the *Kingfisher*, on her way to court-martial and a life of infamy."

AnnaLee truly was evil. But she was not the bird in the back. Melawn couldn't control a surge of anger. "You're surprised? After everything she did on the colony? She broke laws, took followers and isolated them, and disrespected the institutions. She's delusional and thinks she knows more than anyone. More than everyone! How were those crimes okay, but hijacking a shuttle wasn't?"

Thayne was barely audible. "Because I've done all those things." Melawn sat back in his chair. That was true. And somehow hearing Thayne admit it made it impossible to deny anymore. And here he was, right back next to Thayne, feeling sorry for him. Thayne was holding his head in his hands. "I did all those things and no one stopped me."

Melawn slammed his hand on the panel. *"YOU'RE BLAMING US?"*

"Caspia helped! She made me think about it. You would have helped if you cared enough."

"We cared! You're the one who doesn't care about anything except being a hero!"

"I can't help that. It's just natural when you're—"

"A genius? Like AnnaLee?"

"That's why I need your help! AnnaLee turned into a monster! A monster that I could have been. That I'm one step away from being. Unless you help me."

"I can't help you! No one can save you except yourself! You want to be a hero? Be a real one. Go save Seven. But do it without me!" Melawn stood. "Door open!"

Thayne's face went to a dark angry place as he stood, not looking at Melawn, as if Melawn were the betrayer. But Melawn was done. Thayne stomped up the stairs without looking back.

The door hadn't even shut behind Thayne when someone else jammed it open and sidled in. Still breathing hard, Melawn called out, *"What?"* Behind the man, three more people with yellowish hair squeezed in and came halfway down the stairs.

"Sorry. Just gotta ask you—"

"It's the middle of the night!" Melawn complained.

"Bein' as you were up."

Melawn scowled and waved them down the stairs so he wouldn't have to look up at them. Outer sector people for sure. Mechanics. Tektites.

"Sorry, I'm Teeve."

"And I'm Maura. Mika and Coop there. They said you came

from the planet. Just really wantin' to ask about our people." Melawn breathed out slowly, letting go of his anger as much as possible. "They were on the *81-Petals.*"

Melawn nodded. "That crew has come down. They're okay. I've met a few, but there were thousands."

"Sunny? Danny?" Teeve asked.

He shook his head no. "I mostly know singles—unmarried people."

"Oh, ah, Chip and Kente then?" Maura asked.

A flash of crazy hair colors growing out, of slogans scribbled on jackets, two whispering kids sneaking looks at his match-making chart.

"Oh, those two. Yeah, I've seen them. They live in Yosemite."

They smiled with relief, and looked at each other, nodding. "Thanks, friend. We're comin' down with you tomorrow then."

"There's nothing down there for you!"

"Family's down there. That's everything to us."

On the colony

In the morning, when the shuttle took the target team down, the four Tektites hitched a ride, with the Captain's blessing. Thayne nearly had a mindstorm from the craziness of people going down to the planet on purpose.

This time the shuttle landed in the courtyard. The four Tektites gave Melawn friendly nods and walked off like they came to a planet every day, while the rest of them headed for the beach and the terrifying life bubbles.

But at the meeting that morning, there was no agreement to take back the spacers. Pascal flat out told them that only if Humans were declared GenThree would there be any thought of repatriation. Otherwise, everyone on the colony would stay, while everyone in space would be herded back to Sector 1. "However," Pascal said, staring down Melawn. "This one is in agreement that your mind is not on the mission. You will be sent back to the colony." There were gasps around the room.

"No!" Thayne said.

Pascal swerved his head to eyeball Thayne. "Is your mind also not on the mission? Do you need to return?" Thayne went ten shades of pale. Melawn had never seen him actually look afraid. He was totally silenced.

Melawn slipped the pad in his jacket and picked up his gear. "Please let me say goodbye."

"Outside," Pascal pointed over his shoulder with the big claw, dismissing him. "We have work to do."

Thayne was obviously stricken, yet he didn't come out to the corridor. Melawn had a moment of feeling like that deserting child again. But Iricana, Nkiroo, and Danulell had followed him out. Iricana hugged him. "God be with you Melawn."

"Please, if you can, let us know what happens."

"We'll find a way." She slipped back into the meeting.

Danulell put out his hands and Melawn put his on top in the Ramian way. "I'm so sorry Danulell. You're like a brother to me, but I have to go back."

Danulell shook his head, colors yellow. "Never be sorry to follow your heart. I will get our brother Quay back, and you will find a new family and your service."

"Good luck, Danulell. Goodbye."

"Not goodbye. I had a life on a planet. Then I had a life on a finder ship. And then in a pocket for nine years. And then in a ship and then a colony, and then a sailing ship. And now I'm back in space. We're young. We have many lives ahead. Are you so sure of God's plan that you would say goodbye?"

Melawn's eyes filled with tears, but he smiled. "Then no. Until next greeting. Even if it's in heaven."

Danulell left him alone in the corridor with Nkiroo. "I'm so sorry. I know you have to stay. And I have to go."

Nkiroo put his hands on Melawn's shoulders. "You were more than my brother. You were my first real solid person, the first one I could count on." Melawn's tears rolled down his cheeks as Nkiroo squared his shoulders. "But I know, you're not meant to be a prisoner of Thayne. That's not *your* destiny."

Melawn hugged Nkiroo so tightly he thought ribs might break—a hug for a whole life. "Please, if you ever see my parents," Melawn whispered, "tell them I'm so sorry."

And then Melawn's tears mixed with seawater at the bottom of the life bubble as he turned his back on his friends, his family, and ten billion people on Seven, clutching the data that might save the colony.

6-Glory

Colony

Beezan sat in the wetroom, day after day, not trying to stay dry, or following the consultation, not even really paying attention to anything. The "Target Team," Expert, Talker, Thayne, Iricana, and Pascal, spent the time sorting through the many variables of how and where to jump a planet. Veez was there too, but he only came to represent—and sample the seafood.

They would scratch on the wall, use the Navigator's fancy holographic maps, and do a lot of hand and claw waving in multiple languages, plus math. Occasionally, they would ask Beezan how he "felt" about a certain route, or if he thought a particular star would have a strong path from Seven. "Hmmm," Pascal would then say, matching Beezan's answer with a chart that already had all the information they could ever want. After all, the Builders had programmed the control boxes.

Beezan's true purpose in coming was to get away from the *Midnight*, where the crew was watching the convocation nonstop. Every day, a Chike ship, or other GenTwo ship, would pop into the colony system and send a day's worth of convocation recording, which Terina would put on her feed. If he spent all day on the planet and then quickly slipped into his cabin when he got back, he could avoid the worst of it. He didn't even read Terina's summaries, but instead trusted Jarvie to relay basic information that wouldn't break his heart.

Tonight, he was tempted to go to the kitchen, just to have some uncrabby company, but Jarvie brought him dinner and shook his head. "Grim day for the Ramians," he said.

"Oh no."

"Three witnesses testified." Jarvie hesitated. "One was a podpup. I mean, still in podpup form, but really a GenOne. I guess it takes some days or weeks to reform into their true shape."

Beezan ate slowly, signaling for Jarvie to continue. "The podpup was blue. And kind of funny. Like ze still had the podpup spunk." Jarvie smiled. "Ze talked about being well-treated, about how the podpups didn't mind the genetic manipulation of their colors, since they like the colors. Ze was generally upbeat. Ze voted the Ramians GenThree.

"But then . . . a GenOne frog testified. This one had been a bird, one of those with the cameras. But ze had been here long enough to return to its frog form." Jarvie looked down. "I had no idea. The birds have been genetically altered to seek out emotion. And each bird has one eye replaced with a camera."

"Gross."

"And they're expected to fly into dangerous situations, just to get the photos."

"Why don't the Ramians use drones?"

"The Ramians don't use robots."

"*What?*" But Beezan thought about it. He didn't remember ever seeing one. "How did I miss that?"

"Why build when you can breed, apparently. And that's not the worst of it. The last witness was also in frog form, but ze talked about being a "digger." Ze was some kind of animal, bred for mining. Ze had to dig underground all day."

"Horrible."

"It's not that the gens are against domestication, it's just that by the GenOne creed, you have to treat all creatures humanely—properly. You know what I mean. They called it "with loving care." And the podpups are special. No one is supposed to mess with them."

"We figured that out."

"Yes, thanks to the council. But it makes me wonder if they were planted on Azure, for us to find."

"Like a test?"

"Yeah."

Beezan felt bad for the Ramians. "It doesn't look good for them."

"No, but not as bad as some others. At least all their witnesses survived. Not so for some clades."

"The witnesses really made a sacrifice."

Jarvie nodded. "Humanity's witnesses are up tomorrow."

"Humanity did some awful things at one time. Not just to animals."

"I know. Hard to believe. So glad I wasn't around then. But we're being judged on current times."

And later, Beezan considered. For all his heartache, he was happy to be here, in these times, with these challenges, to have the bounty to see the ways. He was grateful.

7-Glory

Back in the wetroom, Beezan contemplated how many more

weeks, or months, he could stand the scary ride through the atmosphere on that hideous Chike shuttle, twice a day. Technological geniuses maybe, but comfort, Chike had no use for.

Suddenly Veez stopped eating his third breakfast and pulled out his p'link device. Pascal frowned as if he were listening to something, and raised a claw. Thayne and Expert froze. Talker held up her spike and it was suddenly broadcasting in the Navigator language. "What's happening?" Iricana asked Veez.

"A ship has just arrived with news. The convocation was interrupted with an emergency announcement."

Talker sent a visual of the announcement to the main wall, so Beezan now had a large view of exactly what he didn't want to see. The speaker was a frog. Beezan slapped his hands over his eyes, but Iricana grasped his shoulder and whispered, "That's not Sky." And it wasn't. Somehow he could tell.

A new frog, also not Sky, leaped to the podium and began the announcement without any sort of greeting. Talker immediately translated. "The GenOne have just completed an emergency test of jumpspace. All indications are that the narrowing of the ways is exceeding historical parameters. We estimate that the ways are in danger of complete collapse—"

They gasped, hissed, and clicked unconsciously. "Hush!" Pascal warned.

Talker went on, "—consequently, all the witness testimony will conclude in two sessions. Harbingers will appear the next two sessions, and deliberation will be finalized in ten sessions. All parties should return to sustainable systems in . . ." Talker paused and looked at Thayne, ". . . 50 Human days. Contingency plans will be announced." The frog had already leaped down the stairs. The convocation was in chaos. Talker flipped off the screen.

"Fifty days?"

"Good," Thayne said.

"*What?*" Veez said.

"That severely limits our choices. It will be much easier to calculate. We need a target that can be reached from a trajectory available in the next 40 days," Thayne said.

"35," Beezan said automatically. "If we survive jumping a planet, we'll need to rest before jumping home."

Thayne nodded sharply and turned back to the wall of calculations, wiping it clean with one hand. Beezan sat up. He scolded himself for his earlier indifference. There was no time to lose here.

8-Glory

Midnight, in orbit around the colony planet

Zahar huddled in the Observation Bay with almost everyone else that was aboard. Her stomach churned. Today, the Human witnesses would testify. And as bad luck would have it, Zombie was first.

Zombie, slightly bigger than she had been, and with more bulging eyes, but still mostly rat-like, took the podium. "The Humans called me Zombie." *This is going to be bad.* "It means a reanimated corpse. And it was true. They killed me over and over. Each time, I survived due to the GenOne core." Her voice was even but angry. The stadium was dead silent, as it had been for previous horror stories of other clades.

"Not just myself, but other innocents were blasted with radiation, given chemicals, genetic treatments, and all matter of sickening, painful procedures. Yes, we got pain meds, but that just made me forget even the remnant of who I really was, until I thought I was one of the rats, a beaten-down, inbred strain of a once-clever, if lower, species." She looked out over the convocation.

"Why?" The chief judge asked.

"They were experimenting on me! On all the rats. But the others were lucky enough to die! All to save a few Humans."

Zahar glanced over at the twins. Euro had his arm around Io, who was slumped in guilt. "She told us it didn't hurt them," Io whispered to Euro, but Euro just shook his head sadly.

"It was terrible!" Zombie continued. "I asked them in every primitive way I knew to stop. But the doctor was relentless."

"Did anyone else come to your aid?"

"The young Humans were kind. Podpups were sympathetic, but none of them had influence. I believe they thought they were treating us well enough."

"How would you rate them?"

"GenFive!" she said without hesitation.

"Your sacrifice does you and your family honor. The GenOne offer our sincere sympathy and thanks for your service. Your duties are concluded."

That seemed to mollify her a bit. She nodded once and leaped down. "Not your fault," many people said to Io and Euro. And it wasn't. But Zahar was older. She should have spoken up more.

The podium was rearranged.

"What is that?" Gola asked as a huge hoofed animal stepped up.

"A horse, of course," Kelson said, with his mischievous smile. It was a beautiful, powerful animal, bronze and white, with a golden mane and tail. It reminded Zahar of Melawn, who'd left without even saying goodbye. The horse spoke through a vocalizer on its neck and had made no attempt to change into a frog.

"The Humans called me Copper, a name I wear proudly. For eighteen years I ran free in the Great Plains. I barely ever saw a Human. I would have nothing to report except one day a woman walked out and greeted me like an equal. She stirred awake my GenOne being. She politely asked me to come, so I followed her. It took many hours. That is how far she walked to find me.

"And when I got to her ranch, there was a young child, crippled on the inside. The woman introduced me and asked if the child could ride. I didn't know what she meant, but then she put the child on my back, and we became one. I spent 52 years with that child—until the Chike called for me. I would not have come back. I wish I could send a message that I never meant to leave them. I wish I could return as a GenOne in this form. If only it were permitted."

"The taboo is not under discussion here. Tell us how you were treated."

"Always with respect, kindness, almost reverence sometimes. I found the Humans to be loyal, gentle, and possessed of keen insight."

"And your judgment?"

"GenThree."

There was a sigh of relief in the room. Zahar hung her head. The horsewoman had sensed the true essence of the horse as a GenOne, even though the horse itself wasn't fully conscious of it. She had walked all that way for that particular horse. Zahar had comforted Zombie, and hated the experiments, but never considered that she might be more than a particularly scrappy rat.

"Next, the last witness of EarthClade."

Jarvie was next to Zahar, although a tumble of podpups was between them. They both took big calming breaths as Sky gracefully took the podium. Clearly it was her, still in podpup form, if slightly larger. Her soft sweet eyes scanned the stadium and then looked at the camera as if searching.

"Greetings friends," she said in Alkulu, to the mumbled consternation of the audience. She nodded and switched to the GenOne language. "My name among the GenOne was Kreedia Onsolay. But the Humans called me Sky."

The podpups stared, gathering around Jarvie. "Sky?" Star asked, puzzled.

Jarvie picked him up and held him. "Yes, grown-up Sky."

"I was born on a ship in the outer sectors, and in the manner of podpups, bonded with a protector, a friend." She paused for many beats. The judges got restless.

"How was your treatment?"

She focused on the judge. "I found myself in the care of an exceptional being. I was taught to speak, allowed to read, to listen to music, to converse. I learned prayers. I had a real life of an intelligent being. I met the Ramians. I explored. I had pack-mates, Human family, food, fun. I was loved."

"What was asked of you?"

"Nothing, other than to follow safety rules."

"And your judgment of EarthClade?"

And here she paused, rocketing up Zahar's heart rate. "The Humans are so diverse. And yet they are united. Goodness and loyalty and adventure run through them. And they possess a vision, a feeling for the ways that even the GenOne do not have. For all our sakes, I beg you to make them GenThree."

It was over for the day. Jarvie dissolved in tears. Katie came to sit by him. "So like Sky in sweet innocence and compassion, and yet somehow mature," she said. Jarvie nodded.

"Sky home?" Star asked.

"No, little one," Katie answered. Jarvie hugged Star and buried his head in white fur. It was probably the last time any of them would see Sky. But the witnesses had been 2 to 1 in favor of humanity. There was hope.

The wetroom

Despite the new deadline and fewer variables, the target team still had an extraordinary task. Beezan was as focused as he could be, determined not to be distracted by thoughts of Sky testifying. *It's over. She's nowhere near here.*

Thayne was the only other person besides Beezan who didn't follow the convo. He seemed truly stunned and regretful that his prodigy had left him. Every night he studied the Navigator math. He had small fits that the others called mindstorms. He ranted at them, and then, shockingly against character, apologized. He banged his head on the table until Caspia threatened to sedate him. She was the only one he listened to. And he hated the shuttle ride as much as Beezan.

This morning, there were storms that swept the shuttle up and down sickeningly. "Old-time piloting!" Veez exulted, never missing a bite of his second breakfast.

Beezan tried to pray, but was distracted by Thayne's nearly tearful ranting. Beezan knew that Thayne had done some terrible things, including transferring that gravity ball on the *Drumheller* without telling them. But he was sympathetic to ordinary human misery. He reached out and grasped Thayne's arm, trying to steady him. Thayne looked up at Beezan, puzzled. Powerful, confused intelligence glittered from his dark eyes. "You see the ways, don't you?" he said, almost sounding jealous. "You CAN jump the planet, can't you?"

"If it's God's Will," Beezan whispered.

"You better!"

. . .

And then, in the wetroom, Thayne argued with Expert, more forcefully than before. "No!" Thayne said, and took the coral spike from Expert's claw and wrote on the wall himself. *He has actually learned their math!* Expert objected, not to the taking, but to the math. A loud discussion erupted, that Talker couldn't translate. Iricana stepped back, unable to follow. But there was a charged feeling in the room like they were on the brink of a breakthrough.

Expert grabbed the spike back, but Talker handed Thayne ziz own, and back and forth they went, objecting, insisting, scratching out, stabbing the rock. Expert poked Thayne with ziz claw and Thayne poked zir right back.

But there was no quick resolution. For hours they went, until Expert gave up and sat contemplating. Or sulking.

Iricana wiped her wet hands on her uniform. "Time to go."

"No," Thayne said. "I'm staying."

"I'm not sure that's a good idea."

"I'll stay with him," Beezan volunteered, having no ambition to return to the *Midnight* and news of the Human witnesses.

So Beezan slept on the driftwood table, immune to the clicking, the sloshing, and the voices of genius math. *Maybe it will help me*, he fantasized.

It was the quiet that finally filtered down to Beezan's consciousness and woke him up. In the soft bioluminescence he could see Thayne, collapsed on a small hammock, and Expert, just under water, eyes retracted, sleeping.

Beezan sat up and looked at the wall. Amid scribbles in two languages, a rough path was sketched. He got up and looked closer. He flicked on the imager to display the actual systems. *That's the path.* A surge of otherworldly fear and confidence collided inside him. Yes, he could jump a ship on that path. *But can I jump a planet?*

9-Glory

On the colony

Beezan was still in the wetroom, thinking about the planet Seven. Apparently, it was in Ramian space, but it was another race of GenFour. One of the troublesome ones. They didn't even have a harbinger at the convocation. And he was supposed to jump that planet, with ten billion people on it, to a different star system. He was staring at the path when a crowd of crabs came in, along with Pascal. "You see the path?" Pascal asked.

"Yes."

"Squishy will never jump the planet," Boss clacked as ze poked Beezan.

"Come with me and find out," Beezan answered, sick of all the poking.

"Tut!"

"Veez says he is the one," Pascal said evenly. "But we will let the pilots choose. Meanwhile, post the timeline."

Talker sent a diagram to the screen. "Twenty-nine days!" Beezan gasped.

"Yes," Pascal said. "We have work to do." And this time, the "we" meant Pascal, who organized big claw and small. Ze demanded action from multiple clades, both on screen and clicking away on ziz pad. Pascal was not some young lackey assigned to lowly Humans. Ze was an all-powerful taboo-free operator.

Ze arranged for the Terraformers to jump ahead to the target system and clear out an orbital zone. "The target system needs a designation / name."

"Target one," Expert suggested.

"It must be auspicious!" Pascal said. Expert's eyes rolled at the top of ziz eye stalks.

"Safewaters," Thayne whispered.

Talker clicked. Expert and boss flexed up and down on their legs, possibly equivalent to shrugging. But Pascal considered and nodded. "Acceptable."

Later that wild day, Pascal checked on the team that would build the planet-steering pusher shuttles. "We will need 200 pilots. We will meet at Seven. It is arranged." Ze turned to Beezan and Thayne. "Say your farewells. We go."

Beezan nodded to Expert, "Thank you for the path," to Talker, "Thank you for translating," and turned to Boss. But before he could come up with anything polite to say, Boss cut in.

"Have a quick trip to heaven, Squishy." Talker hunkered down as ze translated.

Thayne didn't even bother exchanging pleasantries, except for trading pokes with Expert and attempting to leave with a coral spike. Pascal snatched it from him. "With the Chike, genius and immaturity do not go claw in claw," ze commented as they headed for the last shuttle ride, finally.

. . .

By evening, Pascal had compiled all the data, formed a minute-by-minute timeline, gathered the names of 200 pilots, and sent a map to the GenOne for approval. Pilots were already on the way. Pascal got onscreen with some high-up GenOne official. Iricana and Beezan stood beside zir in their best clothes as ze argued for their future.

"Who presumes to jump a planet?" The GenOne frog asked. Beezan's heart pounded, but he tried not to betray his revulsion to the frog form. *Sky is one. Sky is one.*

Pascal argued for something called "Acceptance by Trial," meaning that humanity would be granted GenThree status after performing some great task. There would be no discussion, no committee, no research. "Approve the trial or not, now."

The stern frog rattled off a list of all the things that had to go right. Of the risk, of unforeseen cosmic consequences such as the Destroyer was already pumping out. Pascal stood strong, answering every question.

"There are no a-rings big enough!"

"Humans have freejumpers. Here is one, right here." For the first time, the frog's eyes rolled to Beezan. Ze sat back on ziz haunches and stared.

"This is the one."

"The freejumper, yes," Pascal answered.

"No. The one Kreedia Onsolay spoke of."

Pascal and Beezan exchanged baffled looks. "Sky," Iricana whispered.

"Yes," the GenOne continued. "The witness called Sky."

Beezan clasped his chest, while Pascal quickly affirmed. "Yes. Sky's person. This one."

The GenOne nodded. "Acceptance by Trial approved."

"Can Sky come with us?" Beezan asked desperately.

"Impossible. That one is in transition." And any hope Beezan had of seeing Sky the podpup again was gone.

Lanezi hurried to his cabin where Katie was just cleaning up for dinner. "What's wrong?" she asked.

"The jump meeting," he answered, trying to keep his voice under control. Her face paled with dread.

After all he'd been through. And finally, finally, some peace and love and family in his life!

"You're not the one pilot that has to go down to the planet?" she asked, crossing the cabin to take his arm.

"No," he croaked. "No. Beezan, of course. Jarvie will go with him. Gadi and Gola will take them down in a shuttle." She squeezed his arm reassuringly. "But I'll be leading the 200."

"Is that bad?"

He sat down with her, dropping his head into his hands. "I expected to be one of 200. If anything went wrong, or we ended up in the wrong place, I would just jump back to you, on my own."

"Abandon them?"

"It's part of the deal. No matter what happens, the pilots get to save themselves."

"How?"

"The 200 are each taking a Chike shuttle with the push-along gravity ball. Except these are supergravity balls. We're to fly in a formation near the planet that will cause an interference pattern. The amplified gravity waves will pull the planet into the path."

"Wow."

"Thayne, Iricana, Pascal, and one of the Navigators figured it out." Katie frowned and Lanezi continued. "And then once we're lined up with the path, Beezan will jump us. All of us."

"The shuttles?"

"The planet, the atmosphere, shuttles, everything. Just like we jump ourselves with a whole ship around us. We have to jump it to a system they're calling Safewaters. There's orbital room there."

She looked at him worriedly. "Do you believe it can be done?"

He stared down at the deck. "Faith I have—in God. But that much faith in Honor Beezan? In all fairness, I wouldn't have that much faith in myself, or any person."

"Maybe Beezan's faith is not in himself."

He closed his eyes and nodded. *Truth. Only by the grace of God are we going to do this.* "Tomorrow, we're jumping to Seven. Then the fleet will split up," he whispered, pulling the screen over so they could see the just-posted crew assignments. "*Wheel of Fire* is meeting us at Seven, bringing the other pilots for the 200. The pilots will come aboard *Midnight*. Then you're going ahead to Safewaters System, aboard the *Wheel of Fire*, which is good. We'll be jumping the planet towards our loved ones."

She grasped his hand. "We'll be split up?"

"Yes. The day after we arrive at Seven, *Wheel* will jump to Safewaters. You'll be on it."

"Two days!" She hugged him fiercely as they read the names.

10-Glory

Midnight, in orbit around the colony planet

Zahar stared out of the Observation Bay window at a real live view of the colony planet. It was spectacular, almost like

Earth—probably as close to Earth as she'd ever get. She wished her family could see it.

She was hiding in the Observation Bay until her shift started, trying to calm her rising anger. Everyone else was watching the convo or talking about jumping a planet. All that organizing should be just her thing, but she'd had enough of these crazy schemes. She just wanted to find her family—en route to Firelight, according to the Family & Friends Finder. But since she had been stuck at the convocation and now here at the colony, with no Human ships to take a message, her query sat in the *Midnight* packet queue.

Zahar's only hope was to get off at Harbor. All the Human pilots were gathering there. The *Midnight* would rendezvous there before jumping on to Seven and meeting the Ramian pilots. She'd probably end up on the last refugee ship out of Harbor. But it was better than another misguided adventure. Her p'link chimed the five-minute warning for the crew meeting.

Okay, patience. She headed for the stairs. But just as she stepped into the rimway, Caspia grabbed her and pulled her back onto the stairs. "Have you heard?"

"What?"

"We're going to jump straight to Seven."

"What happened to Harbor?"

"'Waste of time,' says Pascal. They just assume everyone is all in for this, but I know you're not."

Zahar tried to maintain her composure, but it was yell at Caspia or cry. "How am I supposed to get home?"

"Come with me to the captain."

"What's wrong?" Iricana asked immediately seeing Zahar so upset. Caspia steered Zahar to a chair in Consultation Hall.

Everyone was there. She was mortified. But she took a big breath. Now was not the time to cave into these people.

"Captain. I respectfully request not to go to Seven. I have every right to be returned to the sectors."

"Of course," Iricana said. "We'll have to drop you off somewhere safe."

"No time," Pascal said, snapping his jaws shut. "The underling will have to come. Or send her down to the colony."

Underling? Colony? Zahar gripped her hands under the table. Whatever she said now might determine her whole life. She tried to summon that inner captain she had been. "Captain. Honors. Even in emergencies, people have rights. There must be others who don't want to go." She looked around the room.

All the pilots were obviously going. She appealed to Io and Euro. "We're with Lanezi," Euro said quietly.

She looked at Caspia. "I'm so sorry. I'm with Evan."

"I'm with my daughter," Kelson said kindly.

"I'm with my mom—and Beezan," Terina said, determined.

"I'm with Beezan."

"Beezan, Beezan, Beezan," the others coursed.

Tears clouded her vision. She looked at Nkiroo. "I'm with Thayne."

"You promised!"

"I'm so sorry. It's as you said back then; I couldn't really promise."

Suddenly, a large tail wrapped around her. "I will take her."

What? Everyone looked up at Veez, standing next to Zahar's chair, tail gently around her shoulders. "Exempt Pascal, Captain, and my dearest friends, I find myself on the eve of farewell."

"You're not coming?" Iricana asked.

"My ship entered orbit this morning. I'm returning to the

convocation tomorrow. As it turns out, I must deliver Quay's family to the convocation."

"They're going back?" Thunder asked.

"All except Danulell. He will continue on the *Watcher* with Getti Drann and the Ramian pilots. I can take Zahar with me and be sure she is returned to Human space with Honor Oatah. If that is acceptable to all."

"Yes!" Zahar turned to Iricana, "Please, Captain."

There was a long silence as Iricana studied Veez. "Why the sudden change of heart?" she asked Veez.

"My friends, I wish you all the best—and I do believe if anyone can do this thing, your assembled selves can. But I lost many years with my pack and I want to rejoin them."

They looked rattled. Like receiving a vote of no confidence. But Iricana took him at his word. "I entrust my crew to you, Honor Veez. Safe travels."

Caspia hugged Zahar goodbye. "God be with you." Zahar managed to get all the way around the table hugging. Jarvie, Io, Euro, Terina, Gadi, and Gola trailed after her to have one last treat together. Terina passed her a recorder and a notebook. "Be my reporter at the convocation?"

"Of course."

"Why do you think Veez is really leaving?" Terina asked.

"What?" Jarvie was shocked. "You suspect something?"

She narrowed her eyes. "Veez," she said, looking straight at Zahar. "Keep your eyes on him."

12-Glory

Midnight, at Seven

Beezan stood at the exit of the lift, greeting the pilots as they shuttled over from the *Wheel of Fire*. He wished he could say goodbye to Tiati in person, just in case he didn't survive the jump. But Tiati would have none of that, telling him on screen that he'd see him on the other side.

The crew had already said tearful goodbyes to their small delegation headed for Safewaters with Tiati. 194 pilots were coming aboard now, in groups of 10 to 30. Beezan shook their hands, got their names, and whispered a prayer for each one.

With Taj supervising, Gola, Gadi, Jarvie, Lanezi, and Evan got them settled in their cabins. They were young, old, retired, and plain tired. They'd made multiple emergency jumps to meet the *Wheel* in time. Most of them were packet friends meeting in person for the first time, but it wasn't going to be a party.

They looked Beezan in the eyes, holding his hand a moment longer than normal, weighing what they'd heard against the person in front of them. He had no confidence to offer them, no glib assurances, nothing but hope and humility.

Mission Save Seven Feed

Midnight jumping to Seven—crew remaining on the Midnight

Pascal – Mission Consultant
Iricana – Captain
Taj – 2nd in Command
Thunder—3rd in Command
Falcon – Monitor
Caspia – Doctor
Beezan – planet
Jarvie / Star – planet
Pongola – planet shuttle pilot
Magadi – planet shuttle monitor

Lanezi / Whisper – in command of the 200
Io / Summer, Dusty
Euro / Blue
Sequoia – *Midnight* pilot
Evan – One of the 200 shuttles
+ 194 pilots to be transferred from *Wheel*

Wheel of Fire meeting _Midnight_ at Seven, then jumping to Safewaters System

Captain Tiati and family and crew
Kelson – *Midnight* delegation leader
Thayne – Target team
Nkiroo – Target team
Katie – Doctor
Terina / Rocket – Reporter

Watcher at Seven

Getti Drann – Captain
Neah + Sontula / Purple friend
Danulell
Widinmay
Shiwelna
Gosikeen
Kells

Veez's Ship returning to the convocation

Veez and crew
Zahar
Danumae
Zhenulell
Zhenumae
Kavilor
Zhenulor

Zahar's jump back to the convocation was quick in Veez's cozy but surprisingly efficient Scamper ship. It was equipped with the Chike push-along gravity ball, but not the awful striped décor. They'd arrived two hours ago, but were just now getting situated. Sniff and Smaller turned out to be Veez's bridge crew and his grandchildren. Danulell's family stayed in their cabin to watch the proceedings, but Zahar was allowed on the bridge.

"Where are the offspring with the snacks?" Veez complained.

"Probably ate the snacks themselves," Smaller commented, while Sniff studied the ship tracker.

"Fuzz!" Sniff exclaimed. "Lots of ships leaving. We're going to have to stay out of the flight paths."

"The GenOne were positive that we have weeks before the ways collapse," Smaller said.

"But some do have a long way to go," Veez said, "and want to get back to family." Zahar nodded, sympathizing.

"We're only ten hours out," Sniff reported, "but no way are

we going to get down to the planet today." Ze looked up at Veez. "The last of the harbingers will speak in a few minutes."

"What's happened so far?" Veez asked.

"Here," Sniff said and sent the feed to the big curved screen.

A large image of the harbinger platform appeared. The twelve leafy harbinger chairs were partially full. The first nine chairs had large, square, lighted signs above them.

"Look," Veez pointed out for Zahar. "That sign gives the status. These seven clades have all been declared GenThree. Those three slashes are a very old-fashioned way to mark three, but everyone understands." Zahar nodded. Hard to miss. But the signs over two chairs had a dot followed by a slash. "Base four, you know," Veez continued. "Those two, the fifth and ninth clades, were declared GenFive; may the Creator protect them." The three Scampers made slight paw motions, either of blessing or warding. But those two harbinger chairs were empty.

"Their harbingers left?" Zahar asked.

"Oh, they're taken out immediately. They're not part of the leaf."

"Probably on one of those ships out of here," Sniff added.

Zahar used Veez's pad to zoom into Quay. He was looking up at the GenFive symbol above his seatmate's empty chair. He would be the first to speak today. *Good luck*, she wished him.

"It's starting," Smaller said.

As the view zoomed in, Zahar realized that the last chair was also empty. Only Quay and Oatah remained to testify. The Prime approached the platform and said the blessing. Then ze turned and looked at the harbingers. "Last call for LuessClade."

"Foolhardy," Veez exclaimed. "They have not appeared. Historically, this has not gone over well." The entire arena waited in silence, watching the empty seat. Quay and Oatah turned around to look behind them, but no one came. The Prime lowered ziz head. Suddenly, the sign above the last seat switched to a number. Veez demonstrated by counting on his paw. "Dot-slash-slash. Four, five, six."

"Oh no." Even the sarcastic Sniff seemed stunned.

"GenSix?" Zahar asked.

"Terrible." Veez pulled his whiskers back.

"What's the difference between GenFive and GenSix?"

Veez held his paw to his chest in sympathy. "GenFive will be confined to their own planetary system. Their gravity ball will be shut down, control panels destroyed. But the GenTwo and GenThree will still oversee and they'll be reconsidered in 500 years." He didn't go on.

"And . . ."

"Well, the GenSix will be sent back to their primary *planet*. The Gravity ball will be removed. No supervision or help of any kind will be offered. To join the leaf, they will have to develop their own technology. And they won't be reconsidered regard-less, for 5000 years."

"Five thousand! Has that ever happened?"

"No GenSix has joined the leaf in . . . about a million years.

"Have the others survived?"

Veez was quiet a moment, considering. Out of the corner of her eye Zahar saw both Sniff and Smaller turn their heads slightly and give him a warning glance.

"Well, we've no way to know of course," Veez explained with a casual wave of his paw.

And suddenly Zahar realized what sort of spying Veez really did. She tried to keep her face neutral and hope the two younger Scampers were not good at reading Human emotions. "Harsh," she said.

"Maybe," Smaller added. "But consider that without the

gravity balls in their systems, which are basically invitations to join the leaf, they never would have been out here to start with."

"Yes, precisely," Veez nodded approvingly. "It's more of a privilege to join than a punishment not to."

Zahar scowled. She was tired from the jump and anxious to get home. She would hold out hope for humanity, whatever Gen they were assigned.

"Forty-three ships jumping out," Smaller said, attempting to change the subject.

"So what happens," Zahar asked, "when the ways are closed?"

"No one can jump," Sniff said.

"Yes, so what happens to all this Gen stuff? Don't the clades rearrange? Different clades take over?"

"Oh, no," Veez answered. "Like a GenTwo rebellion?" They all laughed. "That will never happen."

"Besides, the ways are only closed for a short time," Smaller explained.

News to me. "Short, like . . ."

Veez considered, "Oh, in Human time, a few years. A hundred at the most."

"So what does it matter?" she said, annoyed. "What difference does it make to be isolated to your system if no one can jump anywhere anyway? Everyone is isolated!"

"That's the spirit!" Veez said.

"My bet is on EarthClade," Smaller said, nodding. And Zahar wondered if they did have a betting ring.

"Ahh," Veez pointed to the screen.

Slowly, Quay stood, holding the banister in front of him. He had regained his visionary look and his colors blazed the blue of destiny. "Oh," Smaller breathed. "That one is a true harbinger."

"Greetings from RamiaClade," Quay announced firmly,

looking out over the arena. "It sorrows me that I cannot consult with my people and must make this statement on my own. As you may know, our society was once very timid, by nature. We have been guided to look to the few bold among us, to align ourselves with the daring. Our people call them, those few, the jik. They inspire all, but their personal helpers are called the tan." He motioned to the other clades. "I see here many clades, brilliant, compassionate, defiant, peaceful, shy, but only one bold." With a strong ringing voice, he turned to the Prime. "RamiaClade announces itself tan, helpers, as a clade. We attach ourselves and put our fate in our new jik: EarthClade."

Oatah's head snapped around to look at Quay, but Quay was slowly sitting down, head humbly lowered. The crowd erupted in hissing. "Oh my God! Veez?" Zahar asked.

"Unexpected," Smaller said.

"But," Veez tapped his own nose with a paw finger. "But yet, a brilliant move, under the circumstances."

The GenFive symbol flashed over Quay's chair, and two Coursers approached him. Zahar's heart went out to him as he was escorted out. Visionary, he may be, but so young to have the destiny of his people on him. She wished she were there to offer support and say goodbye. At least his family would be there soon.

Then the Prime rose and looked at Oatah as the camera zoomed in. "EarthClade, please rise."

"Greetings—"

Suddenly, the Prime put a four-fingered hand up to stop Oatah. "We have a special announcement." The arena went silent. "In the case of EarthClade, the GenOne have agreed to Acceptance by Trial."

Smaller and Sniff gasped. But Veez and Zahar nodded grimly. The Prime went on, with the translator struggling to keep up. "It has been 10,000 years since the GenOne have agreed to an Acceptance by Trial, and 400,000 years since one has been successful. EarthClade has been granted this chance." The light over Oatah's chair went solid red. And then the light over Quay's chair changed from GenFive to red.

"Since RamiaClade has declared themselves helpers of EarthClade, they will share the same fate. Their task will be to save another GenFour clade from certain destruction, or they will both be declared GenSix."

"Oh, no!"

"Excellent!" Veez said.

Whose side is he on? "Veez! This isn't a movie!"

"Oh, no. Entertaining as your people are. This is dead serious. The Exempt Pascal must have been more persuasive than I expected. This is by far the best chance for all of you."

"Alert!"

Sniff practically jumped from ziz seat. "All GenThree ships must exit the system," ze reported.

"They seem quite serious," Smaller noted.

"Well, we have to transfer our passengers to their ships," Veez said, matter-of-factly.

Sniff turned to the ship tracker, running ziz paws over the panel quickly. Ze stopped and did it again. "There are a lot of ships," Smaller commented, helping. There must have been an ultrasonic communication then, as Veez and the two put their noses together suddenly. Then Veez sat back.

"There must be some small delay. There is no Human or Ramian ship in system."

"Humph. Maybe they are hiding?" Zahar asked.

"We have checked for that." *And they would know how . . .*

"But I'm afraid it does not matter. Neither Oatah nor Quay can leave until a final decision is made. Sadly, we are going to have to leave all of you on the planet." And he really did seem sad.

"I understand. It's okay." She glanced at the screen. "Look!" Quay was being escorted back to the harbinger platform, but he didn't sit in his chair. He came to stand behind Oatah. Oatah gestured him forward and they stepped to the banister side by side, looking out over the railing at the Gens.

Midnight shuttle *Snapdragon*, approaching *Wheel of Fire*, at Seven

Rocket whined in his box as Terina and the others approached the *Wheel of Fire* hanger in the shuttle *Snapdragon*. "Almost there, sweetie," she assured him. She flashed back to the day she'd boarded the *Drumheller*. It seemed so long ago. And the *81-Petals*, and then the *Midnight*, and now *Wheel*. And she was not with her mom. In truth, Terina fully expected to see them again soon. Her mom's job, piloting the *Midnight*, was the safest pilot job of the mission. Gadi, Gola, Jarvie, and Beezan had the most dangerous job, going down to the planet. But she had full faith in all of them.

Her grandfather was in charge of their little delegation that would jump ahead to the target system, Safewaters. She had the feeling Thayne was annoyed about it, but couldn't argue with such an elder. Now Nkiroo piloted the shuttle to take them to *Wheel of Fire*, and Thayne sat up front, acting as monitor, as far away from Rocket as he could get.

Grandfather Kelson unbuckled and floated over his seat to face them. Everyone came to quiet attention. Even Thayne turned around to listen. "My friends," her grandfather said mildly, "by all reports, the *Wheel* is a very casual cargo ship and we're likely to be greeted by a slap on the back and a joke." The crew smiled. "But we don't want to convey any disrespect ourselves. So please be prepared for formal boarding. Of course, I will introduce Thayne and Nkiroo as mission specialists, Katie as doctor, and then Terina.

And when they got to the Entry Lounge of the *Wheel* and lined up in seniority order, they were greeted by Hana, the Captain's wife, and two kids, a toddler and a baby. So of course Terina had to let Rocket out, and then it was chaos. The toddler took Rocket and floated out with him first, kids and podpups given priority on this ship.

13-Glory

Sandstorm, at Seven

Pascal's ship *Sandstorm* met the *Midnight* and the *Watcher* at Seven. Now, two hundred pilots were jammed nearly elbow to elbow into a nogee section aboard *Sandstorm*, in a pilot training simulator room, complete with Chike shuttle controls. Four of those pilots were Ramian, and the other 196 were a combination of mid jump, long jump, and retired Humans.

Lanezi pulled off the simulator goggles and let them go. A sea of pilots braced at their nogee stations with tethered goggles tugging away like unhappy balloons. On this run-through they'd spun themselves into a massive virtual pileup, pulling the planet Seven out of orbit, but failing to jump it. Lanezi scowled at Pascal, strapped in ziz throne at the front of the room. His stomach heaved, but he kept his lunch down this time.

"This is not how Humans learn!" a voice rang out.

"Agreed," Pascal said darkly. "You study your native language for twenty years. We have no time for that coddling! We have simplified the controls and reduced the responsiveness as much as possible for your little minds. If you want to do this, you will learn the Chike way."

"Do or die," "sink or swim," "fast and furious," people muttered.

Pascal swung ziz head sideways to give them the one-eye. "Learn and live," ze hissed. "Again!"

Lanezi hauled in his fluttering goggles, settling them back on his face as the program reset. *Left hand, big stick, right hand, little stick.* He had every intention of learning and living. He had to save the pilots, who were putting their trust in him. He did not want to disappoint Raykatoo. He wanted to save Seven, save humanity, and most of all, jump to Katie with a clear conscience.

Midnight, with Sequoia, would go first, in a direct path toward the thread. But the planet was spinning, which would normally tip it out of the path. So they had to create a spinning, twisting path in spacetime with the 200 push-along gravity balls. Lanezi would be in the lead, with 199 ships behind him, spiraling out wider and wider until they circled the planet, all the while following the *Midnight* at top speed.

They were learning impossible pilot skills in alien shuttles, while testing anti-fainting suits and anti-sickness drugs, all at the same time. And this, the day after freejumping halfway across the leaf to get to Seven. In the old days, they'd have rested five days after a mid-jump.

And as their leader, Lanezi had the tightest spiral of all. Like the tip of a diamond drill, he had to pierce the jumpspace, keeping his shuttle and soul intact. And gut-wrenching, heart-pounding, mind-numbing as it was, this was just the simulation.

At the end of the session, nothing better to show for themselves, the pilots hung at their straps, some sick, some crying, all in despair. But every single pilot stayed. Pascal finally took pity. "No one expected you to do it on the first day," ze said quietly. "As long as you do it on the last day."

Wheel of Fire, in Safewaters System

Terina continued her notes, trying to figure out what to put in the feed. Captain Tiati had jumped them to Safewaters, coming in a safe eight days off their target. After a rest, they crowded around the big screen in the Observation Bay with Tiati's command crew, as Thayne explained what would happen next.

"The Terraformers, otherwise known as the Swish, have stabilized the orbits of the other planets in Safewaters system." Thayne pointed to a big map of the system. "There's a gap here in the habitable zone. And this," he drew his finger along an approach, "is the expected path of the incoming planet." He didn't even flinch at the phrase "incoming planet," as if he saw the whole thing as a mathematical exercise. "The Swish will be standing by with their own planet-grade gravity balls to help adjust the orbit."

"What are those?" Tiati asked, pointing to a spattering of red beacons in the outer planetary system.

"Those," Thayne said, "are redirected comets, specially chosen iceballs to add to the atmosphere of Seven. If necessary. With controlled entries, of course."

Terina swallowed. The planet might lose atmosphere? And the plan was to smash it with comets? "What's the expected survival rate?" a now grim Tiati asked.

Thayne scowled. "Expected survival rate, calculated by the Navigators, is zero."

"*What?*" everyone in the room burst out. But before people

could start complaining *why are we doing this?* Thayne continued.

"Zero survival is equal to doing nothing. The Chike are trying to prepare the people of Seven to the best of their unco-operative ability. Everything depends on the pilots. Before they can jump, they have to drag the planet farther from it's star. How long it takes will determine how cold it gets. Then, it's critical to drop out of jumpspace in the right place, so the planet can return to an appropriate distance from its new star immediately. My calculated survival rate is 30-80%."

It all depends on the pilots, Terina wrote.

"And," Nkiroo added, "Any long-term survival over 10% will be considered a success, as far as the GenOne are concerned."

"But make no mistake," Thayne said. "Even that 10% depends on the planet actually arriving at Safewaters."

15-Glory

Convocation

Now that Zahar was not the escort of a witness, or the family member of a harbinger, like Quay's family, she wasn't granted any special privileges and was sent down to the planet alone. After hearty hugs, Veez had sent her on her way with two translator earclips, a credit slider that he said would be good "for anything," and of course, snacks. She landed hours away from the convocation.

At first, Zahar was concerned about making her way from the distant shuttle port to the arena as the only free Human on the planet. But she gradually relaxed. The Coursers were the perfect hosts, friendly and efficient. Every time she thought she needed something, there was a sign, a flashing arrow, an information kiosk, or a helpful Courser right there.

Zahar forgot her clade's worries as well as her own in the wonder of the Courser planet. Courser puppies played in the grass. High-rail trains sped in the open air. Trees, rivers, and fields of flowers had fragrances even she could detect. The

Coursers on the train lifted their noses in the air. Zahar let the wind blow through her hair as she joined them in the joy of the ride.

Back at the arena, Zahar walked in like it was no big deal. Her plan was to circle around to the harbinger entrance and simply request to be let in. She might even meet Quay's family. But as she walked around, she felt eyes watching her, like she was being followed. She turned, but the twenty or so beings behind her were all minding their own business. She shook her head and went on.

"Help me!"

She stopped and turned again. That was Alkulu, not through the translator. She turned in a full circle, scanning the crowd. She pulled the translator out of her ear and walked slowly, close to the inner wall.

"Up here!" She froze, and, before looking up, stepped back into the entranceway of the facilities. Then, quiet as a Scamper sneaking food, a disheveled man dropped from the ceiling beams and landed next to her in a crouch. "Shhh."

He was Human. "Oatah?" He stood up. Not Oatah.

"No! I am Reeder. Please, I need help. I haven't eaten for days." He slid behind her so people wouldn't notice him.

"You don't have to hide."

He looked at her uncomprehendingly. "I'm a stowaway."

"Don't be ridiculous. What are they going to do? Throw you on a ship home?"

"Exactly. I can't leave Honor Oatah."

He really looked desperate. "Listen," she said, as calmly as possible. "You don't have to worry. There are no Human ships in system."

"*What?*"

"Whatever ship finally shows up is going to take all of us home, including Oatah."

"Are you sure?"

"Yes. Veez—my ride—checked. They're having some trouble finding a Human ship willing to come out." He looked horrified. "But they will!" She didn't want to mention Plan B, going out with the Ramians, who also had no ship here. "I'm on my way now to insist they put me with Oatah."

"You're just going to walk up and say—"

"That you and I are the only Humans on the planet, so we're with Oatah." He flinched. "Honor Oatah," she revised. He seemed too dazed to think straight. "Let's get you some food," and she pulled out her Scamper snacks.

Three hours later, the two of them presented themselves to the Courser host at the harbinger hall. Reeder, after food, a shower, haircut and new clothes, all compliments of Veez, was transformed. There was so much credit on Veez's slider that Zahar bought pads for both of them, which they tucked under their arms like they were VIPs. They approached with breezy efficiency, the new Reeder taking the lead.

The host yipped politely. Reeder, now wearing her extra translator, nodded. "Reeder, first assistant of Honor Oatah, Harbinger of EarthClade, and Zahar—"

"—sent by the Exempt Pascal." The Courser's eyes went wide.

Reeder continued. "We understand seclusion is over. Honor Oatah will require our assistance now." Zahar tried not to hold her breath. The Courser checked ziz pad, looked back and forth at the two of them, and finally, sent a message.

Only seconds later, a verbal message came back, which they heard through their translators. "Yes. Humans. Consolidate them in the new section." Zahar tried not to show any relief.

Reeder unconsciously put his hand on his heart. Maybe they would think it was thank you if she did it too, so she copied him. But then Reeder swayed, so she grabbed him by the arm. He straightened and pulled himself together. Then they almost had to jog to keep up with the Courser.

Through fancier and fancier corridors, they were eventually brought to a large set of elegant rooms and left there.

"Hello?" Zahar called out.

"Honor Oatah?"

They peeked into the kitchen, sleeping rooms, and facilities, a conference room and other sitting rooms. "No one," Reeder shook his head in confusion. He looked faint. He had seemed so confident moments before.

"Maybe we should just sit—"

The doors slid open. Quay entered and stepped aside, ushering in Oatah and his own family. They all stood in surprised silence for a moment. Quay looked stressed and tearful, but a smile lit his face when he saw her. She skipped forward to hug him.

Oatah looked at Reeder in puzzlement. Zahar had a moment of concern. *Did I make a mistake? Is Reeder not his assistant?* "You're alive," Oatah finally said. "Thanks be to God. Where have you been?"

"Hiding," Reeder answered shakily. "Waiting to see you."

The Ramian bright happy colors took on a tinge of confusion. Then Oatah reached out and took Reeder's arm. "Good. Thank you. We have work to do." And they sat down at the table, all business.

Zahar hugged Zhenumae and the baby and pressed hands with the rest of Quay's family. "We're to be together to the end," Danumae said. "Actually, we are all officially tan to the Humans, so you may direct us as you like." He said it so seriously, but his family's colors ran to humor so she smiled.

"Well, if someone knows how to get food?"

"Dinner will be soon, they told us," Danumae said.

They gathered together on the couches. Quay sat right next to Zahar.

"I've missed you," they both said at once, and then smiled. Quay was obviously trying to calm down.

"There's nothing I can do now," he said. "It's up to the pilots."

Momentarily, the Courser escorts appeared at the door bringing all of Oatah and the Ramians' luggage. "These will be your new joint quarters, the chief Courser informed them. "Three Humans, this side" ze pointed with ziz nose. "Six Ramians, that side."

Zahar's fingers itched to unpack, to get organized, to make a schedule. "As it is mealtime, we will escort you," the chief went on.

"Thank you," Oatah said. The Courser stood by the door, apparently waiting for them to line up. Oatah stood directly behind him, and Reeder, slightly behind and to his right. But Quay approached Reeder and said gently. "I am tan now."

"What?" Reeder said.

"I am tan to Honor Oatah."

"Reeder," Zahar whispered, realizing neither Oatah nor Reeder would understand the significance. "You need to let Quay stand there."

"This is my place! By Honor Oatah's side. I have risked everything—"

"Yes, of course," Zahar said, feeling for him. "But temporarily, it's Quay's place. The Ramians are tan—helpers of the Humans—until the trial is over."

Reeder looked at Oatah, but he was puzzled. Zahar gave Reeder credit. He swallowed and stepped all the way behind Oatah, allowing Quay his spot. Danumae slipped in next to Reeder, as if to be his tan. Then Zhenulell guided Zahar behind Reeder and stepped beside her. "We'll explain more later," Danumae told Reeder.

"Be advised," the chief said, as the door slid open, "Outside these rooms, all is projected for the convocation."

"Projected?" Quay asked.

"We're on the feed?" Zahar realized. "Everyone is seeing this?"

"Reports go out with the ships. All clades involved should receive them."

Good, she thought. *Because then my parents will know where I am.*

18-Glory

Sandstorm

The 196 Human pilots were so exhausted that Jarvie, Taj, Gola, and Thunder were pressed into service shuttling them over to Pascal's ship. The four of them tagged along, sneaking into the back of the sim room. Neah, who had brought over the four Ramian pilots from the *Watcher*, floated in next to them.

The 200 pilots strapped into their stations, waiting resignedly for Pascal to start the simulation. "How are your pilots holding up?" Thunder whispered to Neah.

"Stubborn, scared, quiet. That's why I came to see for myself. Yours?"

"Grim," Thunder admitted.

"Only twenty more days."

"Esteemed pilots!" Pascal called out, raising ziz big claw.

"Today, you will practice something different." The 200 stirred. Jarvie thought ze looked disapproving, but that could have been normal. "As agreed, this one has ordered the shuttles to be preprogrammed with an escape option." Now the pilots were fully focused. "Should the jump fail, at any location, at any velocity, the pilot can exercise this option—but ONLY after the escape command is given. You will each have two choices: to continue on the path to Safewaters, or reroute to your own sector. The lead pilot," Pascal's eye swung to Lanezi, "will be designated to issue the escape command, only after deter-mining that the jump has irreparably failed."

Lanezi hung his head. What a burden, Jarvie thought. But Pascal swung his head the other way. "We are merely practicing this as an exercise. You will *not* fail. You will *not* quail in the face of difficulty. You will *not* skitter away like *bugs*."

6-Beauty

Midnight, at Seven System

A week later, Beezan was walking around the *Midnight* during the hour it took for the shuttles to go get the 196 pilots and return. It was quiet and he could say prayers without having to stop and greet people. Soon, he needed to get back to the kitchen to help serve their dinner.

He wasn't running late, but suddenly, the lock from ARC 2 opened and the pilots spilled through. Beezan stopped in surprise. Rather than the usual funeral procession, they were tromping along, upbeat and excited.

The pilot in front, Rendra, saw Beezan and smiled. "Suc-cess!" someone exclaimed, and the others shouted "Success!"

"No," Rendra said, stopping in the rimway and motioning for them to calm down. "Barely adequate," he mimicked in

Pascal's voice. "Barely adequate," the rest shouted, turning their heads to look at Beezan with one eye.

Relief flooded through Beezan. He even laughed. He wasn't going to have to drag that planet through jumpspace by himself. He clapped, and as they passed, high-fived everyone. All 196 had come to ARC 1 to see him.

Jarvie squeezed in next to Beezan as they were serving dinner. "They did it," he whispered. "They did the spiraling arc exactly right, and Pascal calculated the jump was perfectly set up."

"Fantastic news."

The night before the jump, Beezan carried his yoga mat and a blanket around to the empty ARC 8. He had to get away from the well-meaning well-wishers and say prayers alone, on this, the last night. That it might be the last night of his own life was of little consequence compared to the pressure of saving ten billion on Seven and the fate of humanity.

The cabins were locked, so he sat down in the rimway lost in prayer. Word had gone through the sectors and even to Ramian space for everyone to pray tomorrow. They would not be alone. He sat a long time, hands on his knees, clearing his mind. The 200 pilots were already in bed. Pascal had them in the pattern of two days practice and one day off. But their performance was always better on the first day, so today had been their day of rest.

Annoyingly, he heard the door open. He sighed inwardly. But the footsteps he heard were tiny patters. He looked over, surprised and pleased. The podpups, all of them, had come. Led by Star and Whisper, they congregated around him. Silver, white, cream, coffee, chocolate, and the three colorful Ramian pups. So many. Some he had never seen before. There was a baby black one that achingly reminded him of Sky. He expected they would settle around him, but instead, they sat down at attention, as if ready for class.

"What is it?" They cocked their heads as one, and he couldn't help smiling. "Star?"

Whisper spoke up. "Bee."

"Yes."

"Follow Bee."

Follow me here, now, or follow me tomorrow?

"I'm going to follow you." They considered that, tipping their heads the other way. "You're all very important." He reached out and patted Whisper, who seemed pleased. He patted them all. Big conversation over, they settled down. When he was done with his prayers, he lay down on his mat and they snuggled around him, Star by his neck. The little black one climbed up on his chest. He slept soundly and peacefully, surrounded by their little humming snores.

At four in the morning, he awoke, mind fuzzy, but heart tranquil, and stomach rumbling. "Okay my friends," he said, picking up each one and looking into their eyes. "Off you go for breakfast. I'll see you on the other side."

They set off in groups, some back to ARC 7 and some coming with him through ARC 9 and into ARC 1, and beyond. He watched the last group go, heart swelling with love for the little ones, and ready for the jump day of all jump days.

19-Beauty

Wheel of Fire, at Safewaters

Terina checked her schedule one more time before kicking off her shoes and going up to the prayer room. She settled in next to Katie with a mutual hand squeeze. It was 07:00 back at Seven, where *Midnight* prepared to jump the planet.

According to her schedule, the 200 pilots had already boarded their special shuttles. Beezan, Jarvie, Gola, and Gadi should be boarding *Larkspur* any minute.

Tiati whispered to the assembled crew, "All jump traffic in the entire leaf was suspended as of last night." And Terina knew that all sectors in Human and Ramian space were starting twelve hours of prayer.

The events of the day would be recorded and broadcast as soon as possible, but in the meantime, Terina's schedule would have to suffice. A Chike relay ship at Seven would jump to the convocation after the planet left, or if they failed to jump it. Another Chike ship at Safewaters would jump immediately to report on the planet's arrival.

The tension aboard the *Wheel* was heart-rending. Thayne was pale and had swollen, red eyes. He clutched a pad of numbers that he compulsively checked, even in the prayer room. Her grandfather was calm, but seemed more resigned than hopeful. Io and Euro were nervous wrecks, so they were making breakfast and watching pups. Of all the people, Tiati blazed with confidence. He caught Terina's eye and they both smiled. *He believes in Beezan.*

Then Tiati started the prayers and they went around several times, the toddler even saying a short prayer in his sweet voice. Then, beside her, Katie inhaled sharply and stiffened.

Kelson held up a hand. "You have an idea," he whispered.

"I'm sorry. It can wait."

"Maybe not; tell us."

"I just remembered something. When the Ramians were jumping into our space and crashing into our a-rings, they said their implants could detect a-rings in operation."

There were gasps all around. Thayne hit his knee with the pad, breaking it. "I knew that!"

Nkiroo shook his head. "It's too late. Even if we could get a message through, they can't swap Lanezi for a Ramian leader now."

"But it might help them tip out in the right place," Tiati said, standing up. "Just before the jump, I'll have my relay ship get in the rings to turn them on."

Kelson nodded. "Breakfast and stations. Let's pray as we are able."

"Yes, Honor," they said as they started down the stairs. But Katie didn't come. Terina felt for her. Lanezi was the lead pilot, but without the Ramian implants, he may not have been the best choice. And if the jump failed, he would have to live with that failure. She knew in her heart that Beezan and Jarvie would die trying, so they would be spared.

Terina ran back up the stairs and knelt next to Katie, taking her hand. Did she fear Lanezi would die rather than live with the failure, even if he had the chance to return?

Katie was in tears. "He promised to come home."

South of Paradise Valley

Melawn, stomach rumbling while waiting for his breakfast ration, was going over the map of today's route with their expedition leader, Jadee, when Fez, the lookout, shouted "Bird!"

Everyone ducked down, drawing their various makeshift weapons. But soon a wide green neckband on the bird became visible. "Sorry!" Fez shouted again. "Messenger!"

Using the killer birds for messengers must have been a Ramian idea, Melawn thought. The bird landed on a rock, and Jagger, the only one tough enough to deal with the winged monsters, put on safety goggles and approached it, managing to get the message without being skewered by the long beak. Eyes glaring, the bird was somewhat mollified by a raw lizard, hastily offered.

Melawn grabbed his already-written update, just for these occasions. He quickly added the date and their location and gave it to Jagger, who reattached the message sleeve while the bird was still eating.

They all backed away, Jagger guarding the bird until it felt like leaving. Melawn had no idea what creature on the planet would threaten the wicked thing, but he sure didn't want to run into it. "Good system," he muttered to Jagger, "but I sure wouldn't want your job."

"Ah, she's one of the mellow ones. They don't use her much, she's so old."

Melawn ran the message over to Jadee, who opened it as the rest of the expedition gathered around, the kids Chip and Kente jostling in front of Melawn. "It's from Paradise Council, addressed to all Valleys and Expeditions," Jadee said and read it out.

Dear Friends,

We have received an unusual message from the Chike. They are informing us of the events of the convocation, which we were already aware of through other channels. At this convocation, humanity and the Ramians are being judged for their suitability to enter the wider community of beings in this galactic "leaf." Judgment was withheld pending what they call an "Acceptance by Trial." The trial will be jumping a planet called Seven to a safe location. For the sake of the people of Seven, for humanity, and the Ramians, for the prosperity of this leaf and for the pilots and their families, we request prayers throughout the sectors. To that end, we have just been given the jump date: 19-Beauty.

"Today!" they gasped as one. Like a native, Melawn glanced at his shadow. It wasn't much past seven in the morning, local time. But who knew what time they were jumping for real?

Jadee folded up the expedition map. "We'll stay here today."

They knew, without being reminded, that if the jump failed, then the colony would be separated from humanity forever. Holding back tears, they created a half circle facing south-south-west. Using the most heartening information from the *Lotus* shuttle landing, the location of Earth, they turned in desperate prayer.

. . .

At the Convocation

Yapat, their Courser host, arrived early on jump day. It didn't matter; all of them had been up praying. Zahar brought him to their sitting room.

"May I speak seriously?" Yapat asked Oatah.

"Of course," Oatah said. Quay took his usual place beside Oatah.

"We apologize for the inconvenience of talk, but arrangements must be made. The events of today will determine the placement of EarthClade and RamiaClade. Either way, you are scheduled to return home in the next three days."

Everyone nodded. Zahar sighed inwardly. Home. She would miss Quay and his family. She would probably never see them again. But by tomorrow, finally, she'd be on her way back to her own family.

The Courser sat down formally. "Unfortunately, no Ramian or Human ships have arrived, although there is a strange rumor of a Human ship en route."

Quay, speaking for Oatah, asked "Strange, Honor?"

"Yes," Yapat answered, still facing Oatah, "apparently a Human ship is coming from the homeworld, which is of course, unnecessary."

"How do the Coursers know this?" Reeder asked.

"The pilots have said; ripples in the ways. Even today, the ship comes. All others abide by the travel ban."

"We have no knowledge of this ship," Oatah confirmed.

Yapat nodded once, and continued. "Although the GenOne said we have time, packs of ships will leave tomorrow. The convocation will close. You must be on a ship in three days. If yours does not arrive, you will go on a Chike ship."

"Go home?" Reeder asked, alarmed.

The Courser stood and gave a little shake. "Wherever the Chike wish to take you."

With that unhappy news, they marched out to their places on the harbinger platform in the arena. All of them were now on display. Oatah sat in a constant state of prayer, with Quay almost trance-like beside him and Reeder stiff with worry.

Around the arena, the GenOne had put up huge photos of Seven. The planet itself was so much like Earth. Even though Zahar had never been to Earth, she felt a kinship. Seven was smaller, warmer, and had no moon. But the oceans, the white clouds, and the continents were familiar. And the land was so green. In drone photos from the surface, they could see trees, even taller than the ones on the Courser planet. Lakes, rivers, mountains too, but it seemed to be a world of trees.

The people, primates similar to humans, lived in a few skir-mishing megacities and an uncountable number of villages trying to stay out of the way. The *Larkspur* was supposed to land far from anyone. Finding a landing spot among the trees was the challenge.

"Earth was once like that," Oatah murmured. The others looked at him, surprised. He nodded. "Before humanity cut them down. It was almost too late when they realized how important trees are to a planet."

Midnight, at Seven

Remembering how Beezan had carried Lander's pilot jacket on the day of his funeral, Jarvie folded his jacket in the same manner. He touched the four ship pins: *Sunburst, Drumheller, 81-Petals, Midnight*. From sun to midnight, his life had gone quickly. He put the jacket on top of his few possessions in the drawer, but kept his small photo album with him.

He was convinced that Beezan could jump the planet. And yet he felt that it was impossible, almost an affront to heaven to even try. But he would not let Beezan go alone. He secured the drawer and hurried down the rimway to the suit room.

On arrival, he found Caspia, Io, and Euro, along with many podpups, including Star. "There you are!" he said, scooping him up, pleased.

"With Bee."

"Honor Beezan made him stay here," Caspia filled Jarvie in. "Apparently, the lot of them stayed with Beezan last night."

"Awww," Jarvie hugged Star as tight as the wiggly pup would tolerate.

"Utter side," Star said.

"Yes." Jarvie teared up for a second. "Be good." He tapped Star on the nose. "See you on the other side."

Caspia needed to help Jarvie suit up, so she handed Star off to Io and Euro, who made small formal bows to Jarvie. "See you on the other side," Jarvie said.

"In His Hands is the destiny of all His servants,"[1] Io and Euro recited together.

"Ready?" Caspia asked, when they were finished.

"Yes," Jarvie said. And he was.

Down the lift, to the Entry Lounge, with Caspia, he greeted Iricana. "Captain."

"Honor Jarvie." She did not ask him if he was sure about this.

Beezan, in full pilot mode, serene and drifting in nogee, slowly spun around to look at him through his open helmet. He did not ask if Jarvie was sure about this, and Jarvie smiled. Beezan grasped his shoulders and looked into his eyes. "Together."

Jarvie grasped Beezan's wrists. "Yes Honor. *Dad.* Together."

Beezan nodded and they proceeded to the *Larkspur*, one of the smaller shuttles, where Pongola and Magadi waited. "Captain," Jarvie said to Iricana as he maneuvered through the hatch.

"See you on the other side," she said, to both of them, but Beezan didn't answer. She smiled, tears in her eyes.

Larkspur

Larkspur landed on the evening side of the planet, in a circular clearing, like a giant well among towering trees. Pangola set them down while Magadi studied the readouts. Both were fully suited up too, but they all had their visors open. "The 200 shuttles are in position," Magadi reported.

Iricana's voice came through the speakers: "Countdown at Jump minus eight hours. Mark."

Jarvie settled into his special seat across from Beezan in the middle of the shuttle. Now was the long period of pulling the planet partially out of its gravity well. It was all up to the Terraformers, zooming past with their supergravity balls, turning them on just long enough to adjust the orbit, hundreds of times over and over. "Slight seismic shifts are to be expected," Magadi said. As long as the giant trees didn't fall on them. Really, they had nothing to do but pray for the next six hours. Magadi turned down the volume so as not to disturb them.

Midnight, at Seven

"Jump minus 1:15," Falcon announced. "Planet is approaching jump zone."

"All crew in chairs," Caspia confirmed.

"Ready for jump," Iricana announced. "To you, Honor Sequoia."

Shuttle 1, at Seven

"Jump minus 1 hour."

Good, Lanezi thought, sparing a neuron to check their progress. Exactly on target. He would have let out a little sigh of relief if not for several sims where that had been premature. Staying in his tight twisting path was all he needed to think about.

Wheel of Fire, at Safewaters

"Jump minus 20 minutes," Hana advised.

Terina captured an image of the tactical displays in the Passenger Lounge for her history. Only Tiati, his monitor Hana, and Kelson were in the Command Bay. Everyone else was in the Passenger Lounge, in the chairs, no brackets but strapped and watching the feeds.

An overall top-down view of Safewaters System was on the main screen. The location of the Safewaters C gas giant, in the same orbit as the a-rings, was safely outside the intended path of the incoming planet Seven, marked by a giant sweep of yellow. The *Wheel* was in the warm zone, interior of Seven's expected new orbit. About six minutes' lag time away, Tiati's relay ship was in the rings. *Watcher* was just outside the orbit of Safewaters C, and Pascal's ship was another 30-seconds' lag time farther out in the system. Forty-five Terraformer beacons identified their ships lined up along the expected trajectory. They were the ones who would use their supergravity balls to adjust the orbit of Seven after it came in.

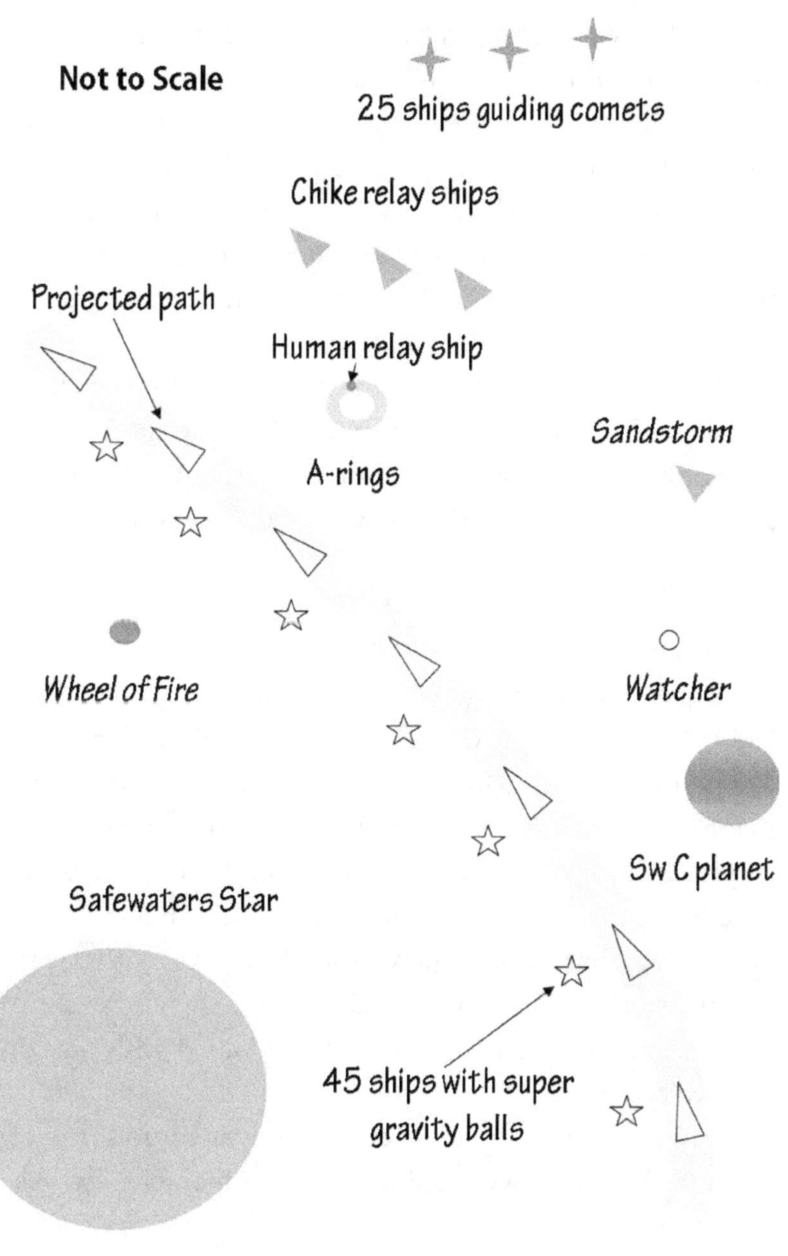
Not to Scale
25 ships guiding comets
Chike relay ships
Projected path
Human relay ship
Sandstorm
A-rings
Wheel of Fire
Watcher
Sw C planet
Safewaters Star
45 ships with super gravity balls

The most nerve-wracking part of this orbital dance was the twenty-five incoming comets. "Small ones," Pascal assured them. They were escorted by more Terraformer ships ready to fine-tune their trajectories for grazing impacts.

The Human ships were marked by blue dots. *Watcher*, the sole Ramian ship, was a white dot. Pascal and his relay ships were orange; the supergravity-ball Terraformers were yellow and the comet escorts were red. When they appeared, the shuttles would be green and the planet Seven itself would have a purple marker. *Please let us see the purple.*

On a separate arrival screen, the 200 shuttles were listed in columns of 40 as if they were at a really busy spaceport. They were only listed as Shuttle 1, Shuttle 2, etc., but on Terina's pad, she had a list of names, from 1) Lanezi, to 200) Evan.

Convocation Arena

There was a loud announcement and Zahar's earclip translated, "Jump minus 10 minutes." She looked up at the screen. Humanity's history would be decided in 10 minutes. She felt sick from the stress and dazed from the hours of praying. She sipped some water to calm herself. And then Quay began to sing. In the silent arena, the sound was audible but thin. It was a prayersong that Zahar knew from her days with Quay on Pascal's ship, so she joined in, along with Quay's family. After only one repetition, Oatah and Reeder joined with amazingly good voices.

Slowly, the other clades joined with them until the arena resounded with overlapping but harmonious waves of prayersong.

. . .

Shuttle 1, at Seven

"Jump minus zero."

"*Midnight* away!" Lanezi reported to the other shuttles as Sequoia freejumped into the path, disappearing. Lanezi saw the thread in his mind, thin and peach, and knew it was the correct path.

Exactly on trajectory, Lanezi held the formation behind *Midnight. Into the path, into the path.* And he slipped in, trailed by 199 shuttles. It was all up to Beezan now.

Larkspur, on Seven

Jarvie felt the *Midnight* go, felt the path and grabbed his armrest. The spinning eddies created by the 200 shuttles were disorienting. Getting Seven in the path was going to be like rolling a giant spinning ball into a moving tube. *It won't throw Beezan off!* Jarvie closed his eyes and felt the path, so strong in his implants. He pushed with all his willpower for the planet to go. He had nothing left in his life to do but this. And slowly, ponderously, possibly taking hours, the planet whirled into the spinning path.

Convocation Arena

"Attention!" Zahar jumped in her seat from a loud announcement in the arena. She put her hand to her earclip. "The planet has jumped." As one, the citizens of Kingdom Leaf leaped to their feet. It wasn't just about humanity now. This was history-making for all the gens. The Prime, on screen, seemed flabbergasted, covering ziz head with ziz little hands.

Within two hours, there was a video showing the planet *disappearing*. To see it was stunning. Unbelievable. Astounding even. But what made it convincingly real was the very concerning puff of atmosphere it left behind.

Shuttle 1

We're going! Lanezi exulted. This was the moment of uncertainty, where destiny hung in the balance. Cautiously, holding his breath, Lanezi let his mind peek behind. YES! A huge mass was in the path. So huge he could no longer detect the other shuttles. *But—oh no!*

Larkspur

Jarvie gasped for breath. Seven was in the path, a gut-wrenching, spinning ride with a blinding spotlight blinking on and off. *Destroyer.* It was pulsing ahead of them. Calculations had shown the paths would not connect. But Destroyer's path was twisting around as if trying to reach them. Maybe the mass of the planet was attracting the deadly pulses.

As Beezan held them in the path, the sentries appeared. Wave upon wave, a massive flood of souls surged right past them. Billions. *For the planet.* And the spinning was slowing. The Destroyer was slowing down Seven's rotation. Their calculations would be off. For the first time, Jarvie had real doubt and fear. Jarvie focused his whole mind and soul on staying in the path. The next pulse from the Destroyer grazed past, but Beezan didn't even flinch from the path. Another and another. Beezan was so strong, but their path was bending. They would be off trajectory, but they had no choice but to stay with it.

How far off the target will we be? Will we even arrive in the correct planetary system? Jarvie cast his mind ahead and could feel a tight rhythm, like a-rings. *Yes!* They must still be on target.

Another huge pulse from Destroyer bent so near it buffeted them alarmingly. Beezan was battling for the way. And then the next pulse hit them head-on. Jarvie screamed as the path ripped open. His implants seared with pain, and they were dumped into normal space. *We're not there yet!*

31 / THE WAYS

Shuttle 1

Lanezi's mind split in two as the pulse from Destroyer twisted around their spiraling path and wrenched the planet away. *No!* Lanezi tried with all his mind to reach out to the planet and pull it along, but it was too late. Seven had dropped into normal space. Now, that thread that Lanezi was riding was unanchored on one side, flinging the shuttles in all directions.

The sentries! He was one of the few pilots that rarely saw them. But he did now, and they were everywhere, even pressing in on him. Terrified, he gathered up his will to live, and pressed forward. Reaching out to guide the pilots behind him, he held onto one thought—Katie ahead! He shook off the sentries as he held on to the wild snapping path. *I've done this before! I can do it again!* He was sure now there were shuttles behind him, but how many?

Wheel of Fire, at Safewaters

Terina knew that travel through jumpspace wasn't exact, so

they didn't really know when to expect the planet. But it had been hours since *Midnight* arrived. Everyone stayed in the Passenger Lounge to watch, fretting and praying.

Finally, there was a small popping sound. All eyes jerked to the shuttle arrival board where the Shuttle 1 light went on. Katie let out a gasp of relief, but Terina held her breath. "Shuttle 1 is off course," Falcon reported from the *Midnight*.

Pop. Pop. Pop. Green lights were appearing on the shuttle arrival board, but on the main screen, they appeared well outside the expected trajectories. Some were farther out, some closer to the star. They were scattered all over. "If they're even farther out, we won't get their signals for a bit," Falcon reminded them.

"*Midnight* to *Shuttle 1*," Falcon said.

Terina glanced at Katie, who was obviously trying not to panic.

"*Midnight* to *Shuttle 2*."

Pascal broke in, sending a message from his ship. "Medical data indicate that pilots are . . . unresponsive. This one is going to reroute shuttles to their closest ship. Except for Terraformers, all stand by for shuttles."

"Ze was supposed to send them home!" Terina said, alarmed.

"Ze can't," Nkiroo said, subdued. "They're unconscious . . . or—"

"—in need of medical attention," Katie finished. "Captain, permission to go to Med Bay?"

Tiati answered immediately. "Yes, Doctor. *Wheel* Crew, emergency stations. Kelson is headed for the Entry Lounge. Nkiroo, go with Kelson. Katie, Terina, Hana to Med Bay. Thayne, take over as monitor."

Terina took a moment to set up an automatic camera in the

Passenger Lounge, and put another scramble cam on a headband. She set her pads to the feeds and turned to go, but just as she was leaving, the shuttle lights started to blink off again. Pascal was using their push-along gravity balls in-system. They would reappear near the ships. She ran to the Med Bay.

"*Wheel*, expect shuttles 1-5," Pascal announced.

"That's Lanezi and the Ramians!" Terina said.

"*Wheel*, get all Ramian medical data from the *Midnight*!" Katie called.

"Recalculating Seven's incoming path based on shuttle arrivals," came Pascal's voice. Terina turned on the big screen in the Med Bay and put up the feed. A new, fiery red path, much wider than the planned path, appeared.

On Terina's pad, shuttles 127, 128, 129 appeared, way farther out in the system. Then the shuttle 1 light went back on, close to them this time. Thayne tried to reach Lanezi. "*Shuttle 1*, report."

A dazed, static-y voice, barely audible, brought Katie to a teary-eyed stop. "*Wheel*. Whoever. Lanezi here." Everyone froze. "We tangled with Destroyer. We lost the planet."

The only sound was Tiati relaying the message to the other ships, Thayne apparently unable to speak. They stood frozen in the Med Bay.

"*Relay Ship* to *Wheel*, should we stay in the a-rings?"

"Yes, please. If you can. A little while longer," Tiati answered. "Let's not give up hope."

Larkspur, on Seven

Vaguely, through the throbbing pain in his implants, Beezan heard Gola and Gadi talking desperately.

"They're unconscious!" Magadi said. "What happened?"

We're not in the right place! Where are we? Beezan wondered.

"Gola, there are no beacons! Wait! One beacon, *Shuttle 200*."
Evan?

"*Larkspur* to *Shuttle 200*, Evan?"

"I'm here. Sorry. Pain. There's no star."

"What?"

"No star. We're in the wrong place. We're not in any planetary system."

The path! Beezan thought, panicked. *I can't lose the path.* "We have to jump again!" But pain was surging through his implants. "Show me the trajectory, on screen," Beezan ordered.

"Just getting it now," Magadi said, putting it up.

"Honor!" Pongola objected. "We only have one shuttle! We can't make the spinning path."

"We have to! Jarvie! Wake up!" Beezan staggered out of his chair, fighting the pain and the gravity and the bulky suit. He shook Jarvie's shoulder. "Wake up, Jarvie!"

"Wait!" Pongola said. "NAV report: the planet is no longer rotating. We don't need the spinning path."

"I still feel it," Jarvie murmured, holding his head through his open visor.

"Destroyer?"

"No, ahead. A pulsing, like a-rings."

"Your Ramian implants!" Hope surged through Beezan. "What's our speed in the target direction?"

"1.72 JV!" Pongola answered.

Beezan flipped down his helmet visor. "Secure your helmets. Let us out."

"Out?" Magadi said, alarmed.

"Evan, give us 10 minutes from my mark. Then use your emergency escape to jump to Safewaters. We're going to follow you."

Magadi, Pongola, and Jarvie all turned to look at him.

"We're going to jump again." Exhaustion, fear, and pain cleared from their faces. They slammed down their visors.

"Yes, Honor," came the answer from Evan.

Jarvie struggled up and stood by the airlock with him. "Why do we have to go outside?"

"I don't know. Trees, I think," Beezan answered, confused himself.

"Secure for both doors!" Magadi called.

"Evan," Beezan said, "Mark!"

"Ten minutes, mark!" he answered.

"See you on the other side!" they all shouted together, and with a surge of energy, Beezan and Jarvie tumbled out of the airlock into the darkness. It was .89g. They struggled to their feet and staggered towards the trees, holding on to each other.

Have I gone mad? crossed Beezan's mind, but it was like a passing dust mote. He had one overriding thought, to get to the trees. Holding onto Jarvie, they maneuvered around rocks, their suit heaters blasting in the frigid black night. Headlights swinging wildly, they made their way to the ring of trees.

"5 minutes, 9 seconds," Magadi reported quietly.

The bright lights illuminated a giant tree trunk, bigger than the main lift. Beezan tried to look up to see how tall it was, but almost fell over. "This tree," he said, putting his hands on it and leaning his helmet against it. They switched off their lights and stood panting.

"Two minutes."

Not enough time! Beezan panicked. *I can't find the path so fast! Calm, stay calm.* He felt Jarvie put a hand on top of his.

Any movement animated by love moveth from the periphery to the center, from space to the Daystar of the universe. Perchance thou deemest this to be difficult, but I tell thee that such cannot be the case, for when the motivating and

guiding power is the divine force of magnetism it is possible, by its aid, to traverse time and space easily and swiftly. [1]

"Ten seconds," Magadi whispered.

Evan: "Activating." And a shutter went through Beezan's mind.

Pangola: "He's gone."

But Beezan didn't need her to tell him. A thin pale path appeared. It looked barely strong enough to take a shuttle, and they needed to take the whole planet. Pressing the tree like a giant joy stick reaching to the heart of the planet, Jarvie's hand pushed on top of his in exactly the same direction. For an eternity of heartbeats, they leaned the planet into the path.

And there it was, waiting for them. Destroyer. *Hold on!* Beezan thought to Jarvie. With every ounce of muscle, of spirit, of mind, of breath, of everything he had in him, as if his whole life and being were for this moment alone, Beezan dropped them so deeply into the path that he feared they would never get out.

It could have been a minute later, or hours, but suddenly, a mind-shattering blast blew the Destroyer star apart. As they rode through the final pulses, the explosion tore up the fabric of spacetime and the path was gone.

Colony

They were having a quiet, subdued dinner after their long day of praying. Melawn sat next to Jagger and the entertaining Tektites, waiting for their food. The Tektite Danny looked up at the twilight sky, "I wonder if the jump is over."

"Would the Chike even tell us?" Sunny asked.

Suddenly, Jagger slumped against Melawn. Melawn

grabbed him to keep him from rolling onto the ground, and immediately knew he wasn't just sleeping.

A clatter from the makeshift kitchen and a cry for Tenshi made Melawn look around. Others were jumping to their feet in alarm, as three people dropped unconscious.

"Stop eating!" Tenshi shouted.

"Jagger hasn't eaten," Melawn said. "Who else is it?"

"Eunji and Ishaan!" Teeve answered.

"The pilots!" Melawn realized.

Jadee put his hands out for calmness. "Make them comfortable over here."

But Jagger groaned and opened his eyes, immediately squinting and grasping his head. "The ways," he gasped. "The ways have closed."

Convocation

Zahar was taking her time walking back from the facilities, meandering along the outer circular corridor of the arena, looking out the big windows. It was just nightfall on one side of the building, and on the other, the last moments of daylight. It was so stunning to see these atmospheric sunsets in real life, rather than on a screen. And to think, those who lived on planets could watch every day.

Suddenly, there was another rumbling announcement. "A Chike relay ship has arrived with devastating news." Zahar stopped breathing, stunned. The planet had jumped. What could go wrong? "The planet did not arrive at Safewaters. It dropped into normal space before reaching the destination." Her hands flew to her mouth to stifle a scream. Everyone else in the rimway outside the arena froze in place, eyes wide, and apparently, tears were universal. "Some shuttle pilots survived.

They reported that the star Destroyer disrupted the path, despite calculations that there would be no interference. It is impossible to know where the planet and its inhabitants ended up. Reconnaissance jumps will be made, but as the shuttle team is broken up, there is no hope to rejump the planet."

Zahar slid to the floor sobbing. They had done the impossible, jumped a planet. And it had killed all those people. Her heart went out to the poor pilots, even to Thayne, who must be mindstorming in misery by now.

Quay dropped onto the floor beside her, colors running dark gray and black. He was pale and shaken. He grabbed her arm and shook his head. "This is not what happens." He seemed confused and disoriented.

"What?"

"The planet makes it. I know it does."

"You can't see the future, Quay!"

Tears rolling down his cheeks, he looked out the window as the sun went down. "I guess not."

On Seven

Beezan awoke, realized that he wasn't dead, and considering the pain, was disappointed. The sentries were doing their job well. Wincing hurt. Groaning hurt. His implants were like knives. He couldn't breathe and he couldn't escape an earsplitting alarm. "Air tank depleted. Prepare for native atmosphere." *What?* "Visor opening in five seconds." *Wait!* But his body was a lump. If he had arms, he couldn't find them. He couldn't form words to countermand the suit.

PWESSSHT! His visor opened and a blast of icy air stung his face. He gulped it involuntarily and it seared painfully all the way down his throat. The shock of it propelled him to his feet.

He tried not to breathe, but couldn't stop, despite the agony. He tried to cover his nose, but only smacked himself in the face with his suit glove. The pain was worse than the pain in his implants. His vision blurred. He finally got his hands to the sides of his helmet and slammed down the visor, making it impossible to see. His suit heaters went to max trying to warm up the air. He fell to his hands and knees and just stayed there, whining until he could see again. And slowly, as his wits returned, he realized it was light out. He turned to see a dim star—and a misty red sky with streaks. Comets!

We're in the right place! We made it! And with a surge of joy, coupled with sudden survival instincts, he was on his feet again. Jarvie was behind him, cowering from falling branches. The ground was shaking. Beezan didn't want to look up at those trees. Together they stumbled toward the *Larkspur*. And then Magadi was there, walking in front of them, so they could each put a hand on her shoulders.

"We have to get out of here! Keep walking!" she said.

Step by clumsy step, they made it to the hatch, where Magadi half-shoved them in. Scrambling in herself, she shut the hatch and yelled "Go!"

Without restraints, they were plastered to the deck as Pongola put everything *Larkspur* had into the launch. Beezan tried to find a less painful position, but gave up and passed out instead. Minutes, or maybe hours later, his visor popped open again. Only this time it was heavenly, warm, recycled shuttle air.

Magadi had dragged herself to the monitor station and strapped in. "We dance with the comets, sister," Pongola said and they swerved, sending Beezan and Jarvie rolling against the side of the shuttle like roughhousing podpups.

"Why do my implants hurt so much?" Jarvie gasped.

"I don't know," Beezan answered. "Maybe it's the price of jumping a planet."

Wheel of Fire, at Safewaters

Terina scrambled to help in the Med Bay, pulling down exam beds and grabbing blankets while Katie skimmed through the Ramian Medical data.

"Terina!" Hana called, "There's no room in here to get people out of suits. Grab a couple of bins and do it in the rimway."

"Medical emergency—Command Bay!" Thayne's strained voice called.

Katie answered, "What's happened?"

"Tiati has collapsed. He was holding his head."

Katie and Hana tore down the stairs.

What is going on? I need to focus. Should I go help? No. I should read that Ramian stuff. She skipped to the part about pain medication. "*Wheel*, can you make these Ramian meds?"

"How many doses?"

"Four patients."

"Thirty-seven minutes. Load these ingredients." A list appeared and Terina scurried around collecting them.

Katie and Hana came back with Tiati on a stretcher robot. They rolled him onto the exam bed. "Vitals are good," Katie reassured Hana.

"I've got to take over the Command Bay," Hana said. "I think Thayne is going to be your next patient."

"Attention!" It was Pascal again, but there was an uncharacteristically long pause. "We have received data . . . indicating that . . . the ways have . . . closed. Yes. The ways have closed. Stand by."

Tiati groaned. "That's why the pilots are in pain," Katie reasoned. But Terina stood frozen. *The ways are closed.* "We're stuck here? Stuck in a system with no habitable planet, with only two Human ships, one Ramian ship, the Chike and Terraformers?" She couldn't keep the horror out of her voice.

Katie took Terina's arms, gently. "We have our families! We have each other! Let's get through the current emergency."

Terina grabbed her s'link to check on her mom when there was a clambering downstairs. She ran down to help.

In the rimway, Lanezi was staggering along, holding himself up with one hand against the wall, no helmet, no gloves. Farther behind, Nkiroo, Kelson, and some of the *Wheel* crew were carrying four Ramians on stretchers. "Suitout here please," Terina said.

But Lanezi didn't stop. "Katie?"

"Up there, but—" Lanezi went for the first step and almost collapsed. "Let me help you!" She backed him out of the stairway and started to wrestle him out of the suit. Shaky, wincing, sometimes jerking in pain, Terina wasn't sure he could get up the stairs even without the suit.

"I can make it." He stood up straight and was instantly tackled by someone from behind Terina.

"Thayne!" Nkiroo shouted, setting down his stretcher and running over.

Thayne knocked Lanezi against the wall. "What did you do?" he shouted.

Nkiroo grabbed Thayne and Terina reached out for Lanezi, but Thayne was much stronger than he looked. Distraught, he shook Lanezi by the arms. Slamming him against the wall again, he shouted, "Tell me what happened!"

Terina tried to gently push Thayne away. "Honor! He's injured." But it was like she didn't exist.

"You lost the planet!"

"We didn't lose it!" Lanezi gasped. "Destroyer—"

"Destroyer's path did not intersect! You were off course!"

"No! Destroyer's path changed!"

"The paths are point to point. Direct arcs in jumpspace! The Navigators told us!"

"Well, what do they know about planets in jumpspace? I'm telling you the path bent!" Lanezi stopped yelling and finished tearfully, "The pulses hit the planet head-on. The planet dropped into normal space."

"You should have stayed with it—"

"Enough," a quiet, but commanding voice said. Tiati, with Katie behind him, stood at the foot of the stairs, swaying on his feet. "There will be no blame. Not for the pilots, not for you, not for Beezan. We have injured." He reached out and took Thayne's hands off Lanezi, who sunk into Katie's arms.

"He saved us," Widinmay whispered, sitting up on the stretcher. "Lanezi brought the pilots through. We were thrown off too far to rejump the planet. He saved us."

"It was Katie," Lanezi said, wiping his eyes. "Knowing that you were here brought us through."

"We can't get these Ramian suits off," Kelson whispered.

"I know how," Lanezi said, slowly letting go of Katie and going to Kelson's aid.

Tiati gave Thayne a stern look. "Honor, you will help here or sit in the prayer room." But Thayne sunk down, sitting right where he was, gasping like he couldn't breathe.

Still shaky from the shock of Thayne's attack, Terina ignored him and helped get everyone up to exam beds while Katie did the pain meds and scans. Katie stood over Captain Tiati, "Honor, there doesn't seem to be any permanent damage for you, but I'd like Caspia and maybe the Ramians to take a look as soon as possible."

Tiati nodded. "*Wheel*, tell Hana she's in command. We're going to want to rendezvous with *Midnight* as soon as we can boost. Also request *Watcher* to join us."

"Try to get some sleep," Katie whispered.

Terina checked her p'link. Message from Thunder. "Your mother is in Med Bay on *Midnight*. She'll be fine." She breathed a sigh of relief and wondered how Caspia was doing with no word yet from Evan.

"Whisper," Lanezi said, from his bed.

"I'll get her," Terina said as she flew down the stairs again, down the rimway, and into the nursery. There, the *Wheel's* children were having a snack with several podpups. Everyone turned to look at her in alarm.

"Oh! Sorry," she said. "I just need Whisper."

She grabbed her s'link and sent a message to Euro aboard the *Midnight*. He answered right away. "We're with Star, and he's fine." Was it possible Star didn't know that Jarvie was separated? Rocket made a flying leap and knocked into Terina's head as a greeting. "Oh Rocket! You stay here. I'll be back in a bit."

She backed out, taking only Whisper. "I don't understand," Terina said to Whisper. "Podpups were distraught when Sky left."

Whisper just looked up, confused. "Ezzi."

"I'll take you, sweetie."

Maybe Jarvie is fine, she thought, *wherever he is*. But it was too horrible to think about. How many hours or days would they live out in the darkness? With the shuttle, they might be able to last for weeks on a dying planet. They would send lightspeed messages for sure. Some future historian would get the whole heartbreaking story.

. . .

Back in the Med Bay, Whisper was curled up with Lanezi, and Katie checked on them constantly. Kelson called Terina over. "I'd like you to organize prayers for tonight—"

Pop.

No one had turned off the screen. They glanced up. A purple beacon. *The planet!*

"How is that possible?" Terina asked. "The ways are closed."

Tiati blinked and pushed himself up on his elbows. "They are. But that was in real time." He struggled off the bed and tapped on the screen. "Lag time is 94 minutes. The planet has been here for 94 minutes . . ." It was well off course, outside the red adjusted path.

Whenever Terina had prewritten this historic moment in her mind, there had been joy, cheering, hugging, tears. But they stood there unbelieving. "How?"

"Attention!" came Pascal's usual shoutout. "The planet's arrival is confirmed."

"Oh my God," they all whispered, grabbing hold of each other.

Pascal went on: "There is sufficient atmosphere for survival at lower altitudes. Atmosphere enhancement and orbital adjustments are in progress."

Pop. Shuttle 200 lit up on the board. "Evan!" The joy and the tears were starting.

Pop. Larkspur. "*Larkspur* to all," Magadi's angelic voice rang out. "Greetings and blessings of the day. Four crew alive!"

Beezan and Jarvie lived! And now there was cheering! Tiati clapped his hands and then hugged them all. The other pilots struggled to their feet and joined the celebration. Only Thayne collapsed on the deck sobbing in relief.

16-Grandeur

Watcher, at Safewaters

Beezan stood in the *Watcher's* Observation Lounge staring outside. He had a fancy blue Ramian shirt with gold birds soaring on the wide floppy sleeves. The shirt hood was pulled up to cover his partially shaved head where the Ramians had replaced his overloaded implants.

Beezan admired the Ramians' gumption, replacing instead of removing. "We will jump again," was their motto. But when? Three years? Thirty? A hundred? A lightspeed message to Firelight would take 57 years. He would probably not see the sectors again.

People kept asking "Are you sure the ways are closed?" Like they still couldn't believe it. But to Beezan, the universe had gone dark. Except for the warm fuzzy glow of Little Red, as they called the Safewaters sun, he was surprised to even see stars when he looked out. They just felt *gone.*

And gone with them was any hope of reunion with Sky, with

the *Drumheller*, or his parents. It was a second sundering, only worse.

He reminded himself to be grateful. He lived. Jarvie lived. He even had his best friend Tiati. And they had saved a planet. Mind-boggling. Humanity didn't even know it, but they were about to be GenThree. As soon as they all shuttled over to Pascal's ship for some kind of ceremony. And then he would be transferred back to the *Midnight*, his new home. Tiati had offered of course, but *Midnight's* people were Jarvie's people, and so now, they were his people. And Tiati would be nearby.

Beezan rested his forehead against the window. He could hardly believe that fifteen days had passed. The planet was now in a stable orbit. A war was averted when Pascal broadcast a stern message to them, that *THIS ONE* hadn't risked everything to save their puny planet just to have them kill each other off. The sight of Pascal giving them the one-eye was probably enough to scare some sense into them.

Getti Drann and the *Watcher* were going to continue their studies of Seven as long as they were here. *Midnight* and *Wheel* were still waiting to sort out their crews, now that all the pilots had the Ramian surgery. The hooded shirt was a popular style.

He'd managed to avoid being made a hero, refusing to let them make a summary. "Let the deceased be heroes," he'd told them. "We still have work to do." But at this ceremony, there would be a lot of people. He said a prayer for calmness.

The door opened. Neah and, surprisingly, Thayne, came in. "Beezan my friend," Neah hugged him, colors deep burgundy.

"Greetings, Honor," Thayne said quietly.

"God is Most Glorious," Beezan replied, puzzled. They were both in dress clothes, Neah in full tokens, and Thayne in the dress black and gold of the *Midnight* crew. Thayne looked even thinner and more fragile in the close-fitting suit, but his dark eyes glittered with gratitude rather than anger.

"Honor Beezan," Thayne said, "we have requested the privilege of escorting you aboard the *Sandstorm*, and received permission if it is agreeable to you."

Beezan was surprised. "I thought I'd just go with Jarvie. Why do I need an escort?"

"For your comfort, Honor," Neah said.

"The others have . . . podpup duties," Thayne added.

"Oh. Of course. I'm ready."

Sandstorm, at Safewaters

Terina wasn't allowed to go ahead to set up cameras in the Chike auditorium, but she had everything with her to record this historic moment. She adjusted her new earclip translator as she flew one of her drone cameras to the front of the processional. Lined up in the Chike rimway, the crews of the *Midnight*, *Wheel*, and *Watcher*, including the 196 surviving shuttle pilots, waited, excited in spite of their caution about the Chike and their recent ordeal.

Her camera hovered at the front, jockeying for position with the multiple Ramian photographers. Their summary artists were here in force. She heard one of them whispering to her pad to delete the green and gold stripes from the background of the auditorium, but, distracting as they were, Terina was committed to documenting the truth of the day for history.

The elders and "dignitaries" were up front, followed by a sea of pilots, all in fancy flowing Ramian shirts, blue, green, purple, and the pink shades of love and contentment. Their shirts shimmered in the harsh Chike lighting. Terina, Io, Euro, Jarvie, more

Ramian summary artists, and a parade of podpups brought up the rear.

A piece of triumphant marching music started. Definitely not Chike music; they didn't seem to have any. Ramian? Human? She had no idea. But on her pad, she could see that the processional had started forward into the auditorium.

Iricana, Getti Drann, and Kelson were followed by Thunder, Taj, Shiwelna, and Widinmay. Then Neah, Beezan, and Thayne. Caspia, Evan, Sequoia, Tiati, Hana, and *Wheel* crew in their fiery orange and yellow jackets and brown pants, and then the pilots in ranks of four. The first row of pilots held out the ship jackets of their four fallen, who had sacrificed when they were hit by Destroyer: Rendra, Sandra, Melina, and Camilo.

It took several minutes before Terina, with Lanezi, Katie, Jarvie, Io, Euro, Danulell, and the pups marched through the door with as much solemnity as they could muster surrounded by the combined podpups of the three ships, at least 35 of them.

Terina's camera now opened up for a wide view of the stage, where Pascal stood in ziz greatest finery yet, a robe of glittering green and gold. Ziz special guard had gold and green sashes, but no masks, and had not turned their faces away. They had been told that the taboo was suspended for today.

And then the camera zoomed in on a tall cylindrical tank—a contained environment. Inside, Terina realized with surprise, was a Terraformer! Ze was beautiful, like an iridescent octopus. No wonder their clade could survive sustained 10g. They were probably quite squishable. Ze had eyes, many of them. Ziz whole body shifted colors like a Ramian headband.

Of course, the podpups broke loose as one and flooded up onto the stage. Pascal stepped back and squinted one eye at them, but the pups ignored zir and gathered around the

Terraformer, putting their paws up on the container and peering in.

The audience froze as if a great intergalactic incident was about to take place. There was no way for Terina or Jarvie to work through the tightly-packed standing crowd to corral them.

The Terraformer gracefully sank down to the podpups' level and pretended to poke one on the nose with a tentacle. At first Terina was alarmed, but then realized ze was playing with them, giving off a little burst of color with each nose poke. The pups hummed and squirmed in excitement and the mood in the giant room shifted from nervous to good-natured.

With a shake of ziz head, Pascal strode to the center of the stage. The Terraformer gave a little flick of light and all the pups but Whisper scampered back to their people, having no trouble finding them in the sea of legs. "Rocket! Be good," Terina whispered as Jarvie picked him up, as well as Star. She saw Lanezi, balancing with a hand on Katie's shoulder, standing on his tiptoes to look for Whisper, who was sitting quietly on stage, next to the Terraformer.

"Citizens of Kingdom Leaf," Pascal began. *Wow. Big change from Lesser ones*, Terina thought. Poles pounded the stage once, and the guard lowered their heads. Pascal offered one of the short Chike prayers, more like a shout to heaven. The poles struck the stage again, and all eyes turned to Pascal.

"This one is honored to present the highest-ranking member of the leaf here present, the Prime's chosen witness, Fleet Commander of the Seven Project, High Exemplar of Waztic Realm, known among the GenTwo as Ziz Great Honor Indigo Waves.

The Terraformer brought all ziz tentacles together and made a small bow of sorts, which seemed humble considering all those titles. "Thank you, Exempt Pascal," the Terraformer said, ziz translated voice sounding patient and benevolent. "Please have the representatives come forward."

Slowly, Iricana, obviously nervous, and Getti Drann, more accustomed to spectacle, walked up to the stage and turned to face the audience. And stood there waiting. Pascal peeked over to ziz honor, who flicked a tentacle at Whisper. "All must be represented." Whisper casually wandered over to Iricana who picked her up. *Please don't let there be three hours of speeches,* Terina thought. But the Terraformer got right to the point.

"Assembled clades, as we cannot go to the convocation for this ceremony, we will proceed here. By the trust invested in this one as witness of the Prime, I acknowledge that the Acceptance by Trial was completed successfully." The pilots smiled, although it was bittersweet. "RamiaClade." Getti Drann stepped forward. "The Kingdom Leaf pronounces RamiaClade GenThree."

"Thank you, Great Honor Indigo Waves. It is our deepest pleasure to serve the leaf alongside diverse and friendly clades." Ze stepped back.

"EarthClade." Terina knew that Iricana was sad that Oatah couldn't have this moment, but stepping forward with Whisper somehow seemed to represent humanity in a sincerely humble way. "The Kingdom Leaf pronounces EarthClade GenThree."

Iricana cleared her throat. "Thank you, Great Honor Indigo Waves. We are grateful to join the leaf. And in the words of one of our Great Leaders, ***'They should manifest gratitude and thankfulness to God, and the best way to thank God is to love one another.'***"[1]

Pascal nodded and raised his claws. "For the leaf."

They all shouted together, "For the leaf."

And that was it. Terina flew her camera around the room to get more shots, while around her the others hugged and high-fived and tried not to step on the podpups. She was about to recall her camera when a strange sensation came over her, and she realized that Jarvie and all the pilots had grabbed their heads.

Jarvie feared his new implants were about to rattle out of his brain. *Are they malfunctioning?* It reminded him of the resonance of the near miss with *Mammoth* and, later, on Lander's moon. But it was more. He gasped in pain and Terina took his arm. "Better sit," she whispered, as hundreds of other pilots collapsed on the deck. Jarvie realized he had dropped the pups, but they were running around excited. And then the non-pilots started to collapse.

Now down on both knees, he saw a bright blurry Being, like the great angel who had sent him back to life when he was so sick. But this Being was *alive*—and speaking to them. The message reverberated along the ways. Ze was speaking to all of them, everywhere, at the same time.

From some kind of ship, the Being stood on a raised platform. Below the Being nine people stood at attention—Humans, humbly escorting the Being. This was not an angel. This was clearly a Divine Manifestation, a Renewer, maybe the One promised after a thousand years, somehow radiating the Message of the Great Announcement into all of space.

Jarvie bowed his head in awe and respect. He was only vaguely aware of everyone around him doing the same, even Pascal, who threw ziz robes aside and prostrated zirself.

Jarvie didn't capture the words, only the brilliance of the Being that had opened the ways, refreshed his heart, and renewed his soul. All their accomplishments were suddenly as nothing. Child's play. Jarvie squinted his eyes, but the vision was in his mind, or his soul. He couldn't see it clearly. And then the vision was gone.

Jarvie blinked and looked around. By the tears and stunned looks it was obvious that every single person had experienced the same thing. The podpups were ecstatic, running in circles, rolling, and nuzzling everyone. And quietly at first, a song started from the front. It was a Ramian prayersong. And it took on a strength and vibrancy he had never imagined.

But Jarvie couldn't join in. He sat down, shaking, along with many others. He didn't know how long he sat. He remembered Mullá Husayn saying discovering the Báb was like a thunderbolt.

Finally, Pascal struggled to ziz feet and touched ziz earclip. The singing stopped. Humbly, Pascal said, "Honored ones, a relay ship has arrived from the convocation. The ways are open."

Yes, yes, I felt that.

"This one has received the message that a . . . Great Prophet / Manifestation / Divine Teacher has arrived at the convocation and is calling / summoning all heads of state. All else are to return home."

Home?

Pascal seemed beyond humbled. Ze looked as if ziz world was upside down. "Return to your ships. A New Day has dawned. The Great One . . . has come from . . . Earth."

Colony

The bells rang up and down Paradise Valley, rang so loud they echoed off the canyon walls. But it didn't matter. Even in the dusty camp they had seen the vision, or the truth, or whatever it was. And when Melawn came to his senses, he was on his knees next to DeeZann, holding her hand.

And for some reason, as he sat, whispering prayers, he did not let go. And neither did she.

The Convocation

Zahar tried to clear her head. *Where am I?* She looked down at her hand grasping a metal bench, but not on a ship; she was outside. Her heart pounded as she tried to trace back her thoughts.

Hoping to distract the distraught Quay, and find some peace of mind for herself, Zahar had gone with Quay, Zhanumae, and the baby Zhenulor to a podpup sanctuary that they'd heard about on the Courser planet. And amidst the rolling green hills, there were thousands of podpups, living together in happy playfulness. She had no hope of finding Kiwi. But then, he'd come to her. Yes, he was happy, and she'd hugged him. Kiwi nuzzled Zhenulor, said "bye-bye," and bounded off.

Happy, and sad, Zahar and the Ramians got back on the open-topped tram. They rode through indescribably beautiful landscapes. If there was a place to be stuck while the ways were down, this was it. But no family. Still, what just happened?

Zhenumae blinked, dazed, on the bench across from Zahar. She looked down at the wide-eyed baby, and then at Quay, cross-legged on the floor, peace and contentment replacing his recent dismay. But he had no colors. Zahar looked back at Zhenumae. Her colors were gone too, as if they were burned out by—the light! The Being! She gasped, realization sinking in as her thoughts sorted into order. They had seen a true vision. A Manifestation of God was here! In the convocation system. Somehow she knew that. The blast of light. "The ways!"

"Yes, the ways are open," Quay said. Then, all around them, the Coursers shook off their stupor and began to howl. Zahar and the Ramians clapped their hands over their ears and shivered. It was joyful, and longing, but it was loud! They just sat there, the three of them with their hands over their ears and the Coursers howling in the tram, stopped on a three-meter-high railing, still a few hundred meters from the convocation arena.

Zahar stood and shielded her eyes. Out at the shuttle pad, she could see an escort of Coursers hastily lining the path from the VIP entrance. "Oh, my God!" she gasped, just as the shadow of a huge shuttle passed over them. "The-the, Ze is coming here!" The Coursers leaped out of the tram, landing easily despite the drop. They ran like wild things toward the landing pad.

One Courser with pups quickly led them to an emergency exit. "Come on!" Zhenumae said, tucking Zhenulor in a carrier and following the pups down the stairs. Together they started jogging for the landing pad as the shuttle set down.

Zahar, Quay, and Zhenumae were completely outpaced by the Coursers, but it didn't matter. They arrived several minutes later, gasping and holding their sides.

From this distance, Zahar couldn't make out faces. But as nine people marched down the ramp, Quay asked, "Who are they?"

And she wondered, *could it be?* "Maybe, they might be the Earth Council. But they never leave Earth."

And then the Being appeared—without the brilliant light. Hooded in a long robe, ze seemed like an ordinary human, but yet, there was something. Some sense of power, of destiny, of purpose, far beyond what Oatah possessed.

Would she have recognized the Being for a Manifestation if she had not first seen the radiance in the ways? She hoped so.

As the Manifestation passed, the crowd bowed their heads, and as much as Zahar wanted to look, she did the same. Just before entering the building, the being stopped and looked up at the Bright for a moment. And then Ze was gone.

The crowd turned to follow, crowding politely through the arena doors, excited and awestruck, wanting to hear the Great News. Zhenumae, Zahar, and Quay shuffled along behind them, but were stopped by a Courser.

"Most Honored Human, Honored Ramians. We have instructions for your immediate care." Zahar glanced at Quay in confusion as the Courser continued. "Your two clades are to board this shuttle for transport into orbit. A Human ship awaits."

Disappointment surged through Zahar. A day ago, she would have jumped off the tram to get to that shuttle, but now, she only wanted to be near the Being. But Quay stood up taller. "We will obey. We are blessed beyond measure."

"Yes," Zahar realized. Out of all the people in the leaf, they actually saw the Prophet with their own eyes. She took Zhenumae's and Quay's arms and they followed the Courser.

"The ways are open," Quay, said. "We can go home!"

"And everything will be different," Zahar said.

"Better," Quay said, smiling.

They were hustled along. At the top of the shuttle ramp,

they were greeted by a somewhat dazed young man in a pilot's jacket, holding an ancient podpup. Standing behind him was an equally ancient woman, rubbing her face as if not accustomed to smiling.

"God is Most Glorious. I'm Captain Ra'Tama, and this is our co-pilot, Alesta Eve."

"God is Most Glorious," they said together, and Zahar took a step inside looking down. There was no doubt she was standing in the same place where the Great Being had just been standing.

"Yes," Ra'Tama said, smiling, "Everywhere, the Blessed One has touched, but especially the hearts."

Ra'Tama walked them to the passenger area. "Please strap in. Your delegations are on their way. And also," he said, looking at his s'link, "a horse."

The witness! "Are we going to Earth?" Zahar asked.

"Not directly," Ra'Tama answered. "I'm to drop all of you at Canyon. The Ramians will pick up Quay and the delegation there. And also, something about your parents being made base commanders?" He shrugged like it was no big deal. She gasped and then he smiled.

"We're going home!" she shouted. Quay's and Zhenumae's colors blazed back to life as they joined her, chanting together and jumping up and down, the baby and Ra'Tama's pup looking on in bewilderment.

17-Grandeur

Midnight, in the Safewaters System

The entire *Midnight* compliment, except Sequoia and Falcon, over 150 people, were jammed into the Observation Bay, standing shoulder to shoulder, squished like friendly podpups. Lanezi held hands with Katie and kept the twins in front of him.

They were shaken, stunned, and yet exhilarated, even now, seven hours after the most momentous event of their lives.

They were in their jump suits, ready to go. Wasting no time, except this one formality. To vote where to go. The captain came in and struggled to the front of the room, but just as she did, a tearful Thayne came up, "Captain, please." Everyone else had been astonished and overwhelmed by the vision, but Thayne was distraught. "Please. I have to beg forgiveness, from you, from everyone."

"Honor, that's not necessary right now," Iricana said.

"I've done terrible things. I see it all now—"

Iricana took his hand as Caspia worked her way up next to Thayne. Lanezi found himself agreeing, *yeah terrible*. But yet, it was terrible in some distant way. He wasn't angry any more. All the faults of others had faded. Even his own faults felt fixable. He could be better. He would be.

"Honor," Iricana repeated. "As individuals. New Beginning. Fresh start. Everyone. The councils will decide the rest."

"But," Thayne said.

"No." And she hugged him, and so did Caspia, and then he was swallowed into the front of the group, with people patting him and murmuring support. Lanezi smiled. He had no doubt about what he had seen, but if he needed any further proof, Thayne's change of heart would be enough.

"So what are we?" Io whispered to Euro. "A new religion?"

"A space religion!" Euro answered excitedly.

"We'll find out soon enough," Katie said. "As soon as Pascal sends us word from the convocation."

Finally, Iricana stood before the crew.

"Suggestions for a destination?" she asked.

Everyone looked around, all eyes settling on Beezan. "Oh, um, I suggest . . . Firelight."

There had been talk of going to Earth, but that was so far away. Not even in the outer sectors. "All in favor," Iricana asked, and over 150 hands went up. They were going home.

5-Mercy

Firelight Station, Docking Ring 2

Beezan hovered near his chair in the little *Midnight* cabin that had been his supposed home. His violin and luggage, long-ago packed, were tethered at the top of the stairs. He could hear Jarvie through their shared open door, last-minute packing, and distracted by continuously checking the *Midnight* crew feed. Beezan didn't have the heart. He knew where some people were going. Lanezi and Katie were taking Io and Euro back to S-tro base. Iricana and Thunder would stay at Firelight Station to help organize the repopulation of the outer sectors. Only Gola and Gadi were remaining aboard, to stay on with the new Captain, Captain Bozenka's grandson. Danulell was being escorted back to Canyon to meet his family. But other crew were uncommitted, or like him, had nowhere to go.

The last three-week run-in had been the happiest time of his life. Their relief, their camaraderie, Thayne's brilliance unleashed from his ego, and their exposure to the Manifestation, now called the Blessed One, had broken down all Beezan's hesitation about being around people. They were his people now, his family, his tribe. And the podpups too. They followed him around as if he were a walking treat dispenser. And it warmed his heart.

Now that they were coming in to Firelight, all that would change, again. How many new lives had he started in the last two years? But he wasn't alone anymore, and humanity wasn't just holding on. They were GenThree and there was a galactic leaf to explore, ships to be built, and habitable planets to be found.

Star came into his cabin, bouncing off the wall and unerringly landing by the drawer that once held treats. His little paws grabbed the handle. "Sorry," Beezan said, holding Star and slowly opening the drawer. "Treats all packed."

"Packed?"

"Yes."

"Unpack!"

"Later." Star gave him the one-eye, like some wannabe fuzzy Chike. Beezan laughed and ruffled his fur. "We're going on an adventure." Jarvie reeled in through the door and hovered nearby, no doubt wondering where this adventure would take him. "We'll put our luggage in dockside lockers and take the 17:00 free shuttle over to the station," Beezan told him.

"Sure," Jarvie nodded, handing Beezan his black armband. It said *Midnight*.

"We're doing armbands?"

"Oh yes. We're back in civilization."

Beezan put it around Jarvie's arm and squeezed it. "Thanks for sticking with me," he whispered.

"Wouldn't miss it." He held out the red overband. "This too." Beezan sighed, but Jarvie laughed. "No worries. Badge of honor now."

"It is. Especially for you. I thought we would go to the pilot center and see if any ships have openings."

"For hire? There are so many pilots, with all the retired ones back in action."

"I can't afford a ship."

Jarvie fished a slider out of his pocket. "I think I might swing a down payment." Beezan pressed it to see the balance.

"*Are you kidding me?*" His ex-stowaway was rich. More than

Lanezi type rich, definitely ship-down-payment rich. "But that's your money."

"Family ship. That's what I want. And you're my family."

Beezan swallowed and handed back the slider. "Thank you. Let's see what we can find. Nkiroo and Thayne are going to OSRI with Tiati. He says it'll be five years before new ships come off the line."

"I can wait."

"Is there somewhere you'd like to go in the meantime?"

"Sure," Jarvie smiled like it should be obvious. "Earth."

"Earth!"

"Don't you want to go? See your parents? See the home planet?"

The last little tightness in Beezan's chest loosened up. "Yes, I'd like that. Maybe we could go with Katie and Lanezi. If we're welcome."

Jarvie smiled. "Of course we are."

"Wait, you've already planned this?"

"Plan A. Let's go, Star." Jarvie spun back to his room to get his gear and Star kicked off Beezan's chest to follow.

So while Beezan had been waffling around about life, Jarvie had simply made a fantastic plan and waited for him to walk into it. He pushed up to the top of the stairs, grabbed his luggage, and left the *Midnight* cabin behind without a backward glance.

Out in the rimway, Beezan helped Jarvie with the empty podpup carrier and headed toward the hatch. They were only an hour or so away from turning over the newly-cleaned ship. Ahead in the rimway a crowd floated, waiting. *Oh, no. More goodbye scenes.*

Kelson, who looked 50 years younger; Sequoia, now Beezan's friend as well as peer; Terina, the newly famous historian; Taj, now in his white headgear; Falcon, still loving the drama; Evan, mind focused, but heart still wandering; and Caspia, overjoyed with the turn of events; luggage bobbing around them, all smiled as Beezan and Jarvie approached. With happy *screes* Star and Rocket bowled into each other mid-air. All of them were now in Sector 5 dress clothes, flowery shirts in full bloom. Only the pilots were identified by their jackets.

"Greetings, friends," Beezan said.

"Greetings, Captain," they responded, and Beezan frowned. He wasn't a captain anymore and they were leaving the ship anyway.

Kelson had mercy on him. "Honor Beezan, it would be our great pleasure to remain with you as your crew."

"Oh. That's . . . I don't have a ship."

"Until you get one. We can stay together. On Lanezi and Katie's ship."

"What?"

"They're expecting all of us," Jarvie said, smiling innocently.

"Lanezi's gone ahead to docking ring 1. He has a possible sale," Sequoia explained. "A ship named *Mammoth*."

Mammoth! Of course, Lanezi could afford that. Good.

"Are you sure?" Heart pounding, he hoped. Nothing would be better than to stay together until he could get a new ship.

They laughed. "Yes, Captain, if you'll have us," Caspia said. "I think we'd be a good crew."

"Yes." He choked up. "A great crew. Thank you."

At the door, they all hugged Iricana and Thunder goodbye. "See you dockside," Thunder said.

Terina insisted on photos, and then they were pulling down the ramp and searching for lockers. "These are all full," Falcon said.

"It's so crowded!" Terina looked around wide-eyed.

"Wow," Jarvie said, grabbing a holdbar and pointing at the Ship Tracker. It covered two walls.

Beezan found *Wheel of Fire* on the departure screen—destination Harbor. Tiati and his big cargo hold would have a major role in the shipbuilding. *Drumheller* might have too, if it were here.

They hadn't heard much from the convocation, but a revised map had clearly shown that *Drumheller* was not in EarthClade space. He wouldn't be allowed out there to get it. Somehow, he felt he'd always known that. His ship. His podpup, left behind. He took a deep breath. Humanity saved. Seven saved. New start in life.

"Hey!" Jarvie pointed. Beezan set himself spinning to look and had to grab a holdbar to stabilize. "*81-Petals!*" Jarvie pointed to the Ship Tracker arrivals board. Sure enough, *81-Petals* just docked at berth 12.

"That's impossible," Sequoia said. "It had no engine."

"Maybe the Chike fixed it," Evan suggested and Caspia patted him on the back, like *nice thought*.

"Wait!" Pure excitement flashed across Jarvie's face. "It's the *Drumheller!*"

"Jarvie!" Caspia scolded. "Don't get his hopes up!" And then the *81-Petals* disappeared from the screen.

"Where did it go?" Falcon asked.

"Let's find out!" Beezan said, looking at Jarvie, shouldering his luggage, and diving across the dock for the conveyorway. Snagging a holdbar, he steadied himself with one foot against the brace.

Jarvie swung on behind him, closely followed by Terina. The others, taken by surprise, were slower. The three of them were way ahead by the time they got on.

Beezan craned his neck to see out the dock windows, but it

was pointless. Most of the berths were full and the ships blocked the view of berths farther along. At berth 12, Beezan sailed off, snagging a holdbar to pull up the ramp, when a guard held out an arm to stop him.

"Sorry friend. Honor. But this is a secure area." Flustered, Beezan fumbled in his jacket for his s'link. "Here." The guard shook his head like it was futile, but scanned it.

Cleared.

Yes! A surge of hope went through Beezan. "They're with me," he waved at Jarvie and Terina.

"And a bunch more people, coming," Jarvie pointed. But Beezan didn't wait. He stopped to let the crazed Star out of his box, then pushed up the ramp, trying to contain his emotions. Star raced ahead. "This could be the biggest disappointment ever," he sternly told himself.

The dock hatch slid open and they tumbled in. They could see the outer door of the ship. Beezan ran his hands over it. The paint was long gone, but that was true of most ships. The lock cycled and they pulled into the ship lock. Beezan peered through the inner window. Impossible to tell. His heart was pounding. Then the inner door slid open.

"Oh, my God!" Jarvie exclaimed. "*Yes! Yes!* You can tell from the smell alone!"

"*Drumheller?*" Beezan dived inside and let go of his luggage.

"Is this it?" Terina asked.

"Yes, I'm sure!" Jarvie said.

"How do you know?" She got out her camera and was looking around.

But Beezan knew. Even though the ship didn't answer, he knew in his bones. Tears started down his face. "*Drumheller?*" he called again.

"Hello?" Jarvie was asking as he pulled ahead, looking for

someone. "Look!" He pointed to the deck, "Where the bricks were glued!"

"Bricks?" Terina asked.

Beezan stopped at a small life support panel and pulled it open. DRUMHELLER, it said, big and bold. Terina shrieked with joy. "How?"

"Someone brought it!" Jarvie said.

Star headed for the kitchen as Jarvie came back and grabbed Beezan in a one-armed hug.

"My ship . . ." And then the others were there, hugging, congratulating, laughing, and crying. "But it doesn't answer me."

They tried the Command Bay, but it was locked. Even Beezan's s'link couldn't open it. "What if it's not my ship anymore?"

"It'll always be your ship," Jarvie said.

Kelson pulled out his s'link. "Let's just call the dock master. The pilot's name will have to be registered."

Yes, that would work. But Beezan left them buzzing in the rimway. "Maybe the guard knows." He coasted back to the hatch, just as it was cycling again. A pretty woman with fuzzy black hair delicately drifted through. "Who—" Beezan grabbed a holdbar and stopped himself from being rude. Was this the pilot? "God is Most Glorious."

"God is Most Glorious," she said, and smiled. "Hello, Bee."

Beezan blinked. He was hovering less than a meter from her. Something about the dark eyes, the fuzzy hair, the voice. *Oh, My God!* He pushed away from her, hitting the opposite wall, and had to grab a holdbar to stabilize. "*Sky!*"

He was struck speechless by her dazzling, joyous, and very Human smile. "I brought you something," she indicated the *Drumheller* with a sweep of her hand.

"But . . . you're . . ." he shook his head in denial and confusion.

"Human," she finished. His chest was heaving. He gasped for air, trying to make sense of this suddenly-too-good-to-be-true world. "Yes, you know, it's been decreed. The generations can mix."

"What?"

"I can be whatever I want to be," and she smiled at him, eyes sparkling. "For life, if I want."

"But—you're a baby."

She laughed. A sound like hope and dreams. "No, I was a trained adult when I took the witness assignment."

He held his hand to his chest, trying not to hyperventilate. "The ship, you brought?"

"Oh, Drummy, audio on. Transfer command to Bee. *Captain Beezan.*"

"Welcome back, Captain. It is very good to see you."

"*Drumheller,*" an indescribable wave of thankfulness rolled over him. ***The best way to thank God is to love one another.***[1] He struggled to get his voice semi under control. "*Drumheller,* I've missed you."

He looked at Sky, grateful beyond measure. "Mix?"

"That's how they put it. The heavens are joined. The taboo is over."

"I've missed you even more," he whispered, and reached for her hand.

Jarvie peered down the rimway, worried about Beezan. "The ship is registered to Captain and Pilot Beezan Mirage," Kelson said.

A cheer went up. "But that doesn't explain anything,"

Sequoia said. Then Star jumped out of Jarvie's hands, sending him into a spin, which Sequoia expertly stopped.

Beezan and a dark-haired woman glided up the rimway, tears and smiles on their faces—and holding hands!

"Who is—" Falcon asked. But Star dive-bombed the woman, who caught him and hugged him tightly.

"Good Lord," Kelson whispered.

"It can't be," Terina said, grabbing hold of Rocket.

"It is!" Jarvie exulted.

"Humph," Star looked up from his hug. "Sky—big showoff!"

And laughter rang in the rimway of the *Drumheller*.

THE END

ACKNOWLEDGMENTS

It's been over 35 years since I started writing a simple, short book set in a future where humanity is at peace, people are basically good, and we've avoided destroying our own planet. But I believe humanity will always have tests. We will always have room to grow. Somehow my little book about future struggles grew into an epic space adventure with over a hundred characters. It's been a long journey. Thank you to all the readers, reviewers, and supporters who have made it worth it.

Special thanks to Brian Burriston, Mojdeh Burriston, and Raeleigh Price for proofreading and encouragement.

Thanks to the Brilliant Star Magazine Crew, past and present, for your support and mentoring in the Bahá'í writing world: Amethel Parel-Sewell, Amy Renshaw, Susan Engle, Annie Reneau, C. Aaron Kreader, Heidi Parsons, Katie Bishop, Foad Ghorbani, Lisa Blecker, Darcy Greenwood, and Dr. Stephen Scotti.

To spaceship designer and artist Tom Edwards of TomEdwardsDesign, thank you so much for bringing the *Drumheller,* the *Cheetah,* the *Watcher,* the *Sandstorm,* and now the *Midnight* to life.

And to Jeff Price, Don Burriston, Shirlie Burriston, Jordan Price, and the rest of my family all over the world, thank you for all your support and encouragement over the years.

'Abdu'l-Bahá said, "When a thought of war comes, oppose it

by a stronger thought of peace. A thought of hatred must be destroyed by a more powerful thought of love."*

I ask you all to join me in thoughts of hope for humanity.

-DRP

*www.bahai.org/r/512608651

What You Win: Stories for the Whole Family

- **How can Mica compete at the science fair when parents are helping the other kids?**
- **Niccolo doesn't want to play in the symphony this summer, but can he bring himself to blow the audition?**
- **How will Jenna and Abby ever become astronauts if they're stuck on the farm, and lost in the maize?**

From silly to serious, here are sixteen hopeful stories about walking your own path, finding friends, and fighting everyday battles.

ABOUT THE AUTHOR

A native of Earth, D Rae Price lives in the San Francisco Bay Area with her family. She has a bachelor's degree in astronomy, but spent her class time thinking up space adventures instead of thesis topics. In real life, she's looking forward to the Lucy mission flybys of Trojan asteroids and finding out more about the origins of our solar system.

For updates, please join my mailing list:
    https://www.draepricebooks.com/contact

amazon.com/stores/D-Rae-Price/author/B09QLLDSCX
goodreads.com/drp99
facebook.com/DRaePriceBooks
instagram.com/draepricebooks
bsky.app/profile/draepricebooks.bsky.social
x.com/DRP191

NOTES

7. THE UNTHINKABLE

1. Bahá'u'lláh, The Seven Valleys
   www.bahai.org/r/233532682

11. THE PROMISE

1. Bahá'u'lláh, Gleanings
   www.bahai.org/r/915437155

21. THE RIVERS CONVERGE

1. The marriage vow: We will all, verily, abide by the Will of God.
   (Bahá'u'lláh, The Kitáb-i-Aqdas)www.bahai.org/r/229859639

24. THE NAVIGATORS

1. Bahá'u'lláh, Prayers and Meditations
   www.bahai.org/r/865529687

30. THE JUMP DAY OF ALL JUMP DAYS

1. Bahá'u'lláh, Tablets of Bahá'u'lláh
   www.bahai.org/r/641599925

31. THE WAYS

1. 'Abdu'l-Bahá, Selections from the Writings of 'Abdu'l-Bahá
   www.bahai.org/r/527494245

32. THE SECOND SUNDERING

1. 'Abdu'l-Bahá, The Promulgation of Universal Peace

www.bahai.org/r/117201530

33. NEW PATHWAYS

1. 'Abdu'l-Bahá, *The Promulgation of Universal Peace*
www.bahai.org/r/117201530

www.ingramcontent.com/pod-product-compliance
Lightning Source LLC
Chambersburg PA
CBHW060613300726
48975CB00005B/1551